One Foot in the Grave

Books by Denise Grover Swank

Carly Moore
A Cry in the Dark
Her Scream in the Silence
One Foot in the Grave
Buried in Secrets

Rose Gardner Investigations
Family Jewels
For the Birds
Hell in a Handbasket
Up Shute Creek
Come Rain or Shine

Neely Kate Mystery
Trailer Trash
In High Cotton
Dirty Money

Rose Gardner Mysteries
Twenty-Eight and a Half Wishes
Twenty-Nine and a Half Reasons
Thirty and a Half Excuses
Thirty-One and a Half Regrets
Thirty-Two and a Half Complications
Thirty-Three and a Half Shenanigans
Rose and Helena Save Christmas (novella)
Thirty-Four and a Half Predicaments
Thirty-Five and a Half Conspiracies
Thirty-Six and a Half Motives

Magnolia Steele Mystery
Center Stage
Act Two
Call Back
Curtain Call

The Wedding Pact Series
The Substitute
The Player
The Gambler
The Valentine (short story)

Discover Denise's other books at
denisegroverswank.com

One Foot in the Grave

Carly Moore Book Three

Denise Grover Swank

Chapter One

"Where's that order, Tiny?" Ruth bellowed from the order counter.

"Sweetie Pie just dropped the burger on the floor," the large, red-headed fry cook grumbled. "It's gonna be another ten minutes."

Sweetie Pie was the newest cook to join Max's Tavern since I'd started working there as a waitress, the fifth in as many months. And just like the others, she wasn't working out so well.

Ruth, the manager and my co-waitress, was fit to be tied. "What's it take to get decent help around here?"

"It's gonna be okay," Lula, the third waitress on Max's staff, said in her soft voice. "She's doin' the best that she can."

Ruth darted Lula a glare, but she stopped short of letting loose on her. Her uncharacteristic restraint could be put down to two things. The first was that the situation was only temporary. Lula was filling in as a favor until we found someone else to take her spot. She'd left the job months ago, and we hadn't felt the need for a third waitress, but the

5

tavern's business had grown exponentially over the last few weeks, now that construction had started on the Drummond Lodge and Spa. With few other dining options around, most of the construction workers came to Max's Tavern for both lunch and dinner. It hadn't taken us long to realize the crowd was too big for one or two of us. We'd both been pulling doubles for two weeks. Max had finally gone behind Ruth's back and called Lula to see if she'd lend a helping hand during the lunch shifts, which would have been great if Lula were more useful. Half the time she screwed up orders too.

Which Ruth would also have yelled at her for if not for reason number two—Lula was the girlfriend of Drum, Tennessee's resident drug czar, Todd Bingham, and she had given birth to his baby daughter only five weeks earlier.

Truth be told, Ruth didn't want Lula working with us at all, but Max had asked, and Lula had agreed. I suspected part of her reason for doing so was that she wanted more of a relationship with him—they'd recently discovered they were half-siblings. Though Max may have regretted making his request. Bingham had shown up in the tavern twice so far to let his displeasure over the situation be known to anyone within earshot—which had been the entire tavern since he'd bellowed at the top of his lungs.

Lula insisted she was an independent woman and no one was gonna tell her what to do. Her incarcerated mother had been controlling her for years from behind bars, but she'd finally shaken free of her hold, and she was claiming her freedom. (Her mother was supposed to have been released this spring, but last I'd heard, her parole hearing had been postponed.) Ultimately, Ruth stood behind Lula's decision, more out of female solidarity than gratitude. Still, we all knew Lula wasn't in it for the long haul, and Max was actively looking for someone to hire. So far, he'd come up with a big fat nothing. Little wonder given how much we'd struggled to find useful kitchen help.

I grabbed my two plates off the counter, grateful neither was a burger so Ruth couldn't lay claim to it, and hurried them out to the table of two hungry construction workers. Both of them were fine-looking, especially the blond guy with bright blue eyes. The other man had brown hair with a beard that was a bit bushy for my taste.

Setting their plates on the table, I gave them both a friendly smile, careful not to appear *too* friendly. "If y'all need anything else, you be sure to let me know."

The guy with the beard shot his companion an encouraging look that had my guard up.

I was used to all sorts of clientele at Max's, from the friendly older people who showed up during the lunch and early dinner shifts to the rough guys in Bingham's motley crew, and I could handle them all, but I had a weakness for cute guys. It hadn't served me well—I had a short list of exes to prove it—and I didn't intend to fall prey to it again.

"Uh, yeah," the blond guy said, looking nervous. "We just got into Drum today, and I was wondering what there is to do around here at night."

His lack of cockiness weakened my resolve. "So you're stayin' in town for the construction of the spa?"

"Just the excavation," he answered, maintaining eye contact. "We're stayin' at the Alpine Inn across the street."

"In that case, I offer my apologies in advance," I said with a teasing grin.

"That bad, huh?" he asked, returning my smile.

I tilted my head and gave him an apologetic look. "Let's just say you'll have a whole new appreciation for Motel 6."

His friend laughed and I started to walk away, but the blond guy called out, "You never told me about the entertainment in this town."

I glanced back at him, shaking my head. "You're lookin' at it. Max's Tavern. There's a Braves game tonight that a good portion of the town will show up to watch." I cocked an eyebrow. "You a Braves fan?"

"Depends," he said with a sly grin. "Are you?"

I knew what he was asking, but it was never going to happen. I laughed. "Who isn't?"

After I checked on my other tables, getting refills for one couple and taking another party's dessert orders, I returned to the guys' table.

"Can I get you anything else?" I asked before thinking it through.

"Yeah," the blond guy said. "Your number would be great, especially if you're free to go out with me tonight."

I shook my head and rolled my eyes. "Well, both of those requests are never gonna happen. I don't have a cell phone and I'm workin' tonight."

His grin spread. "I guess I know where I'll be tonight."

"So the check, then?" I asked.

His friend laughed. "Yeah. The check."

I slipped my order pad out of my apron pocket and put the ticket on the table. "We prefer cash. The internet around here is a little flaky. Makes it harder to run cards."

The blond guy snatched the ticket off the table. As he reached for his wallet, I turned away doing a quick scan of my tables, and saw Marco Roland standing a couple of tables away.

He had a cocky grin, like always, and was wearing his sheriff's deputy uniform.

I shook my head. Marco was too good-looking for his own good, and he knew it and flaunted it. Half the women in Drum and the surrounding area had fallen for his charm, but he wasn't a *use 'em and lose 'em* type of guy. He always made it very clear from the get-go that he wasn't looking for anything more serious than a couple of dates, although *dates* was a generous term. Even if there were places to go on dates in Drum, I highly doubted Marco would have utilized them. Occasionally he brought women to Max's in the evening, but I suspected most of the action transpired at his place. He had to be running out of women, though, because his "dates" had become less frequent over the last couple of months.

A playful smile lit up his eyes as I approached him, and he cast a glance toward the table behind me. "You flirtin' for tips now?"

"Who said I was flirting?"

He leaned closer, a surprised expression on his face. "Don't tell me you're seriously considerin' goin' out with that bozo."

Was I? I shrugged. "I don't know, Marco. It's been a long dry spell."

Sympathy filled his eyes, and I knew we were both thinking about the man who had created that dry spell, Wyatt Drummond.

"It doesn't matter," I said. "I'm working doubles every damn day, so the only date I'd be goin' on would be the horizontal kind, and I'd be too damn tired to do anything but sleep."

He laughed. "And if you fell asleep, it's because he's not doin' it right."

Rolling my eyes, I chuckled. "What are you having today? And I take it the order's to go since you're standin' here."

"I'll take the special of the day, whatever it is. Surprise me. And I'll be eatin' at the bar, so just bring it over there."

"You could have ordered at the bar, you know."

"I know," he said, his mischievous grin returning. "But then I'd run the risk of Lula takin' my order and I wanted it done right."

"Sorry to be the bearer of bad news, but you have about a 33.3 percent chance of Sweetie Pie screwin' it up."

"She's not any better yet?" he asked, casting a glance over my shoulder toward the back.

"Nope," I said with a sigh. "Apparently it's hard to find good help these days."

The blond man and his friend brushed past us on their way to the door, and the bearded guy tipped an imaginary hat, wearing an insulting smirk. "*Deputy.*"

The blond guy laughed.

"Y'all be safe out there," Marco called after them good-naturedly, but as soon as they were out the door, he scowled.

Whatever fleeting interest I'd had in the asshole walked right out the door with him.

Marco wandered over to the bar where Max, my boss and Marco's longtime friend, was standing at the counter, watching us.

Scooping up the ticket and cash off the flirty guy's table, I headed to the back counter to place Marco's order—the special was meatloaf and mashed potatoes. After I hung Marco's ticket, I counted the bills. He'd left me a thirty percent tip along with his name—Blake—and a message: *I'll be back to see you later, beautiful.*

I made a face. If the way he and his asshole friend had treated Marco hadn't turned me off, the cheesy message would have done the trick. The rotten cherry on top was his name. It was too close to my real last name—Blakely—and I wanted as much distance from my previous life as possible.

"Finally gettin' yourself a new boyfriend, Carly?" Lula asked as she walked over with a ticket, grinning from ear to ear. She was stupid-happy in love with Bingham, and she thought everyone else should be in love too. Especially me. She felt responsible for my breakup with Wyatt, no matter how many times I insisted she wasn't.

"God, no," I said with a scowl.

She waggled her eyebrows. "He's cute."

"He's an asshole."

She laughed. "You've gotta find *someone*, Carly. And you keep sayin' there's nothing goin' on with Marco…"

"There's not," I said insistently. "We're just friends. Best friends."

"You can't be friends with a guy. That's not the way things work."

"Well, it works that way for us." And since I'd already had this conversation six or seven times in as many days, I left it at that. I poured a glass of water, dropped in a slice of lemon and another of lime, and took it over to Marco.

He and Max were making small talk, discussing the Braves game and their chance of making it to the World Series this year. As I approached, Max shot me a grin. "I saw that man tryin' to pick you up."

"Never gonna happen," I said. "And don't ask why."

Max lifted his hands in surrender. "I wasn't plannin' to."

"Have you got any more interviews lined up for those waitressing positions?" I asked. "Because I'd *really* like to have a day off. Or at least an evening."

"To go on a date?" Max asked.

I propped a hand on my hip. "Why is everyone so determined for me to go on a date?"

"Because you've been alone too long," Ruth said as she slid behind the bar and started to pull a beer from the tap. "You've got to stop mopin'."

"I'm not moping!" I protested.

Max quickly turned away, his own guilt seeping in. He felt just as responsible for my breakup with Wyatt as Lula did.

"Back to the actual topic at hand," I said, noticing that the customers at another table in my section looked like they were ready for their check. "I want a day off, which means you need to find someone to fill in for me."

"I tried to set some up," Max said, his back still to me, "but Ruth nixed 'em all before I could get 'em on the calendar."

I groaned. "Ruth, we need to hire someone else. We can't keep this up forever."

"We're both makin' good tips," she said, pulling a beer.

"Maybe so, but we've got no time to spend it."

"Hey," Max said as he glanced over at her. "Are you serving that to one of the construction guys?"

She scrunched her face in confusion. "Yeah."

"Doesn't he operate heavy equipment?" Max asked. "Those guys are part of the excavation crew."

She rolled her eyes. "It's *one* beer."

"The construction of the lodge needs to go off without a hitch, Ruth," he said, turning his attention to the dining area. "Which means the construction guys can't be drunk on the job."

"For God's sake, Max," she said in disgust as she headed around the counter. "It's *one beer.*"

I pinned my gaze on Max. "Why are you so concerned with what's going on out at the construction site?"

Max refused to look me in the eye. "Because it's good for business."

But I could tell he was holding something back, which made me leery. Last I'd heard, Max had fallen out with his father, Bart Drummond, early last December, after discovering Lula was his half-sister. Someone had attempted to kidnap her, but she'd managed to run away—and Max had hidden her, assuming Bart was the person who wanted to hurt her. Wyatt had helped him. They hadn't told anyone they knew where she was, let alone that she was safe. Marco and I had been searching for her, and it had nearly gotten me killed. Hence Max and Lula's guilt over the whole Wyatt thing. But Wyatt had been keeping secrets from me long before he'd lied about Lula.

Max had made a big deal of distancing himself from his father. But now I wondered if they'd reconciled. Considering Bart Drummond knew who I was and had threatened to use it against me, I knew exactly how I felt about that.

The lunch crowd died down, and Bingham showed up at around one thirty to take Lula home to nurse her baby. He stood to the side of the doorway, scanning the tavern with his menacing gaze as though trying to figure out if anyone had intimidated or harassed his girlfriend.

Max rolled his eyes and headed to his office to catch up on paperwork, passing Lula as she walked out of the back. She ran over to Bingham, squealing with happiness, and launched herself into his arms.

His glare softened as he looked down at her, and I was amazed for the hundredth time that this deadly man, well into his forties, had such a soft spot for this twenty-year-old woman.

"See you tomorrow, Carly," Lula said as she headed out the door.

Ruth glanced up from the table she was bussing. "Bring that baby around," she called out cheerfully. "We need to see her. It's been too long."

Lula gave her a surprised look, which transformed into a wide smile. "Okay."

I was surprised too, mostly because Ruth didn't usually show any interest in Lula's personal life.

As soon as the door closed behind them, I walked over to Ruth. "What was that about?"

She shrugged but didn't look at me. "We haven't seen her baby in weeks."

I put a hand on my hip. "Since when do *you* have a thing for babies?"

She hesitated, then leaned closer and whispered, "Franklin's makin' noise about havin' one."

He'd also been saying they were going to buy a house, but so far that hadn't happened. Whenever I asked Ruth about it, she always said they hadn't found the right one yet and she didn't intend to settle.

I stared at her in shock. "What? How do you feel about that?"

She shrugged again. "I'm not sure, but I'm not gettin' any younger, you know? I guess my biological clock's a-tickin'."

"So you want to spend time with Lula's baby to help you decide?"

"Yeah, I thought I'd hold Beezus and try her on for size."

"You mean Beatrice?" I said, holding back a laugh.

She waved me off. "Beezus. Beatrice. Same difference."

My brow lifted. "Lula and Bingham would probably beg to differ."

A solo customer walked in, so I broke off to wait on him. After I placed the guy's order with Tiny, Ruth and I headed behind the bar to count out the tip money from the lunch rush.

"We need to find a new waitress," I said to her quietly. "This is gettin' to be too much."

She stopped counting the cash in front of her, then turned to me. "I haven't minded, to be honest. I think part of me is afraid you'll take off as soon as we hire someone."

I snorted. "I'm not going anywhere. You're stuck with me." Of course, technically speaking, I *could* leave. Last fall, I'd only stayed in Drum because my car had broken down nearby and I'd lacked the funds to fix it. But I had a new car—well, a new used car—and I could drive away whenever I pleased. Technically. Unbeknownst to anyone except Marco, Bart Drummond had summoned me to his house to blackmail me into sticking around Drum—if I left, Bart would give information to the sheriff that would incriminate my landlord and friend, Hank Chalmers, and lock him away for the rest of his life. Sadly, the information likely wouldn't be hard to dig up given that Hank had once been the largest marijuana distributer in Eastern Tennessee. Bart seemed to think I could be useful to him one day, but I had no intention of letting that happen.

"Schedule those interviews," I said with a sigh, "or I'll hire someone myself. I need a day off."

She frowned, then left the bar to carry a handful of dirty dishes to the kitchen.

While we were both pulling doubles, one or the other of us would get a few hours off in the afternoon, and it was Ruth's turn today. So she headed off, and I kept busy enough until she came back at five for the dinner shift.

Dinner was usually even busier than lunch now that the construction crew was staying in and around Drum—there was nothing else to do—but tonight, five o'clock came and went with only a handful of the usual customers. By five thirty, I was beginning to wonder what was going on. Then Max took a phone call and his face lost color. I hurried over to talk to him.

He hung up the phone, scowling. "Work's been halted at the construction site."

"What?" Ruth asked. "Why?"

"They found a body buried on the property. It's now the site of a murder investigation."

Chapter Two

Max looked like he was going to be sick, and I had to wonder why. Was he worried about his father? The resort was being built on Drummond land, but a portion of the acreage was a disputed section that the Drummonds and the Binghams had fought over for years. When I'd seen Bart early last December, he'd told me that he'd won a court case granting him ownership, something that had allowed him to proceed with the construction. The question was, which side had the body been found on?

Ruth gave Max a long look. "Now, don't go jumpin' to conclusions."

"And what kind of conclusions would I be jumpin' to?" Max snapped, his eyes flashing. "Do you think my father's stupid enough to bury someone and then put a resort over 'em? He'd go to the trouble of movin' them first."

I scowled. Like that was any better. Then again, I suspected the number of people Bart had actually killed was pretty low, not that he wasn't culpable for quite a few deaths.

I'd learned that Bart ran a kind of barter system—a favor for a favor. The deal was that the person who'd asked for a favor—or, in my case, been cornered into it—had to do whatever Bart requested, no questions asked. I'd done some investigating over the past few months, and I'd found at least eight murders over the past two decades with loose ties to Bart Drummond. Of course, none of the articles mentioned him by name. I'd connected the dots myself.

After my chat with Bart in December, I was fully dedicated to bringing him down. Something that would probably have been easier with reliable access to the internet. I'd spent what little free time I had at the tiny Drum library, searching the online records of the *Ewing Chronicle* for articles about murders over the past two decades. Hours and hours of research. At first, I'd ignored the murders that had been "solved," but it soon occurred to me that I might be underestimating Bart's craftiness.

I knew enough to understand that Bart Drummond was a careful man. Which meant that Todd Bingham's father had probably put the body there. According to Marco, Floyd Bingham had been a mean drunk and had likely killed multiple people. Rumor had it he'd buried them on his own property, two of his wives and his youngest son included.

"Is there any word on who they found?" I asked. "A man? Woman? A child?"

Max shook his head. "Not yet. All I heard was the word body."

"It's probably someone Floyd Bingham killed," I said, trying to reassure him, although for the life of me, I wasn't sure why. "I bet that's where Floyd buried his bodies."

"How do you know about the rumors?" Ruth asked.

I snorted, giving her a sassy look. "Please. People tell me all sorts of things." Then I added, "Marco told me last winter while we were looking for Lula."

The Baxters, a family of semi-regulars, headed in and sat in my section, and I broke away to greet them. I made small talk, asking the two elementary-aged kids how school was going. The little girl, Zelda, told me she was having trouble with her third-grade math, something her parents couldn't help her with since they didn't understand the way her teacher wanted things done.

I winked. "I think I can help you with that. I used to do some tutoring back in Atlanta."

Which was my cover story. Really, I was from Texas, but only a few people knew that.

I checked on a few of my other tables and circled back. Squatting next to Zelda, I ripped a ticket out of my pad and showed her—and her parents—how to break the numbers down into tens and ones before multiplying and adding. We went through several problems I made up off the top of my head.

Understanding sparked in Zelda's eyes, and the knowledge that I'd helped made me nostalgic for my old life. A year ago, I'd been teaching my third-grade class, preparing the kids for their spring PTA performance while I planned my August wedding to my best friend. My father had stolen it from me. On the night of my rehearsal dinner, I'd heard him talking to my fiancé, Jake—it turned out they secretly concocted a savage plan together. Jake would marry me to become my father's heir in his illegal enterprise (something my father didn't need given he was already wealthy several times over with oil money), and then they'd kill me.

I'd done the only thing I could think to do and run.

Six months ago, I'd thought that life—the life of Caroline Blakely, the teacher—was lost to me forever. Then I'd met Wyatt Drummond. He'd discovered my real identity and vowed to help me bring down his father and then my own. Only Wyatt had reneged on our agreement.

I wasn't sure if that meant he'd changed his mind about destroying his father, or only about letting me help, and I didn't care.

I intended to handle this situation on my own. Mostly.

Marco knew that Bart had discovered my secret, and also that I was digging for dirt at the library. He was trying to come up with a plan to protect me, but he hadn't mentioned it in the last month or two. I suspected his efforts had been fruitless.

Both of us worried about what would happen if Bart tried to call in his "favor," but Marco had assured me that I wouldn't have to face him alone.

Todd Bingham was the only other person who knew what I was up to, and since he probably hated Bart more than I did, he'd offered to lend his support. I wasn't naive enough to think the offer didn't come with strings, but I'd deal with those later. At least Bingham still didn't seem to know about my real identity.

For now, my plans, such as they were, provided a much-needed light at the end of the tunnel. And helping Zelda reminded me of what I was fighting for. That I didn't have to settle for a life on the run.

The front door opened and more nostalgia washed through me as Wyatt Drummond, the reneger himself, walked in.

My breath caught as he turned toward me, our eyes locking for a couple of seconds, but he turned away and headed for the bar. As soon as Max saw Wyatt, he slid out from behind the bar, and they headed to the back, presumably to Max's office. Although the brothers had been all but estranged before the Lula incident, they'd made up.

Wyatt came in from time to time, but usually stayed away from me, although he seemed to watch me plenty.

"Carly?" Zelda asked, obviously confused by why I'd zoned off.

"Sorry," I said, turning back to her with a smile. "You get it now?"

She nodded.

"Good," I said. "Next time you come in, bring your homework with you. I'm always happy to help, okay?"

Her mother beamed at me. "Thank you, Carly. You're a lifesaver."

"Not a problem." I got up and greeted another family walking through the door, then headed to the back to check on the Baxters' order.

Some of the construction guys finally came in as I was taking food orders from the new family. The already boisterous men were pulling several tables together, the tables screeching on the wood floor.

"Hold your horses!" Ruth shouted at them, but they ignored her, still talking while they took seats.

Those guys had likely just come from the construction site, and I needed to get over there and find out what they knew. Although I was working on the presumption that the body at the construction site had been buried there by Floyd Bingham, there was still a chance Bart was involved. And if he was, I fully intended to stick it to him.

One of the three tables had come from my section, even if it was now over the imaginary line separating Ruth's side from mine, so I figured that gave me the right to approach them.

"How're y'all doin' tonight?" I asked with a flirty grin.

"We're doin' great!" one of the guys said. He'd been around for over a week, and I was pretty sure his name was Rusty. "Had a bit of excitement on the job today."

"Do tell," I said, propping a hand on my hip. "What happened?" Sure, I knew from Max, but I wanted to hear it from the guys who'd experienced it firsthand.

"Blake was running the bulldozer, and the next thing we know, there was a pile of bones," said a man with a mop of red hair and a stout chest.

Bones. Which meant the body had been there awhile.

"So they called the sheriff," another guy said. "Even though the foreman insisted they were deer bones."

"But they weren't?" I asked, trying to sound like I had nothing beyond a friendly interest. Blake had found them. The crew wasn't large enough for there to be two men by that name. That meant he'd be able to tell me more if he came in.

"Hell, no, definitely human," Rusty said.

"They were bones?" I asked. "Not like a decomposing body?"

"Yep," the guy with the beard said. "Just a bunch of bones."

So how long had the bones been there? I had no idea how long it took for a body to decompose, but thinking about it made my stomach turn.

We got busy after that. Thankfully, Max came out soon, and to my utter surprise, Wyatt worked with him behind the bar.

I stared at him in shock for a few seconds, and Ruth came up to me and said, "Did hell just freeze over and somehow I missed it?"

"I have no idea…" I turned to face her. "When was the last time you saw Wyatt working behind the bar?"

"Back when he was runnin' the place."

Nine years. But based on how deftly he was handling his orders, I never would have guessed it had been that long.

I quickly turned away before he caught me watching him.

The baseball game started and the tavern began to fill. The place was packed, partially because of the game, partially because the construction workers had nowhere else to go, but also because word had gotten around about the body at the construction site. A whole lot of gossiping people wanting to hear the scoop. Every seat in the place was filled.

Ruth and I ran ourselves ragged.

Blake and his friend showed up and filled the last seats at a table, but they sat in Ruth's section. It soon became apparent that I wouldn't need to talk to him in person—he told his tale, loudly and proudly, to anyone who asked, and his version was no more elaborate than what I'd already heard. He tried to gain my attention a couple of times, but I was busy enough that I had an excuse to ignore him.

Blake was a popular guy with his new coworkers. They bought him multiple rounds to celebrate his discovery of the bones. He eagerly accepted them, getting drunker and drunker as the night went on.

Marco showed up around nine, wearing jeans and a T-shirt and looking beat. I took a moment to greet him after he walked in the door.

"You look exhausted, Marco. Maybe you should go home."

He rolled his eyes. "I know it's a school night, Mom, but I promise to leave by ten."

I shook my head. "Sorry for carin'."

His face softened. "I've had a shit day, and I needed to see my friend."

Warmth stole over me, and I gave him a hug. He seemed surprised, and I realized he probably meant Max. They'd been best friends since the first day of kindergarten, and they'd stayed best friends until Max had hidden Lula away and kept it from everyone, Marco (and me) included. They were still friends, but their relationship had been strained ever since. Still, the body had been found on Drummond land, and Marco was probably worried about Max.

I leaned back and grinned. "I know you meant Max."

"I actually meant you too." He hugged me tight. "It really has been a shit day."

I released him and took a step back. "I'll kick Big Joe out of a barstool so you can sit at the bar. He's been here for hours."

He grinned. "I can find my own seat, Carly."

"Well, good luck with that. Every seat in the place is taken. Maybe you can sit behind the bar."

He glanced toward the counter and did a double take. "*Wyatt's workin'?*"

"He showed up, then he and Max went into his office, and when they came out, Wyatt started working behind the bar with him."

Marco shook his head. "Wonders never cease."

"Hey, waitress!" one of the construction workers shouted across the room, sounding pissed. "How about you stop talkin' to your boyfriend and get me a damn drink!"

"Duty calls," I said, rolling my eyes.

Marco's brow lowered into a scowl. "When did Max start lettin' the customers talk to you and Ruth so disrespectfully?"

"He didn't, and since he's not launching himself over the bar, I suspect he didn't hear. Go get yourself a beer, and I'll go take care of this asshole."

Marco shot a glare across the room. "I'm right over there if you need me."

I gave his arm a playful push. "Careful or they'll think you really *are* my boyfriend."

"I don't have to be your boyfriend to look out for you, Carly."

"I know. You've proven that already," I said with a soft smile. "Still, I'm capable of fighting my own battles." I leaned closer. "But it's nice to know you have my back if I need you."

I headed over to the table of the rowdy guys, preparing myself for a confrontation.

"What the hell took so long?" the guy asked. He'd been coming around at least a week, so surely he'd heard the Max's Tavern rules lecture, which Max had issued several times at this point.

Putting my hand on my hip, I shot him my best takedown glare. "My name is Carly or Ms. Moore. Feel free to use either. Being served here is a privilege not a right, so I suggest you pull out the manners you learned back in kindergarten, dust them off, and start usin' them, or I'll kick your rude ass out onto the street."

The men at his table began to laugh, while the man who'd yelled at me turned beet red.

"She told you, Webster!"

"Webster's gettin' schooled by a girl."

I turned to address the man who'd made the last comment. "A *girl*? Do I look like a girl to you? I'm a grown woman who will kick your ass too, so you'd do best to remember that."

The men roared with laughter again.

"Now, if you're ready to behave like gentlemen, I'll be happy to take your order."

I spent the next five minutes taking down their drink and food orders, then dropped off the drink ticket at the counter. Wyatt had been filling my orders without comment for the past hour, but he stopped what he was doing and looked me in the eye. "Are those guys bothering you?"

I released a bitter laugh. "That concern is about four months too late, Wyatt."

He scowled. "I don't like how we left things."

Which meant he didn't like that I'd told him I wouldn't put up with his crap anymore, but this wasn't the first time I'd seen him since our official and final breakup, so I wasn't sure where this was coming from.

"That's a moot point, and this isn't the time or place to discuss it. I'm a little busy." I turned on my heels and headed to the food counter.

Tiny was working alone tonight, but he preferred it that way. We stopped serving anything but bar food after eight, and he ran things like a well-oiled machine, slinging wings and fries and the occasional burger.

I hung up the ticket and turned around, surprised to see Blake standing behind me, albeit a little wobbly.

"I been tryin' to talk to you all night," he said, his speech slurred.

I gave him plenty of attitude. "Well, I've been a little busy, in case you hadn't noticed."

"Why didn't you come wait on me? I got something to show you." There was a gleam in his eyes, and I knew there was a double entendre in there.

Gross. If I hadn't already decided I wasn't interested in him, this would do it. Sloppy drunk was a huge turnoff for me—probably part of the reason I'd remained single for the past four months since all the men I met came into the bar. It took everything in me not to curl my upper lip in disgust.

"Wellll…" I drawled, trying to figure out how to discourage him without pissing him off.

"I can show you now," he said, pushing me back several feet. Before I could react, he had me pinned against the wall in the hallway to Max's office, completely out of sight of everyone. The only way I'd be seen was if Ruth came back to the order counter.

This was unexpected, and I fought every instinct to shove him off me. "Blake, honey," I said in a light tone, giving him a little shove. "I'm workin'."

"This will only take a minute." He leaned his left forearm across my chest, restraining me against the wall, while he reached for his pants. He pressed all of his weight into my chest, making it difficult for me to breathe.

"Blake, let go of me." I used more force this time as I unsuccessfully tried to pry his arm away.

His free hand was between our bodies, fumbling with his jeans.

Panic washed through me, and I had a momentary inner war over how to handle this—his hand would absorb the blow of my knee to his groin and my arms were pinned, which meant I couldn't reach up and claw his face.

The next thing I knew, his weight was gone, and a large figure was slamming his fist into Blake's face.

Blake flew backward and landed on his ass in front of Max's closed office door, staring up in surprise and then anger. He started to get up, but the man next to me growled, "Stay down."

I turned in surprise to see…Wyatt.

27

Chapter Three

Wyatt glared at the man, his hands fisted at his sides.

"What the hell is goin' on?" Marco called out behind me.

I turned to him, still in shock over what had just transpired, and embarrassed to be in the middle of it.

"I caught this asshole tryin' to force himself on Carly," Wyatt growled. Then he turned his murderous gaze on Marco. "Where the hell were *you?*"

"Me?" Marco shot back, his anger rising.

"Stop it!" I protested.

"I could have you arrested," Blake shouted, unsuccessfully trying to get to his feet.

"You're the one about to be arrested," Wyatt shot back. "For attempted rape."

Was he out of his mind? The last thing I wanted was to attract attention. I'd gotten lucky several months back, after the whole Carson Purdy debacle.

"Rape?" Blake shouted in indignation. "I wasn't tryin' to *rape* her! I was trying to show her the pictures of the bones on my phone!" He pulled his phone out of his pocket and held it up as proof.

"You expect me to believe that cockamamie bullshit?" Wyatt sneered.

"Wyatt," I said in an exhausted sigh, "just let it go."

"Let it go?" he demanded.

I held his gaze, shocked to see the fury on his face. "Let it go," I repeated, quieter this time.

"Come on, Carly." Marco reached out to me and I took his hand, on the verge of breaking down. "Let's go out back and get some air."

I nodded as his fingers wrapped around mine and he tugged me to the back door. He shot a look to Wyatt. "Shouldn't you be gettin' back to the bar?"

I didn't get a chance to see Wyatt's face, but he stormed off to the dining area while Marco led me out back.

The cool air hit my skin and I pulled my hand from Marco's. He started to give me a hug, but I pushed him back. "I can't have anyone touchin' me right now."

He slowly lifted his hands. "Okay," he said softly. "Tell me what you need."

"I don't know."

"That's okay," he said, walking over to my car. "How about we just sit for a moment?"

"Okay." I felt foolish over being this shaken up. I was used to dealing with a rough crowd and I rarely got upset, but this one clung to me.

Marco sat on the lid of my trunk, and I leaned my butt against it, staring at the brick wall of the rear of Max's Tavern.

"What did Wyatt walk in on?" Marco asked. "What made him think you were about to be raped?"

I brushed stray hairs from my forehead, glad my back was to him. "I think it looked pretty bad. I wasn't sure of his intentions, so Wyatt's accusation didn't come out of left field. Blake had me pinned to the wall with his arm across my chest, his body leaning into mine, and he was fumbling with his pants."

"Jesus, Carly…" Marco said in horror and disgust. "Do you really believe he was trying to show you some photos?"

"Maybe," I said. "He's been talkin' about those damn bones all night, and he's had more drinks than I could count, which might be why he was leaning into me. He could barely stand upright."

"Why'd you keep servin' him?" he asked with a hint of reprimand.

"Hey!" I glanced over my shoulder at him. "I wasn't the one servin' him. He was in Ruth's section, but truth be told, all his friends kept buyin' him drinks, so she probably had no idea how many he'd had."

He held up his hands in surrender. "You're right. I'm sorry."

I gave him a sharp nod and turned back to face the wall. We were quiet for a few moments, the world completely silent. That was one of the things I loved about Drum, the quiet. It gave me room to think, although sometimes that was as much a curse as a blessing.

"You know what's funny?" I asked softly. "How everyone scrambles to find an excuse to take the burden of guilt off the person accused of rape. What was she wearing? Was she comin' on to him? *Was he drunk?*"

"Jesus, Carly," Marco protested. "That's not what I meant."

I turned back to face him. "Are you sure about that?"

He stared at me, his eyes wide and his mouth open, but I was done with this discussion. I'd gotten what I needed out here.

My fear was gone. I'd replaced it with anger.

Wyatt was behind the bar when I walked back in. He shot me a worried look, but I ignored him.

Blake's friend was helping him stagger out the front door.

"What in the hell happened?" Ruth asked, her gaze darting from Wyatt to Blake. "That customer came out sporting a black eye, and Wyatt's icing his hand. The guy was mumbling something about suing for false accusations of rape, and you and Marco were nowhere to be seen." She sounded pissed, but I could hear the razor's edge of anxiety in her voice.

I shook my head. "I'm fine. I think it was a huge misunderstanding."

"So he *wasn't* tryin' to rape you?" Worry filled her eyes as she looked me up and down.

I gave her a tight smile. I could brush this off, but she deserved to know the truth, so I gave her the fifteen-second version of what had happened, including Wyatt punching him and Marco taking me out back to catch my breath.

"So you're not sure whether he was plannin' to rape you or not?"

"I'm not sure enough to press charges."

"Like you would even if he'd completed the evil deed," she said in disgust, but it was directed at the door Blake had just walked through. "Asshole."

I wasn't sure what she meant (about me—the asshole remark was pretty clear), but it could have been any number of things. That a waitress pressing charges against a customer could be bad for business. That men got away with things like this all the time. Or that we'd follow the unspoken creed of the townsfolk of Drum—they took care of their own, which Max always took one step further with the employees of the tavern. He called us family and he didn't tolerate people hurting his family.

Oh, Lord. Would they seek their own vigilante justice?

"Ruth. For all I know he was reaching for his phone. You have to let this go."

She simply lifted her brow, her mouth pinched into a tight line, a look my mother used to give me when I was in trouble and she wasn't ready to talk about it yet. The thought filled me with an unexpected melancholy.

Eye on the prize, Carly. Take down Bart Drummond, then move on to your father, the bastard who killed your mother and plans to kill you.

My concern about Max and Ruth grabbing pitchforks and running out the door was unwarranted since there wasn't much either of them could do at the moment. Blake was gone, and we were all too busy working for anyone to go after him. His sorry hide would be safe enough until closing time.

Marco entered through the back, taking his seat at the bar, and I kept my head down, trying to get through the rest of the night.

Around eleven, Marco was still sitting at the bar, so I sidled up to him after I dropped off a drink order. "What are you still doin' here? It's past your bedtime."

He gave me an incredulous look. "You really think I'm gonna just go home after the way we left things out back?"

Sighing, I sank into the edge of the counter. "Marco. It's late, and you need your beauty sleep." I gave him an ornery smile. "I can't have you being so tired you get shot again."

His face softened. "I don't think it's exhaustion you have to worry about. More likely I'd be distracted by the worry that I lost my best friend."

I reached up to touch his cheek. "We had a disagreement. We've had plenty before, and somehow we've gotten over every single one."

"This one is different," he whispered, his gaze holding mine. "You think I was excusing what that fucker did."

I pulled back, shaking my head. "No. I know you weren't. I was just trying to make you think about how you were framing the question." Leaning over, I kissed his forehead. "Go home. Get some sleep and rest easy that we're fine. Okay?"

His mouth stretched into a grim look. "I can't. Max called an employee meeting for after the bar closes in an hour."

My brow wrinkled. "An employee meeting? Since when? I haven't heard about this, and besides, you're not even an employee."

"Max called it after Wyatt came out with busted knuckles. And you'll find out the rest after the bar closes."

"Order up," Wyatt called out, giving me a dark look.

Why was he still here, anyway?

The crowd started to thin, finally, but if I were the foreman at the construction site, I'd be concerned about all the men showing up to work with hangovers. It wasn't my place to worry, though, and the tavern was making money hand over fist. Despite Max's earlier concern about serving a worker a beer for lunch, he seemed totally on board with their nighttime shenanigans.

Max had to kick a few stragglers out, and after he locked up, he stood next to an empty table. "Everyone head on over, and we'll get started."

Tiny emerged from the kitchen in back. Wyatt circled the corner of the bar, but instead of leaving, he walked over to the table.

I was about to ask Max why Wyatt was coming to an employee meeting, but then I realized he was *supposed* to be there. Max must have hired him to help with the expanded crowd. The real question was what Marco was still doing here.

Wyatt took a seat at the table Max was standing in front of, but I sat at that table behind Wyatt. Marco sat across from me, with Ruth between us. Tiny took a seat at the table with Wyatt, while Max stayed standing.

"As y'all have noticed, we're busier than a snow cone salesman in a heat wave, so there are going to be a few changes. First off, Wyatt has agreed to work nights and weekends to help behind the bar."

Ruth crossed her arms over her chest. "Is he too good to wait tables with Carly and me? That's where we need the real help. You know Bingham won't let Lula help out much longer, and after what happened to Carly tonight…"

My face reddened at the reminder, but I was struck with the fact that she'd insisted we could handle it ourselves just hours earlier.

"Well," she continued. "Let's just say Bingham wouldn't have been as magnanimous as Wyatt if it happened to Lula."

Max's face blanched as he realized she was right.

"I'm not above waitin' tables," Wyatt said with an expressionless face. "I'll be happy to help wherever I'm needed."

"You ever waited tables before?" Ruth asked.

"I have a bit of experience," he challenged.

She shook her head in disgust.

Max's jaw tightened. "I'm gonna get you and Carly more help. And you're right about Lula. I doubt Bingham will let her help out much longer, although we all know the lunch crowd is tamer than the evening. But for now, Wyatt will help out wherever we need him. And after what happened to Carly, I've made another hire. Marco's gonna be workin' security in the evenings."

"Security?" I asked in surprise.

I turned to Ruth, expecting her to protest, but she quirked a brow. "What? I think it's a great idea."

"You're against it?" Marco asked.

"Bigger bars have them," Max countered before I could answer. "Tiny and I have historically acted as security, which has worked out so far, but now there are too many men coming in. Too many that don't know or follow the rules."

"I'm not protesting," I said. "It just seems like a lot for him. He's working all day, then coming here every night?"

"Hey," Wyatt said. "What about me?"

I frowned. What about him, indeed. How would he and Marco get along? I rolled my eyes. "I'm sure it will be a lot for you too," I said grudgingly.

"Gee, thanks," he grumped.

"This starts tomorrow night," Max said. "And like I mentioned, I'll work on finding a replacement or two for Lula."

"Then are we done?" Ruth asked. "I still need to count tips and get home for some much-needed sleep."

"Yeah," Max said with a frown and a wave of his hand. "In fact, you can leave your tips and I'll count 'em up for you."

She shook her head. "I'll do it. It'll only take a few minutes."

Max gave me a look that suggested I could leave, but I shook my head and pulled out my money and began to count.

We'd made a lot more than usual, enough that it took us fifteen minutes to count it. By the time we finished, the guys had stacked all the chairs upside down on the table. Wyatt had begun mopping the floor while Marco and Max conferred about security in the back. Tiny had already cleaned up the kitchen and left.

I headed to the office with Tiny's share of the tip money and rapped on the frame of the partially closed door.

"Max, it's me. I have Tiny's tip money."

Marco opened the door, leaning over in his chair to do it—the office was *that* small—and Max nodded to me from behind his desk. Marco held out his hand, and I gave him the stack of money and receipts.

Max's gaze leveled with mine. "You okay?"

"I'm *fine*," I said, feeling self-conscious. "But thank you for asking."

"You want me to follow you home?" Marco asked, worry in his eyes.

"Goodness no. I'll be fine."

"If you change your mind…"

I gave him a warm smile. "I'll be *fine*. See you tomorrow."

Ruth was waiting for me by the back door, and she sent a glance toward the dining room as we headed out to the parking lot. "How do you feel about Wyatt workin' here?"

"It worked out just fine tonight," I said with a hint of attitude.

"Good thing he was here to save you."

I put a hand on my hip. "For the record, I could have handled him. That guy was drunk off his ass. All I needed to do was sweep his feet out from under him. Wyatt just showed up before I had a chance."

"Maybe so…" She gave me a speculative look as we entered the parking lot. "He still has feelings for you, Carly."

"And that's just too doggone bad," I said. "Because that ship sailed right on out of the harbor and sunk on a sandbar."

She cocked her head. "I don't think you can sink a boat on a sandbar."

I waved my hand. "You know what I mean."

Pushing out a breath, she said, "And what about Marco workin' here?"

"For the millionth time, we're just friends."

"Y'all looked like more than friends when you were touchin' his face."

I shrugged, both of us coming to a stop as we neared her car. "It's like I told you. We got closer after he nursed me back to health."

"You really expect me to buy that you came down with the flu at the exact time Lula came back? What *really* happened?"

She didn't know the truth about Lula and the Drummonds, and it wasn't my place to tell her. Nor did I intend to tell her that Bingham had helped me find Greta, Lula's friend. He'd dispensed his own brand of justice on those men for the wrongs they'd done—and intended to do—to Lula, and I didn't want to get on his bad side. "I had a really bad case of the flu, and Marco says I nearly died a few times. I don't have insurance, so he took care of me at his place. I owe him, Ruth."

Her eyes narrowed and she studied me closely for several long seconds. "I believe he nursed you back to health and even the nearly dyin' part, but not for one minute do I believe it was the flu. Something happened to you when you were looking for Lula—like maybe you got shot—and Marco took care of you."

I shrugged. Her presumption was close, but I didn't care to confirm or deny it. "Go home to Franklin, Ruth."

She winked. "I'm hornier than a mountain goat in heat, and if I don't get me some, I'll wither up and die."

I winced. "I could do without the visual, but go on. What are you doin' standing here talking to me? Go see your man."

She laughed and hopped into her car as the back door opened. Wyatt walked out, scanning the parking lot, and his gaze landed on me.

Steeling my back, I walked over to him. He clearly had something on his mind, and if we were going to be working together, it would be best to get this conversation out of the way.

"Do you want me to follow you home?" he asked.

"That guy's not gonna bother me," I said. "He's probably knocking at death's door with alcohol poisoning."

He lowered his voice. "Are you okay?"

"I'm fine," I said, forcing a smile. "Thank you for stepping in. I should have thanked you earlier."

"If that guy had…"

"*I'm fine*," I said, adjusting my purse strap. "He only pinned me to a wall."

I could tell he wanted to say more, but he remained silent for a couple of seconds. "So you and Marco…" His gaze held mine.

"My love life is no concern of yours, Wyatt Drummond."

"I'm not asking for myself, Carly. I'm askin' because there's a chance he'll be assigned to help with the investigation of the body out at the lodge construction site."

I blinked. "What?"

"He holds a loyalty to Max that might make him...partial."

"Are you suggesting that Marco might try to cover up murders to protect your father?" It was laughable, but if I said so, he'd just scowl or suggest, again, that Marco and I were involved.

"Just be careful, Carly."

I laughed, but it was bitter. "Oh, that's rich comin' from you. What are you so worried about?" And because he was fraying my last nerve, I couldn't resist adding, "You don't think Todd Bingham will have my back?"

His eyes flashed in surprise. "Will he?"

"You tell me, Wyatt. You're the one who suggested I was on his payroll now." After we'd officially broken up, Wyatt had accused me of being on Bingham's payroll, and I hadn't seen fit to correct him. He'd made up his mind without asking, which had only confirmed I was making the right decision.

He grimaced. "I said a few things that I now regret."

"Well, that's all in the past." Part of me was still disappointed things hadn't worked out with him, if only because his promise to help me expose my father had given me hope at a time when I'd sorely needed it. But he'd reneged on that promise as quickly as he'd made it. "I'm goin' home."

"Is the fact I'm workin' at the bar gonna be a problem?" he called after me.

"Don't flatter yourself, Wyatt," I called over my shoulder. I got in my car and started the engine. He stood at the doorway, watching me pull out of the parking lot.

Working with Wyatt was going to be a challenge, but hell would freeze over before I admitted it.

Chapter Four

The next afternoon was busier than ever. The construction site was still shut down for the sheriff's investigation, and since the crew had nothing else to do, they came to the tavern. Lula called in sick, and part of me couldn't help wondering if Bingham was circling his wagons. I'd presumed the body was connected to his father, but Todd Bingham himself had made several people disappear.

We were all thankful that Sweetie Pie was working, which was saying a lot. Even so, we were too shorthanded for the crowd, so Max made a limited menu that he posted on a whiteboard. Their options were a hamburger or cheeseburger and fries, a club sandwich and fries, or the special of the day—a pulled pork sandwich and fries. No special orders were allowed. They had to put on their own condiments, and if something came on it that they didn't like, they could take it off themselves. We had a few grumpy customers, and I was worried we'd send them off to Watson's Café, which was a block down Main Street, but most were drinking beer, a beverage they couldn't get at the '50s themed restaurant.

Jerry, my friend who lived in the Alpine Inn—and was a regular for practically every meal—came in early and sat at his usual lunch perch at the end of the bar. The other patrons came in between noon and one, setting up at the tables and booths and not making any move to leave as the afternoon wore on. Thankfully, there was no sign of Blake or his friend.

"We can't keep up like this all day," Ruth finally complained around two thirty. "When are we gonna be able to take a break?"

Max studied the room with a frown. "How about you both take off for an hour, and I'll just tell them it's self-serve? They can come to the bar for their drinks."

Ruth frowned, clearly worried Max wouldn't be able to keep up with the drink orders, but I was all for it, especially since I hadn't been to the library in a couple of weeks.

Ruth took off soon afterward, saying she had some errands to run, and I grabbed my sack lunch and headed down the street, casting a glance at the nearly empty Watson's Café. I knew some of the men were frequenting the place, but the majority had been coming to Max's.

I wondered if Greta, who was a waitress at Watson's, would be interested in making a move. Of course, she and Max had history—of the one-night stand variety—so I doubted it would work. Greta might have been interested in him before her kidnapping, but she hadn't been coming around to the tavern. I suspected her new allegiance to Todd Bingham had something to do with it.

The overcast sky started to drizzle as I crossed the street, so I ran and ducked through the library door, smiling when I saw the middle-aged woman at the desk opposite me.

"Carly," she said warmly. "I've missed seeing your friendly face."

"And I've missed *you*, Carnita," I said, noticing all three computers were occupied, not that I was surprised. The library was one of the only places in town where people could reliably access the internet, so it wasn't uncommon for all three to be in use at the same time. There was usually a waiting list.

"I would have reserved one for you if I'd known you were comin'," she said apologetically, "but you haven't been here…"

"Don't worry. We've been slammed with no end in sight, so Max gave me an hour off."

"And this was the first place you thought to come?" she asked with a chuckle.

"I'm behind on my research." And I wasn't going to make much progress today…then again, I could look for some older deaths in articles predating the internet. "Do you have older copies of the *Ewing Chronicle* on microfilm?"

"Sure do, but it's spotty," she said, heaving herself out of her chair. "A few years ago, someone cleaned house while I was on vacation and threw out some of the records, but I'll show you what we have."

She led me to a machine in the corner that looked like it was straight out of the mid-twentieth century. "No one's used this in quite some time. I hope the bulb still works." Leaning over, she flipped a switch, and the fan turned on as well as a light bulb. "Success! Do you know how to use it?"

I nearly told her that I'd reviewed plenty of microfilm when I'd done a research paper on education in the fifties back in college, but that was Caroline Blakely, the woman I'd been for thirty-one years. Carly Moore had waitressed and worked in retail. So I simply nodded. "Yeah."

"Then I'll grab the film rolls out of the back. Is there any particular year that interests you?"

"How about beginning of the year before the online records kicked in?"

"Sounds good." She beamed at me. "I love that you're taking such an interest in Drum and Hensen County history."

I smiled back, hating that I was deceiving her, but there was no way I could tell her I was trying to find evidence Bart Drummond was a murderer once removed. For all I knew, she would wholeheartedly support my endeavor—plenty of people had become disillusioned with Bart—but I needed to keep this quiet.

Carnita went to the back, and I took a seat and opened my sack lunch. Max let us eat whatever we wanted from the tavern kitchen, but most of it was high-calorie, fatty food, something I didn't eat much of anymore. Hank's diabetes had already cost him his leg, and in taking care of him, I had set out to change his diet, incorporating more fruits and vegetables and lean meat. Both of us had become accustomed to eating that way, although he'd never admit it.

Thankfully, Carnita was forgiving of me eating in the library, so I didn't have to feel guilty when she walked up with a box. "Here you go. When you're ready to leave, just put the box on the counter and I'll take care of it." She set the box down, then gave me a questioning look. "Do you think you'll be using this one again?"

"I'll let you know when I leave," I said as I stabbed a forkful of salad in my glass container. "Thank you, Carnita."

She rested a hand on my shoulder. "You let me know if you need anything else."

I set my lunch aside, pulled out the first roll, and threaded the strip into the machine.

The microfilm was dark and sideways, and scanning it was slow going. I was on my second roll when a small article caught my eye on page seven. It was an update on the disappearance of a Drum Lumber employee, Richard Schmidt, who had left work three months prior and hadn't been seen since. Bart Drummond had set up a five-thousand-dollar reward for information that helped the Hensen County Sheriff's Department find him.

Pulling out my notebook and pen, I jotted down the pertinent information, including the fact that the article had been written in February, seventeen years ago. A quick glance at the clock told me I'd been gone an hour, so I put the film back in the box and headed back to the tavern, bidding Carnita goodbye and telling her I'd use the microfilm reader the next time I came in.

Ruth was waiting tables when I got back. Some of the men had left, but the ones who'd stayed were watching ESPN.

A young woman with long dark hair came in close to four. She glanced around the room before walking up to the bar to see Max.

"Oh. My Word," Ruth said, sidling up to me. "That's Molly McMurphy."

"Should I know who she is?"

"I haven't seen her for years," she said with a frown as the woman sat on a stool and leaned forward. "But she is as flighty as they come, and it looks like Max is interviewing her for a job."

A burst of excitement shot through me. If we found another full-time waitress, more of my time would be freed up. "You know we need the help."

"But Molly McMurphy?" she asked in disgust.

"It could be Santa Claus for all I care," I said. "As long as I can stop working doubles and get a day off. Hank has a doctor's appointment in another week."

She gave me a snide look. "You'll be changin' your tune when you think you're gettin' a day off and she doesn't show up to work." Leaning closer, she lifted her eyebrows. "Just like Lula."

That sobered me. As much as I liked Lula as a semi-friend, she wasn't the most reliable employee. Then, before I could stop and think about what I was asking, I said, "How do you know her?"

Ruth rolled her eyes and turned away.

Fair enough. She knew most people in this town.

Max spent about five minutes talking to her, then waved me over. He was grinning ear to ear when I reached him.

"Carly, this here is Molly McMurphy. She's our new waitress, and thankfully for us, she's startin' tonight. Will you show her around, then get her a couple of work shirts?"

"Shouldn't Ruth be doin' that?" I asked, shooting a nervous glance over my shoulder.

"Nah. I want you to do it," he said, but I heard the strain in his voice.

Ruth was watching us with suspicion, and I felt all the pressure of being caught between a rock and a hard place. Well, crap. Ultimately, while Ruth was the de facto manager, Max was the owner. If he said she was our new waitress, then I wasn't about to tell him he was wrong, especially since we needed the help. Besides, I knew Ruth could be hard on people. She hadn't cottoned much to Lula before I'd shown up, and it turned out that Lula had really needed a friend. And yeah, she was a little flighty...okay, a lot, but still...

"Sure," I said, plastering on a smile and stuffing down my concerns as I turned to the woman next to me. She looked like she was around my age—late twenties, early thirties—and she had a friendly enough face, but her blue

46

eyes looked guarded, not that I could blame her if she and Ruth really did have issues. "I'm Carly. Welcome to Max's Tavern. We're happy to have the help."

Some of the iciness left her eyes. "I'm Molly. Nice to meet you. And I'm thankful to be here. I could really use the job."

That made me feel better. Times were tough in Drum, and the fact that she needed a job meant she would likely put in the effort to keep it. "If you want to come to the back, I'll show you where the lockers are and introduce you to Tiny and Sweetie Pie."

She laughed. "Sweetie Pie?"

Grinning, I said, "Tiny, our short-order cook, gives all the cooks nicknames." I nearly told her not to worry about getting to know Sweetie Pie that well since she probably wouldn't be around much longer, but I didn't want to scare her.

Ruth was shooting daggers in my direction as we walked to the back. I showed Molly the back room and where we kept the extra T-shirts. Then I told her she could pick any of the open mini lockers to store her things. After she went to the restroom to change, I took her to the entrance to the kitchen, making sure to tell her that Tiny didn't like anyone in his kitchen during working hours and we weren't supposed to cross the imaginary line at the threshold.

"Tiny," I called out. "This is Molly. Max just hired her as a waitress."

The large man glanced over his shoulder. "Well, I'll be damned. So he actually did it."

"Did what?" Molly asked me in an undertone.

"Hired another waitress," I said. "There's been some resistance."

"From Ruth," she said in a dry tone.

I hated to speak ill of my friend, so I said nothing. I struggled to understand Ruth's attitude, but I knew she had trouble trusting people. Which meant she didn't want anyone new coming in and messing with the status quo. Even if we were working ourselves ragged.

Although the thin woman next to him seemed too intent on the food on the grill to pay attention to us, Tiny turned around to face us. "Welcome, Molly. I'm sure Carly's already filled you in about not comin' into the kitchen. Other than that, I'm pretty easygoin'. Just put your tickets on the wheel, and we'll take 'em down and put 'em with the plates when the order's up. Put the dirty plates and such in the plastic bins outside the kitchen, and we'll load 'em in the dishwasher."

"Y'all don't have bussers?" she asked with a confused look.

Hadn't she been to Max's Tavern before? There weren't exactly a lot of restaurants or bars in the area. Maybe she'd been scared enough of Ruth to stay away.

"Oh, honey," I said with a chuckle. "You must have experience at a fancy restaurant. We're bare bones here. Don't worry, you'll get used to it. It only took me a few days."

"Malarkey," Tiny said, turning back to the grill. "It took you less than a night. On Monday Night Football, no less."

Molly's brow furrowed.

"Monday nights are big in the fall and early winter, thanks to Max's big-screen TVs. Now it's baseball and NASCAR. You got a favorite driver?"

"Who doesn't?" she said as though I'd asked if she knew how to breathe. Then she rattled off the name of one of the drivers I'd heard some of the guys cheer for.

I grinned. I hadn't known the first thing about NASCAR before coming to Drum, but Marco had filled me in, giving me a list of stats and helping me pick a favorite driver. He'd told me it would rake in tips, and he hadn't steered me wrong.

"Who is he?" Molly asked with an ornery grin.

"What?" I asked, realizing I'd zoned out for a moment.

"The guy who put that dreamy look on your face. You were thinking about someone, weren't you?"

"What?" I practically shouted. "I was not."

She laughed. "That's okay. Don't tell me. I'll figure it out soon enough." She pointed to her temple. "I've got really good radar for things like that."

I stopped in my tracks. What on earth was she talking about? Marco and I were just friends. Close friends. When I wasn't working double shifts all the time, we hung out at his place or at Hank's. Or sometimes we went to Ewing to eat or see a movie at the two-screen cinema. A couple of times we'd headed to Greeneville to do some shopping and eat out. But we were only friends. Not once had Marco made the slightest suggestion that he was interested in anything more, and he'd made it very clear that he was a no-commitment kind of guy. And me…given my track record, I'd sworn off men. Which wasn't hard to do when I was working six days a week.

But this wasn't the time to think about my relationship with Marco. "Well, I hope you have a good radar for all these construction workers pouring into town. Especially since the jobsite's been shut down by the sheriff and they've got nothing else to do except sit in here all day and drink."

"Good for business, right?" she said with a smile.

"Yeah," I said, surveying the half-full room. The regular dinner customers would be coming in soon. "When Lula's here, we split the room into thirds, although Lula's section is admittedly smaller and includes the bar. So that seems like the best place to start you, but I'll check with Ruth first." That was one conversation I wasn't looking forward to.

"Wait," Molly said, grabbing my arm before I could head over. "Aren't I shadowing you tonight?"

I released a laugh. "No. My first night they tossed me into the deep end, sink or swim." When I saw her look of terror, I said, "Trust me, it's not that complicated. The menu's pretty limited, and there's always a special. Just write the order down on a ticket, hang the ticket on the wheel, pick up the food about five to ten minutes later, depending on how busy we are, then serve the customers. The drinks are the same—you just take the ticket to the bar and Max'll fill 'em."

My explanation didn't erase the panic on her face, and I didn't want her to quit before she even started. "Okay. How about we work both of our sections together for a bit until you get the hang of it. Then we'll split up, okay?"

She nodded but looked only slightly relieved.

This was going to be a long night.

Chapter Five

Molly was a quick learner, but Ruth was giving me the cold shoulder—likely for helping Molly—but I didn't have time to dwell on it. I let her watch me take a few orders, babysat her through a few orders, then set her on her own, letting her handle the bar and a couple of tables.

We were well into the dinner shift when a family walked in with three kids. I was about to send them to Ruth's section, but the little boy ran up to me and stared up at me with large brown eyes. "Are you the lady who's good at math?"

It took me a second to figure out what he meant. "Oh. Are you friends with Zelda?"

The mother gave me an apologetic look. "I'm Annette. Annette Searcy. I heard you helped a girl in Eric's class and her parents understand how to do yesterday's math problems." She gave me a helpless look. "I really don't understand it." Then she quickly added, "Don't worry. We're here for dinner too."

I cast a glance at the busy dining room and then smiled at the mother. "I'm Carly, and I'll be happy to look at your son's homework and explain it to you when I get a chance. In the meantime, how about y'all find a table in this area, and I'll be over to take your orders."

I grabbed several menus and set them on the table they picked, then checked on my other customers. Molly seemed to be holding her own, so I headed over to Annette and her family. They ordered drinks and three of the special, and I told them I'd be back in a few minutes to look over Eric's homework.

After I hung up their food ticket in the back, I headed over to the bar to get their drinks.

Wyatt was behind the bar, and he nodded toward Molly. "I see Max took my advice."

"Molly was *your* suggestion?" I asked in surprise.

He frowned. "Don't tell me you're about to protest hiring her because I recommended her."

I snorted. "Good help is good help, and so far she seems to be holding her own. I don't care if she showed up on the recommendation of the Grinch, but at least that would explain why Ruth has her britches in a bunch that she's workin' here." The look on Wyatt's face suggested that he might understand the situation better than I did. "Spit it out. Why doesn't Ruth like her?"

"That's between Molly and Ruth."

His words set a fire in my blood. "Don't you dare pull that lame bullshit again," I snapped. "Don't you *dare*."

He gaped at me in surprise, then said, "Molly is the younger sister of Ruth's former best friend, May."

"Why is that a bad thing?"

"The hell if I know."

I narrowed my eyes. "Try again. Why does Ruth hate her?"

His gaze lifted to mine. "Ruth and May had a falling-out, but I don't know many of the details. I'll leave it up to Ruth to tell you."

It seemed like another cop-out, yet I could see it being true. Men were often oblivious to the intricacies of women's friendships, not to mention Wyatt and Ruth hadn't been friendly for years.

I placed the family's drinks on a tray, then slid it off the bar top. "That wasn't so hard, now was it?" I asked in a brisk tone.

He just grunted as I walked away.

I headed over to the Searcys' table and passed out their drinks. "Why don't you get your homework out, and I'll take a quick look?"

Eric was in Zelda's class, and his homework assignment was similar to the problems I'd worked on with Zelda. I squatted next to the table and showed him and Annette how to separate the ones and the tens before multiplying.

It took a few tries before they both got it, and I told them to try the next few problems and I'd be back to check on them.

A few more people had settled in at the bar, but Molly seemed to be doing okay. Jerry walked in and gave me a nod. I noticed he'd been coming in later than usual and not staying as long as he normally would, but he didn't care much for strangers, and the tavern was full of them lately.

I checked on Eric and his family again, looking over the next math problem they'd finished, and corrected their missteps. We'd gotten busier, though, and I couldn't stay for long.

"I'm so sorry, Annette," I said. "We're really slammed tonight."

"*I* should be the one apologizing," she said. "Helping us with Eric's math is above and beyond."

"I actually really enjoy doing it." I paused, wondering if it was a mistake to delve into this part of my old life, but I couldn't deny it felt good. "We're usually slow in the late afternoon before the dinner crowd shows up. If you come back tomorrow, I'll probably be able to actually sit with you guys and help you work through the problems."

"Thank you so much," the mother said. "We'll be here."

They left soon after and the dinner crowd began to thin. It hit me that Marco still hadn't shown up for his bouncer job.

Molly was starting to look frazzled, and Ruth and I had been so busy, we'd barely had a moment to talk except for momentarily running into each other at the order counter, but once I had time to catch my breath, I headed over to Ruth to test the waters.

"It looks like Molly's working out," I said.

She gave me a look through narrowed eyes. "Please. She doesn't even have a full section. You took several of her tables."

"I thought we should ease her into it."

Snorting, she said, "No one eased you in. You took half the room on a football night."

"Yeah, but—"

She held up a hand. "Stop. No excuses."

I released a huge sigh. "We need the help, Ruth. I realize you must have some kind of issue with her, but she did pretty well with the section she had, so let's give her a chance, okay?"

She gave me a long look and her face softened. "Okay. Sorry. I'll give her a chance, but I don't trust her, Carly."

"Fair enough," I said. "You obviously know her and have your own perceptions of her, so I appreciate you putting them aside and giving her a chance." I suspected her problem with Molly stemmed from her falling-out with May, but that wasn't the kind of thing we should be discussing right now. It was likely more of a beer or wine conversation.

"I don't know about putting 'em aside," she grumped, "but I'm lettin' her stay." Then she added, "For now."

I cast a glance toward the bar, where Wyatt and Max were working. "Do you know why Marco hasn't shown up?"

"You'd know better than I would." Our conversation was cut short when she headed over to a table of boisterous construction workers to take orders for refills.

My customers looked content for the moment, so I decided to head over to the bar and check on Molly. "How's it goin'?"

"It's obvious I haven't waited tables in a few years," she said with a wry grin, "but it's comin' back to me."

"You seem to be holding your own," I said. "How's Tiny treating you?"

She shot me a surprised glance. "Okay, I guess."

"He's not very talkative when we're busy, but if he's upset with you, he doesn't hide it. So that's a good thing," I said with a reassuring smile.

"Okay," she said, looking relieved. "Good."

"Don't worry. It'll all come back. And besides, as you already know, we're not a formal kind of place. The main thing is to try to keep the customers happy, but don't take any crap from the guys sittin' around drinkin'."

She got an uneasy look on her face, so I reached out and touched her arm.

"Don't you worry," I said. "If anyone gets out of hand, Max, Wyatt, or Tiny will be on them faster than a tick on a coon dog." I cast a worried look toward the front door. "And Marco Roland when he shows up."

"Wyatt Drummond..." she said with a playful grin. "Rumor has it you two dated."

"Briefly," I said. "When I first got to town. But we've been over for three times longer than we were together, so there won't be any drama." Hopefully.

She nodded. "Okay."

Thinking about Marco had me worried, so I left her and headed behind the bar with my drink tickets, cornering Max while he filled a soft drink order.

Wyatt was a few feet down the bar filling a beer mug.

"Have you heard from Marco?" I asked, my worry seeping into my voice.

"No," Max said with a frown. "Last I heard he was one of the deputies workin' at the construction site."

"Any word on that situation? Will they be able to start construction back up soon?" While the additional business was great, we couldn't keep up at this pace, and a third of the guys in the room had been there all day, getting drunker by the minute. It was bound to turn ugly.

"I heard they took the bones to the state crime lab. They think it's a woman."

"Not a child?" I asked. When he gave me a horrified look, I quickly added, "I wondered if it was Floyd Bingham's son. Or one of his wives."

His brow furrowed. "What do you know about Rodney Bingham?" He released a loud groan. "Let me guess. Marco."

Wyatt gave us an inquisitive look, but a customer waved at him from further down the bar, capturing his attention.

"He told me about it when we were looking for Lula. And then your father told me that he'd won a court battle over some disputed land on the Bingham-Drummond property line. I just presumed the body had been left by Bingham Senior."

Max's eyes brightened. "Hey. You're right."

I raised my brows. "You thought your father was responsible, didn't you?"

He didn't say anything for several seconds. "We both know that Carson Purdy was a murderer."

The story went that Carson Purdy, Max's father's right-hand man, had gone rogue and attempted to start up his own drug empire under Todd Bingham's nose by hauling in drugs from Atlanta in caskets delivered to a funeral home in Ewing. Carson's gang had killed Hank's teenage grandson for trying to get proof to implicate them, and I had witnessed his murder, which had set me in Purdy's crosshairs. Purdy had shot Marco while trying to get to me, but Jerry had ultimately saved us all.

Bart Drummond had denied all culpability, but I sure wasn't taking his word for it.

The look on Max's face shifted to concern. "When did you speak to my father?"

Wyatt glanced toward us with a blank expression.

I hesitated. "Back in December. When Marco and I were looking for Lula."

"Marco never mentioned it. And neither did you."

I shrugged. "He wasn't with me when I saw your parents, and I didn't think it was worth mentioning."

"You saw *both* of them? Together?" Max asked. "Where?"

"Does it really matter, Max? It happened four months ago."

He gave me a dark look. "Humor me."

"I was at Walgreens in Ewing, picking up a blood pressure cuff for Marco. Your parents were there picking up a medication for your mother. She saw me and said hello."

"And my father just happened to mention that he'd won a court case?" Max asked in disbelief.

I shrugged again. "He was in a sharing kind of mood." Without knowing more about his situation with his father, I couldn't risk telling him about his father's threat to Hank, let alone that Bart knew my secret. Besides, Max didn't know my story—he'd only guessed there was one.

"So," I said, eager to change the subject, "since they're done digging up the bones, do you think they'll start construction back up again?"

Max lifted his worry-filled eyes to mine. "I sure as hell hope so."

Was he eager to bring more jobs and money to Drum, or was he worried about his father's investment? Probably both.

Wyatt walked past us. "I'm goin' to get more ice," he said. Then he headed to the back.

I cast a glance out to the dining area, and I could see the drinks were getting low at a table of construction workers. "Will you let me know if you hear anything from Marco?"

"You're worried about him?" Max asked in surprise. "He's literally watching a hole in the ground. There's no danger involved. If anything, he's more likely to die of boredom."

While I knew Max was right, I couldn't help worrying. Marco had almost died on the job, trying to protect me, no less. He'd gone back to work in January, and ever since, I'd lived in constant terror that he'd be shot again. It didn't ease my mind any to know he'd made me one of his emergency contacts.

I was about to head back to my tables when two sheriff's deputies I didn't recognize walked through the door, both wearing serious expressions. They were here for a purpose, and it wasn't a good one.

My heart lodged in my throat, and I pressed my hand to my chest. "Oh, God. Marco."

I felt like I was going to pass out.

Max shot me a horrified look, then turned to the deputies as they approached the counter. The taller deputy stepped up to the bar between Jerry and another of the local customers, his gaze on Max's face.

"We're looking for Wyatt Drummond," the deputy said with a blank expression.

Relief swept through me, making my knees weak, but it didn't last long before a new concern reared its head.

Max froze, then sidestepped to stand in front of them. "And may I ask why?"

"Are you Wyatt Drummond?" the deputy asked.

I didn't hide my surprise. The Drummonds were well-known in these parts, and while Wyatt and Max had similar eyes, Max was blond and Wyatt had dark hair.

"No, I'm Max Drummond, the owner of this establishment." Max leaned his arm on the bar. "Wyatt's not here at the moment."

"Have any idea where he could be?"

Max's face scrunched up as he leaned to the side. "Well…"

Wyatt walked out of the back, carrying a bucket of ice, and paused in the doorway when he saw the deputies. But he only stopped for a second before continuing toward us.

Max shot him a quick glance, then turned back to the deputies. "What's this all about, anyway?"

"We're not at liberty to discuss the matter with you," said the deputy taking the lead.

Wyatt walked behind the counter, keeping an eye on the deputies as he dumped the ice in the bin.

"Wyatt Drummond?" the deputy asked.

Wyatt stood straight, resting the bucket on his hip. "That's me." He shot his brother a warning look. "What can I do for you?"

"We need you to come to the sheriff's station to answer a few questions."

Wyatt's face gave nothing away. "And what would those questions be about?"

"Heather Stone."

Chapter Six

Max looked on in confusion. "What's there for him to answer? Heather left town nine years ago."

The deputy's mouth twitched. "We'd like to discuss this down at the station."

"Is he under arrest?" Max asked.

"No," the deputy said. "We simply want to ask him some questions."

"Then why not ask them here?" Max asked.

"We'd like to do this someplace quiet."

"You can go back to my office," Max said.

"It's okay," Wyatt said, setting the bucket on the floor. "I'll go to the station."

He started to walk around the bar, but I blocked his path. "Not without an attorney you're not."

"That's not necessary, Carly," Wyatt said. "I've got nothing to hide."

Lowering my voice, I said, "You served time, Wyatt. You've already got a strike against you. Call your attorney."

His jaw clenched. "And make myself look guilty? Like I said, I've got nothing to hide." He shifted his gaze to the deputies. "I'll come."

He pushed past me and walked around the counter.

"Max, stop him," I said as he headed out the door with the deputies.

"What do you want me to do?" he asked, sounding frustrated. "Tackle him?"

"We have to find him an attorney!"

"They're just askin' him questions, Carly."

"Don't you think it's a coincidence that they're here asking questions about Heather the day after they found bones buried on your father's property?"

His eyes widened. "Oh Jesus. Do you think…?"

"I don't know *what* to think," I said, putting my hand on his arm. "But we need to get him an attorney. Given his history, he shouldn't be answering any questions without one present. Do you have anyone you can call? Or know who he used before?"

"I only know my father's attorney, and Wyatt would never agree to use him." He gave me a smile, but his eyes showed his concern. "As you know well, Wyatt's a stubborn man. If he doesn't want an attorney, any calls we make will be wasted time and effort."

Unless they arrested him for something.

"Do you think that's why Marco hasn't shown up yet?" I asked. "Because he knew and he didn't want to tip us off?"

Max inhaled deep, then released his breath. "Four months ago, I would have said no, but after Lula…" He cleared his throat. "Things haven't been the same." He nodded. "Looks like that family you were talkin' to is ready for their check."

I swallowed my anxiety and hurried over to Annette and her family to hand them their check. Several other tables needed my attention, but Ruth stopped me and asked, "Why were the sheriff's deputies here, and why did Wyatt leave with them?"

"They said they wanted to ask him some questions."

"About what?" she asked with a suspicious glare.

"Carly, are you gonna get those drinks or not?" one of my customers shouted.

"I'll tell you what I know later," I said before I hurried over to take care of their refills, keeping an eye on Molly, who was busy trying to keep up. If the deputies coming in to ask Wyatt to their headquarters had her concerned, she didn't let on.

A half hour later, Marco walked in wearing his uniform and carrying a duffel bag. He shot a tortured glance at Max, and then they both headed straight for his office. I dashed over to intercept Marco before he disappeared into the back.

"Hey," I said, stopping him by placing a hand on his chest. "What's going on? Why did two deputies show up and take Wyatt to the sheriff's station for questioning about Heather?"

His mouth was pinched. "I need to talk to Max," he said, leaving it at that, then pushed past me toward Max's office.

"What in the hell's goin' on?" Ruth asked behind me. "And don't you dare try tellin' me you don't know."

I dragged her to the storeroom so Tiny wouldn't hear us. "The deputies said they wanted to question Wyatt about Heather."

Her mouth dropped open. "Why?" Then her eyes flew wide. "Oh, my God. Was she *buried* out there?"

"Shh!" I whisper-shouted. "I don't know. The sheriff's deputies didn't say anything about the body. Only that they wanted to talk to him about Heather."

"She was out there," she said, tears filling her eyes. "She's been out there all this time."

We were silent for a moment, because I was thinking the exact same thing.

"Do they think he's involved with her death?" I asked. "Or do you think they're hoping he'll help them pin it on Bart?"

She released a bitter laugh. "They'll never try to pin anything on Bart."

That's what I was afraid of too.

"He needs a lawyer, Ruth," I said. "I told him not to answer any questions without an attorney, but he said he had nothing to hide."

Her lips pursed. "Sounds like Wyatt."

Only the more I thought about the whole situation, it didn't sound like the Wyatt I'd gotten to know at all. Ruth had been familiar with pre-prison Wyatt. I'd gotten to know the post-prison version, and Post-Prison Wyatt wasn't trusting of anything. He certainly wasn't free with information.

So why would he just go like that?

Ruth took a deep breath, then blew it out. "Hidin' in this back room isn't gonna do anyone a lick of good. Let's get back to work." She started to walk out, then turned to face me in the doorway, blocking it. "Oh, and let's keep this from Molly as long as possible. It seems like she's workin' out after all, and I don't want to go scarin' her off."

I nodded, even though I wasn't sure lying was the best course. Nevertheless, it was her first day, which meant she didn't need to be privy to everything going on in the tavern.

Max still wasn't behind the bar when we headed back to the dining room, and Molly looked more frazzled than she had before, not that I blamed her. The entire floor staff had temporarily abandoned her.

Ruth took over behind the bar, so I loosely covered her section along with my own for the next few minutes before Max returned, his face devoid of expression.

I only hoped this didn't set him to drinking again.

Marco emerged a few minutes later, wearing jeans and a snug-fitting black T-shirt, and headed behind the bar to start serving drinks with Max, which surprised me at first, before I remembered what Marco had said about working as a bartender with Max in college. Before Bart and Emily Drummond had called Max home during his last semester of his senior year.

He'd been called home because of Wyatt's arrest. Wyatt had broken into the car repair shop he now owned to steal a baseball his father had sold to the previous owner. The theft charges had been dropped, but he'd gone to jail for driving under the influence. Heather had been with Wyatt, but she'd left town before she could be called to testify against him.

Or maybe she'd never left Drummond land this whole time.

Either way, if her bones had been found, it didn't look good for Wyatt, even if I had trouble believing he would have hurt her.

I didn't have time to talk to Max or Marco because the dinner crowd left and more of the construction guys showed up. I headed over to check on Molly since most of the orders were drinks now. I was ready to fend off a flurry of questions about the sheriff's deputies, but she seemed more taken with the new staff member who'd shown up.

"Damn," she said under her breath, keeping her eyes on Marco, who was pulling draft beers. "That is one mighty fine-lookin' man."

"He's not a long-term sort of guy, if that's what you're lookin' for." I couldn't ignore the unsettled feeling in my gut. I'd spoken the truth, but for some reason, saying the words felt like a betrayal.

"I know I should be lookin' for long term at my age, but short term will do," she said, practically salivating. "I've had a long dry spell. The options around here are limited."

I did a double take, then asked before I could stop myself, "Just how old *are* you?"

"Twenty-eight," she said without appearing offended.

"And you think it's time to settle down and get married?"

She scrunched up her face. "Don't *you*? What are you, around twenty-nine? Thirty?"

In reality, I was thirty-one, about to turn thirty-two in June, but I couldn't give her *that* answer.

"Thirty." I'd just celebrated my new fake birthday back in March. Ruth had baked me a cake and brought it into work, and Max and Tiny had encouraged me to blow out all thirty candles. Marco had shown up at the tavern to give me a bouquet of flowers and a cheesy birthday card. And Hank…he'd gotten Ginger, the woman who cleaned the house and checked on Hank while I was working, to buy me a gift certificate to a salon in Ewing to have my hair cut and colored. When I'd thanked him with tears in my eyes, he'd gruffly told me that he was tired of me filling the house with poisonous gases every time I dyed my hair to cover my blonde roots with auburn, but that was just Hank being his ornery self. When I'd hugged him, he'd held me extra tight.

But Molly seemed to have taken my age to heart.

"*Girl*," she said with her hands on her hips. "You are in *serious* trouble. Those eggs are dryin' up as we speak."

"I wouldn't say that…"

"We're hittin' spinster land."

"Ruth's not married, and she's thirty-seven."

"Ruth ain't *nothin'* like us," Molly said, curling her upper lip.

My protective instincts kicked in. "What's that supposed to mean?"

"It means that Ruth does whatever she damn well pleases without giving anyone else a second thought."

"So?" I asked, starting to let some attitude slip in. While Ruth could be judgmental and bossy, once you got on her good side, she had your back to the bitter end. If I told Ruth I'd killed a man, she'd be the first one to grab a shovel to help bury the body.

"Let's just say that she's never tried to fit in," Molly said with an edge in her voice. "And she's not above breakin' up a happy home to get a man." One of her customers gave her a wave. "Duty calls."

I tried to hide my shock. Ruth had broken up a marriage? Was that what had ended her friendship with Molly's sister?

I didn't have time to ask her what she meant by that, and I didn't want to ask Ruth, so I was left stewing all night until closing time. Max kicked everyone out at midnight, then told Ruth and Molly to be back to the tavern for the lunch shift and me to come in around three. Marco said it looked like the construction site would be shut down again, and Max expected another large crowd in the afternoon.

"Why not have Carly come in for the lunch shift too?" Ruth asked with a hand on her hip.

"You'll have the next day off," Max said in a tone that brooked no argument. "And once the site opens up, you won't need to come in until three."

That must have pacified Ruth, because she didn't attempt to argue.

Ruth, Molly, and I sat down at a table, and I showed Molly how to add up our tips and how much to give the cooks. Then I realized that while Max didn't take tips, it was customary to tip the bartenders. Which meant we needed to be taking some off for Wyatt and Marco.

"Max," I called out. "How do you want to handle Wyatt's and Marco's tips?"

He gave me a long look. "Don't you worry about it. I'll put out a jar for them."

I frowned, but I was too exhausted to worry about anything other than Wyatt. He hadn't come back, and if Max had received a call from him, he hadn't said a word. Nor had I seen him on the phone all night.

Once Molly was done counting her money, I sent her on home. Ruth had left too, and I went to look for Max and Marco in the office.

"Have you heard anything from Wyatt?" I blurted out.

A dark look filled Max's eyes. "No."

I ran my hand over my head in frustration. "Can we call the sheriff's office and find out?" Then I glanced at Marco and realized I already had a source. "What am I thinkin'? Marco, can you find out?"

"No. I'm tryin' to look impartial to all of this."

I could see what he meant. He was Max Drummond's close friend, and they had to worry about Marco being partial. Hadn't Wyatt warned me about that very thing? "Do you know when we'll find out?"

"No," Max said with a sigh.

I turned back to Marco. "Do you think the construction site will open back up at some point tomorrow?"

"I'm not sure. I do know they've been lookin' for more bodies, but so far they've only found the one. It might take another day or it might take a week."

I nodded. "Yeah. Okay."

"Carly," Max said with a sympathetic smile. "You're beat. Go on home and get some rest. I'm sure Wyatt's fine, so stop worryin' and try to enjoy your afternoon off."

"Yeah," I said, then headed out the back door. Easier said than done.

Marco got up and followed me out the back door, seemingly lost in thought as he walked me to my car. When I opened the car door, he lightly touched my arm. "Are you okay?"

I blinked at him in surprise. "Yeah. Why are you asking?"

"You just seem worried about Wyatt."

I stared at him in confusion, unsure where he was going with this. "Well, yeah, I'm sure Max is too."

"Max is his brother."

My eyes narrowed. "What aren't you saying, Marco?"

He shook his head and glanced away. I gave him a moment, surprised to see him like this. Then again, someone we knew had been brought in for questioning after a pile of human bones had been found. The situation was serious, and his mood was warranted. He pulled me in for a hug, and I hugged him back, slightly confused when the embrace lasted longer than usual. When he released me, he gave me a soft smile. "I'm gonna follow you home."

"That's not necessary," I said, still confused. "Blake and his friend never showed up. I don't expect any trouble from either one of them."

"There are bigger worries afoot than two drunk men." He pulled his key fob out of his jeans pocket and motioned for me to get in the car.

He followed me close all the way home, pulling up behind me and watching me get out of the car. I started to walk toward him, but he lifted his hand in a wave goodbye, then left me thinking about what he'd last said to me.

A chill of foreboding ran down my spine as I watched him drive away.

Chapter
Seven

I woke up to someone knocking on my bedroom door. Hank rarely woke me in the morning, so it only took me a second or two to freak out.

Jumping out of bed, I ran to the door and flung it open, scared to death Ginger had found Hank hurt or unconscious from his diabetes. Instead, I found myself standing face-to-face with Wyatt.

"Sorry to wake you," he said with a sheepish look.

"I told him to leave you alone!" Hank shouted from what I presumed was the front porch, his favorite spot to drink his morning coffee.

"You're out," I exclaimed, the previous night rushing back into my memory. Then I shook my head. "I mean, I was worried they were going to arrest you."

"Not yet, anyway," he said. His gaze lowered to my chest, then quickly jerked back up to my face, chagrin filling his eyes.

I was wearing a thin tank top and a pair of short pajama bottoms, so I hastily crossed my arms over my chest. "Did you come to see Hank?"

Wyatt had been a mentor of sorts to Hank's grandson, Seth, and he and Hank had become close. Which was why Wyatt had initially mistrusted me when I'd moved in with Hank as his live-in helper. Now that Wyatt and I weren't together, Hank would only let him come over while I was at work, which mostly turned out not to be a problem since I was almost always at work.

"No," he said. "I came to see you."

My eyes widened. "Oh."

"Can we talk?" His voice lowered. "Maybe not within earshot of Hank?"

"Uh…yeah. Do you want to take a walk? I'll throw on some clothes."

He nodded. "I'd appreciate it."

"The clothes or the walk?" I teased before I thought better of it.

"Both." Then he turned and headed for the kitchen.

I hadn't done laundry for over a week, so I worried about what I was going to throw on, but when I went to check the hamper, it was empty, and my clothes were folded and put away.

Ginger.

God bless that woman and, in turn, Wyatt. He'd decided the housekeeping was too much for me to keep up with on top of caring for Hank's wounds and doing the cooking, and Ginger and her husband, Junior, who worked for Wyatt at his garage, needed the money. He paid Ginger to do light housekeeping a couple of times a week, but now that I thought of it, I wondered if Ginger wouldn't mind picking up a few lunch shifts at the tavern. She wouldn't have to work more than a couple of hours at a time, and the construction workers tipped pretty well. I'd make sure to mention it to her today. And thank her for doing my laundry—something she'd never done before.

I threw on a long-sleeved T-shirt and a pair of jeans, then grabbed my hiking boots and a pair of socks before I ducked into the bathroom. While the Caroline version of me wouldn't have dreamed of leaving the house without makeup, the Carly Moore version of me was much more down-to-earth, and I had to admit I liked it. After I brushed my teeth and hair, I put on a few swipes of mascara and some concealer to help hide the dark circles under my eyes, then headed out to find Wyatt…but first I needed a cup of coffee.

I went into the kitchen and found a travel mug with a lid and a note that said,

I made you a cup of coffee the way you like it. It's the least I could do since I woke you so early.

I couldn't help smiling a little when I lifted the ceramic tumbler to my lips—strong coffee with hazelnut nondairy creamer.

We'd only been involved for a few weeks, yet he'd remembered.

No. No. No. No. I was not going to let this weaken my resolve. Wyatt put my life in danger and never even apologized. Instead, he was full of excuses to justify what he'd done. And then he'd accused me of working with Bingham, something I'd only done because I'd thought we were saving Lula. And the man hadn't paid me squat.

Okay, so he'd paid me about a thousand dollars more than my broken-down car was worth, but I didn't regret it for a minute.

And that wasn't even touching the fact that Wyatt had a dumpster full of secrets.

Which brought me to the question of why Wyatt was here… now. Up until the last couple of days, we'd barely said five words to each other since our breakup. The only thing I could come up with was that he'd come to talk about his interview with the sheriff department.

It was an unusually chilly morning, so I grabbed a heavy cardigan and shoved my arms into the sleeves as I walked out the door.

Wyatt was leaning against a porch support beam, watching the bird feeder he'd put out for Hank last November. Hank was sitting in his usual chair, his remaining leg propped up on a short stool.

"Your leg bothering you today?" I asked, trying to hide the worry in my voice. Hank hated to be fussed over.

"It's my arthritic knee," he said, keeping his gaze on the feeder. "Stop your worrying."

"I never said I was worried," I said, trying to sound nonchalant.

He gave me a pointed look, and I smiled. Six months ago, I hadn't even known this man, but now he was more like a father to me than my own father had ever been.

But Hank didn't do mushy, so I turned back to the bird feeder. A male and female cardinal stood on the ledge. Hank had taught me more about birds than I'd ever wanted to know, especially after I'd gifted him with two bird guidebooks for Christmas, but I found I enjoyed it too. Hank and I had spent countless mornings on the porch, him watching birds while I read. "Wyatt and I are going to take a walk."

"I told that boy to let you sleep. That you're workin' yourself ragged, but he went on in anyway."

I flashed him an appreciative look. "That's okay. I'll talk to him."

I stepped off the porch and into the patchy front yard and waited for Wyatt to follow.

"Want to take the trail?" I asked, still not looking at him.

"Sure," he said, "wherever you want."

"The trail it is."

Hank owned several acres that mostly ran deep into the trees. I wasn't sure about the property lines since there wasn't any fencing, but there was a well-established trail that led to a small pond fed by a creek.

"So you found out about the trail?" Wyatt asked as I headed to the opening in the trees behind the house.

"Hank told me before the first snowfall," I said, keeping my gaze on the ground in front of me. "But I didn't get a chance to check it out until a few weeks ago. Now I come out here a few times a week…if I have time."

I entered the trees, keeping to the narrow path as the scent of pine filled my nose. The first time I'd come out here, I'd been suffused with a sense of peace, something that was in short supply in my life, so if the weather was cooperative, and even sometimes when it wasn't, I hiked out to the creek to clear my head.

Wyatt followed silently behind me until we reached the small clearing. The creek formed a small shallow pool, about six feet wide, before it narrowed to a couple of feet. Several large rocks sat around the perimeter on both sides. I hopped over the narrow section and sat in my usual place—on a large gray boulder with jagged edges on one side, smooth stone on the other. A smaller rock was next to it, the perfect footrest, so I set my feet on it and looked over at Wyatt, who was watching me from the other side. The only sound was the babbling of the water.

I took a sip of my coffee, then asked, "What did the sheriff's deputies want to know? Was Heather buried on that land?"

He made a face, then rubbed the back of his neck, his gaze dropping to the creek. "You sure don't beat around the bush."

"I figured you didn't show up at Hank's at eight in the morning after not speaking to me for months just to have a friendly chat."

"That's not true," Wyatt said. "I spoke to you last night. And the night before that." A dark scowl covered his face, probably from the memory of Blake and what he'd maybe tried to do.

"You know what I mean," I countered.

"Why did you really talk to my father?" he asked, his intense gaze holding mine.

"What are you talking about?"

"You told Max that my father informed you that he'd just won a court case. There's no way he'd volunteer information like that to you at a pharmacy in Ewing. What really happened?"

I snorted, then shook my head. "You could have asked me that question months ago, Wyatt. What does it matter now?"

"Because I didn't know about it months ago."

I shrugged. "It's water under the bridge."

His brow furrowed. "Is it? I'm worried about you, Carly."

I pushed out a frustrated breath. "Sounds like you should be worrying about yourself. Was Heather buried on that land?"

He hesitated. "Yes."

A mixture of grief and confusion stole over his face.

I nodded, grateful for the confirmation, although I wasn't sure why. Maybe I just appreciated that he was being open about something for a change. "Are you a suspect?"

"They didn't come right out and say it, but I have to admit I'd be number one on the list if I were investigatin'."

"Did you do it?" I asked bluntly.

Shock covered his face. "I can't believe you're askin' me that."

I squared my shoulders. "Well, I'm asking."

"I didn't kill her!" he shouted, sounding more frustrated than pissed.

"Now that wasn't so hard, was it?" I asked in a snotty tone that I instantly regretted.

"Did you really think I might have?" he asked in disbelief.

Had I? No. Otherwise I wouldn't be out here alone with him. But I was confused about what he was up to. What he wanted from me.

"Why are you here, Wyatt?" I asked, my voice breaking, which pissed me off.

He ran a hand through his hair. "I wasn't sure who else to talk to."

"That's just sad." He'd lived here his entire life, and he'd only been with me for less than a month. It wasn't like I'd been much of a confidant for him either—he'd told me next to nothing.

"I know."

We stood in silence for several seconds before I asked in a softer tone, "Do you want to sit down?" I gestured to another rock on the other side. "The seats aren't super comfy, but it beats standing."

He glanced at the squatty rock and sat down opposite me.

"Seth used to like comin' out here," he said quietly, his gaze on the pool. A small smile lifted the corner of his mouth. "He'd sometimes sit out here for an hour or more, waiting to get a good shot of a bird or a deer or whatever showed up."

I'd found evidence of Seth's photography skills in his room when I'd cleaned it out. I'd framed a few photos of birds for Hank for his birthday in January. "He was very talented."

"Yeah," Wyatt said in a gruff tone. "He was."

And Bart Drummond had likely arranged his murder, hence our agreement to make him pay for his actions before we did the same with my father. Only Wyatt had reneged, and his father had walked around for the past five months while that talented boy was buried six feet under.

My anger simmered.

"I know I have no right askin' this, but I'm gonna ask anyway," he said, keeping his gaze on the water. "I need your help."

"With what?" I asked, hesitant.

His face lifted. "I didn't kill Heather, and I want to know who did. You know from firsthand experience with Seth's death that the sheriff department won't look into this too hard, which means I'll need to conduct my own investigation."

"And you want me to help prove your innocence?" I asked, my guard still up. "You could just do it yourself."

"People are gonna assume I did it, which means they won't talk to me. And if I hire a PI, they won't talk to them either since they'll be an outsider."

"I'm an outsider."

"Most people have accepted you," he said. "They like you. They'll talk." Then he added, "They talked to you when you were lookin' for Lula."

The mention of Lula only pissed me off more, but he had a point. He'd spent the past several years distancing himself from this town. No one was going to tell him squat.

"Max has got me workin' doubles," I said. "How am I supposed to help you if I'm working all the time?"

"Molly can take some of your shifts."

And Ginger, if she and Max agreed to the arrangement.

I pursed my lips, watching the water from the pool spill over several rocks before it continued downstream. Wyatt and I might not be together anymore, but I didn't believe he was capable of murder. Or at least not the cold-blooded murder of someone he'd once loved. I also suspected he was about to get railroaded, and I didn't want to see that happen. Maybe I really could help. Turned out I'd done a pretty solid job of tracking Greta down, although I'd had Marco as backup. Plus, I couldn't help thinking Bart had played a role in Heather's death, and if I found proof, it might help me knock him to his knees.

"Are you paying?" I asked.

He frowned. "I don't have deep pockets like Bingham does."

I released a bitter laugh. "You think Bingham paid me to look for Lula?" I shook my head, berating myself for getting into this, yet I couldn't seem to stop myself. "I looked for Lula because no one else would. Because I was genuinely worried about her. Little did I know that you and Max had her holed up at your place. You put Greta in danger and you nearly got me killed, all because you, once again, couldn't trust me, so why in God's name would you ask me to help you clear your name? What magic switch flipped that makes you trust me now?"

His eyes narrowed. "Twice now you've said that you were nearly killed, and the day you left me you said you were poisoned. Who poisoned you? What happened, Carly?"

"Those are personal questions, Wyatt, and we don't do those," I snapped. "You want my help? You can pay me with information."

"Carly…"

His tone told me everything I needed to know. He'd used the same exact tone half a dozen other times when he'd hedged and equivocated and circled around the truth, and I wasn't having it. I got up and hopped over the creek, then started down the path.

"Carly!" he called after me.

I kept walking, pissed at myself for wasting my time. He expected me to clear his name for nothing? I told myself that's what a good friend would do. And yet, we *weren't* good friends, hadn't been for months. Where did that leave us?

"Carly!" He grabbed my arm, pulling me to a halt, and turned me back to face him. "Fine. I'll tell you some things."

"*Some* things…"

"You're playing with fire by messing with my father," he said with a tight voice.

"I'm well aware of the danger your father presents to me." I shot him an icy glare.

His body twitched. "What does that mean?"

"You want all *my* secrets now?" I asked with a bitter laugh. "No. That's a two-way street, Wyatt, and you don't seem interested in walking it."

Anger flashed in his eyes. I was about to tell him to go take a flying leap, but my gut still told me that Bart had his hand in this. That looking into Heather's death might help me finally get a foothold, or at least a toehold, on Bart's neck. "I'll do it. But you need to answer my questions about Heather, or you're on your own."

He gave me an assessing look. "I can do that."

I fought hard to keep from rolling my eyes. "That's mighty big of you."

He looked like he was biting his tongue before he said, "Where do you want to do this? I'd prefer keepin' Hank out of it."

Keeping Hank out of it was likely for the best, and I thought about suggesting we head back to the creek, but I wanted to take notes.

"How about we go to my place?" he said. "It's quiet."

I had never been to Wyatt's place before, which was odd given we'd dated for several weeks, but I'd been working nonstop and taking care of Hank, who had been newly released from the hospital, so it hadn't seemed strange at the time.

But I'd be lying if I said I hadn't thought about it over the last four months.

"Okay." I was about to get answers, and probably more than Wyatt bargained for.

Chapter
Eight

Hank usually let me go about my business without much commentary, but he had plenty to say when I announced I was leaving, especially since Wyatt was waiting for me outside. (I'd told him I couldn't leave until I made Hank breakfast.) I whisked together the ingredients for an egg white, onion, and green pepper frittata, and Hank lumbered in on his crutch, leaning his shoulder into the doorway to the kitchen as he watched me pour everything into a pan.

"Does this have anything to do with the fact the sheriff's department called Wyatt in for questioning last night?"

I turned to him with a scowl. "You're one of the worst gossips I've ever met."

"That doesn't answer my question, now does it?"

I sighed. "Hank…"

"Do I need to remind you what happened the last time you went stickin' your nose where it didn't belong?"

Was he talking about when I'd gone looking for Lula? Although he knew part of the story, he didn't know how it had ended, only that I'd "gotten sick" and stayed with Marco for several days before coming home, still sick and frail. It didn't take a genius to figure out something had happened to me, and Hank was an intelligent man. Still, he'd never pried.

I decided to play dumb. "What are you talking about?" I asked, wrinkling my nose. "I don't stick my nose in other people's business."

"Lookin' for Lula nearly got you killed."

Okay, so we were thinking about the same thing… "Hank…"

"I don't know what happened to you, and this town was freakishly quiet about Lula and Greta disappearing then reappearing, but it seems mighty coincidental that the funeral home director in Ewing turned up dead around the same time. The same man who claimed he didn't know anything about a drug cartel using his business to bring drugs in from Atlanta in his caskets."

I shrugged as I flipped his frittata.

"Carly."

His tone was so laden with emotion I couldn't help turning to face him.

"You're playin' with fire, girl."

What did Hank know? "I'm not sure what you're talkin' about."

The bridge of his nose pinched. "Don't play dumb with me. You're a hell of a lot smarter than those blonde roots you're always coverin' up."

"That's a terrible stereotype," I said as I reached for a plate in the cabinet.

"You know what I mean." He hesitated, then said, "Bart Drummond has his hands in this, and you damn well know it. I suspect that's why you're about to go runnin' off after his son like he's a piece of chocolate cake."

I shot him a mock glare. "Really? You're draggin' innocent chocolate cake into this?"

"Charlene." His tone turned harsher.

I couldn't hide my surprise. For one, he knew it wasn't my real name, although he'd insisted he didn't want to know my true identity, and for another, no one had ever called me that before.

"I care about you, girl, and you're dippin' your toe in dangerous waters."

"You think Wyatt killed his girlfriend?" I asked.

"Hell, no. If I did, he'd never have stepped foot into this house."

"But you think his father did?"

"I think his father played some part in it, but it will never be tied back to him." He glanced at the small kitchen table, then back at me. "I know what you're doin', and you need to stop."

"What exactly do you think I'm doin'?"

"You're out to expose Bart, but I'm here to tell you that you'll get burned. Let it go, Carly." His voice steeped with exhaustion, he added, "Just let it go."

I took a step closer and lowered my voice. "I can't let it go."

"Why?" he asked, looking me in the eye. "*Why?*"

"He was behind Seth's death, and you and I both know it."

"That's my vendetta, girl, not yours."

"That's not true!" I whisper-shouted, not wanting Wyatt to hear us.

"Seth's my kin, not yours. There's something else in play here." He paused, then added, "I've seen your notes."

I sucked in a breath, knowing exactly what he was talking about. "You've been through my things?"

"Carly," he said, sounding weary. "You fell asleep on the sofa with your notebook open next to you. I moved it to tuck a blanket around you and a name caught my eye. I wasn't snoopin', but it got me worried. Where are you gettin' that information?"

I could lie or refuse to answer, but I didn't want to do either. "The library."

His face paled. "Such a public place? Who else knows you're investigatin' him?"

"Marco knows a little."

"What about Carnita? She's nobody's fool."

"I told her I'm researching town history."

He frowned. "Those computers aren't very private. Anyone could be watchin' over your shoulder."

"I'm careful."

He still didn't look pleased.

"Look," I said with a sigh, "my research into Bart aside, Wyatt's innocent, and you and I both know the sheriff's gonna pin it on him."

Fear filled his eyes. "You're playin' with fire."

I lifted my hand to his cheek and whispered, "I spent thirty-one years livin' a careful life, Hank, and look where it got me—my own father nearly killed me. Playing safe isn't always the safe way to go. So I'll stand up for what's right because no one stood up for me."

He slowly shook his head, his eyes glassy. "I can't lose you too."

I wrapped my arms around him, pulling him into a hug. "I'll be careful. I promise."

He kissed my cheek and held me away from him. "I suppose that's all I can ask for. Now you're about to burn my breakfast."

Gasping, I turned back to the stove and slid the frittata onto a plate. "You want to eat on the porch?"

"Yep. I'm about to have a chat with Wyatt Drummond." He spun around faster than should have been possible for a one-legged man with a crutch and headed out the front door.

I quickly grabbed a fork and followed him out with the plate.

Hank was standing at the top of the porch steps, pointing his finger at Wyatt, who was leaning against his truck.

"If you're involvin' her in this, then I'm holding you personally responsible for her safety." He jabbed his finger toward Wyatt for good measure. "Do you understand me?"

Wyatt had already moved away from the truck, his gaze on the elderly man. He nodded, then said respectfully, "Yes, sir. I understand."

"I don't think you do," Hank said, his voice harsh. "If anything happens to her, you'll pay the blood price."

"Wait. What?" I stepped in fully, out of the shadow of the doorway, but they were both intent on one another and seemed to take no notice of me. I set the plate on the table and moved next to Hank, giving them both expectant looks, one after the other.

"I wouldn't have it any other way," Wyatt said solemnly.

"What the hell is a blood price?" I demanded.

"Nothin' you need to concern yourself with," Hank grumped, then hobbled to his chair and sat with a plop.

Only it seemed like it *did* concern me.

Wyatt walked around to the passenger door of his truck and pulled it open, giving me an expectant look.

Shaking my head, I went back inside and grabbed my messenger bag and my purse, snatching my keys out of the latter as I walked through the door. I clicked the fob as I descended the steps. "I'll follow you."

Wyatt frowned, but he shut the door and walked around to the driver's side as I headed to my own small car.

"Carly," Hank called out.

I turned back to him and gave him a soft smile. "I'm as stubborn as the day is long, Hank. Just like you. I'll be fine."

He gave me slight nod, then shoved a bite of his breakfast into his mouth before calling out, "She ain't had her breakfast yet. Make sure she's fed."

I snorted as I got into my car. I was perfectly capable of feeding myself, but I also knew it was one thing Hank felt he could control. He was worried I wouldn't be safe, but at least he could make sure I didn't go hungry. It was the fact that he had put Wyatt in charge of it that raised my hackles.

Wyatt pulled out onto the county road and I followed, turning toward town. We drove a short way before he turned right onto another county road, this one in rougher shape than the one that ran by Hank's house. We drove a couple of miles before he turned onto a private road that disappeared into the trees. Branches with leaf buds scraped the top of his truck cab, and I realized the entire road would be engulfed by leaves once they unfurled.

We drove about a quarter mile before the road opened to a clearing at the edge of a cliff, a log cabin to one side. His property overlooked a valley on the North Carolina side of the mountain range.

Wyatt parked on a wide gravel driveway and I pulled in next to him, ignoring him as I got out and walked around the side of his house to see the view.

Storm clouds were dark purple in the horizon, but rays of sun shot through openings, the rays creating spotlights on the pasture below.

"I knew you'd like it," he said beside me, his tone neutral.

I turned to look up at him. "And yet you never once brought me here."

A sheepish look filled his eyes. "The inside was still a work in progress."

I nearly told him he was full of bullshit. The fact was he hadn't trusted me, and while I partially understood why he wouldn't tell me his secrets, his reluctance to bring me to his home was another matter altogether.

"Whatever," I said, my weariness bleeding through. "Let's get started. I have to be at work by three."

He led me to the front door, pushing it open after he unlocked it and letting me enter first. I had no idea what to expect, but the house was more put-together than Wyatt had implied, suggesting he was indeed a liar.

The inside walls were composed of logs, and a smooth rock fireplace extended to the top of the two-story ceiling. Windows at the back of the space overlooked the view. A worn sofa and two chairs had been set up in a conversation area around the fireplace, and a kitchen with maple cabinets filled the opposite wall. A loft extended over the kitchen, with a set of open stairs leading up to it.

I headed to the kitchen island and sat on a stool, pulling my notebook out of my messenger bag and setting it on the counter. "Let's get started."

Wyatt walked around the counter and pulled the pot from the coffee maker. "Let me get a pot of coffee started."

I didn't respond and fought hard to keep my gaze on my notebook and away from the incredible view out of those back windows. Seeing it was like a stab to my heart, one more piece of evidence of how little I'd meant to him.

He was silent as he quickly got to work brewing a new pot, but then he opened a cabinet and pulled out a box of pancake mix.

"What are you doing?" I asked in exasperation.

He glanced at me without missing a beat. "Making you breakfast."

"I never asked you to do that. I'd rather get to work."

"Contrary to what you might think, I'm capable of multitasking," Wyatt said as he got out a glass mixing bowl. "Ask me questions while I cook."

"You're only making breakfast because Hank told you to feed me."

He shot me a glance as he opened his fridge and pulled out a carton of eggs. "I'm hungry too."

"What's a blood price?"

"Nothin' you need to worry about."

"Look," I said in a cold tone. "If I ask you a question, you can do me the courtesy of giving me a straight answer. No more bullshit. Is that clear?"

He turned back to face me. "I'll answer what I can."

I slid off the stool. "Good luck to you."

"Carly," he called after me. "At least stick around long enough to find out what I won't answer. You might fill in some blanks along the way." When I stopped with my hand on the doorknob, he added, "If you leave now, who knows what information you'll miss out on."

At that moment, I hated him. I hated that he was playing me with his dangled carrot, and we both knew I wasn't going to walk away, no matter what my pride was telling me to do.

I turned back to face him. "What's a blood price?"

"It means if anything happens to you while I've sworn to protect you, Hank has the right to seek his own revenge."

"As in *kill* you?" I asked in shock.

"If that's what he chooses."

"It could be something else?"

"Anything of his choosing. Anything."

"Why would you agree to that?" I demanded.

"Because I wouldn't let anything happen to you anyway. It was an easy oath to take."

I struggled to catch my breath, daunted that Hank would ask for such a promise and that Wyatt would agree to it so willingly.

He cracked an egg and dumped it into the bowl. "I'm sure you want to know more about my history with Heather. I suppose that seems like a good place to start."

"Hm," I said noncommittally, then sat back down and pulled out my notebook again. I hadn't used a notebook before, but looking back, I realized that had been foolish. And since I didn't have Marco with me as a backup memory bank, the notebook seemed the best way to keep track of everything.

"You know, I was with Marco when I was looking for Lula," I said. "I wasn't investigating on my own."

"I'll be driving you around," he said in a gruff tone as he whisked the batter, and I couldn't help thinking what a contrast his domestication was to his burly frame and tone.

Nope. Not going there.

I had other issues to think about, especially since I had no intention of letting Wyatt play chauffeur, but we'd cross that bridge when we came to it.

"When did you first start dating Heather?"

He turned on the water faucet, collecting a small bit of water on his fingertips before flicking it into the pan he'd set on the burner. The beads of water sizzled and danced, and Wyatt turned down the heat. "We'd known each other since grade school. Her family moved to the area when she was in third grade, but I didn't pay much attention to her then. It wasn't until middle school that she caught my eye."

I couldn't help noticing the soft smile on his face.

"So you two became a thing in middle school?"

He released a chuckle as he poured batter into the skillet. "No. Believe it or not, I didn't get up the nerve to ask her out until our sophomore year. I asked her to the homecoming dance."

"And she said yes, of course," I said, writing down *sophomore homecoming dance.*

He laughed again. "Actually, she said no. She'd already agreed to go with Herbie Metcalf, but she told me she would have chosen me if she could have. So she went to the dance with Herbie and I went with some friends, but she ditched him before it ended and asked me to take her home."

I blinked hard. "*She ditched him?*"

"We were kids, Carly. Stupid kids."

"And how did Herbie take it?"

Wyatt gave me a long look. "At the time, he seemed to take it okay."

"You were popular, right?" I asked. "You were on the football team. You were good-looking."

"You're forgettin' the part about my father havin' money."

"Oh, I haven't forgotten that part at all, but that's a given."

He scowled. "What are you getting' at?"

"That you were big man on campus. Where did Herbie place in the high school pecking order?"

"That's not fair, Carly."

"What's fair or unfair is irrelevant. I'm looking for facts."

"What the hell does a high school dance have to do with the fact that Heather was buried out there in that field for nine years?" His voice rose then broke, and I realized he wasn't angry with me. He was grieving Heather's murder.

"The fact is someone killed your former girlfriend and her death, it seems, is about to be pinned on you, Wyatt, which means this could be like looking for a needle in haystack. So I'm digging through the haystack."

He turned back to the skillet, flipping four pancakes. "I'm sorry. You're right." He paused, considering, then said, "Herbie was in the middle, I guess. He wasn't unpopular, but he wasn't in the upper echelon."

"How many kids were in a graduating class?" I asked.

"About a hundred to one-twenty," he said. "It's a county school. Kids from Ewing and the surrounding towns like Drum."

I nodded, writing that down. "And where was Herbie from?"

"Ewing. Most of the kids were. There are more kids in the surrounding area, but there's a Christian high school in Ewing, and some of the more rural kids homeschooled, or at least that's what their parents told the school district. No one really pushed them on it."

He grabbed two plates from the cabinet and placed two pancakes on each before pouring more batter into the skillet. He set a plate in front of me, along with everything I would need to enjoy it—a fork and knife, butter, a bottle of maple syrup, and a cup of coffee. "I don't have any nondairy creamer, but I *do* have half-and-half."

"That's fine," I said with a slight frown, feeling uncomfortable with the air of domesticity rolling off him.

He pulled the carton out of the fridge. "Can I get you anything else?"

"Nope. I'm good." I poured some half-and-half into the mug and stirred it with my fork before taking a sip. "Did you have any enemies in high school?"

"Doesn't everyone?" he asked.

"No," I said, harsher than I'd intended. "I didn't."

He turned to face me. "Even with your father being who he is?"

High school seemed like light-years away, and talking about my past as Caroline felt off and wrong. "I went to a private school where everyone's parents had money. I was shy and quiet."

"And from what I gathered, you had Jake looking out for you," he said with a bit of an edge of his own.

My back stiffened. "What the hell is that supposed to mean?"

"It means that you don't have any right to judge me. Was I an asshole in high school? Yeah, I was. I had a chip on my shoulder because in the eyes of the school, I was the kid to knock off a pedestal, even if I never wanted to climb onto it in the first place. But I was a Drummond, and my father had expectations, even in school. Even with sports. And people *hated* that I was a Drummond, so plenty of people stepped up to challenge me. If I didn't defend myself well enough, my father would be quick to rake me over the coals at home for not acting like a leader. So yeah, I was admittedly an asshole with absolutely no real friends. Until Heather."

I set my mug on the counter, my edge softening. "I'm sorry. I'm sure it was difficult."

He shrugged and flipped the pancakes in the skillet. "It was like Heather could see right through all my layers of bullshit." He snuck a glance toward me and just as quickly looked away. "Just like you."

Had Heather been more tolerant of all his secrets? Or maybe he hadn't had them back then. Did it matter?

One thing was certain, I didn't like being compared to her. At. All.

"So you and Heather started dating?"

"Yeah," he said, his voice gruff. "During our junior year, her father got a job in Virginia, but Heather refused to go with them. So her aunt offered to let her stay with her until she graduated from high school."

"Did she go to college?"

"For a while, but she flunked out her second semester. Too much partyin'."

"But you didn't go to college?"

"My father believed it was a waste of time and money. He thinks life teaches you all you need to know. My mother had to convince him to pay for Max's college."

The heir and the spare to the Drummond kingdom. Since Wyatt was the heir, Max had very much been treated like the disposable son. Until he wasn't.

"Did you and Heather break up when she went to college?"

"Yeah. She said she didn't want to be tied down, and my father wasn't all that crazy about her. Heather was much too headstrong to suit him."

"But you got back together?" I asked.

"Not right away. She went to live with her parents for a couple of years after she left college. Then she came back." He made a face. "And so did I."

"You mean you went back to her?"

He nodded. "I was young and stupid. And she had some sort of spell on me."

Something about the way he said that, or maybe the words he'd chosen, made me feel a little prick of jealousy, mostly because I obviously hadn't meant that much to him. I told myself he'd known her for years and me only a month, but still…

"What sort of spell?" I asked, proud of myself for not letting my irritation bleed through.

He put the pancakes on another plate and moved the skillet off the burner, staying on the other side of the island as he started doctoring his pancakes. "Nothing magical," he said with a laugh. "More like she was a master manipulator and she knew how to play me like a fiddle. It didn't hurt that she was wrapped in a pretty package."

"Got any photos of her?"

"Nope," he said, keeping his gaze on his food.

"Come on," I said. "I don't believe that. You were taken with her, spent years with her. Surely you have something. A snapshot of you with friends? Homecoming photos?"

He still refused to look at me. "Nope."

I'd found newspaper articles about her last November when I'd looked up Wyatt's arrest, but none of them had included any photos. "What about yearbooks?"

"I didn't bring any of that stuff with me when I moved out. They're all at my parents' house."

I didn't think marching up to the Drummonds' front door and asking to see Wyatt's old yearbooks was a good idea. "So she left after y'all graduated high school, then came back a couple of years later?"

He took a moment. "She came back to see her aunt for a few weeks over the summer when we were twenty. We hooked up, but then she left for what I thought was good. When she came back the next time, I was runnin' the bar.

We got together, but she said she wanted to see other people, so I started datin' Ruth. What Ruth and I had was nothin' serious, and truth be told, datin' someone who works for you is the worst idea ever. In any case, the next thing I know, Heather was wanting me back. I told her I was done bein' her yo-yo, but she told me she'd done a lot of growin' up and seeing me with Ruth had made her realize what was important." He made a face. "She claimed it was me. And fool that I was, I believed her."

He glanced up at me as though expecting me to reprimand him.

"Who am I to judge?" I said. "I'm the master of playing the fool with men."

He made another face. "I'm fully aware you count me on that list."

I did, but admitting it would serve no purpose.

"When we got back together, she started needlin' me about the bar. She didn't like that I didn't flat-out own it, and suggested I try bein' more assertive with my father. Demand what was mine." He released a bitter laugh. "What was mine." He pushed out a sigh. "I had a small house a few blocks from the tavern, and Heather moved some things in even though she never officially lived with me. We were together for about six months before I found out why she'd ended up back in Drum. She'd had an abortion while she was living with her parents, and they found out and disowned her. She couldn't afford to live alone, so she moved back to Drum, and in with her aunt."

"And back to you."

He shrugged, but he didn't come off as nonchalant as he was trying to act. "Yeah, but she was right. We had done some growing up, and we stuck that time. I think maybe I took her back because I'd dated everyone I was interested in and no one else seemed to fit. For all her issues, I knew what I was getting with her, you know?"

"Yeah." Sadly, I did. I'd done the same thing with Jake.

"We started gettin' serious, but she wanted more…or more specifically she wanted *me* to have more. She wanted me to own the tavern, not just run it for my father." He shook his head with a wry grin. "She had a way of bolsterin' a man to do things he might not ordinarily do. So I went to my parents and told them I wanted them to hand over the bar. My father knew right away it had come from Heather and told me she was a gold digger. I admit, I suspected there might be some truth to it, yet I'd already started the battle, I figured I might as well finish it. I told him if he didn't give it to me, I'd disown the entire family. I should have known better, because he told me fine. I was no longer part of the family. I stopped running the bar, cold turkey, on Heather's suggestion. Show him how much he needed me. Only he never came crawling to ask me back."

He pushed out a sigh, and his voice was tight as he said, "Deep down, I think I knew he wouldn't. Maybe part of me was relieved." He shrugged again and swallowed, refusing to look at me again. "Maybe I was tired of trying to make the old man happy. But Heather was startin' to sweat. She saw me as the Drummond heir apparent and she didn't want to wait for the old man to die for me to get what was comin' to me. She started pickin' fights, tellin' me I hadn't approached him the right way, that I needed to go back and plead for forgiveness. I was close to crawlin' back to him just to get Heather to shut up, and then I caught wind that my father had sold my baseball to Earl Cartwright. The one signed by Joe DiMaggio that my grandfather had given me.

"I'd been drinkin' far more than I should have, feelin' plenty of regret, and I went to talk to my father. He said he was selling off my things since I considered myself too good for the family, only he wasn't givin' me the money. I went home and just got drunker. The next thing I knew, I was drivin' to the garage and breakin' in. I got my baseball back, and I drove Heather and me to Balder Mountain State Park, where we drank even more. The next thing I knew, I was arrested for a DUI and breakin' and enterin'."

"You must have been pretty hurt by his behavior," I said quietly. "Every child wants their father to love them."

He lifted his gaze to mine, his eyes glassy. "You of all people know we don't always get what we want."

I didn't respond.

He shuffled his weight and sniffed, then looked at me with emotionless eyes. "My father had me followed and arrested to teach me a lesson. To bring me to heel. Only I wouldn't fall into line. Heather was furious, and then scared, sayin' my family was pushin' her hard to lie to the sheriff about the drinking and driving and the break-in, with the hope of gettin' me off. My father posted bail, but that's the last favor I accepted from him. When I got out, I wouldn't speak to them and refused their attorney. I told them I was done. Heather didn't stick with me, which came as no surprise. She told me that my father had given her five thousand dollars to leave town and never come back. So she did. Or so I thought. Turns out she was murdered instead."

I listened closely for any hint of sorrow or regret, but all I heard was weariness. Was he really that removed from her death? They'd had a tumultuous relationship. Maybe his feelings had changed after she "left town" and he'd realized he'd dodged a bullet. Or maybe he'd spent the past nine years getting over her. Then again, maybe he'd just learned to control his emotions and hide how he really felt. He was good at that. People were complicated too, and it could be some combination of all three. "Did you love her?"

"I did at one time, but when she left…" He shook his head and pushed out a breath, glancing down at his plate. "I was just grateful she was leavin' me in peace."

"Do you have any idea who murdered her?"

His gaze lifted to mine, holding firm this time. "Nope. None."

"Who did she hang out with? I'd like to talk to them and find out if they knew of anyone who might've had a grudge against her."

He shifted his weight. "She had a couple of friends from high school she kept up with. Mitzi Ziegler and Abby Atwood. I know Abby works at the Drum Veterinary Clinic. Last I heard, Mitzi lives in Ewing."

I nodded. "Okay. I'll start with them. How did you get along with her friends? I know you two broke up multiple times. Did they blame you for the breakups?"

"I don't think so. They both seemed friendly enough. Still do. Abby brings her car to me, but then again, I have the only car repair shop in town, and our prices are cheaper than most places in Ewing. It might just be convenient for her to like me, you know what I mean?"

I nodded. "Yeah."

"So after we clean up here, do you want to drop by the animal clinic? Talk to Abby?"

I gave him a tight smile. "I agreed to help you, Wyatt, but I didn't agree to let you ride along."

"Ride along?" he said, sounding irritated. "I was plannin' on driving you."

"Not happening."

A dark look crossed his face. "You let Marco drive you around."

"Well, Marco just happened to be a sheriff's deputy on medical leave, and he also wasn't the subject of my investigation. Apples and oranges."

"I promised Hank I wouldn't let anything happen to you."

"Guess you shouldn't have made that promise," I said, closing my notebook and slipping it into my bag.

"You didn't eat anything."

"I was too busy taking notes, and while you may have promised Hank to feed me, I never promised I'd eat." I spun and headed for the front door.

"Where the hell are you goin'?"

"To save your ass."

Chapter
Nine

Something about Wyatt's story didn't feel right, although I couldn't put my finger on what. But while I suspected he was fudging about something, I still didn't believe he was a killer. Why would he have murdered his girlfriend? He'd chosen not to fight any of the charges, so her testimony against him would have been a moot point.

While I couldn't help admitting I felt a special thrill about investigating this case—I really, really hoped it led back to Bart in some way—I missed working with Marco. He'd been a great partner, and I'd felt safe with him. I decided to drop by the resort excavation site and kill two birds with one stone.

The resort site was at the northwestern tip of Drummond land, accessed from Highway 25, the road that cut through Drum if you went north, and North Carolina if you drove south. They'd created a gravel road for the construction traffic, so I turned off on it and drove a good half mile until I hit the mostly empty gravel parking lot. A few sheriff cars were parked there, and I could see a couple of deputies standing next to the yellow crime scene tape.

I smiled to myself as I got out of my car and walked over to Marco. He and the other deputy looked as bored as any two people would if asked to babysit dirt. Because that's what it was now that the bones had been removed. Behind them sat multiple bulldozers and earthmoving equipment, all parked around a large rectangular hole in the ground, about ten feet deep on one side, and shallower on the other.

Marco's face lit up when he saw me. "Carly, what are you doin' here?"

"I was drivin' by and thought I'd stop and check on you. Make sure you hadn't died of boredom."

The other deputy, a young man who looked fresh out of high school, laughed. "Not yet, but we're on life support."

"You think they're gonna cut you loose soon?" I asked.

"God, I sure as hell hope so," the younger man said.

"Deputy," Marco admonished, giving him a stern look. "Language."

Chagrin covered the deputy's face. "Ma'am, I apologize."

I laughed. "Please, I've heard worse at the tavern."

"You work at Max's?" he asked, perking up. "Then you must be Carly."

I blinked in surprise. "You've heard of me?"

He grinned. "We know all about you."

Turning to Marco, I cocked an eyebrow. "What's that supposed to mean?"

Marco rolled his eyes. "Don't you have somewhere you need to be, Deputy?"

"Nope," he laughed. "I was told to stick with you."

"Walk the perimeter and make sure no one's tryin' to get under the crime scene tape," Marco said in a harsh tone, but the deputy only grinned.

"Yes, sir."

"What's he talkin' about?" I asked as he walked around the outside of the tape.

"They know about you from the Carson Purdy case. Because you saved me."

"Are you sure that's it?" I asked, not really sure why I was pressing or what, exactly, I was hoping he would say.

He shook his head. "They also know we're friends, yet they don't quite believe it. They can't make sense of me stickin' around you for so much longer than I do the other women in my life." He made a face. "Ignore them. What brings you by, anyway? Wantin' a look at the hole?"

I grimaced. "Maybe? But that's not the only reason."

"That construction guy hasn't given you any more trouble, has he?"

"What?" It took me a second to realize what he was talking about. "No. I haven't seen him since the night Wyatt punched him." I stepped closer, lowering my voice. "Which brings me to the other reason I'm here: Wyatt dropped by Hank's this morning. Lookin' for me."

Marco's eyes darkened. "What for?"

"He wants me to help clear his name. While he wasn't arrested, he's sure he's suspect number one."

"He is," Marco said with a frown. "How'd he take it when you turned him down?"

"Well…"

Disappointment filled his eyes, but it quickly disappeared. "You didn't turn him down."

"No."

He nodded and turned his gaze to the giant hole in the earth. "Why are you helpin' him?"

"Because I don't think he killed her." When he didn't answer, I said, "Do you think he did it?"

"No."

"But you're not happy I'm lookin' into it."

"I'm not," he said. "It's an active investigation, for one thing, which means you could get slapped with a charge of obstructin' an investigation."

"They can do that?" I asked in surprise.

"Yeah, Carly," he said, sounding irritated. "They can do that."

"Why are you mad at me?" I asked, trying not to sound hurt.

"I'm not mad at *you*. I'm pissed at *him* for puttin' you in this position. He had no right to ask you, Carly, but he was countin' on you bein' too nice to say no."

"Is that why you think I'm doin' it?" I asked, starting to get pissed myself. "Because I'm too nice to say no?"

He gave me a sad smile. "No. I think you'd say no if you didn't want to do it."

"But you're disappointed in me for saying yes."

"No," he said, but then he shrugged. "Yes. Look, I don't want to see you get hurt again."

He had a point—he'd been there to help me pick up the pieces of my heart after it had been broken in December.

"I have an ulterior motive for doin' this, Marco," I said in a whisper. "I know Heather's murder has ties to Bart Drummond. I'm gonna figure out how."

His eyes widened. "What?"

As if on cue, Bart's voice called out from the trees. "Why, is that Carly Moore I spot on my property?"

I gave Marco a tight smile, then turned to face the Drummond patriarch. I hadn't seen Bart since the meeting he'd summoned me to in his office, and I sure as hell didn't intend to cower to him. I only hoped I didn't get Marco in trouble.

"Curiosity got the cat?" Bart asked as he strolled toward us.

"Over an empty hole in the ground?" I asked in a bored tone. "You've seen one, you've seen them all. I'm here to see Marco."

"I heard you two are an item, yet *not*," he said, his gaze jumping from me to Marco then back again.

A shiver ran down my back. It didn't surprise me that Bart was aware of our friendship—he was the kind of man who made it his business to know things—but it was still unnerving. I'd already landed a target on Hank—would my friendship with Marco put him in danger too?

"We're just friends," I said.

"Very good friends," Marco said in a deep voice.

Bart grinned, but it didn't quite reach his eyes. "Relationships these days. All that swipin' right and left."

"Not much of that goin' on in Drum," I said before I could stop myself. "Not with the limited access to internet and cell phone coverage."

"Funny you should mention that," Bart said, his eyes lighting up. "All that's about to change. I've got a commitment from two cell phone carriers to add towers close to the resort. We'll soon have access to the outside world."

My blood ran cold. I'd heard rumblings about that before, but the way he said it made it sound like it would be happening sooner rather than later. I knew what he was telling me. Or rather threatening. My anonymity wouldn't last much longer.

"What are you doin' back at the crime scene?" Marco asked, and I was sure he used the term crime scene to antagonize Bart.

From the look on Bart's face, it had worked. But the irritation quickly faded, replaced with the fake-as-could-be pleased look he seemed to wear most of the time. "I'm eager to get construction back on track. What's the word, Deputy Roland?"

"I'm hearing it should be released any time now."

"Perhaps you could give them a call and see what's what?" Bart suggested.

Marco was about to say something when the radio close to his shoulder squawked. He picked up the mic and pressed the button. "Deputy Roland."

There was a second of static, then a male voice. "Deputy, the all clear has been given for the construction site."

"Copy that." Marco hooked his mic back onto his shirt and gave Bart a deadpan look. "Well, what do you know? It's like you're psychic."

Bart smiled. "Oh, a little birdie might have told me the order had been given to release the construction site. You'll always be a step behind, Marco. Always. Best keep that in mind." He grabbed the evidence tape and gave it a hard jerk, his eyes glittering with evil.

I was about to blast him when the other deputy rounded the corner and shouted in alarm, "You can't do that!"

"He can," Marco said. "We just got the all clear."

"Carly, would you like to see where the bones were buried?" Bart asked, "Oh, come now. Don't be shy. Or perhaps you're frightened," he cajoled,

I was scared, but not of the hole or the bones. I was scared of what Bart Drummond had up his sleeve now. "Sure," I said, trying to sound breezy. "Why not?"

"Carly," Marco warned in a low undertone I was fairly sure Bart couldn't hear. The radio squawked again, and he cursed under his breath.

Ignoring him, I stepped over the ripped-down yellow tape, toward the right side of the hole.

"I hear the bones were buried over here in that shallower area to the left," Bart said as I approached, waving his hand in a sweeping motion. "About three feet deep. Why do you think that is?"

"I couldn't say, Mr. Drummond."

He smirked. "Mr. Drummond. So respectful."

I held my tongue. Any answer I gave him would only feed his ego.

"I'm not a law enforcement officer," Bart said in a slow drawl, "but I would think it meant whoever did it was in a hurry to dispose of her body."

"I suppose you would know," I said in a dry tone.

He laughed. "I know you don't have a high opinion of me, Ms. *Moore*, but I'm not a stupid man. And only a stupid man would hire an excavation crew to dig in an area where he'd buried someone."

"Perhaps you didn't know where she was buried," I challenged.

"I would make it my business to know where every body on my property was buried," he said with a gleam in his eyes. "Hypothetically speaking, of course."

"Let's not forget that the man who ran your many acres of property was a known killer. Perhaps he buried bodies in locations you're unaware of." I gestured to the shallow location. "Case in point."

He chuckled. "Carson Purdy was not a murderer."

"I'm sure Bitty, the former cook at the tavern, would disagree. But she can't since she's buried in the Drum Cemetery."

"We have no proof that he killed her," he scoffed.

"Actually…" I said, tired of this game. "I *saw* him kill her. And so did Wyatt. Not to mention Carson shot Marco twice and fired at your son in the woods." Why was I having this conversation with him? It was pointless. "This has been a lovely chat, but I need to be on my way." I turned to head back to the parking lot.

He called after me, "I want you to tell me what you find out about Heather's death before you take it to the sheriff's department."

I turned back to face him. "Excuse me?"

He took a step closer. "I know you'll be lookin' into it. You can't help yourself. I'm offering you my encouragement and support. In fact, Emily would love to have tea with you this afternoon. She can tell you anything you need to know about Wyatt and Heather." When he saw my surprise, his grin spread. "Now, does that sound like a man guilty of murder?"

"Not until you said you wanted me to take the information to you before I talked to the police."

He laughed. "That doesn't make me a murderer, Caroline. It makes me controlling."

I whipped my head around to see if anyone was within hearing range. Marco and the other deputy were by one of the patrol cars.

"Your secret is still safe with me," Bart said, although the *for now* had obviously been left unsaid. "Shall I tell Emily to expect you at three?"

"I have to be at work at three."

"I'll call Max and tell him you'll be a little late."

"I can handle my own work hours," I said, my tone short. "I don't want Max knowing we had this chat."

"Or Wyatt?" he asked with a grin. He cast a glance toward Marco. "I might not tell Max, but he likely will." Then he added, "Not that it matters to me one way or the other."

But it did matter to me. The less they knew about my interactions with their father, the better. While they both claimed to be estranged from him, I didn't totally trust that. I knew they disliked him—*hated* him—but that didn't mean he lacked power over them. Plus, I didn't want them to know that he'd threatened me. I didn't have a solid reason for that, except Hank had warned me months ago that knowledge was currency. I needed to stock up on my currency. Everyone else in this town seemed to do a good job of that, especially the Drummonds.

"Emily will have tea ready and waitin'," he said in his sly tone. "She'll be very excited to chat with you. I hope you don't disappoint her." With that, he strolled off, whistling a happy tune.

And that was the clincher to let me know I'd just been conned.

Two could play that game.

Chapter
Ten

Marco was still talking on his radio, but as soon as he ended the conversation, he turned to me with a frown. "How bad was it?"

I checked the time on my useless cell phone—or at least useless for now. "Do you know when you'll be free for lunch? I would love to bounce some things off you."

"And here I was hopin' you wanted to have lunch with me because of my charming personality," he said with a grin. "Still, I'll take what I can get. I need to wrap some things up around here, but I can be free in an hour. Want to meet at Watson's?"

"Sounds good."

I headed to my car and drove into town. Since I had an hour to kill, I figured I might as well make the most of it. I could stop by the veterinary clinic and talk to Abby Atwood.

There were only three cars parked in the lot when I pulled in. I still wasn't sure what excuse I was going to use to talk to Abby until I saw a small sign out front that read, *Free kittens.* If I pretended to be interested in a kitten, it might give me an opening to find and talk to Abby.

The vet clinic was an old bungalow that had been converted into a business space. The waiting room looked like it had once been a living room.

"Hello," a young woman said from the front desk. "Welcome to Drum Veterinary Clinic. How can I help you?"

She looked to be in her late teens or early twenties, too young to be Heather's high school friend. "I saw the sign out front," I said, thumbing toward the windows. "Free kittens?"

Her face brightened. "Oh, they're so cute! Let me take you back so you can have a peek."

I followed her down a hallway to a kitchen. Several crates lined the wall opposite the one with the cabinets and appliances. The crates held multiple animals—a yellow lab that lay on the floor, a fluffy white mutt with a cone around its neck, and a gray and white cat curled up with multiple gray and black kittens.

"They're not quite ready to leave their mother yet," the receptionist said, "but they only need another week," she said as she squatted next to the cage. "Do you see one that catches your eye?"

I peered into the kennel, overwhelmed. "Oh, my. How does someone choose? They're all adorable."

She laughed. "We have a play area out back. How about I take you out there and let you play with all of them and see if any of them fit."

"Okay."

"I'm Sasha, by the way," she said as she opened the kennel and scooped out a couple of kittens and handed them to me.

"Carly." I held them with both hands, then watched in surprise as she gathered four more on her own.

"Can you open the door?" she asked.

I shuffled the kittens around and turned the knob. When I walked out the door, I found myself looking at a covered back deck, half of it protected with baby gates.

"Right in there," Sasha said, leaning over the baby gate and lowering the kittens to the deck. Then she opened the gate so I could walk in with the other two. "I've got to get back to the front desk even though hardly anyone shows up," she said, sounding disappointed.

"You should get a bell for the door," I said as I sat cross-legged on the wood slats. "Or one of those electronic chimes. Then you can step away."

She made a face. "Dr. Donahey doesn't like it. She prefers to keep things quiet for the animals."

Considering that I didn't know much about animals, I just nodded. "Well, thanks." But as she started to walk away, I called after her, realizing I could use my lack of animal knowledge to my advantage. "I've never had a pet before, so is there any way I could talk to someone about what to expect? Like a vet tech?"

Her face brightened. "Yeah. I'll send someone out to you."

As the back door closed, I gave my full attention to the wiggling kittens crawling on top of my legs. I'd never had a pet as a kid, and my teaching schedule had kept me from my apartment for long hours, which had never seemed conducive to caring for a pet. But I had to admit the kittens were tugging at my heartstrings.

A dark gray one seemed fascinated with my fingers, batting at them and then crawling under my hand as though trying to force me to pet it.

I picked it up and held it to my chest, giving it some good pets, and grinned when it started to purr.

"Looks like you found my favorite," a woman said as she walked out the back door onto the porch.

I glanced up to see a woman in her mid-thirties. Her long blonde hair was pulled back into a ponytail. She wore a pair of pale-yellow scrubs covered in parakeets and cockatiels.

"*He* seems to have picked *me*," I said.

"*She's* really good at that," the woman said with a friendly smile, but the corners of her mouth looked like she was holding them a bit too high to be natural.

Why was she acting strangely? Was she worried I'd take the kitten away?

"Is this one taken?"

"No, they're *all* available. It's hard to get people to take kittens or puppies around here. Dime a dozen. We'll probably be stuck with them for months."

I cringed, hating the idea of the kittens being stuck in a crate for that long.

"I was thinking about getting a pet for me and my landlord, but I work long hours and it would be difficult for him to chase around after a puppy. I've heard cats are pretty self-sufficient, so I figured a kitten might be a good option." I'd had no intention of adopting a kitten when I'd walked in, but now I was beginning to give it serious thought. Maybe a kitten could keep Hank company while I was gone all day. "I've heard cats don't want much attention, but this one seems to like it."

"Cats are a lot like people. Some people are huggers. Some people don't want to be touched. If you actually *are* here looking to adopt a kitten and want a snuggler, that one is the way to go."

Frowning, I said, "What makes you think I don't really want to adopt a kitten?"

She put a hand on her hip. "I know who you are, Carly Moore. You work at the tavern and you used to date Wyatt Drummond. You've never stepped foot in this place, yet you walked in two days after Heather Stone was dug out of the side of a mountain. It's as plain as day you aren't here for a cat. You're here to see me."

"So that would mean you're Abby Atwood," I said.

"Dr. Abby Atwood Donahey," she said. "DVM."

"I love your clinic," I said, still stroking the kitten. "Very homey."

"It's way too small, but there wasn't much available in Drum and I don't see a ton of patients, so the cheap rent works to my advantage." She frowned. "I take it you're here to ask me questions about Heather."

"What makes you think that?" I asked out of curiosity.

She leaned closer. "Rumor has it that the last time Lula Baker took off, you got it in your head to go looking for her, not knowing her history, and put Greta in danger with your snoopin'."

The official story was that Lula had taken off and come back on her own—not entirely untrue—but the other part of the story was a whopper: our explanation for Greta's kidnapping was that her ex-boyfriend had kidnapped her for a few days until Todd Bingham found out and made him let her go. Greta's abusive ex was one of Bingham's men, and Bingham had convinced him to go along with the lie. And he'd given him a well-deserved beating to go with it.

But I was betting Abby Atwood Donahey knew none of that. "Greta's kidnapping had nothing to do with Lula. Her ex-boyfriend got tired of her refusing him and tried to force the issue."

She shrugged.

Something told me honesty would go a lot further with her, so I said, "Look, you're half right. I would like to ask you some questions about Heather, but I'm also interested in a kitten. I'm working far too many doubles, and my landlord's usually alone for hours. He might like a pet to keep him company. From what I understand, kittens litter box train themselves, and I'll only have to change the litter box every few days."

She studied me as though trying to discern my truthfulness. "It does sound like a kitten would suit your home life better than a puppy. Especially if Hank's havin' trouble gettin' around with one leg."

So she knew I was living with Hank. I wasn't exactly surprised considering everything else she knew. Although we'd never met, the town gossip mill was strong. "He's getting around better than you might expect, but that's not to say he's fit to chase down a puppy."

"How does Hank feel about gettin' a cat?"

I gave her a half smile. "He doesn't know yet."

Fighting a smile of her own, she said, "Well, maybe you should make sure he's okay with a new addition to the family before you commit." She tilted her head. "You know, most people were surprised when they found out you were living with him."

"So I heard." Some had claimed I was there to cheat Hank out of his money, although the man lived frugally in a house in major need of updating. But Hank had been the top marijuana dealer in Eastern Tennessee, and rumor had it he'd acquired a fortune. I'd seen no evidence of it, nor was I interested in his money other than to make sure he had all he needed to live comfortably. Truth be told, *I* was the one supporting *him*. I paid for groceries, took him to his doctor's appointments in Greeneville, and had started slowly replacing some of his threadbare clothes—not that I minded one bit. Hank and I were a family—the way family was intended to be. But men were proud in these parts and I would never admit to any of it. "He needed help when he came home from the hospital, and I needed a place to stay. It worked out for both of us."

"Carnita says you're always looking for diabetic recipes for him. And Ellie Smith says she sees you checkin' out with fresh fruits and vegetables at the Dollar General. She said you were even asking about a farmers market."

I made a face, glancing down at the cute kitten cuddled in my hands. "He had the diet of a teenager, and I want him to keep his remaining leg, as well as live a long, healthy life."

"She also says you buy his food with your own money."

How would she know that? Max only paid me in cash, so I wasn't using my card. "He doesn't charge me rent."

"Ruth says you bought Jerry a coat."

My eyes narrowed in exasperation. I didn't like that the town was gossiping about me, even though it wasn't exactly malicious gossip. Where was she going with all of this?

"Sounds like you're a good person, Carly Moore," she finished, tilting her head as if to study me.

I wasn't so sure about that, but I wasn't about to protest. If she thought that, she'd be more inclined to help me.

A playful look filled her eyes. "I'll tell you what you want to know on one condition."

I cocked my head. "And what's that?"

"If you decide to take a kitten, you have to choose two. It's gonna take me forever to find homes for them, and I know you'll give 'em a good one."

I shrugged. What was one more? Besides, maybe they'd be happier if I kept two of them together. "Deal."

She opened the baby gate and walked in, sitting on the floor across from me. Picking up a kitten, she said, "So what do you want to know?"

"How long did you know Heather?"

"Most of us were born here, but occasionally we got a newcomer. Most of them were treated as outsiders, interlopers, but Heather was pretty and vivacious, and soon she had most of the girls eating out of her palm. Half the boys too."

"What grade did she move to town?"

"Third. Me and Mitzi were the closest to her. The three of us were best friends all through high school. Or so we thought."

"What does that mean?"

She pushed out a sigh. "Heather could have taught a master class in gaslighting and manipulation. She loved to play us against each other, sometimes to get what she wanted, but I'm sure sometimes she did it for sport."

"So a lot of people didn't like her, then?" I asked.

"Well, that's the weird part. She didn't really have any enemies. She could lay on the charm as smooth as silk and as sweet as honey. When we were out of her orbit for a while, we'd realize that she'd held us under a spell and tell ourselves that we wouldn't fall for it again. But we always did." She gave me a pointed look. "I'm not a stupid woman. You have to be pretty intelligent to get into vet school let alone make it through, so take my word for it when I say that Heather could get *anyone* to do *anything*. She had a way of pulling people's strings like they were puppets. Of course, when she came back the last time, I was in vet school in Knoxville, but Mitzi was still here and I'm pretty sure she got roped back into her nonsense, although she's never admitted to it, and after Heather left, we had this unspoken agreement to not talk about her."

"Everybody believed that the Drummonds paid Heather to leave town. Why do you suppose no one considered that she might have been murdered?"

Abby lifted a shoulder into a shrug. "Maybe for the same reason most people don't think too much about it when Lula takes off." She shook her head a little, with a rueful smile. "I can't believe you thought someone had snatched her."

I tried hard to look nonplused. Someone *had* tried to snatch Lula, and she'd gone into hiding. "So everybody just figured Heather had left and that was the end of that? No one ever tried to contact her or wondered why she never called or visited?"

"You have to understand," she said, leaning forward. "Heather was an out of sight, out of mind kind of girl. She was your best friend when she was there *with* you, but once you fell off her radar, it was radio silence."

"Do you think Mitzi would be open to talking to me?"

"I don't know," she said. "I suspect you're here to help Wyatt, and Mitzi's not too fond of him. Especially after Wyatt crashed Heather's goin'-away party."

I blinked hard. "Going-away party?"

"Yeah. Heather told everyone she was leavin' for Tulsa and got Mitzi to throw her a party. She told everyone the Drummonds had paid her to leave town, showed them the check and everything."

"Why Tulsa?" I asked. "Did she have family or a friend there?"

"Dunno," Abby said, glancing down at the kittens. "All I know is what Mitzi told me. Rumor has it that Wyatt showed up, drunk off his ass, and they went into a bedroom.

When they came out, they were fightin' like cats and dogs. Then he took off."

"Wyatt drove drunk. *Again?*" That would have been after his DUI arrest.

"I guess so, if he was drunk when he got there. Mitzi said he didn't stay very long. Long enough to screw her in the bedroom, then yell at her as he left."

"So a half hour or so?" I asked, my voice rising at the end.

She laughed. "I couldn't tell you, but if he was as drunk as Mitzi said, it might have taken longer."

I couldn't believe that Wyatt had left out that pertinent piece of information from his version of things. Then again, he'd long since proved he was a man more inclined to partial truths than full ones.

"You think he's innocent, don't you?" she asked bluntly.

I tried not to cringe. "I just know that when Seth Chalmers was murdered, the sheriff's department was pretty eager to find a way to pin it on me. I had to find his killers on my own to clear my name. And while Wyatt and I aren't together, we're still sort of friends. I had the day off, so I figured I'd ask around and see what people know."

She shrugged and gave me a look I interpreted as, *Whatever, you do you.*

"Do you think you could give me Mitzi's number?" I asked, already falling in love with the kitten that had fallen asleep in my arms. "I'd like to ask her some questions too."

She made a face. "I'm not sure I should just give you her number. She may not want to be harassed."

"I don't want to harass her in any way," I said in a rush. "I just want to have a conversation. You haven't felt harassed, have you?" Had I come on too strong?

"No, but Mitzi knows more about when Heather came back the last time. And she's the one who threw the party for her." She was quiet for a moment. "Mitzi's not taking Heather's death well, and she was already fragile. I don't want her to get hurt."

"I promise to be gentle with her," I said earnestly. "I'm not out to coerce people to protect Wyatt, if that's what you're worried about. I'm out to find the truth. So if Mitzi tells me information that paints Wyatt in a bad light, I'm not going to go after her to change her story. I just want to ensure the sheriff's department finds the real murderer."

"Why?" she asked with narrowed eyes. "You didn't even know Heather. Why would you care?"

"Because whatever flaws she might have had, Heather didn't deserve to be murdered, and the person who did it needs to be brought to justice." When I could see that didn't sway her, I added, "And I guess I like playin' PI."

As I suspected, that was the answer she was looking for. A wide smile spread across her face. "You weren't obtrusive, and I really *do* think you're trying to find out the truth. I'll put in a good word for you with Mitzi and have her call you."

This was one of those times I wish I had a reliable cell phone. "She can call me at Max's Tavern, although I won't be going into work until three." Then I remembered Bart's invitation to have tea with Emily. "Or maybe even later. And after I leave here, I'm meeting someone for lunch at Watson's. What if I drop by after lunch? That will give you time to call Mitzi, and you can let me know whether she agreed. I'd really like to talk to her this afternoon."

"Okay..." But the look on her face suggested she was reluctant.

I glanced up at the clock on the wall. "I suppose I should be going soon, but these little guys are *so cute*."

"Are you serious about adopting?" she asked as she got to her feet.

"Yeah," I said, holding the gray kitten in front of my face. "As long as Hank agrees, which I don't think will be a problem. If I promise to take care of all the responsibilities and let him have all the fun, he'll likely be on board. I'd like this little girl to be one of the two."

Abby's face lit up. "Then I'll put in a good word for you. You can leave the kittens in the pen when you're done and just walk around back to your car. Sasha'll be out later to bring them in. The fresh air and space will do them good."

Then she went inside.

I hoped I'd just bought myself an interview.

Chapter
Eleven

I was five minutes early, but Marco was already sitting at a table at Watson's.

"I need to wash my hands before I sit down," I said, placing my purse and my messenger bag in the booth seat opposite him. "Get me an iced tea if Angie or Greta comes by to take our drink order."

"Already did," he said with a grin.

I hurried off to the bathroom to get cleaned up, and when I returned, there were two drinks on the table.

Marco gave me a suspicious glance. "What were you up to?"

"I figure it's pretty obvious what happens in a bathroom, but my main reason for going was to wash off the kitten germs."

"Kitten germs?"

"I was playing with kittens."

The look on his face made it clear he thought I was lying.

"I swear," I said, holding up three fingers. "Girl Scouts honor."

"I'd call your bluff on being a Girl Scout, but I suspect you actually were."

"I was until my—" I cut myself off, realizing I was about to reveal a fact about Caroline's life rather than Charlene's made-up backstory.

But Marco knew my truth and must have realized why I'd stopped myself. He reached across the table and placed his hand over mine. "I'm sorry, Carly."

I held his gaze, and the understanding and warmth flooded me. He'd become so important to me. He knew about my mother's death and how much it had changed my life, which saved me from saying the words. Flipping my hand over, I twined our fingers together. "Thank you, Marco."

"You two are the *sweetest* couple," Greta said next to our table. She was wearing a pink vintage-looking diner outfit, with a white collar and white trim on the pockets. Her long blonde hair was pulled back in a ponytail. And she was beaming as her gaze went from our hands to my face.

Marco gave my hand a squeeze and released me. "For the umpteenth time, Greta, we're just friends."

"Friends who hold hands? And stare into each other's eyes?" Her eyes danced with amusement. "And I know for a fact you haven't seen another woman for over a month, Marco Roland, so why won't you two just admit that you're seeing each other?"

"Because we're not," I said good-naturedly. "We're just very good friends. Marco was the one who helped nurse me back to health after the whole…situation with Lula, and we bonded over it, is all."

Her smile faded as her voice lowered. "I'll never be able to repay you for savin' me."

We rarely spoke about it—especially in public—but I suspected hearing about Heather's murder had made an impact on both of us.

But her bounce wasn't gone for long. "You two are like an old married couple, and if you're not sleepin' together, I sure as Pete don't know why not." She shook her head. "What can I get you?"

My thoughts were lingering on her comment about us sleeping together, and I shot Marco a long look as he ordered the special—fried chicken and mashed potatoes. Why was it so weird for a man and a woman to just be friends? And why didn't Marco seem annoyed by the constant questions about our relationship status?

Greta turned to me with an expectant look, and I realized she was waiting for me to order, not an explanation about my love life or lack thereof.

I asked for a chef's salad, which historically consisted mostly of iceberg lettuce, but the only vegetables at Max's Tavern were the potatoes Tiny used for fries and cucumbers made into pickles. I craved a good salad, but a mediocre one would suffice.

As soon as Greta walked away Marco turned serious. "What happened with Bart at the construction site?"

I ran my fingertip over the condensation on the outside of my iced tea glass. "Bart knew I planned on looking into Heather's murder, and he wants me to tell him what I find before I turn it over to the sheriff."

His gaze darkened. "So he can destroy the evidence?"

"He didn't say."

"How'd he know you were lookin' into it?"

"I don't know, but he knew. And he invited me to have tea with Emily today at three. He told me I was free to ask questions about Heather and Wyatt."

"Are you plannin' to go?" he asked in shock.

"I don't know," I admitted. "I'm tempted, but I'm also supposed to be at work at three." I gave him a questioning look. "What do you think I should do?"

"Obviously you don't go," he said as though explaining something to a fool. "He's playin' you."

I pursed my lips. He was right.

"You're considerin' goin' anyway," he said, his voice tight.

Looking up at his blue-green eyes, I said, "I guess I am."

His emotions shuttered. "Why is he so important to you?"

For a moment I wasn't sure who he was referring to. Bart was important to me, but only in the sense that I wanted to make him pay for all he'd done. For all he planned to do. Then it occurred to me that he meant Wyatt. "Wyatt's not important to me in the sense you're thinking. But I would hate to see him railroaded." I lowered my voice and leaned closer so I couldn't be overheard. "And I realize this is a good opportunity to get more dirt on Bart."

His face paled.

"Surely you knew I was looking to find some."

"Yeah." He looked like he was about to be sick. "And while I understand *why*, I'm still worried, Carly. Bart Drummond is not a man to be trifled with."

"And that's why this is good cover to be lookin'," I said. "So truth be told, I have ulterior motives for doing this."

He gave me a long, hard look and twisted in his seat, glancing around the room. Lifting his hand, he called out, "Greta, we're gonna need our lunches to go."

She gave us an odd look but nodded. "Okay."

Marco was silent while we waited, his jaw tight.

I watched him, worried I'd pissed him off.

Greta brought out our food and Marco took the ticket, something he usually did when we ate together, and slapped down some cash. He told Greta to keep the change and was out of the booth in a flash.

I followed him out the door, my nerves a tangled mess. I knew he was upset that I was putting myself in danger, and while I wanted to ease his concerns, I couldn't. I refused to give this up.

Out on the sidewalk, he stared down at me, still holding our lunches. "We need somewhere quiet to talk. Why don't you get in my car and we'll drive over to Old Mill Park so people aren't gawking at us while we eat."

"Okay."

I got into the front seat of his sheriff's car, and he drove the short distance to the edge of Drum's downtown, then turned onto a road that ran along a creek at the edge of downtown proper. A couple of blocks north was a dilapidated waterwheel attached to a small building with faded red paint. Rumor had it the Drummonds had built it for the town over a hundred years ago as a gift—and proceeded to use it for their moonshine business.

I took it as a reminder that if someone was offering you something for nothing, they usually had other motives in play. Especially in Drum.

Turned out I was adopting that philosophy as my own.

The building needed to be torn down, but a few women had created a historical society and convinced the citizens it was an important part of Drum history. And while the townsfolk had agreed to keep it, they hadn't loosened their purse strings to fix it up either.

You couldn't go in it, nor anywhere close to it—it was surrounded by a chain-link fence, covered by a thick canopy of tree branches—but there was a picnic table a few feet from the fence. There was a small parking area in front of it—trampled grass—and it was a known picnic area...or make-out spot. Often both.

"Did you bring me here to make out, Marco?" I teased as he put the vehicle in park.

He turned off the engine and stared out the windshield at the creek. "I might try if I thought it would make a difference."

"Your skills are that magical?" I asked in a wry tone.

He turned to look at me, but there was no teasing glint in his eyes—I saw all the marks of a tortured soul. "I think it's time for us to come up with a plan to get you out of town."

I jolted, unprepared for his statement. "You want me to leave Drum?"

"Selfishly, no. *God, no.*" He ran a hand through his hair in frustration. "I don't even want to think about life without you, but I *care* about you, Carly, and you're not just playin' with fire, you're takin' on a ragin' inferno."

"He's one man, Marco. One man."

"He is *not* just one man, and underestimatin' him will be your downfall." He took a breath. "Bart Drummond is cunning. You think Max and I never tried to best him over the years? It became a competition to Max, his F-you for all those years Bart overlooked him and rained down all his blessings on Wyatt. He never succeeded, Carly. *We* never succeeded. Bart found out every. Damn. Time. He knows exactly what you are up to right now—before you've even started doin' it. Why do you think he invited you to tea with Emily? Why do you think he took you over to that hole and asked you to tell him what you found? He knew you'd look into Heather's murder, and he knows you intend to use it against him."

"So you're tellin' me to just let it go? Let the sheriff's department arrest Wyatt for a murder he didn't commit?"

"How do you know he didn't commit it?" he said, his voice rising. "What makes you so damn sure?"

I was taken aback by his anger. "Because the man I got to know wouldn't do that."

"People can surprise you, Carly. In bad ways as well as good. Think about your childhood friend, the one you were supposed to marry. Did you ever think he might be capable of murder? Of murdering *you*?"

Tears stung my eyes, because he was right. About all of it.

He grabbed my hand and held on tight, his eyes burning green with intensity. "I will never hurt you, Carly, and I will never lie to you either. Because I know you'll never, ever trust me again the moment you catch me in a *single* lie. I'm tellin' you right now to leave this alone. Let it go. I've racked my brain tryin' to figure a way to get you out of this, and all I ever come up with is a lot of nothing. Which is why we should move on to plan B," he said, glancing down at the food bag. "We need to get you out of Drum."

"What about Hank?"

"I'll find a way to protect Hank, even if it means gettin' him out of town too."

"He'd never go, Marco, and if he did agree to leave, I'd bring him with me."

His gaze lifted to mine. "You can't do that, Carly. Do you know how conspicuous you'd be together, a beautiful thirty-year-old woman travelin' with a one-legged older man? When you run, you need to *hide*."

I didn't say anything, because as much as it hurt to admit, he was right. When I ran, I'd lose everyone I cared about. Again.

The thought lit a fire in me. I was done being jerked around and manipulated. I wasn't losing Hank and I wasn't losing Marco. I was standing my ground. I was getting justice.

My jaw tightened. "No. I'm not going."

"Why?" he pleaded. "To save Wyatt? A man who lied to you and broke your heart?"

I looked up at him, my voice breaking. "It's complicated, Marco."

"I'm in no hurry. Why don't you explain it to me? Help me understand."

"It started off as helping Wyatt, but you're right. Most of his lies have been lies of omission, but they're lies nonetheless." I paused for a moment to consider it. "Several people want me dead, Marco. And if Bingham hadn't found me last December, for all I know, I'd be buried in a mountainside too. Right next to Greta." I shivered at the memory. "They probably would have pinned our deaths on Bingham—on the obvious suspect—and doing that wouldn't have brought me justice, just like it won't bring Heather justice. I want the person who really killed her to be held responsible."

"You mean you don't trust the Hensen County Sheriff's Department to conduct a fair and thorough investigation?" There was just a hint of humor in his voice—both of us knew there were probably more corrupt cops than not. He'd admitted as much in the course of our search for Lula and Greta.

"Can you honestly say you do?"

He pushed out a long sigh. "What else is pushin' you to do this?"

"That threat hangin' over Hank's head. If I can't figure out a way to make Bart pay for all he's done, he's going to keep playing me like a fiddle. Do you expect me to leave him at Bart's mercy? How do you expect me to leave him *at all*?"

"Hank would hate that Bart's usin' him as a threat to you."

"Which is why we can't tell him," I insisted. "Because then he'll force me to go."

"Don't you see you're lying to him too? One of those lies of omission?"

I covered my face with my hands, realizing he was right.

He pulled my hands away, lowering his head so we were eye to eye.

"I don't want to leave him, Marco. I have to stay."

"I know he's like a father to you, but he wouldn't want you riskin' your life. You *know* that."

"I'm tired of running," I said in a whisper. "I've been running from my father like a coward. Maybe it's time to take a stand."

"Then I'll help you take a stand against your father, but leave Bart Drummond out of it."

My mouth parted in shock. "You'd help me take on my father?"

"If that's what it takes to make sure you're safe, then yeah." He sat up straighter. "Isn't that what Wyatt promised and failed to deliver?"

I didn't answer. I didn't need to. It was a rhetorical question. "My father is part of an international drug cartel. You think Bart's tough? He's a cakewalk compared to Randall Blakely." I shook my head, my voice calm and even. "No. I start with Bart because he's practice for the big leagues and he was behind Seth's death. He may not have pulled the trigger, but he was part of it, and I'm going to make sure he pays for that."

Marco was silent for several long seconds. "You're gonna need help."

My eyes flew wide. "You're gonna help me?"

"What kind of friend would I be if I let you do this alone?"

"But how?" I asked. "They won't make you a detective, and it looks like they're keeping you away from the real investigation."

"I can't help with that part, but I can keep my ears to the ground in the department. See if I can find out what's goin' on with the investigation. That part's gonna be hard since they think I'm loyal to Max."

"Aren't you?" I asked in surprise.

"Yeah. But not blindly." Which I already knew. He'd made a point of considering every angle when Lula disappeared, including the possibility that Max, who'd been acting strange, was involved. "I don't want you goin' out on your own, though. You need to take someone as backup. Someone who will protect you."

"Who?"

"Someone with a vested interest in this."

I was confused for a moment. Then it hit me like a brick. "Wyatt?"

"I know he still cares about you—the way he took out the guy attacking you proved that—which means he'll be good backup."

"Maybe I could get Bingham to loan me a guy." When Marco's eyebrow shot up, I said, "What about Jerry? He protected us from Carson Purdy."

He looked even more dubious. "And his hand was shakin' the entire time."

"You really think it's a good idea to take Wyatt while I'm interviewing witnesses? Won't it look like intimidation?"

"With the easier ones, yeah. But the tougher ones, no. You'll need someone with confidence."

Which Wyatt had in spades.

"You were flat-out against this five minutes ago."

He shrugged, grabbing the bag between us and digging into it. "If you're dead set on doin' this, I figure I'd prefer to support you than to leave you unprotected."

"Hank knows I'm looking into this," I said. "And he's none too pleased either. He told Wyatt he'd have to pay the blood price if anything happened to me."

"A blood price? I haven't heard that term in years. The Drummonds used it quite a bit back in their bootleggin' days. It was their version of a handshake deal. If the other party reneged, the offended party got to take their blood price." He was silent for a moment as he handed the Styrofoam container of salad to me. "Wyatt actually agreed?"

"Yeah, which was why he was none too pleased when I ditched him and went to see you at the construction site."

He looked past me through the passenger window, squinting. "That would explain why Wyatt's truck is parked on the side of the road the next block down."

Spinning around, I peered through the tree branches, and sure enough, Wyatt's F-150 was parked on the side of the road. "He's following me."

"If he agreed to a blood price, I'm not surprised. He's got a lot hangin' on you stayin' alive." His lips pursed. "We'll just let this ride. He's providin' backup and thinks you're none the wiser."

"But he's following me!"

"I know. And that's good. For now."

I started to protest but stopped. He was right. Wyatt was my backup, yet I didn't have to deal with him. The contentious side of me wanted him to know I knew, but I could tell him later.

"You see the wisdom in it too?"

I opened the lid to my salad. "You got a fork in there?"

He handed it to me, holding my gaze.

"I'm not protesting, am I? That's the best you're gonna get out of me."

He smiled, but it didn't quite reach his eyes. He was appeased, but barely.

"So what's your investigation plan?" he asked as he opened his own container. "And why were you playin' with puppies?"

"I was holding *kittens* at the Drum Veterinary Clinic. Apparently they have a litter of six kittens that will be ready to be adopted next week." I gave him an appraising glance. "Have you considered getting a cat?"

He released a snort. "Hell, no. And I don't believe for a minute that you were there to adopt a kitten."

"Okay, it started out as a cover to get me in the door. I was there to speak to Abby Atwood, who is now Dr. Donahey, DVM."

"Why'd you want to talk to Abby?"

"She and Mitzi Ziegler were best friends with Heather in school."

"No one could ever accuse you of lettin' grass grow under your feet," he said with a chuckle. "What did you find out?"

"If you're really going to help me with this, then I should share everything with you," I said. "Then we can look at all the information together, and you can help me decide where to look next."

He nodded, looking pleased, so I launched into an account of everything that had happened from the moment Wyatt had knocked on my bedroom door this morning to when I'd left his house. I left out nothing except for my hurt feelings. They were a moot point for this investigation.

"That man has a lot of nerve asking for your help," he finally said.

"I know."

"I think you need to ask yourself what you hope to gain if we prove his innocence. His gratitude? The answers he's refused to give you? Are you hopin' he'll tell you he fucked up and he's sorry and he wants you back? Because you want *something*. You need to figure out what it is and try to determine how heartbroken you'll be if he doesn't give it to you."

"Marco…"

"You don't have to tell me, Carly, but you definitely need to figure it out for yourself."

He was right, and it burned.

I was such a fool when it came to men.

"After I left Wyatt's, I headed to the construction site to see you, had my encounter with Bart, then dropped by the vet clinic to see Abby." I told him what she'd told me.

He stopped me when I got to the part about Wyatt's presence at Heather's going-away party. "He didn't tell you about that?"

"No."

"One of those lies of omission."

"It seems like a pretty big thing to leave out, doesn't it?" I asked.

"Yeah, it does, which leads me to why he did. He told you about her two best friends, so he knew you'd go to them first and get the truth."

"I know. It doesn't make any sense." I stabbed a forkful of lettuce. "I need to talk to Mitzi, but Abby said the news of Heather's death has upset her and she's fragile."

"What does that mean?"

"Good question. She was worried I'd upset her, but I assured her that I'd be perfectly cordial. So Abby agreed to call her and see if she'll be willing to talk to me. I'm supposed to drop by the vet clinic after lunch to find out what she says."

"Are you going to go have tea with Emily?"

"I haven't decided yet."

He looked grim. Then his lips tipped up into the hint of a smile. "What's Wyatt gonna do if he realizes you're heading to his parents' house?"

"It's almost worth going out there to see his reaction."

"If you decide to go, be careful. Don't let your guard down. Know that Bart isn't one step ahead of you. He's *six feet* ahead."

"I know."

He was silent for a moment, his gaze locked on the dilapidated mill. "As I mentioned, if you do this, you could get in trouble for interfering with an active investigation, but on the off chance the sheriff's department catches wind that you're looking into Heather's death, just blow it off as gossip. They'll likely buy it and give you a warning."

"Yeah, good idea."

"Let's drive to the vet clinic together," he said, reaching to turn on the engine. "I'd feel better if I know what you're doing and where you are."

"So you can track me down if I disappear?"

135

"Exactly," he said with a grim expression.

As morbid as that sounded, it filled me with a sense of security. Of course, it was likely misplaced. I'd been kidnapped from the tavern last December.

"Let's finish our lunch first," I said. "We can drive Wyatt crazy a little longer."

He grinned. "I'm good with that."

Chapter Twelve

We'd already eaten some of our lunches, so it didn't take us much longer to finish. Marco purposely drove away from the creek a couple of blocks before returning to Main Street so Wyatt could go on thinking we were oblivious to his presence. Sure enough, he kept following us. We weren't far out of town before we saw his truck in the distance in the rearview mirrors.

"He's probably wondering why I'm goin' with you in your sheriff's vehicle," I said, spotting the clinic ahead.

"I'm more worried what the staff at the vet clinic's gonna think about it," he said, turning on his signal before he pulled into the parking lot.

"I think it might give me more credibility. Abby wasn't worried about the truth coming out. She was more worried about why I was looking."

He nodded and put the vehicle in park. "Go work your magic."

I made a face, then got out of the car and headed into the building. When I walked through the door, Sasha and

Abby were both standing at the window in the waiting room, staring out at Marco's car.

"Is that Marco Roland?" Sasha asked.

I couldn't tell from her tone whether she considered that a good thing. For all I knew, she was one of his multiple conquests, although he didn't seem to have many disgruntled ex-lovers. He always made a point of telling the women he saw he wasn't looking for anything more than a few dates.

"Yeah…" I said hesitantly.

"I thought so," she said, still peering out the window. "Are you two a thing?"

"Because if you're not," Abby interjected, "I'm gonna need you to give me his number. I haven't had good sex since my divorce three years ago, and Marco Roland is known for amazing sex."

I flushed a little as my stomach twisted. So the sheriff's car had affected them, only not how Marco had anticipated.

"Um…he's taken," I said with a tight smile. A wave of horror washed over me. What had possessed me to say that? And what was this unsettled feeling in the pit of my stomach?

"Girl, then what are you doin' tryin' to prove Wyatt Drummond's innocence?" Abby asked.

"Because Marco's not a long-term kind of guy," Sasha said, "although rumor has it that he's stuck with Carly for a few months."

Abby looked at me as though seeing me in a whole new light.

"Did you get a chance to talk to Mitzi?" I asked.

"Yeah," Abby said, peering out the window again. "She says she'll meet you. Is Marco takin' you to see her?"

"No. We were having lunch together, and he offered to bring me by after we finished."

"Oh!" Sasha exclaimed. "We should make a calendar of the hot men of Drum holding puppies and kittens. We could sell those to keep the clinic afloat." She turned to me. "Can you ask him to do it for us? Abby'll even spay or neuter your kittens for free."

Abby started to protest, then shrugged. "But he has to do it shirtless."

"I can ask him," I said hesitantly, not too keen on the idea of them using Marco as eye candy. "But I can't guarantee he'll say yes." In fact, part of me hoped he'd say no. Marco was more than just a good-looking face on a built body. He was my friend and I hated to think of them using him like that. Or at least that was what I told myself.

"You work with Max Drummond too," Sasha said. "Ask him too."

"Okay." No harm in asking, although I had no idea if either one of them would agree. "Do you have Mitzi's number and/or address?" I asked.

Abby frowned as she walked over to the receptionist desk and grabbed a folded piece of paper. "If you go this afternoon, she asked that you knock lightly instead of using the doorbell. The baby might be down for his nap."

"Okay," I said, taking the paper from her before she could change her mind. I opened it and gave it a quick glance—Mitzi's name, address, and phone number—then tucked it into my front pocket. "Thank you."

She gave me a pointed look. "Sasha's onto something with that calendar idea. Be sure to ask Marco and Max if they'd be willing to pose."

"And if they have any hot friends," Sasha added as I reached for the door. But something flickered in her eyes, and she pushed past me. "Or I could just ask him myself."

I hurried after her, worried about her ambushing Marco. He looked surprised when he saw her, but he rolled down his window as she approached his car with purpose. It was only when I stopped by the car that I realized Abby had followed us.

"Hey there, Deputy Roland," Sasha said in a seductive voice as she thrust her hip out to the side.

"What can I do for you?" he asked, shooting me a questioning glance before turning back to her.

"We were wondering if you'd be open to letting us take your photo to put in a calendar. It's for a good cause."

His forehead wrinkled and he gave me a perplexed look.

"They want you to pose holding puppies or kittens," I said. "With your shirt off."

"We want her to ask Max too," Sasha said, leaning her arm against the base of his window. "But I wanted to *personally* invite you."

I couldn't believe she was being so flirtatious after I'd let them assume Marco and I were seeing each other. Then again, Sasha clearly knew about his reputation with women, so maybe she wanted him to know she was ready and willing whenever he kicked me to the curb.

"Well, thank you," Marco said in a slow drawl. "I'll be sure to give it some thought."

Sasha's bottom lip stuck out. "You can't just tell me now?"

He rubbed the back of his neck. "Nah, I need to think it over a bit."

"If you think you have to ask Carly if it's okay, she's given us her blessing. She even said she'd try to get Max to help us."

That wasn't exactly how things had gone down, but his eyes lit up. "Did she now?"

"How long have you two been a thing?" Sasha asked. I could practically hear what she wasn't saying: *And how long until you'll be movin' on? Because I'd like to submit my application.*

Or maybe my imagination was getting away from me. She didn't look overly flirty.

Marco looked like he was about to burst out into laughter.

Before he could correct her about our relationship, I said, "I told her you were taken."

If possible, his smile spread even wider. "So you're ready to share us with the world now?"

"You've been keepin' your relationship with this man a secret?" Abby asked behind me. "*Why?*"

"I can't say that I blame her," Marco said. "I *do* have a reputation for cycling through the ladies, but I don't plan on ending things with Carly anytime soon, so she and I will need to have a discussion about me posin' for anything."

I stared at him in shock, then quickly realized he was backing up my story. "I wanted to make sure he stuck."

He gave me a sweet smile. "I'm good and stuck."

This was getting cheesy quick, so I walked around to the passenger door and got in.

Marco started the engine.

"I'll be sure to get back to you…?" His voice rose at the end.

"Sasha," she said. "You can call me here at the clinic. Or stop by." She batted her eyelashes.

"Will do, Sasha," Marco said as he rolled up the window. When he backed out, Sasha was still standing there, waggling her fingers, but Abby had headed back inside.

Marco headed toward Drum.

"So you told them we were a couple?" he asked with a grin.

I nearly told him I'd only done it because they'd wanted him to pose half naked, but I didn't want to lie, especially after his proclamation that he wouldn't lie to me. "I don't want to talk about it."

"You know word's gonna spread," he said.

I felt my cheeks burning. "Feel free to tell people we broke up. In fact, I can spread the word tonight at the tavern. I'd hate to put a damper on your love life."

"I haven't been out with anyone in months," he said. "No damper."

Months. I'd noticed this last month or so, but I hadn't realized it had been that long.

"Why not?" I asked, scared to hear the answer.

"Dunno. I guess I've cycled through everyone." He shot me a grin, having used the phrase he'd used with Sasha.

"You haven't cycled through Sasha or Abby."

"I'm runnin' out of women," he said with a chuckle. "I decided to pace myself."

I glanced in the rearview mirror. "Looks like Wyatt's back."

"Oh, he never left. He drove past the clinic, then turned around and parked down the road."

I shook my head.

"Did Mitzi agree to meet with you?"

"Yeah. I got her address and phone number. As soon as you drop me off at my car, I'm going to head to Ewing to meet with her."

"And where will you go after that?"

"I'll have some time to kill, so I might stop by the nursing home."

He flashed me a smile. "You bringin' Gladys another puzzle?"

"Maybe."

I'd met Gladys in December, on a visit to Greta's grandma, Thelma, at the Greener Pastures nursing home. Gladys had given me and Marco information about one of the nursing home's employees. I'd taken to visiting both of them whenever I was in Ewing, but today I had an ulterior motive. Today I planned to finally ask Thelma—who seemed to know a lot about the happenings in Drum decades before—what she knew about Heather.

"Tell her I said hello."

"I will."

As he crossed the bridge over the creek into town, he said quietly, "You said you had time to kill. That means you're plannin' to see Emily Drummond, doesn't it?"

I didn't hesitate. "Yeah."

"Please be careful, Carly. And call me as soon as you get to the tavern. Since I'll be out on patrol, I likely won't get the call, but I'll check my messages as soon as I get to a spot with cell reception."

"Okay."

He was silent as he pulled into a parking spot a few spaces from my car. "You must be nervous about Drum opening to the rest of the world."

I gave him a wry grin. "I suspect Drum isn't opening to the world—it's Bart Drummond's resort. Do you think cell service is going to extend to downtown Drum?"

"Good question," he asked. "I have no idea how far those towers send out signals."

I laughed. "Can you imagine how many people are going to start hanging out at his resort—people who aren't paying customers?"

He grinned, but it quickly faded. "Maybe more of a reason to leave."

"And go where? How many remote towns will be as accepting of me as all y'all have been?" I shook my head. "No. I'm taking a stand, and it's starting with Bart." I reached for the door handle. "But this isn't your fight, Marco, so maybe you should stay out of it."

Because I couldn't stand it if something happened to him—again—because he was trying to protect me.

I opened the door and got out before he could answer, but he rolled his window down and called out to me as I walked toward my car. "You can't say something like that and just walk away!"

Turning to face him, I gave him an imploring look. "Just think about it, okay?"

His jaw set. "I don't need to."

I wasn't going to argue with him from the sidewalk, so I waved goodbye before I turned to walk the rest of the way to my car.

He remained in place until I pulled out of my parking place, then followed me to the turnoff for Ewing before branching off and heading toward the state park.

I continued out of town, not surprised when Wyatt's truck came into view two cars behind me, but I had more important things to think about than my tail. Like what I was going to say to Mitzi. I made a mental list of things to ask her and decided to wing it from there.

Part of me wanted to take notes, but I'd rethought the wisdom of that after talking to Marco. A gossip didn't take notes, and it would be hard to write things down on the sly, without drawing the attention of the people I was talking to. Still, I worried about forgetting things, and my junky cell phone didn't have the capacity to take audio recordings.

Maybe I could get a smartphone at some point, just so I could use it for taking notes and pictures, something I'd also been missing, but for the time being I didn't have enough money to justify the expense.

I decided I should try to find a handheld recorder instead, so my first stop in Ewing was at the Helping Hands Thrift Store.

I approached the woman at a register and asked, "Do you know if you have any handheld recorders?"

She gave me a strange look. "Why would you be wantin' one of those?"

I shrugged, playing dumb. "I'm trying to record my husband talkin' in his sleep. He keeps sayin' another woman's name and I want to prove it to him."

Her brow furrowed and righteous indignation flashed in her eyes. "If we have one, it's gonna be in aisle 6. That's where we keep the electronics, but some of them are pretty vintage, if you know what I mean."

Thanking her, I headed to aisle six, trying not to get my hopes up. It was no surprise when I encountered a table covered with rummage sale rejects—huge, blocky computer monitors and some computer towers. A ragtag assortment of keyboards and mouses, old cassette players, and even a knockoff Walkman. Off to the side sat a handheld recorder that looked like it had seen better days. The buttons were well-worn, but there was a cassette inside, even if it wouldn't work when I pressed the play and fast-forward buttons.

"You're gonna need to get batteries," a man said from behind me.

I turned to see a guy in his twenties pushing a broom. His name tag said Red.

"We have to take the batteries out, but you can ask Tammy at the front to pop some in to verify it works before you buy it."

I tightened my hold on it. "Thanks."

Sure enough, when I headed to the front, Tammy—the cashier I'd spoken to upon entering—fished out AA batteries to stick in the back. Once she pressed the play button, we could hear a man's voice droning on about the American Revolution.

"Sounds like a stuffy lecture," Tammy said.

"Agreed," I said, eager to make my purchase and record my conversation with Mitzi.

But Tammy took the batteries out and put them in her drawer. When she saw my crestfallen face, she gave me an apologetic smile. "Sorry. Batteries aren't included."

"That's okay," I said as I dug out my wallet. "I'm just thankful you had a recorder."

She rang me up and I handed over a ten-dollar bill to cover the six-dollar device. I dropped my change into my purse along with the recorder as I headed for the exit.

"I hope you nail the bastard to the wall!" she called out after me.

For a moment, I thought she meant Wyatt, but then I remembered my cover story. Some PI I was turning out to be. I gave her a wave. "Thanks."

She held up a fist. "Solidarity!"

I grinned at her and held up my fist too. "Solidarity."

As I walked to my car—mindful that Wyatt was parked in the next lot over—I wondered how much solidarity Bart Drummond had left in Drum. Despite the promise of the new resort, many people were disillusioned with him. That might work to my advantage.

I needed to get to Mitzi's house quickly so I'd have time to pay a visit to Gladys and Thelma.

But first I had to get batteries. Groaning in frustration, I turned on the car and headed to Dollar General, where I picked up AA batteries, two new puzzles that had shown up since the last time I'd scoured the puzzle assortment, and a bag of candies I knew Thelma liked.

After I inserted the batteries and made a test recording to ensure the recorder worked, I plugged Mitzi's address into the GPS built into my car. It told me it was a five-minute drive to her house on the other side of town.

Wyatt was trailing behind as I headed to Mitzi's. I parked in front and turned off the car. I started the recorder and tucked it into my purse. I wasn't sure it was legal to record a conversation with another person in Tennessee without their knowledge or consent, but it wasn't like I planned to hand it over to the sheriff. Any recordings I made were for my own personal notes.

I started walking toward the front door, fully aware that Wyatt was parked at the end of the street. When I approached the porch, a man in his late thirties stepped out of the house. He wasn't tall, but he looked muscular. His light brown hair had begun to recede. He was wearing a T-shirt that read, *Live Hard, Die Young*, and his hands were fisted at his sides. Not a good sign.

"She ain't gonna talk to you."

I stopped short, caught by surprise. "Excuse me?"

"Abby said you was comin' over, but now Mitzi's a nervous wreck all over again. I ain't lettin' you talk to her."

"I'm not here to upset her, Mr...." I figured his name wasn't Ziegler, but I hadn't gotten Mitzi's married name... if she had one. For all I knew this was her brother, not a significant other.

"My name ain't important," he snarled, then spat into the bushes in front of the porch. "What's important is that you realize you ain't talkin' to her."

"Did someone tell you not to talk to me?" I asked. "Was Mitzi threatened?"

He marched down the steps and pointed a finger only a few inches from my face. "Get the hell off my property," he said through clenched teeth. "You stay away from Mitzi, or I'll make your life a livin' hell. Trust me, girl, I've got the power to do it."

I took a step back, holding my hands up next to my head but maintaining eye contact with a nonthreatening gaze. "I don't want to upset her or put her in harm's way. I only want the truth."

"Well, you ain't gettin' it here."

I took another step back. "If Mitzi changes her mind, tell her to call Carly Moore. I work at Max's Tavern. She can reach me there."

His upper lip curled. "I knew you worked for *them*."

Then he turned around and walked into the house, slamming the door behind him. Seconds later, a baby started crying.

Damn. I should have considered that the fact that I worked for a Drummond might paint me in a bad light.

I'd started toward my car when I realized Wyatt was making a beeline for me.

So much for keeping his cover.

"Are you all right?" he asked, his eyes blazing.

"I'm fine," I said in a huff, although I had to admit it was nice knowing that if things had gotten hairy with Mitzi's enforcer, I would have had backup of my own.

Nevertheless, I was back to square one.

Or was I?

"Meet me at the Dairy Bar," I said, not giving him a chance to respond.

The glare he shot me told me he didn't like being bossed around.

Too damn bad.

Chapter Thirteen

I was at the counter ordering a hot fudge sundae when Wyatt pulled into the parking lot. He walked up behind me and slapped cash on the counter to pay for my order before I could get out my wallet.

"I would have gotten something for you, but I realized I didn't know you well enough to know what you'd like," I said in a curt tone.

The older teen who handed me the ice cream bowl gave me a confused look. "No need to get me anything. We get to eat ice cream for free."

I gave him a tight smile, realizing Wyatt had already drifted away, then turned and headed for a picnic table at the edge of the outdoor dining space, away from a couple eating at a table on the other side, not that I needed to be too concerned with them overhearing. They were too wrapped up in each other to take notice.

Wyatt sat across from me, resting his forearms on the table, waiting.

I took a bite of my sundae, then said, "You lied to me."

"About what?"

"Heather's going-away party."

He didn't show a single sign of remorse at being caught. "I didn't lie. I just didn't tell you."

"Yeah," I said more calmly than I felt. "You seem to be extraordinarily good at that."

"You talked to Abby."

"I did."

"And Mitzi's husband won't let you near her."

"Was that her husband?" I asked nonchalantly before I took another bite.

"Probably. I don't know him. Only that she got married." He paused. "So what are you gonna do now?"

"What can I do?" I said with a shrug. "You gave me two leads and I followed them. Now I'm at a dead end." I didn't really believe that, but part of me wanted to see him sweat.

"Seriously? You're giving up?" he asked, sounding incredulous.

The way he said it pissed me off, but I just shrugged. "This is your problem, Wyatt. Not mine."

"You were all over Lula's disappearance," he snapped. "Chasing every lead. You were like a bulldog."

My fury spilled over, more of it than had been provoked by his remarks, and I realized I'd been holding on to it for months. "Don't you *dare* go there."

His eyes lit up. "There's the Carly I know."

I got to my feet, worried if I stayed here any longer I'd resort to physical violence. "Don't you pretend like you know me. You don't know *anything* about me."

Except that wasn't quite true. He knew plenty about me. I just didn't know him.

"I thought you wanted answers," he said, lowering his voice. "If you don't want to help me, fine. But at least get your answers."

"Fool me once, shame on you," I said with a sneer. "Fool me twice, shame on me. I don't believe for one minute that you're gonna tell me anything. You're playing me, just like your father plays everyone. Guess you're more like him than you thought."

I spun around and stomped toward my car, throwing my ice cream in a trash can with a satisfying thump. As I opened my door, I called out, "Stop following me or I'll call the sheriff's department and have you arrested for stalking."

"Yeah, I bet your new boyfriend would be first in line to put me in handcuffs."

I nearly corrected him for the umpteenth time, and it was tempting to tell him that Marco was fully aware that Wyatt was tailing me. Instead, I said nothing at all. The less he knew, the better.

I would have loved a minute to pull myself together, but he was watching my every move and I wasn't about to give him the satisfaction, so I headed straight to the nursing home. Grabbing my reusable shopping bag, I headed inside, continuing on even as I noticed Wyatt pulling into the back lot. I couldn't say I blamed him for following me. I had no idea what Hank would ask for a blood price, and Wyatt had been foolish to agree to it. Especially if he was going to withhold key information about Heather's disappearance.

Gladys was sitting at her usual table with her grumpy friend, Roberta. I still wasn't sure whether they were truly friends, or two people who'd formed an acquaintance over puzzles. Some days they didn't seem to like each other all that much.

Gladys's face lit up when she saw me approaching. "There's my girl."

"Hey, Gladys," I said, leaning over to give her a kiss on the cheek. "Hey, Roberta."

Roberta scowled. "Tryin' to buy our affection with jigsaw puzzles again?"

I gave her a cheesy smile as I pulled out a box with a tropical scene on the cover and set it on the table next to the puzzle they were working on. They'd only gotten the border and a few sections of the inside pieced together. "Is it working?"

Her scowl deepened.

"I'm gonna take that as a yes," I said with a forced cheeriness that was excessive even for me.

"What's goin' on?" Gladys asked, her cloudy eyes pinned on me. "What's got you upset? Does it have anything to do with the fact you haven't been here for weeks?"

"No. I haven't been coming around because the new construction at the Drummond resort site has brought a bunch of workers into town. I've been working doubles every day for weeks. But Max finally hired someone to help out, and I don't have to go in until three today."

"And you came to see us?" Roberta grumped as her arthritic hands fumbled to open the box.

I took it from her and used my car key to slit open the paper seal. "I was running some errands in Ewing, so I decided to stop by and pay a visit." I darted a glance down the hall, then returned my attention to the box as I worked on another side. "I also want to speak to Thelma Tureen."

"Greta was here just the other day," Gladys said, picking up the box for the puzzle they'd started and sweeping the loose pieces inside. I wasn't surprised they were abandoning it for the new one. They spent so much time building puzzles, they'd pieced together most of the ones owned by Greener Pastures at least a dozen times. "Brought her some pretty flowers."

Roberta started to break apart the border of the old puzzle. "The kind you get at grocery stores."

"Well, it sounds very sweet," I said. "Greta's a good granddaughter."

"And so are you," Gladys said, reaching over to pinch my cheek. A few visits back, she'd told me that I spent more time with her than her real family and declared me to be her adopted granddaughter. "And how is that handsome Marco doin'?"

"He's great. In fact, he's going to be moonlighting at the tavern for a while. He said to tell you hi."

"I take it he's workin' as a deputy today?" Gladys asked, helping Roberta break apart the puzzle. "Otherwise he'd be here with you."

I chuckled. "Yes, he's working, but I had lunch with him."

"I do love a man in uniform," Roberta mumbled under her breath, and my brow shot up as I turned to Gladys.

She tried to stifle a smile. This was the first hint Roberta had given that she liked Marco…or anyone for that matter. But there was no denying Marco *did* have charm.

"It's a shame you two aren't screwin'," Gladys said as she swept the last of the pieces into the box.

"Gladys," I said with a sigh. "How many times do I have to tell you that we're just friends?"

She glanced up. "Then why aren't you screwin'?"

It seemed like everyone was asking me that lately. "I'm not really sure," I said, deciding to be honest. "A lot of reasons, I guess."

"Such as?" Gladys asked thoughtfully as she set the box aside.

I sighed again. "Well, for one thing, Marco told me he wasn't a commitment kind of guy, and I told him I wasn't a fling kind of girl."

"And when did he tell you that?"

"Early last December, when we were looking for Greta."

"And when was the last time he hooked up with another woman?"

"I don't know," I said, really not liking the direction this was going. "This morning he said it had been a few months, but according to him it was because he'd cycled through so many women. He wants to pace himself."

Roberta snickered.

"What?" I asked.

"He likes you, you stupid fool. He doesn't want anyone else. He wants you."

I frowned.

"I've seen the way he looks at you," Roberta said. "And I've seen the way you look at him. Gladys is right. Why aren't you two hookin' up?"

Were they right? Did Marco want to be more than friends? The thought left me devastated, although I had no idea why. I only knew this wasn't the time to figure it out.

I gave them a coy smile. "And what if we hooked up and it was terrible? Then I'd lose my best friend."

"Or you might get to spend the rest of your life with him," Roberta said wistfully.

"When did your husband die?" I asked.

"Three years ago," Roberta said, keeping her gaze down. "Incompetent fools at the hospital killed my sweet Bernard."

155

"I'm so sorry," I said, seeing a whole new side to her.

Her gaze snapped up, eyes blazing. "I didn't tell you for sympathy. I told you so you'd stop wastin' your time. None of us know how much time we have left. What if you're missin' out on something wonderful?"

"Like a really good roll in the hay," Gladys added.

I released a short laugh, but my gaze drifted back to Roberta. "I'll definitely keep your advice in mind."

She nodded. "Well, I can lead a horse to water, but I can't make the damn fool drink."

She had a point. About all of it. But I couldn't take the chance. Losing Marco would break me in a way losing the others had not.

You might lose him anyway, a voice in my head whispered.

What if he told me how he really felt, assuming they were right, and I couldn't bring myself to commit to him? Would he pull away?

"There, there, child," Roberta said in the kindest tone I'd ever heard her use. "There's no sense borrowin' trouble before it hits. The key is to listen to your heart. Truly listen. Then you'll know."

I gave her a watery smile. "Thank you, Roberta."

Her face morphed into a scowl. "All right. Be gone with you. Go see Thelma."

She made a shooing motion as she shifted her focus back to the table.

Gladys, I noticed, looked as surprised as I felt.

Suddenly eager to get away from them, I rose to my feet. "I'll say goodbye before I go."

"Like you could sneak out," Roberta scoffed. "We're right by the front door."

I laughed, slightly relieved Roberta was back to her grumpy self.

Thelma's room was down the main hall. She seemed to spend most of her time in there, not that I was surprised. She had a view of an angel fountain and a courtyard full of rose bushes. Her door stood open, and I could see straight through the window—while the roses weren't blooming now, someone had planted pansies and the fountain was gurgling and spurting water.

"Miss Thelma?"

She was sitting in her chair—a faux leather recliner—with a soft pink knitted throw over her lap, her knitting needles and an unfinished project on top of it. She stirred and turned her head toward me, and I realized she'd been napping.

"I'm *so* sorry. I can come back another time."

"Don't be silly," she said, gesturing for me to come in. "I was just dozing. I don't want to sleep too long or I'll never go to sleep tonight."

"Are you sure?" I asked. "It's no bother for me to come back."

"Please. I always love visiting with you."

"At least I come bearing gifts," I said, lifting my arm to show her the shopping bag, the straps hooked over my arm.

Her face lit up, and I noticed the vase full of mixed cut flowers on the dresser in front of her.

"It's something very small, but something I know you love," I said, pulling out the bag of butterscotch candies.

She beamed and reached for them. "Between you and Greta…both you girls spoil me."

"I love your company," I said as I sat in the empty guest chair in front of her. "How have you been?"

157

"My hips have been actin' up again, a sure sign spring is here to stay. But I've been good otherwise. Tired."

"You need more exercise."

"That's counterintuitive, dear," she said, tearing open the bag and digging out a candy.

The next time I was here, presuming I had more time, I planned to encourage her to walk out to the courtyard. Maybe I could bring some bedding plants and a trowel. She could guide my efforts. I'd be sure to ask the director for permission, but I wasn't worried. Thelma had told me that the families did most of the planting. Landscaping wasn't in the facility's budget.

"To what do I owe the honor of this visit?" she asked. "I get the feeling you want to discuss more than the weather today."

This was something I loved about Miss Thelma: while she was a very sweet woman, she always told the truth, no sugarcoating. Also, she could write a secret history of Drum based on her knowledge alone. Back in December, she'd told me about Bart Drummond's favors. She'd described him as a crossroads demon—only desperate people sold their souls to get a favor from him—but she'd refused to name names, saying she didn't want to air the dirty laundry of lost souls. Although I'd been back plenty of times, I hadn't told her about my research yet, wanting to find more solid evidence first. Maybe it had been a mistake to wait. It was time to share some of my research with her and see if she'd give me some answers.

"I really *do* want to see you too," I insisted.

She waved her hand. "All I do is sit in this daggum chair and knit all day. Let my mind be useful. What do you want to know?"

I pulled the recorder out of my purse. "Do you mind if I record this? It's just for my own notes. I'll destroy it when I'm done."

While I couldn't call it out to everyone I talked to, I trusted Miss Thelma wouldn't throw me to the wolves.

"I don't mind. No one's comin' for me here," she said with a grin.

"I'd like to talk to you more about Bart's favors. Only I need specifics. I can give you some names and what I know, and you can verify if I'm right or not."

Her mouth twisted. "You really shouldn't pry into that dark business, Carly."

"Maybe so, but will you tell me anyway?" When she didn't answer, I said, "I'll tell you about one instance I know about and then leave it to you to decide, okay?"

She gave me a nod.

Reaching into my purse, I pulled out my notebook and flipped through the pages. "I've been doing some research in the *Ewing Chronicle*, looking for strange incidents."

"And what would you label strange incidents?" she asked, undeniable interest in her voice.

"People getting arrested for doing inexplicable things. Such as Roger Pierce."

Her eyes widened at the mention of his name. "What about him?"

"He killed a postal worker in a murder-suicide about twenty years ago."

Her mouth pinched. "Unfortunate business."

"Especially since the articles said the police couldn't find a motive. As far as everyone knew, Roger Pierce had never met Dudley Franken. He wasn't even Roger's mail carrier. It was a totally random act."

"And you don't think it was?" she asked.

"You tell me," I said. "Was it?"

She was silent for several long seconds, and I was sure she was going to blow me off, but then she surprised me. "Roger had a gambling problem. He made good money workin' as a foreman at the lumber yard."

"Drummond Lumber? That wasn't in the news articles."

"Well, he didn't work there anymore at the time of the murder. His last job was at the convenience store at the corner of Walnut and Rally in Ewing. Back when he worked at the lumberyard, he was deep in debt and on the verge of losin' his house. Then suddenly he came into a windfall, or at least enough money to catch up on his mortgage payments. There were a lot of rumors goin' around about where he got the money, but his wife said a guardian angel had given it to them. Of course, Roger didn't learn his lesson, as is often the way with addicts, and soon he was in debt again."

I considered telling her that addiction was a disease but decided not to stop her.

"This time his wife left with their kids and moved to Nashville, and he lost his job. No one was surprised he killed himself. He was a bitterly unhappy man who refused to accept responsibility for his actions. It was the fact that he killed Dudley first that caught everyone by surprise. As far as anyone knows, Dudley never even went into the convenience store where Roger worked."

"Why do you think Roger killed him?" I asked.

She gave me a pointed stare. "You're wantin' me to say that Bart Drummond called in a favor. I can't tell you that, but it's mighty suspicious. The sheriff never came up with an answer, although to be honest, I'm not sure how much they tried."

Once again, nothing solid to link the crime back to Bart.

"Can you tell me about any others?" I asked. "I know you don't like gossiping about things that can't be proven, but I'm tryin' to find people who might have been Bart's victims. I need to figure out a way to stop him."

"Stopping Bart Drummond is like tryin' to stop lava flow from a volcano. It will only get you burnt to a crisp."

"Then I'll wear a protective suit," I said. "Please, Miss Thelma."

She sighed, looking none too pleased. "This one's more personal." She cleared her throat. "One of my husband's second cousins got into trouble with the law for a DUI, and he couldn't afford an attorney. So he went to Bart."

"What did Bart give him?"

"He got the charges dropped."

"And how did he repay Bart?"

She made a face. "Well, that part's a little fuzzy. Bart would never want his favors broadcast, but it's easy enough to guess based on what happened. Oscar got arrested for burning down a house."

"What? *Why?*"

She shook her head. "Rumor had it that the woman didn't follow through on her end of a bargain with Bart."

"So he had Oscar burn her house down?"

"I can't think of any other earthly reason why he'd do it. He didn't even know the woman. He must've been worried about what Bart would do to him if he didn't follow through, but he got caught." She held my gaze. "Her two kids were inside."

"Oh, my God! Did they get out?"

She shook her head. "No, and Oscar couldn't live with it. He took his own life as soon as he got out on bail."

Or Bart called in another favor and had made it look like suicide before Oscar could tell his side of the story. "And the woman?"

"She became a drunk and died a few years later when she ran her car into a tree."

I felt sick to my stomach.

Her hands twisted in her lap, as though she was wrestling some inner emotion, and then she stopped. "I hesitate to say more, but not all of his favors are so ghastly. I heard of a man in Ewing who needed a loan to open a restaurant, and it thrived. Bart always has a table if he wants one."

Wow. His choice of table in a restaurant in Ewing. My father would laugh his ass off at that.

"Will you tell me about more specific cases?" I asked as I flipped to a new page. "What about Betty Villanova? She was arrested for breaking into a pawn shop in Ewing about five years ago. The newspaper said the sheriff couldn't figure out what she was there to steal, and she never told. She's currently in prison after pleading guilty."

"I don't know anything about that," she said, shaking her head.

"Does it sound like something Bart would have someone do?"

"Rumor has it that Bart asks for all manner of favors, and most of what I've heard is speculation and gossip. Might he have been behind it? It's not outside the realm of possibility. I just can't confirm it."

I'd hoped for more information, but I suspected the relatives of the people on the list I'd made at the library would be able to fill in some blanks for me. Presuming they didn't call Bart as soon as they heard from me. Time to move on to the primary reason for my visit.

"What do you remember about Wyatt Drummond's DUI and robbery arrest?"

Her eyes lit up. "Oh, you're here because they found that poor girl's body."

"Heather Stone."

She nodded. "Yep. Everyone was sure she'd left town. It's so, so sad, but it's not all that surprising when you think about it."

"Why?"

"Because it's hard to believe Bart Drummond would let someone get the best of him like that. Rumor has it he paid her off, but I can't imagine him doing that. It would make him look weak."

"But I heard she was showing off a check at her going-away party."

She seemed to give that some thought. "I could be wrong, of course, but it sure doesn't seem like his style."

"So why didn't he squash the rumors?"

"Good question. Makes you think maybe he *did* have her killed."

"Maybe, but if he did, he certainly didn't have her buried there. Do you know anything about her?"

She frowned. "It seems wrong to speak ill of the dead."

"I'm sorry."

Waving a hand, she let out a sigh. "I'll tell you what I know." She rested an arm on her chair, leaning closer to me. "She was a wild one, that Heather. Her aunt was likely sorry she'd agreed to keep her after the girl's parents moved. Caused her nothin' but trouble."

"What kind of trouble?"

"This and that, mostly juvenile stuff. Underage drinkin' at the state park. I'm pretty sure there was a vandalism arrest in there. She slashed some poor girl's tires, but the charges were dropped. Never home by curfew. Hilde tried groundin' her, but Heather never paid her any mind. I told Hilde to send her back to her parents, but Heather would always manipulate Hilde into believin' she was gonna follow the straight and narrow. And she would for a bit, then go back to her old ways."

"And those incidents happened when she was in high school?" Which would be the reason I hadn't found any arrest records for her when I'd searched for her name last December. Juvenile records were sealed.

"Oh, yes. She caused trouble when she came back the other times, but nothin' illegal... not that I knew about anyways."

"You said she manipulated her aunt. Multiple people have told me she was manipulative."

"Yep." She shook her head with a sigh. "And boy, was she a master at it. I've never seen so many people bamboozled by one girl. That Drummond boy to boot. Why, I wouldn't be surprised if she was the one who broke into that garage and stole the baseball."

"Do you remember any of the rumors going around when Wyatt was arrested?"

"Only that he turned his back on his family after his arrest. Wouldn't even accept an attorney from them. Rumor had it the judge gave him a stiffer sentence than normal, but folks figured he was one of the few people not bought and paid for with Drummond money."

"Do you have any idea where Heather's aunt lives?"

She frowned. "You plan on talkin' to her?"

"Is that a problem?" I asked, caught off guard by her question.

"No, I guess I'm just surprised. But that would be awfully sweet of you, dear. I'm sure she'd appreciate the condolences."

Well, crap. I hadn't even thought about that, and now I felt guilty for letting Thelma believe my reasons were so selfless.

"Hilde Browning. I don't have her address, but she lives in the pale yellow house off Freeman Road. About a mile off the county road. Do you know where that is?"

"No, ma'am, but it shouldn't be a problem. I'll bring her some flowers when I go."

"She loves Gerbera daisies," Thelma said, her voice trailing. "Be sure to give her my condolences as well."

"I'll tell her they're from the both of us."

Tears filled her eyes. "You're such a sweet girl."

Guilt tightened its grip on me, forcing me to admit, "That's not the only reason I'm going, Miss Thelma."

Her eyes brightened. "Well, of course not, dear. You're goin' to ask her questions about Heather's murder, but there's no reason you can't offer your condolences to start."

I stared at her in disbelief.

"Please, give me more credit than that." Then she said, "How's Greta? She says she's not seeing the other Drummond boy anymore."

"I don't know anything about her love life, but I just saw her a few hours ago when I had lunch and she looked great."

Thelma nodded. "She seems happy, but I can't help thinkin' she's lonely. She says she doesn't see much of Lula now that she's had the baby."

"Bingham keeps a pretty close eye on both Lula and the baby, from what I can tell," I said. "But I haven't talked to

Greta about that either." It occurred to me that perhaps I should. What if she was lonely?

A quick glance to the clock on the wall told me that I needed to leave soon if I was going to get to the Drummonds' on time. I also remembered that I hadn't told Max I was going to be late. I turned off the recorder, shut my notebook, and put both into my purse.

Standing, I gave Thelma a warm smile. "Thank you so much for letting me dig into the past."

"I'm not sure how helpful I've actually been, but if I think of anything else, I'll be sure to call you at Hank's."

Her offer caught me by surprise, mostly because she apparently had Hank's number. Then again, maybe she'd been friends with his wife. Or perhaps she had an old phone book lying around. I was sure Hank had used the same phone number for decades. "That would be great. Thank you."

As I headed for the door, she called after me, "Be careful where you poke. Something tells me you're about to wake up a sleeping bear."

Chapter Fourteen

Gladys and Roberta looked eager to see me when I emerged from the hall, and Gladys frantically waved me over.

"You've got company," she told me when I neared, and pointed out the blinds covering the plate glass window.

Looking out the window, I frowned when I saw a man standing next to my car. "Wyatt."

"You know him?" Roberta asked. "Because we can go out and rough him up for you."

My mouth hung open in shock, but I quickly closed it. "That's not necessary. I know him, and I'm not surprised. I abruptly ended a conversation with him right before coming over here, and I suspect he's here to continue it."

"Are you safe?" Gladys asked with worry in her eyes.

I gave her a reassuring smile. "Totally. Wyatt would never hurt me. In fact, he's out there because he wants to protect me."

"Does he have somethin' to worry about?" Roberta asked.

Did he?

"No," I said truthfully. But I suspected that could easily change—the more I snooped around, the more dangerous things were bound to get. "Thanks for looking out for me."

"Always," Gladys called after me as I headed for the exit.

"You be careful!" Roberta shouted. "You're our puzzle hookup. If anything happens to you, who knows when we'll get another one."

I shot her a grin before I walked out the double glass doors, putting on my game face.

Wyatt was leaning against my driver's side door with his arms crossed. His dark gaze was trained on me as I headed toward him.

"Do I want to know what you were doin' in there?" he asked, remaining in place. His pose sent a clear message. *You're not leaving until I let you.*

I stopped several feet away, hooking my hand on the strap of the purse slung over my shoulder. "I don't see what difference it makes to you."

"We need to finish our conversation."

"Okay," I said, shifting my weight. "It's simple. If you want me to continue looking into this, you need to give me something else to chase down, along with some kind of incentive to put up with your bullshit. You said you were going to give me answers."

He glanced away, into the trees surrounding the property, then turned back to me. "I asked Heather to marry me. That was what really caused my big fight with my parents. My father actually respected me for demanding ownership of the tavern, and he would have probably given it to me, only I told him I wanted it because I planned to marry Heather and we wanted to start a family."

I stared at him in shock. "Why in God's name didn't you tell me any of that earlier?"

"Because I was embarrassed. She refused to marry me if I didn't get ownership of the tavern, and no one else knew."

"Not even her friends?"

"Did Abby mention it?" he asked with a questioning look.

She hadn't, but then again, she might not have known. According to her, Heather had operated by an out of sight, out of mind policy, and Abby had been out of town when all that went down. If Heather shared the news with anyone, it was likely Mitzi. Who refused to talk to me.

I shook my head. "How the hell do you expect me to clear your name if you won't be honest with me?"

He glanced away. "I want you to find out most everything from other sources. That'll help you see this through their eyes, not mine." He turned back to me. "I didn't kill her, Carly. I swear. And if you come to that conclusion on your own, maybe you'll find it in your heart to trust me again."

"That is such bullshit, Wyatt," I said, raising my voice and not caring a bit. "You don't give a shit whether I trust you. You made that clear when we broke up last December."

"That's not true!"

"I believed you when you told me you'd help me," I said, feeling angrier with every word. "I believed you when you said you'd share your past. Like a damn fool! Then you stonewalled me at every turn. You *had* to know I'd call you on your bullshit. You had to know how much it would hurt me, especially since you knew I'd been deceived before."

He studied me with wary eyes.

"Well, say something!" I shouted, taking a step closer.

"I can't," he said, his voice thick. "Because you're right. About all of it."

That was what I wanted to hear, yet somehow it made everything worse.

"Do you realize how badly you hurt me?" I asked, my voice cracking. "You convinced me to trust you, and then you screwed me over just like every other guy before you." Tears stung my eyes. "You broke me, Wyatt Drummond. I'll never trust another man again, and now I'm destined to be alone for the rest of my life. So *fuck. You.*"

Dismay covered his face. "Carly…"

Embarrassment washed over me like hot tar. I hadn't even realized I felt that way until that very moment, and now I'd confessed it to him. He knew the power he'd had over me, the power he still had. I had to get away from him. I couldn't stand to look at him for another moment. "Get the hell away from my car."

"Carly."

I reached into my purse and pulled out the can of pepper spray Marco had gotten for me, and held it up, aiming it at his face. "I'm not afraid to use this, so I suggest you get away from my car."

He held his hands up in surrender. "Carly, I didn't mean to hurt you. I swear."

"Go swear to someone else, because I'm done talkin' to you," I said, my Southern drawl coming in strong.

"Carly." He showed no sign of budging.

I didn't want to talk to him. I wanted to talk to Marco. I wanted to tell him about this—about the vulnerability that threatened to choke me—and it was then that something else dawned on me.

Part of the reason I was so upset was because I *did* have feelings for Marco, and no matter how much that man bent over backward to show me that he would always be honest and have my best interests in mind, I would never fully trust him, at least not with my heart. Wyatt really had broken me.

Tears welled in my eyes, and I felt close to breaking down into sobs. The sympathy in Wyatt's eyes wasn't helping.

"Hey, tough guy," Roberta called out from behind me, "you want a piece of me?"

I glanced over my shoulder to see Roberta hobbling with her walker, coming toward us much faster than I would have thought possible. Gladys was marching right behind her, holding a flyswatter.

Wyatt's eyes flew wide in surprise. "I'm not a threat. I'm Carly's friend."

"Then why's she cryin'?" Gladys demanded. "It looks like you're blockin' her from gettin' into her car."

What did Gladys plan to do? Swat him? If I hadn't been so close to breaking down, I probably would have burst into laughter.

"I just need to talk to her, is all," Wyatt said.

"It looks like she don't want to talk to you," Roberta said, still approaching.

"Carly, call off your posse," Wyatt said in a low growl, not looking amused.

"That's right! We're her posse," Gladys shouted, whacking the handle of the flyswatter on her hand, then releasing a curse as she shook out her fingers.

"Gladys. Roberta," I said, turning to face them. "I can handle him." Then I spun around to glare at Wyatt. "Get out of my way."

"We can't just leave things like this," he protested, holding his hands out at his sides to keep me from going past him.

"Get out of my way, Wyatt!"

But he refused to move. "Not until we're done."

"How dare you?" I shouted, anger rushing through my head. He'd set the rules for our relationship, and now he thought he could determine when I could leave?

Roberta reached us and rammed a foot of her walker onto Wyatt's boot.

He yelped and jerked backward, but he was still blocking my car door. "Carly."

I was pissed, more pissed than I'd ever been in my life, and before I could even think about it, I pressed the tab on the can. My aim had lowered, and it sprayed on his abdomen.

He let out a cry and stumbled away from the car, covering his face with his hands. "Jesus! What the hell did you do that for?"

"I warned you," I said, already feeling guilty as I moved out of his path.

"Fuck!" he shouted, stumbling a few more steps. "This burns like hellfire!"

"I think that's the point. Imagine what it would have felt like if I'd sprayed you in the face." I clicked my fob and covered my face with my purse in case any lingering spray was in the air.

"Don't you dare leave!" he shouted, more out of panic than anger, but I ignored him, getting in the car and turning on the engine.

He spun and turned toward the car, blindly reaching out to stop me as tears streamed down his face. What *would* have happened if I'd sprayed him in the face? "Carly!"

I quickly backed out straight so I didn't accidently run him over or the two older women, then turned before he could reach the car. I gunned it, looking into the rearview mirror.

He was still stumbling around, probably because Gladys was now smacking him with the flyswatter and Roberta was jabbing him with her walker, and my guilt returned. Then I told myself that he'd brought it on himself. Maybe he'd take me seriously next time. Because something told me that Wyatt had picked up some tactics from both his father and his girlfriend, and he'd been using them on me.

I was done being manipulated, and God help the next person who stood in my way.

I figured it didn't bode well that my next stop was at the home of the master manipulator himself.

Chapter Fifteen

As soon as I pulled away from the parking lot, I called Marco's cell phone, not surprised and actually grateful when it went to voicemail. I wasn't sure I could handle talking to him right now.

I listened to his message and took a deep breath to calm my nerves before I started to speak.

"Hey, Marco. Just calling to give you an update. I went by Mitzi's house, but her husband came out and said she wasn't going to talk to me. Like we discussed, I dropped by Greener Pastures to see Gladys, but I also talked to Thelma Tureen about Heather. She told me where Heather's aunt lives, so I'm hoping to visit her tomorrow before my shift. Oh…if you think of it and you're in Ewing, can you get a bunch of Gerbera daisies? If not, that's okay, but Miss Thelma said they're Hilde's favorite, and I was hoping to bring some to offer my condolences."

I paused and took a breath, wondering what I should say about Wyatt, if anything. But if Wyatt showed up at the tavern tonight, Marco was sure to pick up on the tension between us.

"Say, just so you're not blindsided later. Wyatt pissed me off in the nursing home parking lot, and I might have pepper sprayed him in the stomach. So good news, the pepper spray worked," I said with a fake cheery voice. "But don't worry, he didn't try to hurt me or touch me or anything untoward. He just pissed me off with his usual bullshit. Like the fact that he was apparently *engaged* to Heather when he demanded his father give him ownership of the tavern. I told him I was sick of his lies, and when he wouldn't get out of my way, I sprayed him." Then a new thought hit me. "So if someone from the nursing home calls the sheriff on him, he didn't do anything worthy of arrest, because last time I checked, irritating the hell out of someone wasn't an actual crime."

I realized I was rambling, but I couldn't seem to stop.

"In any case," I said with a sigh, "I wanted to give you an update and to thank you for being such a good friend. Thanks for putting up with my crap. Okay. Bye." I hung up.

I called Max next, trying to hurry before I left Ewing and lost cell phone service.

"Max's Tavern," he answered in his good-natured voice.

"Hey, Max, it's Carly. How are things workin' out with Molly?"

"Well…" he drawled, and I knew it wasn't great. "She's slower than you, and she's made a few mistakes, but it's Ruth that's the wrench in the engine. She's ridin' her hard."

Great. "I'll talk to Ruth when I come in, which is why I'm callin'. I'm gonna be about an hour late."

He was silent for a moment, then hesitantly said, "Okay…"

I knew he wanted to know why, but I really didn't want to tell him, and I also didn't want to lie. "Thanks for your understanding, Max. I'll be in as soon as I can. Promise. Oh! And before I go, I think we should consider hiring Ginger to help with the lunch shifts. I figured it would probably work with her kids' schedules."

"Huh," he said as though mulling it over. "That might be a good idea, and as far as I know, Ruth doesn't have a beef with her." His voice was becoming staticky.

"Well, there's a good sign," I said. It was a sad day when you hired people based on their ability to get along with a contrary waitress.

The connection dropped after that, and I didn't see Wyatt in my rearview mirror, not that I was surprised. Marco had told me that pepper spray would incapacitate a person for a good length of time—plenty of time to get away, although I was fairly certain this wasn't what he'd had in mind.

As I drove through Drum, I saw Emmaline Haskell sitting in a chair on the sidewalk at the street corner by the library, and I said a quick prayer of thanks. She was an older woman who sometimes came to town with a five-gallon bucket of bouquets of flowers she grew on her land. Today I could see white, red, and yellow tulips sticking out of her bucket. I couldn't see any parking spaces, so I waved to her when I got to the stop sign, feeling bad when she hobbled over, trying to drag the bucket with her.

I usually walked to her from the tavern when I knew she was in town, always eager to buy a couple of bouquets to brighten the house. Most people in town didn't buy them, thinking they were a frivolous expense, but she was a sweet old woman, living alone and trying to get by on a small social security check, and I loved flowers. It was a win-win situation. Some days I was one of her only sales if people driving through didn't stop.

"Oh, Miss Emmaline!" I shouted through my open passenger window. "Stop right there! You don't have to bring the bucket to me! Just give me three of your prettiest bouquets."

She leaned into my open passenger window and gave me a stricken look. "But that's $30, Miss Carly."

"I'm just plain Carly, Miss Emmaline," I said, hating that she thought me better than her because she was poor as dirt and I had enough money to buy flowers. I dug into my wallet and pulled out two twenty-dollar bills, leaning over to hand them out the window. "You keep the change."

She took the bills and looked them over. "Are you sure?"

"I have a couple of friends I want to give them to, and you have the prettiest flowers." Then a thought hit me. "Miss Emmaline, would you be interested in a small job next week? I'd have to take you to Ewing, but I have a friend—Thelma Tureen—at the Greener Pastures nursing home and she loves flowers. I was going to take some bedding plants out there and help her plant them, but I don't know the first thing about growing flowers." (Not entirely true since I'd worked in a plant nursery in Arkansas for a month, but that wasn't part of my official story.) "*You're* clearly an expert. I could pick you up and we could go to the Piggly Wiggly in Ewing to pick up some plants—I'd pay you of course, and pay for the plants—and then you could tell me how to plant them in the courtyard. I'll pick up something for lunch, and we can make an afternoon out of it."

The look of shock on her face made me question whether I'd offended her somehow. I was about to backpedal and apologize when she gave me a watery smile.

"You don't have to pay me, Miss Carly."

"Carly," I said insistently. Then I gave her a wink. "My momma taught me to respect my elders. Even if they are only slightly older than me."

"Your momma did right by you, girl," she said, wiping a tear from her eye. "I ain't seen Thelma in over five years. I'd be honored to do it. No pay needed. And I'll bring some of my own plants. I have a mess of 'em in my greenhouse."

Of course they knew each other—both of them had lived in Drum for over sixty or more years. I had no intention of just taking her plants, but I figured we could work out some kind of payment later if she'd be willing to sell them without cutting into her own plantings. Right now I needed to get my flowers and get out to the Drummonds' place.

She handed me four beautiful bouquets since I'd overpaid her, the stems in a bread loaf bag with a tiny bit of water so they didn't wilt, and I told her I'd be in touch to figure out which day worked best for her and her flower-selling schedule.

I felt better having a gift to give to Emily, but my stomach still clenched the closer I got to the Drummond property. I definitely wasn't dressed for tea in my jeans and long-sleeved T-shirt, but I hadn't had time to change, not that Bart would care about my schedule. I was sure he'd see it as a sign of disrespect.

There was nothing I could do about it now. If I went home to change, I'd be late, and I'd barely make it in time as it was.

I turned onto the Drummond property and took the lane up to the circle drive in front of the large stone, two-story monstrosity the Drummonds called a house. The first time I'd seen it, I'd struggled to envision the men I knew growing up in this house. It looked like a grand estate, totally different from the way Wyatt and Max lived now. Hell, Max's apartment over the tavern was a remodeling disaster. But I knew the Drummonds had hit hard times first when moonshine became legal, and then once and for all when their lumber business had gone belly-up over a decade ago. The Drummond Lodge and Spa was Bart's wing and a prayer to turn it all around, which seemed like further confirmation that he'd never have put the resort in its current location if he'd known that his son's ex-girlfriend was buried there. He couldn't really afford the bad publicity at this point.

I parked in the drive and looked in my rearview mirror. My hair was longer than it had been on my last visit, slightly past my shoulders now, and it didn't look too bad. I did a quick finger comb, and considered putting on some lipstick, but that was Caroline. Carly was usually makeup-free, or just mascara and a bit of concealer. I hadn't taken the time to apply anything this morning, so Emily was getting me *au naturel*.

I pulled the recorder out of my purse, flipped the cassette over and pressed record, ~~play~~, then set it back in my bag. I only had thirty minutes left. I would either need to get more tapes, or review what I'd recorded and start taping over it.

With my purse slung over my shoulder and a bundle of white and red tulips in my hand, I walked up to the front door and rang the doorbell next to the large double wooden doors. They opened about five seconds later. A woman in her late fifties—the same one who'd turned up her nose and pointed me to the servants' entrance at the end of the house last December—answered, looking just as disgusted by the sight of me today as she had before. At least I'd worn a dress last time. Today I looked like a ranch hand.

"Mrs. Drummond was expecting you for tea," she said, her gaze sweeping my attire. She looked extra revolted when she took in the bouquet of flowers dripping water on the front step.

"I hadn't realized there was a dress code," I said in a breezy tone I hoped would piss her off.

For a moment or two, I thought she was going to turn me away, but she backed up with a look of utter disgust and let me in.

The entry way was two stories tall with a massive wooden chandelier over our heads. If the Drummonds wanted to kill someone and make it look like an accident, they could pull it off with that light fixture. All they'd need to do was arrange for someone to cut the chains at the right moment. A curved marble staircase was off to the right, a pair of open French doors to the left.

The woman released a huff of disapproval—I wasn't sure of what: my attire, the flowers, my existence?—and ushered me through the doors into a very fancy living room with twelve-foot ceilings and a large stone fireplace with an enormous hearth. Perpendicular red velvet couches formed a little conversation area near the fireplace, separated by a coffee table with a white marble top and a gold base. A black grand piano was to the left of the massive, nearly floor-to-ceiling windows overlooking the drive. Multiple other seating arrangements filled the nearly thirty-foot-deep room, with windows on the opposite wall, which I presumed looked over the backyard.

A silver tray with a silver tea pot sat on the coffee table, and a three-tiered silver caddy filled with tiny cakes and cookies sat on a gold and marble cart next to the sofa, along with a stack of two blue and white china plates. Two blue and white china teacups were arranged on the silver tray next to the pot.

Emily sat at the end of one of the sofas wearing a black and white tweed blazer and skirt, a black-and-camel-colored scarf wrapped around her presumably bald head.

"Mrs. Drummond, *Miss Moore* has arrived," the housekeeper said in a condescending tone.

"Now, now," Emily said with a wave of her hand. "Be nice, Annie."

Annie pierced me with a dark look, then shut the doors.

"Oh, Carly," Emily said in delight. "I'm excited to host you today. You have no idea how happy I was when Bart said you asked if you could call for tea."

An interesting way of putting it, given Bart had been the one to invite me. I hurried toward her when I saw she was struggling to get up.

I leaned over, extending my hand. "Thank you so much for having me. I'm sorry I'm not more dressed up. I had some errands to run earlier, and I never made it home to change."

"Don't you worry about a thing," she said, dismissing the matter with a flick of her hand. "No need for formalities. We're friends here."

"I brought you these," I said, holding them out. "Emmaline Haskell has the prettiest flowers, better than you'll find in any shop. She sells them on the street corner in downtown Drum."

She took the flowers and sniffed. "Ah, Emmaline. She's still around? She's been selling them for years. I'll ring the bell and have Annie bring a vase." She picked up the bell from the side table before I could stop her.

"I could have gotten you one," I said, taking a seat opposite her.

"Nonsense. You're my guest. It's Annie's job."

The French doors opened, and Annie stood in the doorway. "You rang, ma'am?"

"I need a vase for Carly's bouquet. She got the flowers from Emmaline Haskell. Can you believe she's still selling flowers downtown?"

"No, ma'am," Annie said in a dry voice. "I'll get your vase right away." Then she walked out and shut the door.

The tension in the room eased after Annie left, but I still resisted the urge to glance around the room for Bart. Hopefully, the fact that there were only two cups indicated we'd be alone. "I take it that it's just the two of us today."

"Bart *so* wanted to be here, but he was called back to the construction site. We're all so relieved it's been reopened." She reached for the tea pot and poured some into a cup. "I'd have Annie serve our tea, but she's on the grumpy side today." She leaned closer and held the edge of her hand to her cheek as though hiding her mouth from the doors. "I think she's going through *the change*."

I suspected her attitude ran deeper than some errant hormones but held my tongue. "I can get you something from the cart."

"Oh, that would be good. Go ahead and put the two plates on the coffee table, next to the teacups."

I realized both cups had been poured and set before our respective seats. I passed out the two plates.

"Now grab the tray and bring it over. I suppose we'll just serve ourselves," she said with a sigh as though she'd been asked to climb Mount Everest. Personally, I'd much rather serve myself than have someone else do it. Especially Annie.

But as though she were Beetlejuice and could be summoned at the mere mention of her name—or, in this case, a manifestation of my thoughts—she walked into the room with a crystal vase with a small amount of water at the bottom. She snatched the flowers off the side table where Emily had placed them and dropped them into the vase as though touching them were offensive, and I knew it was partly because I'd bought them off the street.

It took everything in me not to snatch them back, not on my account but Emmaline's.

Once Annie set the vase on the fireplace mantel, she practically bolted from the room.

Emily selected a cookie and a white petit four with pink frosting and put them on her plate. I took a petit four too before setting the tray back on the cart.

"Did you and your mother have tea?" Emily asked as she placed a lump of sugar in her cup.

"Uh… no." I wondered what she knew about me, if anything. Did she know my real identity? I suspected not, but then a forgotten memory surfaced, one that caught me off guard. "But I remember having a tea party with my dolls." I swallowed the lump in my throat. "With my dad."

"How lovely. I always wanted a daughter, but I'm not sure Bart would have lowered himself to having tea parties," she said wistfully, stirring her tea. The spoon clanged daintily against the thin china. "I would like to think he would have treated his daughter different than he did his sons."

I wasn't prepared to hear her admit he'd treated his boys so poorly, and thankfully, she didn't give me a chance to respond.

"I miss my boys. They rarely come around these days." Her gaze lifted to mine. "I keep telling Wyatt to bring you to the house for lunch on a day when Bart's not around, or arrange for us to meet at a restaurant in Ewing, but he insists your schedule is too busy, and when I pester Max to let you off, he always has an excuse."

She clearly thought Wyatt and I were still dating, four months after we'd broken up. Why hadn't they told her the truth? "Mrs. Drummond—"

"Call me Emily, dear. Mrs. Drummond is much too stuffy."

"Emily, Wyatt and I…" But something held my tongue. If the lies or evasions had come only from Wyatt, I might have written it off as his usual mysterious behavior, but Max? Was the fact that Emily thought Wyatt and I were together keeping me safe? That made no sense, especially since Bart thought I was seeing Marco. "Max is right. It's been especially busy lately with all the construction crews coming in. This is the first half day I've had off in weeks."

"And you came here to see me?" She placed a frail hand on her chest. "That means more to me than you could possibly know."

Now I was filled with guilt. Damn Bart Drummond. I wanted to ask her about Heather, but if I jumped right into the questions, I'd look like a jealous lover—a crazy jealous lover since Heather was dead. Which made me wonder if Emily knew the truth. Although the news was all over town, she didn't get out frequently, and Bart clearly didn't feel the need to keep her informed.

"Has Bart told you much about the bones they found?" I asked, picking up my teacup and taking a sip.

"Not much. He thinks they came from Floyd Bingham." She curled her nose. "Nasty man."

"I thought so too." When she gave me a curious look, I added, "Marco told me how awful he was."

"It's a wonder that Todd survived living in that hell," she said. "I couldn't believe his stepmother didn't take him or Rodney."

She didn't know about the rumors about Floyd's wife? Or she didn't believe them?

"Emily, do you have any idea about the identity of the person they found buried out there?"

"Bart says it was likely an ex-employee of Floyd's. He didn't believe in firing people. Once you worked for him, you were his for life." She made a face. "Which makes it all the more strange that his wife ran off."

"Emily," I said before I could stop myself, "do you really think he'd let her go?"

Sadness filled her eyes. "No... I suppose he didn't."

Just how sheltered was Emily? I knew Wyatt had come back to Drum because of her, and both he and Max had spoken of her fragility from the cancer. But did it go deeper than they let on? Was she emotionally fragile too?

I found myself thinking of what Abby had said about Mitzi, and how her husband had acted like I had the potential to break her.

Seems to be a weirdly common ailment in these parts.

"Do you think his wife is buried out there?" she asked, her voice breaking. Then horror filled her eyes. "Rodney! Oh, that poor dear boy."

"No," I rushed to say. "They didn't find a child. I asked. Marco confirmed it." But I was sure he was buried somewhere.

Her eyes sank closed and she set her teacup on the tray. "I had nightmares after he disappeared. I dreamed of my own boys going missing. I dreamed of Rodney being buried in the ground." Her gaze lifted to mine. "He was friendly with Max and Marco, although Bart didn't like it much. I saw him during my room mother functions at school. He was such a quiet boy. He had a haunted look. Too many kids in these parts do." Tears swam in her eyes. "I asked Bart to put up a reward to find him, but he wouldn't hear of it. Said it would be unseemly, and it could cause a war with Floyd. He was already dealing with enough trouble from Hank, he didn't need to go courting any more. And that poor boy was never found."

"I'm sure that must have been very hard for you as a mother. Especially since your son was friendly with him."

She gave me a tight smile. "Bart accused me of smothering the boys for a while after that. I had a hard time letting them out of my sight. Wyatt was easier—he was twelve, goin' on twenty-two." She chuckled. "Kids seem to be in such a hurry to grow up, Wyatt in particular. But soon Bart put a stop to my fussin' and decided to send Max off to summer camp in North Carolina. Wilderness training. Said I was makin' him into a sissy and it would toughen him up." She shuddered.

"Did he want to go?" I asked, in disbelief she would share all of this with me.

"Oh, dear. No. Wyatt was loud and boisterous and larger than life in everything he did, just like his father wanted. But Max…"

That was so unlike the Wyatt I knew; I had a hard time imagining it. Wyatt was quiet and withdrawn. Was that a result of his break from his father or his time in prison? Maybe both.

A soft smile covered Emily's face. "Max… he was more easygoin'. Less intense. Bart called him a momma's boy who needed toughening up. But Max went to camp because his father had asked it of him. He would have done anything to make his father proud, but I knew he was scared. So I snuck behind Bart's back and offered to send Marco to camp with Max, unbeknownst to Bart. His mother was hesitant at first—no one wanted to face his wrath—but I convinced her in the end."

"Did Bart ever find out?"

"Good heavens, no," she said, picking up her tea again. "And Max never mentioned Marco while he regaled us with tales of his adventure. He had his father's attention for three days, and those were three of the happiest days of Max's life."

I stared at her in shock. "Mrs. Drummond—I mean Emily…why are you telling me this?"

She looked at me with tear-filled eyes. "Because while Bart has been a good husband, especially in our later years, he's been an equally terrible father."

"Again, I have to ask—"

"Every bad thing that has happened to my boys is because I didn't protect them from him. I let him convince me that he knew best. That he was makin' them into real men. By the time I realized what was happenin', it was too late. I was trapped, and so were they." She lowered her voice and leaned closer. "Even if I wanted to leave, I couldn't. I had no money to support myself let alone both boys. And if he'd found me, he would have taken them from me. So I stayed to keep them close. And over time, they convinced me they were glad we had stayed. That they had the life I wanted for them, and that I'd given them that by staying."

"Emily…" I said, not knowing how else to respond.

"I'm not sure what Wyatt's told you about his childhood or his relationship with his father, or with me for that matter, but my boys haven't had an easy life. I did the best I could. I'm sure the boys have kept you away from me because of Bart. Worried about what he might do to you."

She tsked. "He would never approve of you for a wife. Just like he didn't approve of Heather. Only you're as sweet as molasses and Heather was a viper."

"Bart paid Heather to leave town after Wyatt's arrest?"

"Yes. He paid her five thousand dollars. He was shocked she accepted an offer that low. He was prepared to go quite a bit higher."

"He doesn't approve of me. Do you think he'd try to pay me off to leave?" I knew the opposite was true—he'd blackmailed me into staying—but I wanted to see how she'd respond.

"Oh, no, dear. I told him if he tried that stunt with you, I'd leave him." She poured more tea into her cup, then held the pot out to me. "A refill? You haven't even touched your cake."

I forced a smile as I set my teacup on the table. "I had a late lunch."

In reality, my stomach was churning. If Wyatt and Max were attempting to hide the fact that I'd broken up with Wyatt to keep me safe, they'd done a poor job of it. Bart knew.

What were they all up to? Why were there so many secrets?

"Do you think Heather left town?" I asked as she topped off my cup.

"Of course she did. We never saw her again. She told us she was headed to California."

California? According to Abby, Heather said she was going to Tulsa.

"You were at the meeting with her?" I couldn't hide my surprise.

"It was my idea," she said, picking up her cookie and taking a nibble. "I had to protect my son."

"And you don't think he needs to be protected from me?"

"Don't be silly," she said with a laugh. "Why would he need to be protected from you? Everyone—including Bart—tells me how sweet you are. That's the kind of woman Wyatt needs. Someone soft enough to round off his rough edges."

Wow. That sounded like the basis for a great relationship.

"Did you see Bart give her the check?" I asked.

"I filled it out myself and handed it to her," Emily said, her chin lifted. "On that topic, Bart and I were united. In fact, it drew us back together, reminding us why we'd married in the first place."

"Love?"

"Don't be silly," she scoffed. "Bart was inheriting his father's fortune. He needed wise counsel, not a nitwit."

I wondered how well that had worked out given that he'd bullied his sons and her wise counsel had been dismissed again and again.

"I see the look on your face. I know what you're thinkin'," she said, sipping her tea with a satisfied smile. "You think I'm powerless."

I couldn't hide my shock at her accusation.

"We all have our strengths and our weaknesses. I can still get one up on Bart from time to time."

It hit me full in the face why I was here. Bart was using me against his wife. He expected me to give her the news that Heather had never left Drum after all. This was yet another game he was playing.

"Emily," I said, trying not to show how unnerved I was. I was here for information, and I still intended to get it. "Do you know if Heather cashed her check?"

"Well, of course she did. Why wouldn't she?"

"Just curious," I said with a tight smile. "She seems like she's fond of games. Maybe her request for money was a game too, and she just wanted to see if you'd pay."

"Oh, no. That's not Heather at all. She's a conniving gold digger," she said with a sweet smile. "She was interested in Wyatt for the money. Nothing more. Nothing less. Once we cut her a check, she moved on."

"But like you said, five thousand dollars doesn't seem like very much… given all she thought she had to lose."

"I'll agree with you there," she said with a nod. "I have no idea what changed her mind. We were all just grateful she left."

But something else was going on. Someone else must have promised her more money, because I didn't believe she'd walk away from what she saw as the Drummond fortune for such a pitiful amount.

"Could I ask you a favor?" I asked. "And it's going to seem strange, but could you make sure Heather actually did cash the check?"

"That's silly," she scoffed.

"I'd love it if you indulged me," I said, pouring on the charm. "And I'd love to come back for tea."

As I suspected, her face lit up. "You will?"

"Yes. When you find out about the check, you can leave a message with Max at the tavern and tell him I'm invited for tea, but please don't let on that we've been discussing Wyatt's ex. I don't want him or Wyatt to know I've been asking questions about her." I feigned a shudder. "Nothing like a jealous girlfriend to sour a relationship."

"You have no reason to be jealous," Emily said, looking pleased. "Heather is ancient history. Don't worry even a little bit that she was prettier than you." Her eyes lit up with kindness. "It's what's inside that counts."

I studied her in disbelief. Was she playing me or was she serious? Oddly enough, I was fairly certain it was the latter.

"Well, thank you, I think."

"Now, now. Don't be offended. Know your opponents' strengths and weakness, but also know your own."

Did she see what she perceived to be inferior looks as a weakness? It was time to end this conversation, even though our talk had left me with even more questions.

"I wholeheartedly agree," I said with a genuine smile. "But now I have to go. I'm late for work, and we're always busy now that the construction crews have moved into town."

"I haven't been to the tavern in ages," she said wistfully.

"You should come in sometime," I said as I got to my feet. "I'm sure Max would be thrilled."

Happiness lit up her face. "Maybe I will."

"This has been lovely, Emily. I look forward to chatting again."

"Yes, I'll look into the check matter, even if I think it's silly."

"Thank you." I headed for the door, and then impulsively stopped and turned back to face her. "Emily, if I could ask one more thing. When you came to see Max at school after Wyatt's arrest, what did you tell him that convinced him to come home?"

Her smile wobbled, and although it quickly righted itself, it no longer looked genuine. "I reminded him of his obligations to his family. Of course."

Her answer shook me, so I gave her a wave and hurried out of the house and to my car, holding my breath until I was off the Drummond property.

Emily had reminded Max of his family obligations, which had sent him on a multiday bender that had ultimately brought him back to Drum.

What were his family obligations? One thing was certain—nothing good.

Chapter
Sixteen

Ruth was watching for me when I walked in the back door close to four, and she followed me into the back room.

"Where the hell have you been?" she snapped.

"I had a lot of errands to run," I said as I shoved my purse into a small locker, then unzipped my duffel bag to retrieve my Max's Tavern T-shirt. I paused, considering, and asked, "How hot is the dining room today?"

Her forehead wrinkled. "What?...Oh. Warm."

I nodded, then quickly stripped off my long-sleeved tee and pulled my work shirt over my head.

"Damn, girl," Ruth said in an appreciative tone. "Just strip that shirt right off."

"It's the same as hanging out at the pool in a bikini. Besides, we're friends and I'm late." I sat down and jerked off my shoes and made quick work of putting on my athletic shoes with the cushioned insoles that helped keep my feet comfortable—or at least more comfortable—during a long shift. "Is Molly still here?"

"She took off an hour ago."

"How'd she do?" I asked with some hesitation.

"Better than I would have expected, but she's not up to speed."

"Well," I said, lacing my shoes. "Let's give her a few days."

Ruth made a face like she'd consider it. "There's a family out in the dining room askin' about you. They ordered drinks and fries and nothin' else. The mother said you offered to help her kid with his homework?"

Oh crap. I'd forgotten about Annette and her son.

"Yeah. I'll take care of them. Have they been here long?" I finished tying my shoes and jumped to my feet, starting to push past her.

She grabbed my shoulders and held me in place. "Whoa. Slow down." She cocked her head to study me. "Something's not right with you. You seem a bit unhinged, and you're never unhinged."

I wasn't about to admit that I'd had tea with Emily Drummond, especially since our conversation had given me some worries about Max. Like the timing of when he'd been summoned home and what, exactly, he'd been asked to do. "This whole Heather thing has got me spooked."

"You think the Drummonds are gonna come after you next?" she asked, half serious, half derisive.

"You think *they* killed her?" I asked. "Not Wyatt?"

She snorted. "Why would Wyatt kill her? At that point, he was probably happy she was leaving."

"Did you know she had a going-away party the night before she supposedly left town?" I asked.

Her eyes flew wide and she pointed a finger in my face as she took a step back. "I knew it! You *are* investigatin'!"

"Shh!" I practically shouted. "It's an active investigation. If the sheriff department thinks I'm looking into it, I could get arrested."

"I get why *they're* lookin'. The question is, why are *you* lookin'?" she asked.

"I just want to know what happened," I said, then for good measure added, "And I'm nosy."

"No," she said thoughtfully. "You're not nosy...not unless you're tryin' to get to the bottom of something. Are you doin' this to try to save Wyatt? Did he ask you to do this?"

That was the reason I'd started looking into it, but if he told me to stop, I'd keep right on pushing. Especially after my conversation with his mother. I sensed there was more to this—that I could truly find something that implicated Bart. Still, I wasn't ready to admit any of that. I had questions for Ruth, but I'd ask them later.

"I've got to get to work." I hurried past her and came to an abrupt halt at the entrance to the dining room—Wyatt was sitting at the end of the bar closest to the back room, his dark gaze aimed at me. He'd changed shirts since I'd last seen him hunched over in the nursing home parking lot. His eyes didn't look very bloodshot, which confirmed I hadn't reached his face with the pepper spray.

"I meant to tell you," Ruth said in an amused voice behind me. "Wyatt's waitin' for you, and he's got his undies in a twist."

Not surprising.

"Did he mention why?" I asked quietly enough that I hoped he wouldn't hear me.

"Nope. He just took a seat and ordered a coffee. He's on his third cup, so now he's *extra* wound up."

Great.

"Thanks."

She laughed, but I knew if she thought he was a threat to me, she wouldn't be so jovial. It was more likely she was hoping to watch me hand him his ass on a platter.

Too bad she hadn't been in the parking lot of Greener Pastures a couple of hours ago.

Ignoring Wyatt, I headed for the family sitting in the booth at the front of the tavern. Annette and Eric were seated across from each other, and relief filled her eyes when she saw me coming toward her.

"I'm so sorry I wasn't here earlier," I said, sliding into the booth next to Eric. "This was my first afternoon off in weeks and I got detained running errands."

"Oh, you don't need to apologize," she said. "I think I should apologize to *you*. I think one of your bosses is upset about us being here."

"Max?" I asked in surprise. While I probably should have cleared this with him, I doubted he'd care. We had lots of empty tables at this time of day, and I was usually trying to find work to do. It looked like Annette had ordered drinks for her and Eric as well as a basket of fries. Max was a shrewd businessman. He'd see it as money he wouldn't have had otherwise. Hell, some of the nightly regulars took up tables for hours and spent less than this.

I glanced over to Max at the bar, and he responded with a grin.

"No, not the guy behind the bar right now," Annette said. "The guy at the end. With a cup of coffee. He was servin' drinks when we first got here and I asked for you."

"Ohhhh," I said, drawing it out. "That's not my boss. That's my boss's brother, and while he's been helpin' out lately, he won't be here much longer. You don't need to worry about him."

Her eyes flew wide. "*That's* Wyatt Drummond?"

"You don't know him?" Given how large the Drummonds loomed over Drum, I'd figured everyone in the area would know him by sight.

"I've heard of him, but I've never seen him. My husband takes our car to Greeneville for maintenance and such."

Which meant she likely had a newer car.

She still looked uncomfortable. "I don't want to step on any toes."

"No toes or any other appendages have been stepped on," I said with a laugh. "Wyatt's not very happy with me today, and I suspect he was taking it out on you. I'm sorry you were made to feel uncomfortable. I'll make sure it's handled."

"I don't want to get anyone in trouble," she said with a frown.

"Don't you worry about *that*," I assured her. "How about you get out Eric's work, and I'll help you both figure out how to do the problems?"

Relief washed over her face, and we spent the next fifteen minutes working through a few problems together until Annette and her son felt comfortable trying some on their own.

I left them to get started and headed over to the bar to check in with Max. As I slid behind it, Wyatt shot me a deadly glare.

"Where the hell have you been for the last hour and a half?"

"You have no right to ask me that," I said in a short tone. "We're not together anymore, and even if we were, you wouldn't have the right to dictate my comings and goings.

The fact is, I didn't ask you to follow me. I didn't want you anywhere near me."

Fury filled his eyes. "I'm tryin' to keep you safe, Carly. Maybe if you weren't acting like *a child*, you would put aside your hurt feelin's and see that."

My mouth dropped open, but I decided not to blast him, however much I wanted to stab him with my words. I inhaled deep, refocusing my energy. "What did you say to that mother siteating in the booth in the corner?"

He darted a glance in that direction, and a sheepish look washed over his face. "Let's just say you weren't my favorite person when she asked to speak to you."

Max stepped over, eyeing us like we were a pair of skittish horses. "Is havin' you two in the same place gonna be a problem?"

Wyatt grunted "no" as I said "yes."

Max put his hands on his hips and pushed out a sigh. "Funnily enough, when I pictured myself becomin' a daddy, I didn't see myself disciplinin' a couple of grown adults, and I sure as hell didn't expect for one of them to be my older brother."

Wyatt gave Max a look that should have brought him to his knees.

"I don't have time for this nonsense," I said. "I only came over to tell you that I'm helpin' a little boy with his math homework."

Max did a double take. "Say what?"

"He didn't understand how to do it, so I showed him and his mother." I made a face. "Actually, I helped a little girl the night before, and the mother of the little boy caught wind of it and brought her son in for dinner last night to see if I could help him. They didn't quite get it, so I'm showing them this afternoon while we're not busy."

"Let me get this straight," Max said, resting his hand on the counter. "You're helping a kindergartner with his math homework."

"Not a kindergartner," I said in exasperation. "A third grader, and it's the new math, which is totally confusing when you don't know how to do it, but once you get it, it makes higher math easier, which is why it's so important for the parents to understand so they can help their children."

Max stared at me like I'd started speaking Russian. "Where did *you* learn how to do this new math?"

I shrugged, the neurons in my brain scrambling to come up with an acceptable answer. "I tutored in Atlanta as a side job. Retail doesn't pay much."

"Huh," he said, shifting his weight and casting his gaze to the booth.

"Sounds like several of the kids don't know how to do it," Wyatt said, turning his head sideways to look at his brother. "Maybe you could have Carly host a tutoring session in the afternoons, after school. The kids and their parents would likely order food while they're here, and it's a dead time anyway. Great opportunity to give back to the community but make some money too."

Wyatt turned to me, his expression softer, and part of me wanted to push him off his barstool. He knew I'd been a schoolteacher, and I'd confessed how much I missed teaching. Just when I was sure I hated him, he went and did something nice.

My eyes burned and I had to look away.

"You know," Max said, sounding excited. "That's actually a good idea." He turned to look at me. "Can you help with other subjects besides math?"

"Yeah," I said. "I can help with it all."

"We could call it Max's Homework Club," Max said. "We could host it a couple days a week from three thirty to five, which would clear them out before the dinner crowd."

"The families just might stay for dinner," Wyatt suggested. "And maybe we should name it something else since Carly's gonna be helpin' with the homework and not you."

Max rubbed his chin. "Yeah, maybe so."

Annette glanced over at me with a look of panic.

"Excuse me," I said, heading around the corner of the bar. "Duty calls."

I spent the next ten minutes helping Eric work a few problems before they left. Some customers came in with the dinner crowd, and I kept glancing at the door, watching for Marco. I hadn't spoken to him since I'd left my long, rambling message. I was eager to tell him about my encounter with Emily, but that would have to wait until later. The last thing I wanted was for either of the Drummond boys to overhear me.

Ruth was at the food counter when I headed back there to pick up the plates for table three. Neither of our orders were up, so I leaned against the counter and glanced toward the front.

"What are you watchin' for?" she asked. "Or should I ask *who*?"

Not much got past her. "Marco."

"I heard he was guarding the construction site."

I nodded. "He was until they gave it the all clear. The construction guys must still be out there."

"Max says they got a late start, so they'll probably be out there for a while yet. Bart's gonna push them to get a full day's work in to make up for the lost time."

That stood to reason, but it also meant there'd likely be a late dinner rush.

"Say, Ruth, I know you and Heather weren't friends, but do you happen to know who went to her going-away party?"

She looked uncomfortable. "That was a long time ago."

"Not really. Not like decades. You were working here. Surely you heard rumors."

"I was older than her and her friends," she said, curling her upper lip. "And they were trouble with a capital T."

"Abby and Mitzi?" I asked in surprise.

A grin stretched her mouth as she turned to face me. "Someone's been doin' her homework. Should I start calling you Veronica Mars or Nancy Drew?"

"Neither," I said, rolling my eyes as I laughed. "But if you know anything, I'd really appreciate hearing it."

She was silent for a moment, her gaze drifting to the dining room, and I realized she was watching Wyatt behind the bar, but this time without her usual animosity. "I didn't know Heather well. I mostly just knew *of* her, but not until she came back after high school. She moved in with her aunt. My mom knew Hilde. Heather had given her grief in high school, and it didn't sound like Hilde was too happy she was back. I don't know much, because my mom and I weren't seein' eye to eye back then. She was hooking up with a particularly disgusting guy and hittin' the bottle pretty hard."

My face softened. "Ruth, I'm sorry."

Her mouth was all smirk, but I could see the pain in her eyes. "What are you sayin' sorry about? None of that is your fault."

No, but she rarely talked about her mother. I knew she'd died from a drug overdose a few years ago, although she hadn't been a drug addict all that long in the scheme of things. Based on what Ruth had told me before, her mother's vices of choice had been alcohol and men who were bad for her.

"Do you remember anything else?"

Her mouth twisted to the side as she scanned the counter to see what was holding up her order. "I heard Dick Stinnett was at that party. He dated Molly's sister, May, after Heather left. May was there too."

"Do you know where Dick lives or where I might find him?"

Her brow lifted. "You want to talk to him?"

"I have to find out what happened at the party," I said. "From what I've heard, she supposedly left the next day. I need to find out who saw her last."

Tiny put two plates on the counter, and Ruth shot me a dark look before grabbing them. "I think he's workin' at a used car lot in Ewing." She started to leave, then hesitated. "Carly, just remember that the very last person who saw her was also the person who killed her."

A shiver of fear shot down my spine. She was right, and apparently Wyatt had also considered that little tidbit—likely why he was being so protective in his overbearing way.

Tiny handed me a couple of plates but held my gaze. "You lookin' into Heather Stone's murder?"

His curiosity caught me off guard. He rarely made small talk during the dinner rush. "I'm just askin' people questions."

"You know the Drummonds weren't the only ones who wanted her gone. I hear she had a thing with Todd Bingham before she and Wyatt got back together the last time."

"Todd Bingham?" Well, crap. That shouldn't have surprised me, yet it did. But it added a new element to the case. She was buried on the disputed Bingham-Drummond land, after all, and Lula had called in sick after Heather's body had been found. "Thanks."

"You thinkin' about goin' out to talk to him?"

Was I? Dammit, I was.

"Maybe take the baby a gift to get in the door," he suggested. "We've all seen Bingham has a soft spot for that baby."

"Thanks, I'll keep that in mind." Although I was pretty sure Bingham would see right through that approach. He was a shrewd man who'd taken his father's bare-bones criminal enterprise and run with it. I knew he was capable of murder, but I didn't for a minute think he'd killed and buried Heather Stone. If he were responsible, he would have dug those bones up and moved them before the ink was dry on the judge's signature releasing the land to Bart. Or maybe Bart was the one who'd killed her, and he'd hoped to pin it on Bingham.

Still, I wouldn't be surprised if Bingham knew something. It wasn't a bad idea to pay him a visit tomorrow morning before I went to work at noon.

I took the plates out to my table, pleased that I now had three people to talk to—Bingham, Dick Stinnett, and May McMurphy. I'd talk to Bingham first and then figure out where to go next.

I grabbed glasses from one of my tables to get refills, and as soon as I set them on the counter in front of Max, he gave me a perturbed look.

"What?"

"Got any idea why Marco called a few minutes ago, frantic to make sure you were safe from Wyatt?" he asked with a raised brow.

I grimaced. "What did he say?"

Exasperation covered his face, and he sounded irritated when he said, "Like I said, he asked if you were safe from Wyatt."

"And what did *you* say?" I asked.

"I told him you two were bickering like usual, but everything was fine other than that. Was I wrong?"

So Marco hadn't told him I'd pepper sprayed Wyatt, and Wyatt hadn't mentioned it himself. Once again, I was caught in a tangle of omitted information.

I was about to tell Max myself, but both of us were distracted by the sight of Bingham and Lula walking in with their baby. Four of Bingham's men followed behind them.

Talk about lucky timing. I'd wanted to arrange a meetup, and here he was at the tavern.

"That's a first," Max said, his brow furrowed. "He's dining with his family."

Bingham had been a regular customer ever since I'd started at Max's Tavern, but he'd never once come in with Lula, let alone the baby.

Tables were self-seating which Bingham and Lula were both well aware of, but apparently Bingham wanted his men close to their table, because he scanned the room, looking for two tables together. There were two in Ruth's section, but he made a couple of younger men at a four-top table get up and move so there would be an empty table in front of an available booth in my section.

It was an obvious maneuver to get me to wait on them, and Max didn't look happy about it. Neither did Wyatt, who was pulling a draft beer.

Ruth hurried over with a drink ticket and gave me a worried look. "It looks like Lula's over whatever fake illness she had. You good with waiting on 'em?"

I'd had multiple encounters with Bingham, most of them here in the tavern. Ruth knew he was sometimes trouble for me, but I could handle him. "Yeah."

I grabbed the refills that had brought me to the bar, and after I placed them on the table—they were for the two guys who had moved—I walked over to greet Bingham and Lula.

"Hey, Carly," Lula said with a bright smile. She was holding her sleeping daughter in the crook of her arm.

I couldn't help oohing over the baby. "Beatrice is getting so big already!"

"Like a weed," Lula said, looking at her baby with so much love it took my breath away.

I wanted a baby someday. Multiple babies. I just didn't see that happening. I couldn't bring a baby into the mess of my life, and after everything I'd been through, I didn't see me ever "settling down" with a man, let alone placing enough trust in him to have a baby with him.

"Oh, somebody's gettin' baby fever," Lula cooed.

I snorted, shoving all my dreams back into the chest I kept them in. There was no room for children in my life. Thanks to my father. The irony was he likely needed a grandchild to carry on the legacy of the Hardshaw Group.

"Nah," I said softly. "Just admirin' yours. She's so beautiful, Lula. You've truly been blessed."

Lula's gaze lifted and locked with Bingham's. "Trust me, I know."

I really didn't want to stick around for their lovefest because, to my surprise, jealousy rose up in me again. Not of Bingham—I resisted a shudder—but of what Lula had. Of what I likely never would.

"Can I get you something to drink? Or I can go ahead and take your order if you know what you'd like," I said, digging my order pad out of my apron pocket. Bingham was here enough to know what we had available, and Lula had worked here.

"Tryin' to rush us out of here?" Bingham asked in a low growl.

I was about to respond, but Lula beat me to it. "You hush now, Todd. She means no disrespect." She glanced up at me. "Ain't that right, Carly?"

"Of course," I said in shock. I wasn't sure if I was more surprised that she'd spoken to him like that or that he'd clamped his mouth shut. "I was just thinking you might want me to get your food out quickly so you can eat in peace while Beatrice is sleeping."

Lula beamed up at me. "You are just the sweetest."

She proceeded to give me her order and Bingham's. I expected him to contradict her, but he remained silent with his arms folded over his broad chest, his gaze on the baseball game on the TV in the back corner of the room.

I turned to the table of bodyguards, and Bingham told them to order their food with their drinks. They seemed taken by surprise and a couple of them had a hard time settling on what they wanted so quickly.

I ran the food orders back to Tiny, then took the drink orders to the bar. Most of the men had ordered beer, so, lucky for me, I got to take their ticket to Wyatt, whose gaze was firmly on Bingham.

"I need five beers and a coke. And don't provoke him," I said, glancing around my section to see if anyone needed my attention. Shockingly, everyone seemed good. Which meant I didn't have a reason to walk away.

"It's pretty damn obvious he came here to see you," he said in a dark voice as he grabbed a mug and started to pull the draft. "He cleared a table of customers to sit in your section."

"Orrr," I said, drawing out the word, "he really wanted to sit in a booth with the baby."

"There's a booth open in Ruth's section with a table in front of it."

"Calm down," I said, slightly exasperated. "If he picked my section, it's probably because of Lula. She and Ruth don't exactly see eye to eye."

His lips pressed together, and his gaze seemed to turn more intense as he set the first beer on the counter.

"Stop that," I said as I grabbed a tray for the drinks. "You're gonna piss him off."

"Good. I don't want him thinkin' he can mess with you."

That stupid blood price. It was making him crazy.

A flood of anger washed through me, and I leaned closer, lowering my voice. "I can handle myself. Todd Bingham's no threat to me. I've spent more time with him than you and I did when we were dating."

Jerry caught the corner of my eye as he walked through the door, far later than he usually came in. He sat at his usual perch at the end of the bar, but something about him seemed different. His posture maybe, or the way he was sitting.

"I don't need to be reminded of your relationship with a criminal," Wyatt growled.

My brow shot up, and I said in a deadly calm voice, "Be careful, Wyatt. Think very carefully what you say about him and my *relationship* with him from here on out, or I might not be so inclined to keep helping you."

Wyatt looked like he was about to choke on his own tongue, so I headed to Jerry, leaving Wyatt without a backward glance.

"Hey, Jerry," I said, trying to shake the weird feeling squeezing my chest after my encounter with Wyatt. "You're coming in late tonight. Want me to get you a beer to start?"

"I got me a temporary job," he said, beaming.

I couldn't hide my surprise. "A job? That's so exciting, Jerry. Where is it? What are you doin'?"

"At the construction site. I'm just sort of a gofer, but they kept me busy this afternoon." He jutted his head toward me. "The construction site opened back up today."

"Yeah, so I heard." Something about his job offer made me feel unsettled. "How did this all come about?" I asked excitedly, because Jerry was beaming and I didn't want to take that from him. He'd felt beneath everyone for so long, and while he'd been coming out of his shell over the last five months, I'd never seen him like this.

"One of the construction foremen was here during lunch. He spotted me and asked if I wanted a job. He said it's only temporary, but I don't mind because it's more money than I had before and it's something to *do*."

The arrangement sounded fishy. I didn't mention it because if I did, I'd sound crazy, but I couldn't shake the feeling that Bart had arranged this. But I sure hoped not. It would kill Jerry to know he'd been used, even more so if it was Bart Drummond doing the using.

"This calls for a celebration," I said with a huge grin.

Jerry's face glowed with pride.

Max must have heard because he came down to the end of the bar. "What are we celebratin'?"

"My new job," Jerry said, looking pleased with himself. Then he started to tell Max about his duties for the day while Max listened, excited for him too.

But an oily feeling took hold of me. The more I thought about it, the more certain I felt that Bart had somehow arranged this.

He intended to hurt Jerry to get to me. And I was powerless to stop it.

Chapter Seventeen

It was after seven when Marco showed up, still in his uniform. His gaze found me instantly, as though his inner radar could detect my presence.

I was at the bar, getting refills for Bingham's goons. We locked eyes, and for a split second, a sensation of warmth washed over me.

No. I couldn't feel this way about him. I couldn't risk losing him as my friend. The tug of yearning I felt was only because I wanted the comfort of being near him. Everyone needed to stop running their mouths about our friendship.

Wyatt was pulling the drafts, and Marco's eyes darkened at the sight of him.

I hurried over to him, grabbing his arm. "I suppose we have a lot to talk about after my message this afternoon."

"And your tea appointment," he said, his gaze still on Wyatt.

"Yeah, that didn't turn out as I'd expected."

He eyes jerked to mine, filled with worry.

I shook my head. "Nothing to worry about... at least I don't think so. You can help me decide when I tell you all about it later, but I don't think we should discuss it here. Do you want to come over to Hank's after work?"

He hesitated, then said, "I was thinkin' you could come to my place for a sleepover. I have the day off tomorrow. I don't go in until the evening. I can help."

I gave it a thought. "I'd have to go by Hank's for some things."

"You already have a toothbrush at my place. And shampoo and conditioner too."

Marco had gotten me those things when I'd spent days recuperating at his place after I was drugged, but I'd stayed at his house several times since for what we called sleepovers—which usually consisted of us sleeping on the sofa after watching movies. He'd introduced me to Star Wars and Star Trek—both of which I'd enjoyed, to my surprise.

When I hesitated, he added, "We can throw your clothes in the washer and dryer, and you can wear one of my T-shirts and sweatpants to sleep in." His smile spread. "Come on, it'll be fun."

I had to admit that hanging out with Marco tonight and tomorrow morning was exactly what I needed. And I could really use his insight into everything.

"Well, when you put it that way," I said, "I could use a little fun."

Wyatt's scowl deepened as Marco grinned at me and headed to the back to change. Ignoring Wyatt, I picked up the drinks he'd finished pouring, dropped them off, then checked on Lula and Bingham.

Beatrice was awake, and Lula was cooing to her. Bingham's gaze was on both of them, his guard up.

"Bingham," I said in a low tone as I took their dirty plates. "I'd like to make an appointment to see you tomorrow morning."

A smirk spread across his face. "Is this about Heather Stone? Are you playin' Nancy Drew again?"

"I need a little insight into some Drum history, and I figured you might be able to help."

His brow shot up. "You gonna accuse me of burying her body?"

"I know you didn't bury her," I scoffed. "You're smarter than that. Her body wouldn't have still been there if you'd put it in the ground."

His smile stretched. "You think Old Man Drummond did it?"

"Unfortunately, no. But again, I'd like to pick your brain, if you'll let me."

"Figuratively, I hope," he said with a wink.

"You hush now, Todd," Lula said, then turned to me. "Of course you can drop by and talk to him. How about ten?"

I turned to Bingham and waited for him to confirm his agreement. He gave a slight nod, his gaze pinned on me.

"Well, all righty then," I said, my attention fully on the baby. "Before I take these plates back, can I get you anything else?"

"I think we're good," Lula said, then smiled. "Do you want to hold her?"

I sucked in a lungful of air. "Me?"

I glanced around to see if anyone needed me.

"They'll be fine," Lula said, turning toward me. "She needs her godmother to hold her."

"*What?*"

"I want you to be her second godmother. Greta's one, of course, but you were the only one in this town to go lookin' for me. If you'd help me like that after just meetin' me, I can only imagine what you'd do to help Bea."

"I...I don't know what to say."

"That's why we came in tonight. I should have told you sooner..." She leaned closer and lowered her voice. "But Todd and me couldn't see eye to eye on some of the people we picked. Beatrice is being baptized this Sunday at church."

"Oh," I said, still in shock. Being a godmother came with responsibilities, but they were usually ceremonial. I knew of very few godparents who ever did anything beyond giving their godchild a birthday gift every year and bragging about being a godparent. Which, thankfully, made it feel less morally reprehensible to accept and then turn around and leave Drum... because if I didn't accept, I'd have a whole lot of explaining to do to Bingham. "I'm honored. Do I need to do anything? I've never been a godmother before."

"Just show up at the church," Lula said. "And promise to look after my baby should anything happen to Todd or me. And Greta. She's first in line."

Bingham and Lula were a whole lot more likely to come to harm than Greta, so at least I'd have her as a buffer. Plus, Max and Wyatt would surely be first in line, given they were Lula's half-brothers.

"Do Max and Wyatt know about the baptism?" I asked, and Bingham released a grunt.

"Not yet," Lula said, lowering her voice. "We're asking them both to be godfathers, but we haven't talked to them yet."

"Your secret is safe with me." I'd wondered if I was the person she and Bingham had argued over including, but now I suspected the dispute had been about Lula's half-brothers. Bingham and Max tolerated each other with a live-and-let-live philosophy, but he and Wyatt couldn't stand each other.

"Here," she said, "you need to hold her." Then she lifted the swaddled baby toward me and placed her in my arms.

She weighed next to nothing and looked so fragile I was afraid I'd hurt her, but she stared up into my face as I cradled her to my chest, and my heart melted.

"She likes you," Lula said.

"She likes everyone," Bingham grunted.

"She's so beautiful, Lula," I said, falling in love with her already.

"She's a good baby," Lula said with obvious pride.

Bingham kept quiet, but his guarded gaze was firmly on me and Beatrice.

Ruth was a few tables down, and I motioned her over to meet the baby since she'd asked Lula to bring her around. She stepped over cautiously, staring at the baby as though she were a space alien.

"Do you want to hold her?" Lula asked Ruth.

"Me?" Ruth asked, taking a step back.

"Yeah, of course you." She got out of the booth and took the baby from me. "Carly, can you ask Max and Wyatt to come over?" She shot me a wink.

"Yeah," I said, reluctant to give up the baby. At the same time, I didn't want to be anywhere near them when Lula popped her question.

Max was watching me as I slid behind the bar. "You got to hold the baby, huh?"

"She's so sweet. It's a wonder we got Lula to come work at all. I'd probably just sit around holding her all day."

He gave me an inquisitive look. "You got baby fever, Carly?"

"Someday," I said, working to keep my voice level. I suspected that "someday" would never come, and the reminder stung. "Say, Lula wants to talk to you and Wyatt."

"In the back room?"

"No, over at her table."

"*Wyatt too?*"

"Yep. The both of you. I'll cover the bar while you go over." I laughed at his perplexed expression. "But you have to be the one to tell Wyatt."

He snorted. "Fine. I'm not workin' on any orders, so nothin' for you to do at the moment."

He sidled over to Wyatt to relay the message. Wyatt gave me a questioning look, then steeled his back and followed his brother.

Marco had changed clothes and was sitting at the end of the bar next to Jerry, so I wandered over to check on them. Marco had a basket of wings and fries, and a glass of iced tea, which suggested that Max had put in the order for him.

"How're you boys doin' over here?" I asked.

"Lula's baby is cute," Jerry said.

"She's precious." Even I heard the wistful tone in my voice.

Marco gave me a concerned look, and I smiled.

He smiled back, the smile that lit up his face and made his eyes dance like he was the happiest man in the world, only right now his eyes were more subdued. Deeper than happy.

Content.

Butterflies fluttered in my stomach, catching me off guard. Foolish butterflies. Marco and I couldn't be anything more to each other than we already were. But it was hard to remember that when he was looking at me that way,

215

especially in the wake of holding Lula's baby and thinking about all that I'd planned for and lost.

"How are you doin'?" he asked quietly. *"Really?"*

"I'm okay. Eager to go home with you, though."

Jerry glanced back and forth between us. "Tell me again why you two aren't datin'?"

I laughed and took a step back. "Because we're just friends. Sleeping together would only screw everything up."

Jerry shook his head, muttering something about not understanding the youth of today.

The rest of the evening flew by, especially since a bunch of the construction workers came in for late dinners but didn't linger to keep drinking. I called Hank when things settled down around nine to tell him I was spending the night with Marco and wouldn't be coming home.

"There's some breakfast casserole in the freezer," I said. "Wrapped in foil. Just set it in the fridge tonight, then put the whole thing in the oven for a half hour at 300 degrees."

"I'm perfectly capable of feedin' myself," he grumped. "Did Wyatt stick close to you today?"

"Closer than I liked. Why on earth did you force that man to agree to a blood price?"

"Because I needed him to know how much you mean to me, and if he's puttin' you in danger, then he better do everything in his power to keep you safe."

Of course, I'd been thwarting him at every turn.

"Well, I don't need him tonight. Can you call him off?"

"He made a vow and he's bound to it until I release him. Did you run into any trouble today?"

"None, other than Wyatt himself—and don't worry, he's just being his usual overbearing, withholding self."

He was quiet for a moment. "You don't need to do this, girl. Makin' Bart pay won't bring Seth back."

A lump filled my throat. "No, it won't, but justice still needs to be meted out."

"Just be careful what you wish for." Then he hung up.

What was he talking about? Did he think he deserved some sort of punishment for the things he'd done?

I got busy after that and didn't have time to dwell on it. Max sent Ruth home at ten, but first he told us that Ginger had agreed to help with the lunch shift. Molly would be there too, so Ruth wouldn't have to come in until five.

By 11:30, the tavern was mostly empty, so Max decided to shut down early.

Marco was mopping the floor and Max was cleaning behind the bar, and I sat at a table to finish tallying my tips. Thankfully, I'd already done most of them before we closed.

Wyatt sat down in front of me. "I need to talk to you."

"There's nothing to talk about," I said in a breezy tone as I kept my attention on my tickets.

"You plan to just ignore the fact that you pepper sprayed me?" he asked, incredulous.

Lifting my face, I said, "I gave you fair warning, then followed through."

"You pepper sprayed him?" Max called out from across the room.

Marco stopped mopping to watch us.

Wyatt ignored his brother. "Where did you go after you left me in the parking lot gettin' beat up by two old ladies?"

"If I wanted you to know, I would have told you."

"Don't you think I have a right to know given that you're lookin' into something that directly affects me?"

"You're presuming I did something pertaining to Heather's murder."

"Well, didn't you?"

"Again," I said, "if I wanted you to know, I would have told you."

"You heard her, Wyatt," Marco said, walking over from across the room, still holding the mop. "Let it go."

Wyatt spun in his seat to face him. "This is none of your business, Roland."

"And as Carly herself told you, it's none of yours either," Marco countered, resting the mop on the floor and leaning against it.

"Marco," I said, "thank for your intercession, but Wyatt was just leaving."

"I'm not leavin' until you tell me where you went," Wyatt said, his hand clenching into fists on the table.

"Wyatt," Max said in a low tone. "Enough."

Wyatt stood, his face red. "Don't let your pride get you killed."

Then he stormed out the back door.

We all stood in silence for a few moments before Max said, "Will someone please tell me what's goin' on?"

Marco glanced at me, waiting for my cue.

"Wyatt came by Hank's this morning," I said, pushing the tickets toward the center of the table. "He asked me to look into who killed Heather, but he expected to chauffeur me around. So he's pissed that I didn't allow that to happen."

But it was more than that, and I knew it. I just didn't like it.

Chapter Eighteen

Marco insisted on following me to his house in his sheriff's SUV, just in case someone decided to run me off the road. I thought he was overreacting. I hadn't poked any bears yet. Or at least I didn't think so.

I pulled into the driveway behind his Explorer. Marco pulled in next to me, and we met in front of the steps to his front porch. He stretched his arms wide as I got close, and I went to him, letting him engulf me in a hug.

"How are you really, Carly? Because you're not the type of woman to just pepper spray somebody because they pissed you off."

"I don't want to talk about it. Not yet. Give me a minute."

"Okay," he said, holding me close.

We stood like that for a long time—me clinging to him, Marco holding me up as the silence surrounded us.

"You don't have to do this, you know," he finally said.

"Are you talking about trying to figure out who killed Heather or staying in Drum?"

"All of it. What happened when you went to see Emily?"

The night was chilly, but I liked being out under the stars. "Can we sit outside for a bit?"

"Yeah," he said, pulling away and rubbing my arms. "Do you have a jacket?"

"No, but—"

"Come inside and change into something warmer," he said. "Then we can sit out on the porch."

"Okay."

I headed to his room and helped myself to a pair of sweatpants and a sweatshirt from one of his drawers, then tossed my jeans, shirt, and undergarments into his washing machine and turned it on. When I emerged from the bedroom, I found Marco in the kitchen making two cups of tea. He handed one to me.

Balancing his own tea, he grabbed a blanket from the sofa and headed out the door to sit on the two chairs on his front porch.

I settled in my usual chair, and he dragged his seat closer to mine and threw the blanket over both of our legs. I took a sip of tea. "Teatime with Emily wasn't what I expected."

"So you mentioned."

"Bart wasn't there, so small blessings, but Emily didn't know they'd found Heather's remains."

"Seriously?"

"I think Bart assumed I'd tell her, but I didn't. I'm still not sure that was the right call, but Bart was using me and I didn't want to play by his rules."

"Sounds like a Bart move."

"Emily was more open than I expected and shared things I didn't even ask about. She confessed that Bart was a terrible father, even told me she'd considered leaving him at some point but she'd stayed for fear he'd maneuver to get full custody."

"Yeah, that was a good call," he said, lifting his foot to rest it on the porch railing.

"I asked her about Heather, and she seemed willing to answer my questions. She didn't approve of her either. In fact, she was the one who suggested they pay her off. She even wrote the check. According to her, Bart was surprised she left town for so little money. He'd expected to pay more, and she sounded like an opportunist. Which makes me wonder why she took so little."

"The way you said that makes me think you have a theory," he said, then took a sip of tea.

"What if she was working with someone else, with the hope of making more money?"

"And who would that be? To what purpose?"

"I don't know, but I *do* know that she left for a shockingly low amount."

"Only she didn't leave. She was killed."

"True," I acknowledged.

"What if she agreed to leave but changed her mind?" he suggested. "And the person who killed her didn't like that she'd decided to stay. Who would have wanted her gone?"

"Likely a lot of people. Emily and Bart." Then I added, "Probably Wyatt."

"Did he say he wanted her gone?"

I gave it some thought. "When he talked about it this morning, he didn't give an opinion about it one way or another. Just stated that she'd left. Or so he thought. They'd broken up by then. He said it happened sometime after he was arrested." I took a sip of my tea and turned to him. "In the nursing home parking lot, he told me he was engaged to her when he went to his parents to ask for the tavern."

He frowned. "I don't think Max knew that."

"I don't think *anyone* knew," I said. "Abby didn't mention it, and Ruth sure hasn't. I think maybe she changed her mind after Wyatt came back empty-handed."

"She really *was* a gold digger," Marco said.

"Which is why it doesn't make sense for her to leave for so little money." Then I added, "If she even cashed the check. Supposedly she was waving it around at her going-away party. I asked Emily to look into it. When she has an answer, she's going to call Max's and leave a message for me to come to tea. Even if I still don't want Max or Wyatt to know I went to see her, not yet. But it was better than asking her to call Hank's house. I can only imagine what Bart would do if he found out."

He nodded. "And you got her to talk about all of that without mentioning Heather's body? She didn't find that suspicious?"

"No." I turned in my seat to face him. "The first two times I met Emily, she seemed like such a sweet woman, and I couldn't understand why she was with Bart."

"You say that like you changed your mind."

I twisted my mouth to the side as I thought it over. "She still seemed sweet, but much more calculating than I expected."

"I'm still surprised she admitted that she wanted to leave him, but like I said, she made a good call," Marco said. "He saw those boys as possessions, and he never would have stood for her taking them from him. Hell, I can't even see him letting *her* go."

"Like Floyd Bingham?"

He was quiet for a moment. "No, I don't think he would have killed her. People were afraid of him and his power, but Emily had a way of softening his edge, just enough so people didn't think he was a monster. He needed her."

"He was really that evil?"

"Not evil, per se. There were just so many secrets and rumors about the favors. And of course, the murders and the strange, unexplained things goin' on that people attributed to him, even if the sheriff's department claimed they never found a link."

"Thelma Tureen told me that her husband's cousin went to Bart for a favor." I told him about the whole episode, starting with the man's DUI and ending with the way he'd burned the house down and then ultimately killed himself.

"Yep," he said with a grim face. "That all fits with Bart and his favors."

"When did the favors stop?" I asked and shivered a little from a chill.

"They never really stopped, I don't think," he said, leaning over to tuck the blanket around my legs. "But he lost most of his money and, along with it, his power. Plus, he got old. He just seemed to lose the things that lent him his air of intimidation. But I think he still grants and calls in favors, just not as often as in the past."

"Emily said she was worried about what Bart was doing to Wyatt and Max while they were growing up. I think she was worried he'd break their spirit or make them into monsters too."

"Definitely a valid concern," he said slowly. "I'm just surprised she was so free with that information. Max always suspected she wanted to leave and take them with her, but he never knew for certain."

"I wasn't sure why she was telling me any of it. Maybe because she still thinks Wyatt and I are together?"

"You're kiddin'," he said in a flat voice.

"Wyatt never told her we broke up. She told me she's been beggin' him to bring me to lunch. Wyatt always tells her I'm too busy, and she said that Max backs him up."

"Why would they both lie about that?" he asked, sitting up straighter.

"I don't know," I said, "but she told Bart and Wyatt that she likes me. She thinks I'm good for Wyatt, and she told Bart she'd leave him if he ran me off. Do you think that Wyatt or Max know that and are lying to protect me?"

He sat back in his chair. "Wow…maybe."

"But none of that makes sense because Bart *knows* we aren't together. He thinks I'm sleeping with *you*. He told me so today at the construction site."

He was quiet for a moment. "Was he threatening you?"

"No, I don't think so. More like he was trying to get me to admit it." I paused, then added, "It surprised me to realize Emily's manipulative too."

He was slow to respond. "It stands to reason she would need to develop that trait to survive."

My heart skipped a beat. "They all would, the boys included."

He frowned. "I guess, although I've never thought Max was manipulative. He's mostly 'you get what you see.'"

"Mostly?"

"I suppose you can't grow up in that house without being damaged somehow."

"His drinking," I said softly.

"Yeah."

"It sounds like Wyatt was his mini-me until their falling-out," I said. "He wanted to please his father. Which means he would have learned the art of manipulation at the knee of the master."

"You think he's been manipulating you?" he asked, but without the heat I would have expected.

"Yeah, I think he's been manipulating me ever since he discovered my secret."

He reached over and placed a hand on my lower thigh in support.

"He's definitely been yanking me around all day. He wasn't forthcoming with information. And when I confronted him with it, he claimed he didn't want to tell me everything because he wanted me to form my own opinion."

"That sounds like a bullshit answer."

"No kidding."

"He still cares about you, Carly."

"Does he?" I asked, seeing him in a whole new light now. "Or does he see me as someone new to play with?"

"I think he sees you as someone new, someone who didn't know him before or during his legal mess. You saw him with fresh eyes, and obviously liked what you saw."

I started to contradict him, but I suspected he was right.

"I know he promised to tell you his secrets, but I would have been surprised if he'd actually followed through. He was raised with the mindset that knowledge is power, and giving you information would have leveled the power structure. At the moment, he holds the power. He ultimately decided not to pull you up to his level."

I gasped. He was right, because even now, Wyatt was doling out his information like they were precious gold nuggets. I closed my eyes. "My father played games. I refuse to do it with anyone important in my life. I need honesty. I need trust. Wyatt gives me neither of those things." He didn't answer. "Why am I still trying to figure him out, Marco? Why do I care what happens to him?"

"I don't know. Maybe because you saw something in him and you're trying to save him. Maybe that's why you're helping him."

"Yet you haven't tried to stop me."

"I'll never tell you what to do. I might ask you to explain your reasoning, but I'll ultimately support whatever you decide to do." He dropped his foot to the floor. "What happened in the nursing home parking lot?"

I wasn't proud at my outburst of temper, but I didn't want to flinch from the truth. "He was upset I wasn't being agreeable. I brought up the fact that he'd reneged on our deal. I asked him to move several times, and he refused."

"There's more to it," he said quietly.

I took a drink of my now-cool tea. "I told him that he knew my history with men, yet he still lied and withheld information from me. That he broke me." My voice cracked and I took another sip. "That I wasn't sure I'd ever be able to fully trust again. When he still refused to move, I sprayed him." I paused. "I'm not proud of it, but I'm not sorry either."

We sat in silence for a bit, and I was relieved he didn't try to smooth it over or convince me that I'd be okay. Instead, he left me to my feelings, which was exactly what I needed, further proof he knew me well.

Finally, I asked, "Do you remember going to a summer camp with Max?"

"Survival camp?" He released a short laugh. "Emily mentioned that?"

"She told me that Bart sent Max to the camp after Rodney Bingham disappeared. He thought that Emily was hovering over the boys too much and it was making Max into a sissy. He thought the camp would toughen him up."

He grimaced. "Sounds like Bart."

"Emily said she went to your mother and offered to pay for your tuition if she'd send you too."

He nodded. "I knew, and Max suspected. He's always been pretty intuitive. Even back then. It wasn't Max's kind of thing. He'd much rather have had his nose in a book, but he tried for his father."

"Did you like it?"

A smile spread across his face. "Loved it. The outdoors. Physical activity… I was in my element, and Max even liked it some."

"You two are more different than I first thought."

He gave me a pensive look. "I suppose, but we always had each other's backs."

"Until I got between you two when I was looking for Lula."

"No," he said, gazing out toward the thin view of the valley. "The crack started when he came home from college. He would never tell me why. Before that he told me everything."

"When I was leaving, I asked Emily what she told Max to convince him to come home."

His eyes widened. "She told you?"

"Kind of." I took a breath. "She said she reminded him of his family obligations." I leaned closer. "Do you have any idea what those could be?"

"No," he said, shaking his head.

"Do you think it could have anything to do with Heather?"

He turned to look at me. "Are you suggestin' that Emily asked him to come home and murder Heather?"

Was I? The thought had occurred to me, but only in a fleeting way, and it refused to stick. Ultimately, I just couldn't imagine Max doing such a thing. "No, but she requested something he couldn't refuse."

"Agreed."

"Bart gave Jerry a job," I said, the new worry popping to the surface.

Marco sat up straighter. "He what?"

"It didn't come directly from Bart—Jerry said a foreman asked him if he'd be interested in a job—but it sure sounds fishy. With all the guys who need work around here, the foreman just happens to ask a seventy-year-old man if he wants a job as a gofer?"

He frowned. "You're right. It does sound fishy. What did you say when he told you?"

"That I was happy for him, of course. I've never seen him so excited and proud, and I hope it's on the up an up…"

"But?"

I turned to face him. "What if Bart plans to hurt him to get to me? What if he knows I'm fond of him?"

"How would he know that?" he asked.

"How did Abby Donahey know I gave Jerry a coat?" When he started to say something, I added, "Yeah, she brought it up as evidence that I was a good person."

He laughed. "You say that like it's a bad thing."

"It's not that. It's just weird to know strangers are gossiping about me. But if Abby knew, you can bet your boots Bart knew."

He was silent for a moment. "We'll keep tabs on the situation, okay? We won't let anything happen to Jerry." Then he added, "He had our backs with Carson Purdy. We'll certainly have his."

"Thanks, Marco." It took everything in me not to reach out and snag his hand.

After a few seconds, he set his mug on the porch railing and asked, "Do you have anything to look into tomorrow before you go into work?"

I yawned. "I have an appointment with Bingham tomorrow at ten."

"*Bingham?*"

"Tiny told me that Heather went out with him before she got back with Wyatt the last time. I doubt he killed her, or he would have moved the body. Same with Bart."

"So why go talk to him?"

"Because he's an observer, and I suspect he's always been hungry for power. Which means he likely watched everything going on in Drum, especially anything that had to do with a Drummond."

"You think he might have information other people won't?"

"I know you probably think it's dangerous…"

"Maybe for someone else, but Lula just asked you to be one of her baby's godmothers, and she'd be furious if he hurt you. Not to mention Bingham seems to treat you differently since the whole Lula and Greta mess. Make no mistake, he has no loyalty to you, but he has a new respect for you. If anyone can talk to him, it's you."

I stifled a yawn. "Thanks for the vote of confidence."

He grinned. "Just don't expect him to tell you much. He might be open to a trade, though."

"A trade of information?"

"Who knows with him. Just keep it in mind. You can expect a whole lot more game playin' with him."

"I suspected." The people in this town were good at it. "I have two other leads to follow after that. Dick Stinnett.

Ruth thinks he was at the going-away party. The second person is May McMurphy."

"Molly's sister?"

"She was at the party too, and she dated Dick after Heather left. I'll approach her after I talk to him."

"Do you know where to find Dick?"

"Ruth said she thinks he works at a used car lot in Ewing."

He nodded. "We'll figure out which one tomorrow."

"You can't openly help me with this, Marco," I said gently. "You yourself said if I get caught doing this, I could be charged with interfering with an investigation."

He was silent for a moment. "I know."

And I could tell it was killing him, not only because he was worried about me, but because he loved investigating. The department never gave him much of a chance. They underestimated him, or maybe they knew he was good and they only sidelined him because half the department was in someone's pocket.

I stood and reached my hand out to him. "Let's go inside."

He took my hand and stood, clutching the blanket with his free hand as he looked down at me.

Heat rose up in me as I stared into his eyes. I wanted to kiss him. I wanted him to kiss me back. I wanted to take him to his bed and do more than sleep next to him. But I couldn't do any of that for a whole host of reasons. Most of all, because every romantic relationship I'd ever been in had been poisoned, and I couldn't bear to lose Marco.

"What are you thinkin'?" he asked in a careful voice, his face swathed in shadow.

I swallowed the urge to tell him the truth, worried I was lying by omission, but I didn't want to risk scaring him away.

"I'm thinkin' how grateful I am to have you as my friend. You have filled my life with happiness, Marco. Thank you."

He grinned. "Hey, you're not so bad yourself."

Grabbing his mug, he ushered me inside. "Do you want to watch a movie before we go to sleep?"

I was exhausted, but I wasn't ready to let him go yet. "Yeah. I'll even let you pick."

He must have had mercy on me because he picked a Sandra Bullock rom-com he seemed to like. We settled onto his large sofa with another blanket covering us, sitting side by side, his body heat soaking into me.

You have to accept this, Carly. This has to be enough.

But I was so very tired of settling.

Chapter Nineteen

We fell asleep on the sofa. I was pretty sure I'd only made it about fifteen minutes into the movie before I passed out. When I woke up, Marco had moved to his recliner and I was stretched out on the sofa, covered with a blanket.

I got up and went to the bathroom, then checked the time—it was after seven. I considered trying to sleep longer, but my mind had already started thinking about everything I needed to do before I went into work at noon. I doubted I'd have time to see Dick Stinnett today, because in the light of day I remembered I still needed to pay a visit to Heather's aunt—and also that I'd left the rest of the tulips in my car.

Marco was still sleeping, so I started a pot of coffee, then slipped my feet into a pair of his slippers and walked out to my car to see if the tulips could be salvaged. I'd just reached the back door of the car when I noticed a pickup truck parked partially down Marco's long, winding drive. I nearly ran back inside to tell Marco, but then I recognized the truck. It belonged to Wyatt.

He was watching Marco's house.

I opened the car door and found the limp and wilted flowers on the floor behind the driver's seat. I picked them up, hoping they might revive if I put them in water, and cast another glance down the drive. Wyatt was sitting behind the steering wheel, watching me.

I decided to ignore him as I went inside to take care of the tulips. After I put them in a pitcher with water, I set them on the table. I'd been quiet, but Marco started to stir.

"Do I smell coffee?" he asked, rubbing his eyes.

"Guilty as charged," I said. "It's almost ready."

"Where'd the flowers come from?"

"I bought some from Emmaline yesterday, and then I forgot about them. I took a bunch to Emily when I went for my visit."

He laughed. "Emmaline Haskell? Did Emily know that?"

I cringed. "Yeah. Is that a problem?"

"I'm pretty sure they had a spat about flowers a few decades ago. Emily grows her own flowers in her backyard. She's quite the gardener."

That might explain her housekeeper's attitude, although I suspected the woman would have acted that way regardless. "She didn't mention it." I pushed out a sigh. "But I got some extra bouquets, one of them for Heather's aunt, in case you didn't have a chance to get to a florist." I'd meant to take one home to Hank, but that was looking doubtful now.

"Lucky for you, I got the daisies," he said as he walked into the kitchen and opened the refrigerator. He pulled out a bouquet of cut daisies and handed them to me.

"You put them in the fridge?"

He shrugged as he pulled out my creamer and put it on the counter. "I don't know what to do with flowers, and they

233

were in a refrigerated cooler when I bought them. I remembered they were in the car after we started watching the movie, so I went out and brought them in."

The daisies were still wrapped in their plastic sleeve and looked about a hundred times better than the wilted tulips. "Thanks, Marco."

"Helpin' you where I can." I could hear the guilt in his voice. It was killing him that he couldn't do more.

"I'm trying to decide if I should go see Hilde before or after I see Bingham. I guess it depends on whether she's an early riser." I considered calling Ruth to see if she knew, but she was likely still sleeping herself.

"I'll call my mom," Marco said as he grabbed two coffee mugs out of the cabinet and poured coffee into both.

"You never talk about your mom," I said, taking one of the mugs and pouring creamer into the coffee. I knew his parents had moved away after they got divorced twelve years ago. His mother had moved to North Carolina, and his father was in Knoxville.

"We talk now and again, and I know Mom was friendly with her."

"Then did *you* know Heather?"

"Not really. Max and I were several years younger than Wyatt and Heather, and I really didn't give her any thought. I was in college when she came back and she and Wyatt were together," he said as he grabbed the creamer and put it back in the fridge, "and she was gone by the time I came back from school. I'll call Mom in a bit." He motioned to the door. "Do you want to sit outside while we drink our coffee?" He knew about my morning ritual with Hank.

"Um...before we decide on that, I need to mention something I noticed while I was outside." I made a face. "Wyatt's truck is parked at the end of your driveway."

"That doesn't surprise me," he said with a look of resignation.

"You're not angry?"

"Why would I be angry? I'm not gonna invite him in and serve him breakfast, but if he wants to provide an extra layer of protection for you, I'm not gonna fight it."

"I don't need protecting," I said. "I've hardly talked to anyone yet."

"But if the real killer finds out you're lookin', they might try to stop you."

I still didn't think I had much to be worried about, but I wasn't about to argue with a sheriff's deputy.

"I think we should go sit outside," Marco said with a mischievous grin. "It looks like a beautiful morning."

"You're terrible." I shook my head. "Call your mom, and I'll go take a shower. *Then* we can sit outside."

I tossed my clothes into the dryer before I went into Marco's bathroom. My shampoo and conditioner were still in the shower from the last time I'd stayed over. When I got out, I blow-dried my hair, then put on a clean pair of his sweatpants and one of his T-shirts.

Marco was talking on the phone when I came out, and he cracked a smile, pointing to the phone and mouthing *Mom* as he flapped his hand to pantomime that she wouldn't stop talking.

Grinning, I refilled my coffee, while Marco said, "I've got to go, Mom...yes, I'll come see you soon... love you." He hung up and lifted his brow. "And that is why I don't call her very often."

I leaned closer and said in a conspiratorial tone, "Perhaps she wouldn't spend so much time talking to you if you called her more often."

He refilled his own cup and took a sip. "Ah, the age-old chicken and the egg mystery."

"You're lucky to have a mother, Marco. Don't take her for granted."

He placed a kiss on my forehead. "Touché. Thanks for the reminder." He took a sip of his coffee. "Mom says that Hilde's a very early riser. Like five-in-the-morning early. You can go anytime."

"Okay."

"But I'm going with you."

"Marco… we discussed this last night."

"No, I agreed it would be best if you talked to Bingham and other people on your own, but Hilde's different. Mom wants me to give her condolences on her behalf." When I gave him a dubious look, he said, "Carly, I'm going. My mother will kill me if I don't."

"Okay," I said, trying not to read too much into the relief washing over me. I had to admit that I'd felt awkward about dropping by Heather's grieving aunt's house unannounced to pepper her with questions about her niece's death.

"But I have to take a quick shower, so give me fifteen minutes."

I laughed. "My clothes are still in the dryer, so unless I go in your clothes, I need to wait anyway."

He gave me a playful grin. "They look way better on you than they ever have on me."

Then he headed around the corner to the bathroom.

I was tempted to let Molly and Ginger handle the lunch rush on their own so I could go to Ewing to talk to Dick and May—I suspected Max wouldn't give me a hard time for trying to clear his brother's name—but Molly had just started and it was Ginger's first day. I didn't want to toss them to the wolves. I'd figure out what to do after I talked to Marco.

I peered out the window and saw Wyatt's truck still parked at the end of the drive. Giving in to a moment of weakness, I found a travel mug and filled it with coffee, then headed out the door toward the truck.

Wyatt sat up straight when he saw me, rolling down his window. "Now, Carly, before you say anything…"

"Here," I said, handing him the mug. "You probably need this."

His eyes widened in surprise as he took the coffee.

"I know why you're here. And I know I led you to believe I hit a dead end, but I'm planning to do more digging today. I'm visiting Hilde Browning first. Then I have an appointment with Bingham at ten. I'll see if I have time to do anything else before I go to work."

His eyes darkened at the mention of Bingham's name. "Why the hell are you visiting Bingham?"

"Look, you asked me to do this, so that means you have to trust me."

He didn't respond.

"I didn't have to tell you anything, Wyatt, but I felt guilty that you spent the night out here." I paused, and when he didn't say anything, I added, "Marco's a deputy sheriff. If I need protecting, he's perfectly capable of doing the job."

"I'm sure he's protectin' you," he murmured in a deep voice.

"What's that supposed to mean?"

"You're standing in front of me, wearin' his clothes."

Rolling my eyes, I spun around and started back to the house, but then I turned back to face him. "I don't want you anywhere near Bingham's while I'm there."

His anger flared. "Are you crazy?"

"He's not going to do anything to me, and it might screw things up if he knows you're there. I mean it, Wyatt. If you feel the need to follow me, then stay off Bingham's property."

"What the hell kind of arrangement do you and Bingham have?" he shouted after me. "Why would he make you his baby's godmother?"

Ignoring him, I headed back to the house. The dryer was done, so I changed into my clean jeans and a shirt I'd left at Marco's a few weeks ago before seeing to breakfast.

Marco was done soon after that, coming into the kitchen wearing a navy blue thermal shirt that clung to the muscles of his arms and chest underneath. I forced myself to avert my gaze.

"Something smells good," he said.

"I made breakfast." I placed two plates of scrambled eggs with salsa and toast on the table.

"I'm tempted to ask you to move in with me," he said as he sat down.

"Ha!" I said as I grabbed some silverware and placed it next to him. "I think Hank might have a thing or two to say about that." With the thought of Hank, I said, "You go ahead and start while it's hot. I'm going to check in with Hank and let him know I'm okay."

I grabbed the cordless phone and placed the call, but when I started to leave the room, Marco motioned me over to the table. "Carly, eat while you talk. Don't worry about being rude."

Hank answered right away, which surprised me since it usually took him several rings to get to the phone.

"Chalmers," he answered in a gruff tone.

"Hank, it's me," I said, caught off guard because he hadn't answered with his typical hello. "What's going on?"

238

"I was just about to call you at Marco's," he said. "There's a warrant out for Wyatt's arrest, and a couple of deputies just came here lookin' for him."

My eyes widened, and I turned to Marco as I asked Hank, "What did you tell them?"

"The truth. I don't know where he is, and I haven't seen him since yesterday morning. I didn't tell them he asked you to look into the murder, but they might find out."

"Okay," I said, my heart racing. I knew I couldn't let them arrest him. I had to find the real murderer, with evidence to back it up, because something told me that if Wyatt got locked up, he wasn't coming out anytime soon. If ever. I'd already cycled through the possibility that Bart had set up Bingham (or vice versa), but I hadn't stopped to consider that one of them might have intentionally set up *Wyatt.* "Thanks for the heads-up."

"Will you warn him if you see him? I know the two of you aren't seein' eye to eye, and I've been givin' him a hard time for months, but there's no way he killed that girl. Not Wyatt."

"Yeah," I said, trying not to freak out. "I know he didn't do it. I'll warn him."

"You stay safe, girl." Then he hung up.

I placed the phone on the table and stood. I had to talk to Wyatt.

"What's goin' on, Carly?" Marco asked with concern in his eyes.

"Hank said the sheriff's department was at his house this morning, looking for Wyatt."

His face paled. "Shit."

"Hypothetically speaking, if you knew there was a warrant out for someone's arrest and you happened to know that person's whereabouts, would you be obligated to detain them?"

He put down his fork, his face grim. "Perhaps you should take a walk and make sure we don't have any visitors before I step outside and get in my car to go to Hilde's."

I nodded, then hurried out the door, my mind frantic with worry. Where could Wyatt hide that the sheriff's department would never think to look for him? I was almost to his truck when I figured it out.

He got out and shut the door, standing next to his truck with a blank expression. "What happened?"

"I just spoke to Hank—"

"Is he okay?" he asked, sounding more worried than I'd expected.

"He's fine. Just concerned. The sheriff's department just paid him a visit. They're looking for you, Wyatt. They have a warrant for your arrest."

He showed no reaction whatsoever.

"You have to hide."

His gaze shifted to the house. "Is Marco on his way out here to arrest me?"

"No! But you have to leave now. If he sees you, he'll be obligated to take you into custody."

He gave a hard shake of his head. "I'm not leavin' you."

"Oh, for God's sake, Wyatt!" I shouted. "Forget the damn blood price!"

He took a step toward me, his hands clenched at his sides. "You think I'm sittin' out here because of the blood price?"

I shook my head. "No, but don't you dare go there. You need to get out of here. Now. Marco's off today. He's going with me to visit Hilde, and I'll make sure he follows me to Bingham's. *You* have to go somewhere the sheriff's deputies won't find you. If you don't know where to go, I have a suggestion."

"I'm not hidin', Carly!"

"Do you think you can protect me, or anyone, if you're stuck in a jail cell? For once in your life, stop being a stubborn ass and listen to reason."

He started to say something, then stopped, some of his anger fading. "Where?"

I held up my hands. "Now, hear me out before you tell me no."

"That bad, huh?" he grunted, shoving his hands into his pockets.

"It's somewhere they'll never think to look... Bingham's."

"It's somewhere they'll never think tolook...Bingham's."

He jerked his hands out of his pockets. "*What?*"

"You took Lula in when y'all thought your father was looking for her. She'll be more than happy to protect you now."

"Bingham won't."

"He will if Lula tells him to. How else do you think you and Max ended up being Beatrice's godfathers?"

He was silent for a moment. "I'm not a coward."

"No one said you were, but I also thought you weren't stupid. Now go."

He hesitated and cast a glance back at the house. "Does he love you?"

"Oh, for heaven's sake!" I shouted, throwing my hands out to my sides. "Why won't anyone believe we're just friends?"

Pain filled his eyes. "Because I've seen the way he looks at you, Carly."

"We're *just friends*."

Which was true, even if it wasn't the whole story. But I needed him to leave, to get to safety quickly. He didn't say anything for several seconds. Then he got into his truck and turned around to head back to the county road.

Marco was waiting for me when I went back inside. "Is it clear for me to come out?"

I nodded. "Thanks for giving me a chance to warn him."

He rubbed the back of his neck. "Max would kill me if I arrested his brother."

"Would you do it if you thought he might be guilty?"

He hesitated. "He isn't. Wyatt isn't perfect, but I know he didn't kill Heather Stone."

He hadn't exactly answered my question, but I let it go. "Since the sheriff's department wants to arrest Wyatt, I'm thinking about calling Max and telling him I won't be in today. Or," I added, "I might go in for the busy lunch rush, then do more investigating before the dinner shift."

"Why don't you talk to Hilde and Bingham, then we'll decide?" he asked as he picked up the bouquet of daisies from the table.

"Yeah," I said. "Good idea." I grabbed my bag and headed outside.

"You follow me," Marco said as he locked his front door.

"Okay," I said, "then you can follow me to Bingham's and wait on the side of the road. We'll figure out where to go from there."

He nodded with a grim expression. "I'm gonna take my own car. I don't want to be calling attention to myself in my deputy vehicle."

I was parked behind his Explorer, so I tossed my bag into the back of my car and got in. After backing up and turning around, I got onto the county road leading to the highway.

Marco followed, and I stopped about twenty feet from the stop sign at the highway and let him pass me. He headed toward town, but it wasn't long before he turned off onto a county road. Several minutes later, he pulled off and parked in front of a pale yellow house set back about thirty feet from the road.

I parked next to him and got out. My nerves were on edge as I walked toward him. Now that we were here, I wasn't so sure I could go through with asking Hilde questions about her niece. She'd only just found out Heather had been murdered.

Marco gave me a reassuring smile after I told him my concerns. "How about you let me take the lead at first? Then we can suss out how she's feelin' and go from there?" He leaned closer and lowered his voice. "Heather's been missing for nine years. While I'm sure she's upset, it's not like her niece has been part of her everyday life. It might actually give her closure to know why she hasn't heard from her."

I nodded. "Yeah. That's true."

We walked toward the front door together, and Marco knocked, holding the flowers in his other hand.

The door opened right away, and an older woman answered with a cautious look on her face. "Hello?"

"Hi, Miss Hilde," Marco said in his friendly voice. "I'm not sure if you remember me, but I'm Marco Roland, Beth Roland's son."

She clasped a hand to her chest. "Beth? Oh, my word! How is she? I haven't talked to her in years."

"She's good," Marco said. "After she heard about Heather, she wanted me to come by and offer condolences on her behalf." He held up the bouquet.

Tears filled her eyes. "Gerbera daisies. They're my favorite."

"A little birdie told me," I said. "A birdie named Thelma Tureen."

"You know Thelma?" she asked in surprise.

"Carly likes to visit some of the residents at Greener Pastures," Marco said. "And she wanted to come offer condolences on Thelma's behalf."

Hilde turned her attention to me.

"Hilde," Marco said, "this is my friend, Carly Moore. I hope it's okay I brought her along."

"Of course," she said, backing up. "Where are my manners? Come in. Come in."

We followed Hilde inside, and she gestured to a worn sofa against a wood-paneled wall. Marco handed her the flowers and she took them into the small kitchen, opening a cabinet and pulling out a vase.

"Is Beth still in Wilmington?"

"Yep," Marco said, resting his hands on his knees. "She got remarried. Did she mention that?"

"She sent me an invitation to the wedding. I was sorry to miss it." She put the flowers in the vase and filled it with water.

"Well, it was pretty short notice," Marco said, glancing around the room. "I had trouble getting time off work to go."

"Is she happy?" Hilde asked, setting the vase on the peninsula separating the kitchen from the living room.

"Yes," Marco said. "She and Herb are very happy."

"And your father?" she asked, sitting in a recliner across from us.

"He's got his head in the clouds in Knoxville. Just like when he was here in Drum."

She shook her head, clucking. "That man never realized what he had."

Marco didn't respond, but his body tensed, and I wondered what had happened in his past to make him close up like that. He rarely talked about his childhood, and when he did, it was usually about Max.

I covered his hand with mine, and he flipped his hand over and linked our fingers. He gave my hand a squeeze, then released it.

"We were surprised to hear that Heather had been murdered," Marco said. "Everyone thought she left town."

Hilde nodded. "Me too."

"You didn't find it strange that she never contacted you after she left?"

"That's just it," Hilde said. "She *did* contact me. She sent a postcard about a month later. She told me she was in Tulsa and had gotten a job at a Walmart."

"Did you keep the postcard?" Marco asked.

"I did, but the sheriff's deputy took it," she said. "I told them about it when they came to tell me that they'd found her." She sucked in a breath, as though struck anew by the news of her niece's death.

"You never suspected she'd been killed?" Marco asked.

"No. Never. Not hearin' from her wasn't all that unusual. I never once heard from her directly after she left for college. Not until she showed up on my doorstep, askin' to move back in."

"Thelma told me that Heather gave you trouble when she lived with you back in high school," I said.

She nodded. "That girl was as wild as a banshee and a compulsive liar. I can't say I was sorry to see her go away to college. The only one of her friends who was ever respectful to me was that Drummond boy."

"Wyatt," Marco volunteered.

She nodded.

"Who else did she spend time with?" I asked.

"In high school or once she came back?" Hilde asked.

"Both, I guess."

"Abby Atwood and Mitzi Ziegler were her closest friends, along with Wyatt. But she had a parade of boys and girls comin' and goin' in high school. There were fewer of them once she came back. I think many of the kids had moved out of town …the smart ones, anyway. Mitzi was still around though, and she added a few new friends. May McMurphy. Dick… I can't remember his last name."

"Stinnett?" Marco asked.

She nodded. "Yep. And a couple of others whose names escape me. Most of them never came here. She went to them."

"And Wyatt?" Marco asked.

"Yeah, and her other boyfriend. The one at the end before she left."

My brow shot up. "She had another boyfriend? Todd Bingham?"

She wrinkled her nose. "I'm pretty sure she was sleepin' with that Bingham boy during one of her breakups with Wyatt, but no, not at the end. She claimed he was from Ewing."

"You don't have a name?" Marco asked.

"No. She was secretive about him. I think she met him at her job."

"What was she doin'?" Marco asked.

"After she flunked out of college, she lived with her parents and went to beauty school in Virginia. When she moved back, she got a job as a nail technician at Carolyn's House of Style in Ewing."

"What makes you think she met him at work?" I asked. Ewing didn't seem progressive enough for men to get mani-pedis, especially nearly a decade ago.

"She was still with Wyatt when she first mentioned him. One of the beauticians cut his hair, and Heather talked to him while he was waitin'. She got a kick out of flirtin' with him. She said he flirted back. Honestly, I think she was foolin' around on Wyatt before they broke up. I caught her wearing low-cut shirts the days she mentioned that he came in, and sometimes her clothes would smell like men's cologne. Wyatt never wore cologne."

He still didn't.

Marco shifted on the sofa. "Did the detective who came to talk to you ask you about her other boyfriend?"

"Oh, no," she said, shaking her head. "He never asked anything about that. He only wanted to know about the last time I saw her, whether I'd talked to her after she left, and whether she felt threatened by Wyatt."

"And when was the last time you spoke to her?" I asked. Part of me wondered if we were being too obvious in our approach, but I felt the pressure of time bearing down on us. With that warrant out for Wyatt, we needed to move fast.

"The night before she was supposed to leave. When she went to her goin'-away party at Mitzi's."

"She didn't come by to get her things?" Marco asked.

"I suppose she did, because they were gone. She must have grabbed them after the party and then just left without sayin' goodbye."

Marco's chin lifted slightly. "Is it safe to say you're not sure who picked up her things?"

She shuddered. "I guess you're right. It gives me the creeps to think a murderer might have been in my home."

"We don't know that they were," Marco assured her. "Heather could have picked up her belongings and then encountered the person who killed her."

Hilde nodded.

"Did Heather feel threatened by Wyatt?" I asked.

She snorted. "No, and I told the detective that. She thought she was playin' him. I heard her tellin' someone on the phone right before Wyatt was arrested for drivin' drunk and breakin' into Earl Cartwright's garage."

"Do you know who she was talking to?" I asked.

She gave me a penetrating look, as if to determine why I was asking her, then said, "I told the detective I wasn't sure, but after he left, I spent a good amount of time thinkin' about it, and now I suspect it was her other boyfriend."

"And you don't remember his name?" I asked. "Maybe a nickname?"

"Sometimes she would call him Peep. But never a given name."

I glanced at Marco. I wasn't sure whether that would help us or not, and judging by the look on his face, he wasn't either.

"Did Heather leave anything behind?" Marco asked. "Anything we could look through?"

Her body stilled. "Are you trying to find who killed her?"

Neither one of us answered at first. Then Marco finally said, "The sheriff's department is convinced that Wyatt killed her, but we think someone else is guilty. We're trying to figure out who."

I turned to him in surprise. He wasn't supposed to be any part of this. He was only here because he'd insisted on offering his condolences.

He gave me a grim look. "I'm in this now."

Chapter
Twenty

Marco turned back to Hilde. "But I have to tell you that even though I'm a deputy, I'm not lookin' into this in an official capacity. That means you're under no obligation to tell us anything."

"I've got nothin' to hide," she said. "And I'm not sold on the theory that Wyatt killed her either. I'll help you however I can."

I pushed out a sigh of relief.

"Did she leave anything behind that we can look over?" Marco asked.

"She took most everything—" she made a face, "—or at least someone did, but there's still a box of odds and ends in the closet in her old room. You're welcome to look through it." She got out of the chair and led us to the first doorway of several down a long hall, flipping on an overhead light as she walked into the room—what appeared to be a guest room with no personal ornamentation. Just some framed cross-stitch samplers hanging on the walls.

"Let me just get it out of the closet," Hilde said, crossing the room and opening a sliding closet door. She started to reach for a cardboard box over her head, but Marco made his way inside and pulled it down for her.

"Just put it on the bed," she said, pointing to a solid peach comforter.

He set it down, and she opened the tucked flaps and rifled through a couple of items at the top before standing upright.

"Yep. That's it. Mostly a bunch of papers and letters and such. Feel free to dig through it." She walked back to the wall and leaned against it, giving Marco an expectant look.

Marco and I exchanged a glance, and then we both sat down on the bed, one on either side of the box. He reached in and pulled out a small framed photo. He glanced at it, then handed it over. It was a photo of a smiling younger Wyatt and a woman with brown hair that hung slightly past her shoulders. His arm was slung around her, and she was leaning into him in a way that spoke of possession. She was pretty—*very* pretty—and I tried to not let Emily's comment about my own looks burn. Both of them seemed happy. They were standing at the overlook with the valley behind them.

As I stared at the photo, it occurred to me that I'd rarely seen Wyatt smile. Had he been happy back then? I knew from Ruth that he'd always had a tendency to keep secrets, but surely it had become more pronounced after his arrest.

Marco's gaze held mine as though asking if I was okay, and I gave him a soft smile.

He grabbed a handful of papers next and started to sort through them.

Hilde had given Marco permission to look through the box, but I wasn't sure if I was included in that invitation, so I turned to her and said, "You were very kind to take in your high school niece when her parents moved away."

She made a face. "I was young once, and she seemed so happy here, especially since she was datin' Wyatt. She was devastated when her father announced he'd found a new job. And I was all alone, so I figured it might be nice to have the company. My Artie had died a couple of years before and we never had kids. I think some small part of me hoped she'd be like a daughter."

The disappointment in her eyes let me know that had never happened.

"Her parents were okay with her staying?" I asked.

"At first they put up a fuss, which I'd expected, but they came around before too long. In hindsight, I suspect they realized their lives would be a lot more drama-free if she stayed behind."

"Did Heather realize they felt that way?"

"She never said, but how could she not? She rarely talked to them on the phone, and she didn't want to go spend the summer between her junior and senior year with them. Or the summer she graduated. She went from here directly to college."

"Did you consider sending her back to her parents?" I asked.

"Sure, I considered it, and even threatened it, but she'd cry and plead with me to give her another chance. And then she'd follow my rules and do her chores and come home before curfew, and I'd soften, but soon it would all start all over again."

"So you were relieved when she went away to college?" I asked.

"It seems wrong to admit to such a thing, but yeah. But then she showed up on my doorstep several years later, completely unannounced. She said she'd had a fight with her parents and asked if she could stay with me for a few days until she figured out what to do. So what could I say? I let her stay, and days turned into weeks and weeks into months. Only I'd married Phil by then, and he wasn't too keen on Heather bein' here. He was never so happy as the day she said she was leavin'."

"Can we talk to Phil?" Marco asked as he handed me his stack and grabbed another.

"He died last year," she said in a subdued tone. "Heart attack."

"I'm so sorry," I said.

She frowned. "We got six good years. I can't complain."

I started leafing through the pile Marco had handed over. There were several receipts and birthday cards, one of which was from Wyatt. It was a cheesy, sentimental card, which he'd signed, "Love, Wyatt," and nothing else. There was a warranty for new tires for a Toyota and an invoice for nail supplies. Nothing of use.

Marco went through the next pile even quicker before he handed it over. It proved as benign as the first pile—a few credit card bills, a receipt from a dentist. Marco was going through the last pile when he went still.

"What did you find?" I asked.

"I don't know," he said. "Maybe nothin'…"

"But maybe something?"

"It's a receipt for the Mountain View Lodge. It's dated the week before Wyatt's arrest."

I squinted in confusion. "Do you think Wyatt and Heather spent the night there?"

"I can't see Wyatt doin' that," Marco scoffed. "You've seen those rooms."

"So she went there with her boyfriend?"

"Maybe."

I glanced up at Hilde. "Do you think Heather sometimes spent the night with her other boyfriend?"

"She was gone a lot. She never moved in with Wyatt, and I'm sure it was because she was meeting her boyfriend on the side. Kept Wyatt from noticing."

We needed to talk to someone who was close enough to Heather to possibly know who her side boyfriend had been. Since Mitzi was out of the question, I wondered how well Dick Stinnett knew her. Or May McMurphy.

Marco put everything back into the box with the exception of the hotel receipt. "Would you mind if I hold onto this?"

"You can keep the whole box for all I care," Hilde said. "It ain't like she's comin' back to get it." Her voice cracked, the first sign that she was upset. "I guess I could ask her momma and daddy if they want it, but it's just a box of paper. Can't see why they'd care."

"Thank you," Marco said. "The receipt is all we need for now. But I'd appreciate it if you'd let me take a picture of the photo."

"Of course," she said with a wave of her hand. "You can take it if you like. Maybe Wyatt wants it. I'll probably just end up throwing it away. I can't imagine her folks will want all that junk."

I was pretty sure Wyatt wouldn't want it either, so I said, "I think this will do for now."

Marco took the picture out of the frame and set it on the bed, then snapped several photos before tucking it back into the frame.

"Will you let me know if you find anything?" Hilde asked.

"Of course," Marco said, getting to his feet and putting the box back on the shelf. "Thank you for answering our questions. If you think of anything else, could you call and leave a message?" He closed the door, then reached into his pocket and pulled out a business card to hand to her. "My personal number is written on the back."

She took it and looked it over, then nodded. When she glanced back up, her eyes were full of tears. "Heather had her flaws, but she didn't deserve to be killed and buried like that. I hope you find the monster who did this."

"We're definitely going to try," I said.

Marco and I walked outside and stopped in front of my car.

"We need to figure out who this second boyfriend was," Marco said.

"I wonder if Wyatt has any idea."

Marco gave me a dry look. "Do you really think he'd tell you? He isn't what you'd call an open book."

"Maybe he'll talk with an arrest warrant breathing down his neck."

He pushed out a sigh. "Do you know where to find him?"

"I do, but I have an appointment with Bingham at ten." It was on the edge of my tongue to tell him that Wyatt was probably there too, but I didn't want to put him in a sticky position. He'd already bent and flat-out broken plenty of rules to help out.

"Do you really think that's the best use of our time?" he asked. "Maybe we should focus on finding Dick Stinnett."

"I considered it," I said, "but I suspect that Bingham has useful information. You know he has it out for Bart. It stands to reason he might have been keeping tabs on Wyatt."

"That's not creepy as shit," Marco groused.

I shrugged. "You can't tell me you're surprised."

Rather than respond, he looked down the road.

"So I'll talk to Bingham. Then we'll head to Ewing." If I didn't change my mind and go to work for an hour or so. I hated to just throw Ginger and Molly in the deep end. But I'd decide after I talked to Bingham. "Don't forget you need to wait off Bingham's property."

"I don't have to do that now," he said. "Since I'm officially helpin' you."

I shook my head. "You and I both know I have to do this alone."

The expression on his face said he wasn't any too happy about it, but he nodded after a moment. I hopped in my car and headed back to the highway, leaving Marco to follow.

He pulled onto the side of the road, and I left him behind as I made the turn onto Bingham's property and drove toward the white bungalow house with peeling paint that sat in front of a giant metal building surrounded by cars in varying states of rust decay. I knew the large building housed the body shop that he also used as a chop shop.

I parked out front, noticing that Wyatt's truck wasn't anywhere to be seen, not that I'd expected him to be so obvious. I hoped that meant he'd hidden it well and not that he wasn't here.

The front door of the house opened as I got out of my car, Bingham filling the doorway.

"You know what I've figured out about you, Carly Moore?" he asked with a sly grin as he shut the door behind him. "You're a shit stirrer."

My eyes widened and I stopped in place.

He took a couple of steps toward me across the covered porch. "You've been stirring up shit in this town practically since you crossed the city limits, and you're still at it."

I held up my hands, but I kept my back straight. "I'm not trying to cause you any trouble, Bingham, and I'm sure not here to accuse you of anything."

"Yet here you are, darkening my doorstep, days after they found Heather."

"I already told you that I know you're not stupid enough to have left a body out there. You didn't kill her." I took a step closer. "But I think you might know something about who did."

His eyes hardened. "So you think I'm a snitch?"

Dammit, this wasn't going as I'd hoped. He had his dander up.

"No, Bingham, I think you're an intelligent man who pays attention to the world around him."

His stance suggested I hadn't buttered him up much.

"Come on, Bingham. We both know that Wyatt didn't kill Heather, and while I'm not insinuating that you know who did, you might be able to point me in the right direction so I can figure it out."

His jaw relaxed slightly, and he leaned a shoulder against a pillar next to the top of the steps. "And why would I do that?"

"Because I can't help thinking Bart Drummond played a part in this, and it would be in your best interest to help me prove it." I nodded to the front door. "You gonna invite me in?"

His hard look was back. "I told you last time you showed up at my front door that I don't conduct business in my house."

And I'd assumed it was just an excuse to keep me out. "Then can we sit down instead of standing across from each other like we're about to have a showdown at noon?"

He cracked a grin and backed up, taking a seat in a wicker chair that looked like it would collapse under his weight. I climbed the steps and sat in the chair next to him.

"So I know you dated Heather during one of her breakups with Wyatt."

He burst out laughing. "You don't waste time with small talk."

"You're a busy man. I figured you would appreciate skipping the small talk."

He nodded. "True enough." Releasing a sigh, he sat back in his chair. "Sayin' I dated her would be generous. Sayin' I fucked her would be more accurate."

I resisted the urge to cringe at his crassness. "So it was a hookup situation."

"If that makes it more palatable for you. Sure."

"How long did it last?"

"A month or so? We hooked up a couple of times a week. She had an itch and I was happy to scratch it."

I had to be careful with my next question. "Did you ever get the impression she had ulterior motives for being with you?"

"You mean other than tryin' to make Drummond jealous?" he asked.

"Was that her motive?"

He pushed out a breath. "I'm sure that was part of her intention, but you're right. I got the impression she was tryin' to get information out of me."

"Did you tell her anything?"

"I told her I didn't mix business and fuckin'."

Apparently he had a lot of rules about how he conducted business.

"So she eventually got back together with Wyatt," I said, "but I'm sure you kept an eye on her."

His eyes darkened. "Why would I keep an eye on a gold-diggin' bitch?"

"Because she went from you back to Wyatt."

He released a short laugh. "You think I was jealous?" He sounded incredulous.

"Hell, no," I scoffed. "But you're smart enough to keep tabs on her. Just in case she accidently stumbled upon something that could be used against you."

He didn't respond, but the corners of his mouth ticked up.

"I'm trying to figure out a timeline here—she went back to Wyatt, then nagged him into demanding that his father give him the tavern. But instead of getting it, Wyatt disowned his family."

Bingham gave me a long look. "What comes next? You're the one tellin' this story."

"A week or so later, Wyatt drove drunk to Earl Cartwright's garage and stole back the baseball his father sold."

He continued to watch me.

"Then they went to Balder Mountain State Park, and the sheriff showed up and arrested him."

"That's the story."

The way he said it implied there was a lot more to it, and that he knew a thing or two about how it had gone down. Wyatt had said his father had contacted the sheriff after having him followed, but what if he was wrong? What if it hadn't been Bart?

I looked Bingham square in the eye. "How'd the sheriff know where to arrest him? I'm sure the arrest report would tell me, but you could save me the trouble of looking."

A slow grin spread across his face. "An anonymous tip was called in."

"Any idea where that tip might have come from?"

His grin spread. "I can see you're dyin' to pin it on me. I'm sorry to disappoint, but I didn't do it. I generally like to handle things my own way. No need to bring in a middleman, especially law enforcement."

"Yet you knew it was an anonymous tip. Surely you gave some thought as to who called it in."

He leaned forward, resting his elbows on his thighs as he stared out into the trees beyond my car. "I always suspected Heather set him up. It was no secret she wanted the Drummond money. The tavern closed for a few days. Then Bart had Carson Purdy run it for a bit, tellin' everyone that Wyatt was sick. It wasn't hard to believe since he stuck to his house. Wyatt was arrested not long afterward, and then Max came back from school, not only runnin' the place but ownin' it, just like Wyatt had demanded. How's that for karma?"

Heather must have been furious. "Why would she have had Wyatt arrested if she wanted the money?"

"Rumor had it Wyatt was done. He'd put up with a lot of shit from his old man, and he'd reached the breaking point. But Heather had invested a lot of time in her trust fund project, and she had no intention of walking away empty-handed."

"So her plan all along was to blackmail the Drummonds?"

"I don't know that for a fact, but I've always suspected."

"So why make all that fuss about the Drummonds pressuring her to change her testimony?" I shook my head, realizing the answer myself. "Because she fully expected them to pay her off. And the Drummonds didn't pay up because they expected Wyatt to use their attorney, and then they'd grease the wheels of justice and get the charges reduced or dropped."

Bingham winked. "But it turned out the oldest Drummond boy wasn't the team player his daddy raised him to be."

"The Drummonds gave her five thousand dollars to leave town," I said. "But that's got to be a far cry from what she expected."

"She was probably just cuttin' her losses," Bingham said. "Take the money and move on to the next mark."

I shook my head. "I don't think so. I think she had another plan." I turned to glance at him. "She had a boyfriend on the side. Any idea who it was?"

He snorted. "It sure as hell wasn't me, so you can stop barkin' up that tree."

"I know it wasn't you," I said. "You're too smart to get caught up in someone else's machinations."

"It could be argued that you're gettin' me caught up in some now."

"Nah," I said. "I'm not involving you in anything. I'm only borrowin' your ear."

A guarded look crossed his face. "I don't allow many people to borrow my ear."

"I'm not using you, Bingham," I said. "We're both working toward the same end."

"Damn straight," he said in a growl. "*No one* uses me."

"I'm not using you," I said insistently.

"What am I gettin' out of all this?"

That was a good question. I was about to tell him that the information he could provide me might help me bring down Bart, but I was beginning to wonder if Bart had anything to do with Heather's death after all. Even through a favor. What if Heather and her boyfriend had set Wyatt up, expecting the Drummonds to pay her big bucks to go away? What if they'd fought about the low payout and he'd taken out his frustrations by murdering her?

"I don't know," I said, deciding to go with honesty.

"I ain't a charity."

"Consider it a gift to your baby's godmother."

His eyes darkened, and it was clear that Lula had forced me on him, not that I'd expected differently.

I knew I was opening a huge can of worms, but I asked anyway, "What do you want?"

A sly grin spread across his face. "A favor that I can call in later."

Ice flooded my veins. "I never knew you were in the favor business, Bingham."

"I'm typically not. Maybe I've been inspired by our mutual *friend*."

Owing Bingham a favor was the worst idea, yet I was tempted. What if he knew the identity of Heather's boyfriend? What was that name worth?

But I still hadn't spoken to Dick or May, and it was possible I could get the information I needed without his help. I wouldn't make myself beholden to Bingham unless I had no other option. "No."

He chuckled. "No? You don't want to know what I know?"

"Of course I do, but I'm not going to indebt myself to you to get it."

He stood. "Then I guess our appointment has ended." He started for the door but turned back before he reached it. "If you change your mind later, the price goes up, so consider this your second chance."

"No," I said. "I'm not going to put myself into the exact same position as all of Bart's victims."

"Victims? Many of those people purchased their fates with their own bad choices."

"Which is why I'm trying to make only good decisions." I stood and glanced at the door. "Is Lula home?"

"You gonna go cryin' to her?" he growled.

"This business is between you and me. I need to speak to her about the baptism."

His forehead creased in an annoyed, or maybe unhappy, look, but he opened the door and called out, "Lula?"

"Shh!" she called out in a whisper-shout from inside. "Beatrice just went to sleep." Then her face popped into the opening. "Hey, Carly." She stepped out onto the porch and glanced up at Bingham. "Is your meetin' done?"

"Yep. Carly said she needs to speak to you about the baptism." He gave me a nod. "You think about what I said." Then he went inside, closing the door behind him.

"What do you need to know?" Lula asked.

I'd figured she would know I wanted to ask about Wyatt, but as it happened, I did have a question. "What time should I be at the church?"

"Oh, I forgot to tell you, didn't I?" she said with a laugh. "The service starts at ten, but the minister wants us there about twenty minutes early."

"Okay," I said. "I'll be there." I paused, then asked, "Have you heard from Wyatt this morning?"

Guilt filled her eyes. "I can't talk about it."

"Lula, I'm the one who sent him to you."

She shook her head. "I don't know what you're talkin' about."

"I need to talk to him, Lula. It's important."

She lifted her chin. "Then tell me, and if I see him, I'll be sure to pass on the message."

Dammit. She was stonewalling me too. "Tell him that I need to talk to him."

Except I had no idea how he was going to contact me if I was out on the road. "Tell him I'm working the lunch shift," I added, deciding on the spot. "I'll be there from noon to about one thirty. He can call me there." It might be a waste of time if Wyatt didn't call, but at least I could help Ginger get acclimated, and Molly might know something useful. She was May's sister, after all.

"Okay." Then she added, "If I see him."

Shaking my head, I headed for the steps.

The Drummonds were infuriating.

Chapter
Twenty-One

I knew Marco was dying to know what I'd found out, so I parked my car behind his and got into his Explorer.

"I'll take the fact that you seem to be in one piece as a good sign," he said, relief washing over his face.

"Yeah, but I don't have all the answers I hoped to get."

"What did you find out?"

"Bingham and Heather had a month-long hookup relationship. He thinks she was after information, but his direct quote was he doesn't mix business and fucking. Interestingly enough, he doesn't conduct business in his house either."

"Quite the gentleman."

I made a face. "One thing I hadn't known was that the sheriff's department found Wyatt and Heather at Balder Mountain State Park after an anonymous tip was called in, but that doesn't seem like Bart's style. Also, it's noteworthy that they would have just gotten him for breaking and entering, not the DUI, if the sheriff's deputy hadn't found them in the car."

"Who do you think called in the tip?" he asked. "Bingham?"

"Bingham swears it wasn't him, and crazily enough, I believe him."

"So who did it?" he asked.

"This is purely speculation, but I think it was Heather's behind-the-scenes boyfriend. Bingham thinks Heather was in on it—that it was a setup for Wyatt—and I have to say it makes sense."

He was silent for a moment. "For what purpose?"

"What if Heather was upset because Wyatt had disowned his family? She was counting on the Drummond money, but he messed that up for her."

"So she punished him by turning him in to the sheriff's department?"

"No," I said, "I think she was trying to get the money she thought she was owed directly from the Drummonds. I'd even go so far as to suggest she blackmailed them."

"But she only got five thousand," Marco countered.

"Because things didn't work out the way she was hoping. Bart and Wyatt are both more stubborn than she realized. Bart wanted to use an attorney to make the whole thing go away, and Wyatt didn't want a thing to do with his family."

He was quiet for a moment. "We really need to find her boyfriend. Let's go back to my place to make some calls. Then we can head to Ewing to talk to Dick Stinnett. After we talk to him, we can find May."

I hunched my shoulders. "Actually, I need to go in for the lunch shift. I need to talk to Wyatt."

He stilled. "And why do you think he's gonna show up at the tavern?"

"I don't," I said. "But I suspect Lula knows how to get ahold of him, and I told her to have him contact me at the tavern between noon and one thirty."

He gave me a long look. "Are you sure talkin to him is necessary?"

"I need ~~to~~ him to answer some questions."

"Assuming he'll tell you anything at all. You're busting your ass to try to help him, and he's not doing a single thing to make it easier on you," Marco said, anger creeping into his voice. "While I don't think he did it, he needs to start being a hell of a lot more up-front with what he knows."

"Agreed," I said quietly. "But what's the alternative? Stop trying to help him?"

"I'll admit that part of me is tempted, but *you* won't because you're worried he'll get railroaded."

"Marco," I said, something tugging on my heart.

He gave me a soft smile. "I'm not mad, Carly. I admire your dedication to finding justice. I'm just not sure he appreciates everything you're doing for him, and I don't want to see you get hurt again."

"I'm not emotionally involved, Marco. Not like I was before."

He looked into my eyes for a moment, as if considering that, then gave a nod of acknowledgment. "You don't have to be at the tavern until twelve, so we still have time to make some calls. I'll follow you to my house."

"Okay."

I got out and walked back to my car. Then we drove to his place. After we went inside, he found a phone book for Ewing and started calling used car lots, asking for Dick Stinnett. It only took three calls to locate him, and Marco set up an appointment to meet with him at two.

"Marco, are you sure about being involved in this?"

"I've been thinkin' about trading in my Explorer."

That was a bald-faced lie. His SUV was less than two years old and he loved it.

"Okay," he said. "Let's move on to May McMurphy."

"Our best bet is to ask her sister," I said. "She's working the lunch shift."

He nodded. "Okay, but we still have about a half hour to kill before you need to be at work. Anything you want to do between now and then?"

I found myself thinking of Emily Drummond, and of the look she'd given me when she talked about Max and his duty. Max. Why hadn't we asked him about any of this?

"I say we head into the tavern and ask Max what he knows," I said.

His eyes widened. "Shit. I didn't even think about that."

"I know. Me neither. It just occurred to me."

"Of course, he wasn't here when Wyatt was arrested," Marco said, "but he was here when Heather left."

"Let's head to town," I said, getting up and grabbing my purse. "You'll follow me again?"

He gave me a pensive look. "Yeah, but after you get off work, maybe you should leave your car in the parking lot so we can ride together in the Explorer."

"Is that really a good idea?" I asked. "I mean, I'm glad you're coming with me, but maybe we should take my car."

"I'll think it over," he said, moving for the door. "We can decide when you get off."

When we walked in the back door to the tavern, Tiny gave us a wave from the kitchen, where he and Sweetie Pie were prepping for the day, and we found Max in his office.

Max looked up from his computer, startled, and turned his chair to face us. "What are you two doing here together?"

Marco gestured his thumb behind him. "We'd like to ask you a few questions about Wyatt and Heather, but can we do it in the dining room?"

"Are you serious, Marco?" His face hardened. "The ink's barely dry on the warrant for Wyatt's arrest."

"You know about that?" Marco asked, rubbing the back of his neck.

"I had a friendly chat with some not-so-friendly deputies who dropped by to see if he was here or if I knew where they could find him."

Marco released a groan. "For God's sake, I'm not here to arrest Wyatt." When Max didn't say anything, he added, "I'm helpin' Carly with her investigation. We're here to see if you can give us any leads."

Max inhaled deeply, then said, "I don't know anything about any of it."

"You might know more than you think," I said. "And if we're asking questions, we might help you jog something loose."

Max's gaze lifted to his friend.

"He's your brother, Max. I'm not out to arrest him," Marco pleaded. "I know he didn't kill her. I'm tryin' to help him, even if he doesn't seem to be doin' much to help himself."

"What's that supposed to mean?" Max asked, his jaw clenching.

"It means he hasn't exactly been forthcoming," I said. "He has information that could help me clear his name, yet he's barely told me anything." I held out my hand. "Max, I'm trying to figure this out before the sheriff catches up to him. *Please.* Anything you tell us will help."

He studied us for a moment before nodding. "Okay." Then he closed out the spreadsheet he was working on and stood. "I'm gonna need more coffee for this." He picked up his stained, nearly empty cup and followed us out of the office. He slid behind the bar and refreshed his cup. "I'd rather do this standin' up, if you don't mind. You two can sit at the bar if you'd like. Either of you want a cup of coffee?"

"Sure," Marco said as he pulled out a barstool.

"No, thanks," I said, taking a seat next to him, and pulled my notebook and recorder out of my purse. I felt no need to hide the fact that I was taking notes, given they knew exactly what I was up to, plus it occurred to me that I probably didn't have much time left on the tape.

Max stared at me like I'd grown two heads.

"What?" I said, clicking the recorder on. "I want to be able to go back and listen in case I missed something."

Max shot a glance at Marco, then shrugged.

Opening the notebook to the next available page, I said, "Wyatt and Heather dated while you and Marco were in eighth and ninth grade. What did you think of her?"

Max's mouth curved into a derisive grin as he poured some coffee for Marco. "What I *really* thought of her or the watered-down version?"

His answer took me by surprise. "The truth."

"I thought she was gorgeous and had big tits. You can only imagine what a boy that age would do with an image like that."

I cringed. "Gross. Maybe not *that* honest."

Max laughed and Marco covered his mouth to hide a grin.

"Okay," I said, "besides inspiring you to perfect your masturbation technique, what kind of impression did she make?"

Max laughed. "I was a stupid, barely pubescent boy. At the time, I was envious of my brother. It wasn't until college that I realized she was a first-class manipulator. She knew I was attracted to her, and she played me like a fiddle when Wyatt wasn't around. She tried to play our parents too, but my father seemed especially immune. After finding out that he had so many girlfriends spread out over the area, part of me is surprised he wasn't more taken with her. She definitely knew how to play Wyatt, homing in on his need to prove himself to dear old Dad. She encouraged it so that it became an unhealthy obsession for both of them. I think part of Wyatt was glad to see her go to college. He was relieved to not have pressure from both sides anymore."

"So do you think she was interested in Wyatt for his money, even in high school?" I asked.

"I never really thought about it at the time, or even much later," Max said, leaning his forearm on the counter. "I always thought she was interested in Wyatt because he was tall and good-looking. He was on the football team, he lifted weights, and he was popular. I'm sure every girl in high school wanted to date him on that basis alone. But for Heather, in hindsight, yeah, she was probably interested in the money from the start."

"So you knew her to be manipulative?" I asked.

"Again," Max said, shifting his weight, "I didn't put any of this together at the time, and if I'm being honest, I didn't make the connection until I started dating a few girls who were just like her." He turned to Marco. "What do you remember about her?"

Marco cast me a sidelong glance and cringed. "I'll admit that her looks were…distracting, but I never spent any time around her. Wyatt didn't hang out with us much, and Max's interactions with her were all from family dinners and hanging out at their house."

"You didn't see her when you were over?" I asked.

Marco and Max were both silent for a moment. Then Max said, "Marco wasn't over much. I tended to go to his house."

"Was that your choice or your father's?" I asked.

Max's face reddened.

"It's okay, Max," Marco said. "I always knew your father didn't care for me."

"Why?" I asked.

"We were a lot poorer than most of the families in town," Marco said. "My father was a dreamer, always working on some cockamamie project or another that he was sure was going to be a huge success. The gadget to finally make us rich. Bart Drummond considered him a joke and a blight on the town. I was guilty by association."

Max looked embarrassed. "By middle school, my father decided I needed a new friend group, so Marco and I would hang out at the ball fields or his house, which was a few blocks away. Other kids hung out there, so it was a good cover. I'm sure my mother knew what we were doin', and my father was pleased as punch that I was takin' up an all-American sport and was hopefully becoming more like my brother. So I joined the team and my father came to one game. I sat on the bench for most of it and struck out once. On the drive home, he told me to let him know when I was actually worth watchin'."

"Max." My heart broke for him.

He shrugged. "Life with dear old Dad."

I found myself thinking again of what Emily had said, about his family obligations. Why had he felt any if his father had treated him so poorly? Had he gone home just for Emily?

"In any case," he said, sounding weary, "he stopped paying attention to me after that, and I'd just hang out at

272

Marco's house. Mom knew, of course—she loved Marco—but it was our secret from Dad. Long story short, that's why Marco wasn't over much."

But I had to wonder if it was really a secret. Hadn't Marco himself told me they'd never once pulled the wool over Bart's eyes? Were there many secrets in Drum he didn't know?

I had a million more questions for them both, but none pertained to Heather. Molly and Ginger would be here soon, which meant I needed to stay on topic. "Did you come home from college while Wyatt and Heather were back together?"

Max was silent for a moment. "I came home for Christmas and summer. Wyatt and Heather weren't around much, and I spent a lot of time working on the land with Carson, but she was around some. Mom and Dad couldn't stand her, and it was obvious to everyone except my brother that she wasn't with Wyatt for love."

"How could you tell?" I asked.

Max was silent for a moment. "She wasn't very affectionate. You know how you can tell when a couple is really into each other? I never got that vibe from either of them. Wyatt seemed to be in it because…maybe he didn't see a better option? She was a habit? She was with us when we opened presents on the last Christmas Day she was in town, and when she realized there was no ring-sized box in her present pile, she looked furious. She claimed she had a migraine and made Wyatt drive her home before Christmas lunch. As you can imagine, Dad was furious. Mom disapproved, but in her typical private way. Of course, Heather convinced Wyatt to propose shortly after. And then it all snowballed from there."

"You knew they were engaged?" I asked.

"Mom told me. As far as I know, not many people knew, and the information didn't spread like wildfire."

Part of me was dying to ask Max how his mother had convinced him to come home, but I suspected that was a surefire way to shut down our conversation. "When you came back to run the tavern, did Heather ever show up?"

"Not at all in the beginning, but then she came in a few times with a group of friends. One time she was drunk off her ass, and she cornered me in the back and tried to come on to me, telling me that she'd always thought I was hot back when she and Wyatt were together in high school. Of course, she had given me little attention back then, and I reminded her that if she'd really had those thoughts, it might have been considered pedophilia. As you can imagine, she didn't appreciate that much."

Marco sat up straighter. "You never told me that."

Max's lips pursed and he shook his head. "You were still at college, and it was disgusting. I turned her down, of course. I figured it was best to pretend it had never happened. I didn't feel like joking around about it."

"I would have taken it seriously," Marco said, then shrugged. "But I might have laughed a little later."

Max nodded.

"Did she ever mention it again?" I asked. "From what I've learned about her, I suspect she wouldn't take rejection well."

"The next time I saw her she pretended like it had never happened," Max said with a faraway look. "Now that I think about it, that was a week or so before she left town." He grimaced. "Or was murdered, as the case may be."

"Who did she come to the tavern with that last time?" I asked.

His mouth twisted to one side. "Dick Stinnett and Molly's sister, May. A guy named Kyle and a few more I can't remember."

"Were Heather and Dick seeing each other?" I asked. "I keep hearing his name in connection with hers."

He snorted. "No, Dick had it bad for May, only she didn't seem to notice him until after Heather left. There was a guy who'd occasionally come in with them, and Heather would be hangin' on his every word, but I don't know who he was."

"Could he have been from Ewing?" Marco asked.

"Yeah," Max said. "Likely not from Drum."

Marco shot me a glance, confirming he also thought it could be our guy.

The back door banged shut, and Molly called out cheerfully, "Hey, everybody! Good morning!"

"Thanks, Max," I said as I stopped the recorder and closed my notebook. "This was actually helpful."

He nodded. "Glad to help. I hope you find the bastard who killed her."

"Yeah," I said as I glanced over at Molly in the doorway. "Me too."

Marco leaned closer and whispered, "Do you want to talk to her alone or with me?"

I gave it a moment's thought. "I think alone might work better. I'll introduce it with small talk."

He nodded. "In that case, I figure I'll work behind the bar with Max."

Which reminded me I wasn't done talking to my boss. "Max, I'm going to need to take off for a few hours this afternoon. I'd like to leave around one thirty, and I'll try to be back at five for the dinner shift."

He simply nodded, not that I'd expected anything different. He knew what I was doing with my time.

"One more thing," I said, holding his gaze. "I might get an important phone call this afternoon, and if it comes in, I'm going to need to drop everything and take it. No one can know anything about it."

"Okay." I knew he wanted to ask questions, but I wanted him to maintain plausible deniability. The less he knew, the better.

I got up and headed toward Molly.

"Molly, I hear you did really well yesterday."

She beamed. "Thanks. Even *Ruth* didn't seem to mind me so much." But she said her name like it had a bad taste.

"Did Max tell you that we have a new waitress starting today? She'll only be working the lunch shift with us."

"No, but that's great. We could sure use the help."

We only had ten minutes left before the tavern opened, so we got busy refilling salt and pepper shakers.

"Say," I said, trying to appear nonchalant. "Where does your sister May work?"

She gave me a cautious look. "She doesn't. She stays at home with her two kids."

"How long has she been married?"

"About five years."

I was hoping she'd volunteer more information, but it was obvious I was going to need to be more direct.

"Did she marry someone local?"

"He's from Ewing. She and her husband live in Piedmont."

Piedmont was about ten miles northeast of Ewing.

"I know why you're askin'," she said with a hint of attitude. "This is about Heather Stone."

"I'm curious," I admitted. "I'd like to talk to her, if she's willing."

"Why?"

"Because I know she was friendly with Heather. I'm trying to find out what happened."

"Why don't you ask Wyatt Drummond? I suspect he had something to do with it."

"I don't believe he did," I said. "Which is why I'd like to talk to May."

She shook her head. "May won't want nothin' to do with it. She was only too happy to leave Drum and all the shit that went down here behind her, especially after what happened with Ruth."

"What happened?" I asked, scared to hear her answer.

"Ruth's not who you think she is, you know," she said, her eyes flashing. "She's no angel."

"I have no doubt about that," I countered. "I have no idea what she's done in the past. But we've worked together practically every day since I started five months ago, and she's a great coworker and a good friend."

"That might be the person you know now, but it's not the person my sister knew."

"And I have no idea what she did to your sister, so unless you give me specifics, I can't let that cloud my judgment."

"How about the fact she slept with May's first husband while they were married?"

Molly had alluded to this a couple of days ago, but I still had trouble accepting that Ruth would sleep with a married man. Especially since she'd held an almost decade-long grudge against Wyatt for kissing Heather while he was still dating Ruth.

"Is there a problem over here?" Max asked, walking over to us.

"Nope," Molly said in a snippy tone. "We're hunky-dory."

Max gave her a dubious glance, then turned to me. "Ginger's in the back changin' into a work shirt. I don't want her to think we're anything but one big happy family."

I set the saltshaker I'd just filled on the table. "I'll go say hi and show her the ropes. Max, can I talk to you for a moment? I forgot to tell you about an incident last night."

That wasn't entirely truthful, but I didn't want Molly to know I intended to grill him about her sister.

"Yeah, sure." He glanced back and forth between us, as if trying to understand the nature of the problem he had on his hands, and we headed to the back.

"What was that about?" he asked under his breath.

"Molly's sister. I need to talk to her, but Molly's resistant to the idea. Plus, she claims Ruth slept with May's first husband."

"Ruth *did* sleep with May's first husband."

I stopped in my tracks in the hallway to his office. "*What?*"

"Carly," he said, turning to face me. "May's first husband was Tater."

In response to my blank look, he said, "Franklin."

My mouth dropped open as if it were hinged.

"No one told you?"

I felt sick to my stomach. "No." I shook my head and stared at him in disbelief. "What were you thinking hiring Molly?"

Wyatt had condoned it too!

"Molly claimed it wouldn't be a problem, and Ruth...she's like a robot."

"That's bullshit," I hissed under my breath. "Max!"

He scrunched up his face, clearly perplexed. "Do you think it's gonna be a problem?"

"Of course it's gonna be a problem! I can't believe they've gotten along as well as they have so far."

He frowned, then glanced in the direction of the back room. "I know you have to leave early, but can you take Ginger under your wing today?"

"Yeah, of course."

"Good, you're in charge of the dining room until you leave," Max said, then headed back out to the bar.

When I got to the back room, Ginger was pacing the small space in a Max's Tavern T-shirt, radiating nervous energy. "Do you really think I can do this?"

"I don't see why not," I said. "You're an intelligent woman who's used to juggling three kids, a husband, and Hank," I teased.

She laughed. "True."

"Thanks for doing my laundry the other day."

She waved it off. "You've been working crazy hours. It was the least I could do, although you have to know I didn't expect to get a job offer out of it."

"We need help, and you could use a job that works with your kids' schedule. I see it as a win-win."

We headed into the dining room, and I told Molly she was taking Ruth's section, which earned me a dirty look. I told Ginger she would shadow a few orders with me, then I'd let her loose on the bar and a couple of tables, just like I'd done with Molly her first night.

I unlocked the door, not surprised to see a line outside, but not prepared for the grumbling.

"We've only got an hour," one of the men griped. "You need to open sooner."

I supposed that might be possible if Molly and Ginger worked out, but I had other things to worry about...like a group of cranky men and two barely trained waitresses.

The men got seated, and we started taking orders—Molly keeping up with the rush, and Ginger picking up the rhythm of it quickly enough for me to set her loose after only a few orders. Marco helped out by bussing tables and refilling drinks.

When we were at the height of the lunch rush, Max motioned me over, holding up the phone.

Crap. Talk about bad timing.

Molly noticed as I made my way to Max's office, and she said, "Are you seriously takin' a phone call now?"

"Yes. I am." I understood why she would question the timing, but I'd been around months longer than her and had often worked the lunch shift alone. I sure as hell didn't need her policing me.

Once I was in Max's office, I shut the door behind me and picked up the phone, pushing the blinking button for line one. "This is Carly."

"Is everything okay?" Wyatt asked. "Lula said you needed to talk to me right away."

"I didn't say right away," I said, taking a seat in Max's chair, "but yeah, I have to ask you some questions and I need some straight answers."

"What do you want to know?" He sounded guarded, not that I was surprised, but I didn't have time to beat around the bush, and neither did he.

"Tell me about Heather's other boyfriends."

He was quiet for several seconds. "Based on your tone and your appointment this morning, you've already figured out there were several."

"Several? I only know about two, and only one by name. Fill me in."

"I'm sure you know she had a fling with Bingham. She was up-front about that after we got back together."

"I know about Bingham, and I know she had a boyfriend before she was murdered, but I don't know much about him other than that he was from Ewing and she met him at the salon where she worked."

"Well, you know more than me," he said in a dry tone.

"What *do* you know?"

"That she was seeing him after I was arrested."

"From what I learned, it might have started before that."

He didn't respond.

"You said you knew about him. What can you tell me?"

"Like you said, I'm pretty sure she met him at work. I figured he was a client at the salon."

"Do you have a name?"

"No."

I tried to rein in my frustration. "Look, Wyatt, if you want me to do this, you have to be more forthcoming. I shouldn't have to drag every damn answer out of you."

"I knew she was unhappy," he snapped, but then his tone softened. "She wanted me to propose at Christmas, but I wasn't sure I loved her. I just couldn't seem to pull the trigger. I think deep down I knew she was wrong for me."

"So you didn't follow through, and she found a boyfriend on the side?"

"I didn't know the timing overlapped, but I'm not surprised."

"What do you remember about the night you were arrested?"

"Really? We've already covered this, Carly."

"No. Not completely. You said your father had you followed and arrested to drag you back into the fold. Did he tell you that?"

"No, but we weren't exactly speakin' at that point. I knew the sheriff got an anonymous tip. It stands to reason it was Dad."

"What if it was someone else?"

"Who else would do it?" he asked, sounding unconvinced.

"Heather's boyfriend. What if he had you arrested so Heather could coerce your parents into paying her not to testify against you?"

Silence hung over the line for a moment. Then he asked, "Do you have any proof of that? Because my parents *did* pay her off to leave, but I'm pretty sure they offered, not the other way around."

"But only five thousand dollars. That's not much in the scheme of things. You know she was banking on so much more."

He didn't respond.

"I need to know what happened at her going-away party." I steeled my back, preparing to put up an argument if he tried shooting me down. "Were you invited?"

"No," he scoffed.

"What made you decide to go?"

He was silent for several seconds. "I heard she was pregnant."

My stomach dropped. I hadn't been prepared for that.

"I went to confront her," he said. "To make sure it was mine."

"What did she say?"

"She laughed at me. Told me she'd lied about takin' the pill for the last six months of our relationship, tryin' to get pregnant so I'd have to marry her, but it didn't happen because I had bad sperm."

"She tested your sperm?" I asked in disbelief.

He snorted. "No, but Heather couldn't take responsibility for anything. Not even failing to get pregnant, so of course it had to be my fault."

"I heard you were in a room with her for half an hour. What did you do in there all that time?"

"There was no way in hell I was there for that long. More like ten minutes. Fifteen minutes tops. And we were in the room because I didn't feel like discussing her possible pregnancy in a room full of people."

"You discussed the fact she wasn't pregnant for fifteen minutes?" I asked.

"There was a lot of rehashin' about how I'd screwed her over and wasted her life. But she told me she was leavin' Drum in her dust, and she'd never give me a second thought after she left."

"Did you know she was going to Tulsa?"

"No. She never said anything about it to me, but I tried to pay her as little attention as possible after we broke up."

"If you weren't paying attention to her, then who told you she was pregnant?" I asked.

"I don't know."

"What does that mean?"

"I found a note in my mailbox that said Heather was pregnant."

"How long did you have the letter before you confronted her?"

"The same day. I don't know how long it was in my mailbox. I hadn't checked it in days."

"Did it look like a man or a woman had written the letter?"

"A woman, I guess," he said. "It had swirly handwriting."

"Were you drunk when you confronted her?"

"What?"

"A witness said you were drunk."

"I wasn't drunk," he said in disgust. "I'd had a beer before I found the letter, but I sat with it for a good hour before I went to the party."

"Did someone drive you?"

"No, I drove myself." Then he added, "I wouldn't drink and drive, Carly. Not after my arrest."

"What did you do after that? Where did you go?"

"Home," he said. "And no, I don't have an alibi for the rest of the night."

I should have asked sooner, but it stood to reason he didn't given the fact he had me trying to find the real murderer. "The night you were arrested, what time did you break into the garage?"

"Carly…"

"Answer the question, Wyatt," I snapped.

"Around midnight. Maybe later."

"You went and confronted your father and came home and started drinking. What made you decide to get your baseball?"

"I don't know," he said, getting angry. "I was furious with my father."

"But whose idea was it to go? Did Heather plant the seed?"

He hesitated. "Maybe."

"And you drove? She let you drive knowing you were drunk?"

"Yeah."

"She didn't try to stop you. She let you drive. She probably planted the idea in your head." I paused. "She set you up, Wyatt."

"Well, congratulations, Carly," he said in a wry tone. "You can call up the sheriff and tell him I had motive to kill her."

I pushed out a sigh. "Look, the key is finding out who helped her, because she didn't orchestrate your setup alone. Someone had to make that call."

"Unless she prearranged it with the sheriff's department. But she still would have needed an accomplice."

Then a new thought hit me—what if her boyfriend worked for the sheriff's department?

"Who was at the going-away party?" I asked.

"I didn't pay much attention. I went there to talk to her. I let her berate me, then I left."

"Whose house was it at?"

"Mitzi's. She was furious when I showed up."

I *really* needed to talk to Mitzi.

"You're in hiding now, right?" I asked. "You're not trying to hide in the shadows and follow me around, are you?"

"It's shortly after noon," he said in a teasing tone. "There aren't many shadows."

"You know what I meant."

"I went to Lula like you suggested."

"How are you getting along with Bingham?"

"Trust me, I'm staying as far away from him as I can." I heard the sound of a car in the distance. "I've got to go. I'll call Max later to check in." Then he hung up.

I knew I needed to get back to work, but first I looked up the number for Drum Veterinary Clinic and called Abby.

"Dr. Donahey," she said after Sasha transferred the call.

"Abby, it's Carly," I said. "I have another couple of questions for you."

"Ask away," she said, "although there's no guarantee I'll know the answer."

"You said that Mitzi told you Heather was going to Tulsa. Are you sure?"

"Yeah. Did you ask Mitzi?"

"She wouldn't see me."

"What?"

"I guess it would be more accurate to say her husband wouldn't let me see her."

She was silent for a moment. "Paul is a controlling asshole."

"I was surprised he was home."

"He works nights for the sheriff's department. He's a deputy sheriff."

I gasped. "You're kidding. What's his last name?"

"Conrad. Paul Conrad. Trust me, if he knows about this, you'll never get to talk to her."

I let that soak in for a moment—both that he was a sheriff deputy and that Abby was sure he wouldn't let me talk to his wife. What was he hiding something? "Do you happen to know who Heather's boyfriend was? The one she was seeing right before she left town?"

"She had another boyfriend? That's news to me."

"I think she was meeting him at the Mountain View Lodge. They spent a night there the week before she left. I have the receipt."

Abby was quiet for a moment, and when she spoke again, she sounded more subdued. "Wow. I didn't know. Mitzi would know better than I would."

Or maybe Dick or May, but I didn't need to mention that. "And Paul won't let me talk to her."

She paused again. "Maybe you should just let it go, Carly. I worry this is dredgin' up a lot of memories she would rather forget. Just let the sheriff's department do their job and leave it at that."

"But they're pinnin' this on an innocent man," I said.

"Can't Wyatt come up with an alibi?" she said, her voice strained. "I just know Mitzi didn't sound good on the phone. This is *really* upsettin' her." Then she said, "Hey. A client showed up. I've gotta go."

She hung up and I thought about what she'd said about Mitzi and Paul. I didn't want to cause her grief, but I suspected she had more answers than anyone. I wanted to talk to her more now than I had before.

I just needed the element of surprise.

Chapter
Twenty-Two

I headed out to the dining room and found absolute chaos. A large group of construction workers had come in and filled every single chair at the bar. Ginger was handling the rush as best she could during her first hour of waitressing, and Molly looked furious.

"Where the hell have you been?" she barked as I tried to figure out where to start first. Marco had taken some of the drink orders for my new customers, so I started taking food orders and getting them in so the laborers could get back to work on time. I was dying to talk to Marco, but I knew it would have to wait.

It was nearly one thirty before we had everything under control. Molly had survived the rush, even if she'd fallen behind for a bit, and Ginger had jumped right in and handled all of the customers at the bar—with a little help from Max and Marco.

When we got a breather, Molly cornered me at the server counter. "What makes you think you're special enough to walk off the floor for nearly ten minutes?"

I gaped at her in disbelief. "And just how long have you worked here?"

She lifted her chin in defiance. "That's irrelevant."

"Did *you* have to cover my section?" I demanded.

"No, but—"

"Are you my *boss*?"

"No—"

"Did my absence hurt you in any way?"

"People were complainin'."

"To you?"

"Well, no, but—"

"Let's get one thing straight, Molly," I said with a cold tone I rarely used. "You worry about *you* and let me take care of *me*. Max was fully aware that I had something I needed to deal with, but instead of taking off the entire shift and letting *you* deal with it all, I took off a few minutes to handle it. With his permission. I've worked here for *months*, while *you* are still on probation."

She stared at me in shock.

"I suggest you spend more time handling your own customers and less time supervising *me*."

"Order up, Molly," Tiny said with plenty of judgment in his voice.

Molly gave him a hateful look, grabbed her plates, and stomped off to the dining room.

"You gonna tell Max about that hissy fit?" Tiny asked, leaning in the window.

"Tiny…"

"That's a fat no." He sucked in a deep breath, then said, "I know the dining room is none of my business, but she's never gonna work out here. She's got a mile-long grudge against Ruth, and now she's buildin' one against you. I know y'all need the help, but I don't trust her."

"I'm not gonna be responsible for getting someone fired, Tiny."

"You think I don't know that? That's why I'll be tellin' Max every bit of nonsense I've heard that woman spout." Then he turned back to deal with his own employee, who, for all her incompetence, was at least respectful.

Tiny placed my order on the counter, and I delivered it to my customers before checking in with Ginger. I'd thought she might be flustered, but her eyes were glowing with excitement.

"Is it like this every day?" she asked.

"Not quite this crazy," I said, "but it's been hopping lately with the construction crew."

"I can't wait to come back tomorrow."

I hoped what I was about to tell her didn't make her change her mind. "I really hate to do this, but I'm going to need to take off early, and I'd like you to cover my section too."

Her smile fell, and I was sure she was about to blast me too, but instead she lowered her voice and asked, "Are you leaving to help clear Wyatt's name?"

I hesitated, not sure how much she knew.

She leaned closer and whispered, "Junior's covering the garage so Wyatt can tail you, although now I hear he's hidin' from the sheriff. You're helpin' him, aren't you?"

"Yes."

Taking a step back, she said, "Then what are you doin' here? We'll handle this. You go save our boy."

Our boy. Wyatt wasn't my boy, and the look on her face said she realized her mistake.

"Carly, I'm sorry. I know you two broke up, but since you're helpin' him, I thought…"

I shook my head. "We're not getting back together. That man has too many secrets. Too much baggage. I'm only helping him out as a friend."

"He's a good man," she said with an imploring look in her eyes. "He's always gone above and beyond for Junior and me, and he's so good to Hank too. I know he misses you."

"I agree that he's a good man in many ways, but I deserve more than he's willing to give me." As soon as the words left my mouth, I regretted revealing so much, but I also needed her to understand. "I don't have to tolerate a man who is only willing to meet me part of the way. I deserve a man who's all in."

"Like Marco?" she asked, her gaze drifting over to him. He was bussing another table and chatting with customers. "He's a good man, Carly, but he's not Wyatt."

"Maybe that's what I like about him." This conversation was beyond inappropriate, especially on the dining room floor. I handed her my ticket book. "I'm going to give my cash to Max. He'll help you cash out for the both of us before you go." I started to walk away but turned back. "Oh, and you did great, Ginger. Thanks for helpin' out."

Nodding, she grinned, although there was a slightly uneasy edge to it—like she knew she'd overstepped. But the next moment, she turned to ask one of my customers if they needed a refill. She was a natural.

Untying my apron, I walked behind the bar and handed my money to Max, telling him that Ginger was taking over. "I'm not sure if I'll be back by five," I admitted. "I feel like I'm racing a ticking time bomb."

He gave me a serious look. "Don't worry about us. We'll deal with things here. Just clear Wyatt's name."

"I'll do what I can," I said.

I found Marco dumping off another batch of dirty dishes in the kitchen. We parted ways so he could wash his hands and I could change my shirt in Max's office. Then we met at the back door.

He held up a large paper bag. "Lunch."

"Good idea," I said, following him out the back door to the parking lot. "I didn't realize how hungry I was."

"Who said I got some for you too?" he asked, looking back at me with a sparkle in his eyes. I gave him a fake shove, and he grinned, but it quickly slipped away. "You're right about taking your car," he said. "We're more likely to get noticed in mine."

"Okay."

I got into the driver's seat and Marco got in beside me. He handed me a turkey sandwich, while he opened a cheeseburger.

"When I told Tiny we needed lunches to go, he said he'd handle yours."

Tiny definitely knew what I liked.

While we ate, I told Marco everything I'd learned from Wyatt and Abby, saving the information about Mitzi's husband for last.

"Mitzi's husband is a sheriff's deputy. Paul Conrad. He works the night shift."

"Paul Conrad?" he asked in disbelief.

"So you know him?"

His face hardened. "He's an asshole."

"How long has he been in the sheriff's department?"

"Longer than I have."

"So it's possible he was on the force when Wyatt was arrested?"

He turned to glance at me. "You think he was Heather's mystery boyfriend?"

"I don't know," I admitted. "He ticks some boxes."

Marco was silent for a moment. "Let's talk to Dick first, then figure out where to go from there."

"Agreed," I said. "I'm glad you're helping me, but we can't let anyone know. It has to look like you're only with me for support. If you don't ask questions, then maybe they can't nail you for investigating." It was a thin argument, but at least it was something.

"We'll give it a try," he said.

When we reached Ewing, Marco gave me directions to the used car lot. I pulled into a parking space about five minutes after two. We got out of the car, and a man in his mid-thirties walked out. He was several inches shorter than Marco, and the front of his button-down shirt stretched across his belly. He had light brown hair and a tan.

"Marco?" he called out as he headed toward us.

"That's me," Marco said, reaching out his hand as the man came to a stop in front of us. "And this is Carly."

The man shook Marco's hand. "Dick Stinnett. Thanks for reachin' out. What are you and your wife looking for? A family car? We got a real nice minivan in last week."

Marco frowned, and I wasn't sure if it was because Dick had ignored me or suggested we get a minivan. Maybe both.

"Actually, Dick," Marco said in a congenial voice, "we're here about Heather Stone." Then he added, "We'd like to ask you a few questions."

The smile on Dick's face froze in place, and he glanced between us. "Are you with the Ewing Police?"

"No," I said, deciding this was a good place for me to take over. "We're friends of Hilde Browning, and we're trying to figure out what happened to Heather." It wasn't the full truth, but she *had* told us that she wanted to know what we discovered.

His face paled. "I thought the police were lookin' into it."

"The sheriff," I corrected. "But Hilde doesn't quite trust them to conduct a fair and impartial investigation, so we're talking to people who knew Heather, trying to get an idea of what happened."

He swallowed. "And you want to talk to me?"

"Hilde said you were one of her friends."

He rocked his weight from the balls of his feet to his heels and back. "I wouldn't say we were friends."

"The current owner of Max's Tavern says he remembers you coming in with Heather."

"We were always with a group, but that doesn't mean she was my friend."

"So then how *would* you describe your relationship?" Marco asked.

I cast a warning glance at Marco. He wasn't doing a great job of staying silent, and I wasn't so sure it had been a good idea to take a direct approach.

"I knew her through Mitzi. I didn't really like her," he said. "No offense to the dead, but she was kind of a bitch. Bitter as the day is long. Couldn't stop talkin' about how the Drummonds screwed her over."

"Did she give details about how they'd screwed her over?" I asked.

"She would whine about wasting her time on Wyatt, even when she was with him. After his arrest, she shifted to whining about his parents not payin' her money to say she hadn't seen him steal the baseball and that she was the one who'd driven the car. Then they finally agreed to pay her on the condition she left town, and she coerced Mitzi into throwing a going-away party for her."

"So Mitzi didn't want to host the party?"

"Hell, no. Mitzi knew she'd be stuck providing all the food and alcohol, and she'd just lost her job at the Mountain View Lodge and hadn't found a new one. She couldn't afford to host a party, but Heather always had a way of getting what she wanted."

"Who else was at the going-away party?" I asked.

"Mitzi, Heather of course. Anna Faith Kennedy, Kyle Timmer, and May McMurphy." His face flushed.

"You and May were romantically involved at some point, weren't you?" I asked.

"After Heather left, but not for long. She set her sights on Franklin Tate, and when he became available, she dropped me like a hot potato."

"They got married," I said.

"They did, although we weren't talkin' at that point. I heard she got divorced before her first anniversary. She's remarried to Pete Agnew, and last I heard, they're living in Piedmont."

"Were Heather and May friends?" Marco asked.

"Heather really wasn't friends with *anyone*," Dick said. "But I think she got as close to people as she was capable of. She was too narcissistic to be a real friend."

"Did she have any enemies?"

"Lots of people felt used by her, but all she had to do was circle back in their orbit and they'd fall under her spell again. Me included."

"So you don't know of anyone who held a grudge against her?" I said.

He shrugged. "It's complicated. I know people were annoyed with her, but I don't think anyone wanted to kill her."

"How well did you know Wyatt?" I asked.

"Not well."

"But you saw him when he showed up at her going-away party," I said matter-of-factly, leaving little room for argument.

He grunted, then nodded once in lieu of a yes.

How did he seem?" I continued.

"He seemed agitated at first, insisting he had to talk to Heather. She laughed and told him he'd better get his closure now, as she was taking off the next day. They went into a room together—at that point he didn't seem as angry. He just seemed tired."

"Did he look like he was drunk?" I asked.

He made a face. "No. He was pissed when he first showed up, but he wasn't drunk."

"It was rumored that he was drunk, but it wasn't anyone who was at the party who told me. It was a friend of a friend."

"Let me guess," Dick said in disgust. "You heard it from Abby."

I didn't respond.

"Mitzi told a lot of stories after Heather left, saying Wyatt had been drunk and he and Heather had sex in the room." He shook his head. "Never happened. Heather was shouting at him too much for that to have happened. We could hear them through the door."

"Do you know what she was shouting about?" Marco asked.

I shot him a dirty look.

Dick lifted his shoulder into a half shrug. "That she'd wasted her time on him. That she deserved more than five thousand and she had a plan to get it."

Marco glanced at me, eyebrows raised.

"Do you know *how* she planned to get more money?" I asked.

"I wasn't privy to Heather's schemes," Dick said. "Nor did I want to be."

"Was Heather's new boyfriend at the party?" I asked.

"I'd heard rumors of a new boyfriend, but I never saw evidence of him," Dick said. "He never showed up at anything. Heather claimed he was private and wasn't ready to go public with their relationship."

"Do you know his name?" Marco asked. "Surely she called him by something."

"Yeah, she had a nickname for him." Dick scratched his head. "It was different…what was it? Peep."

"Peep?" Marco asked as if baffled.

"Do you know if Heather stayed at the Mountain View Lodge with her boyfriend?" I asked.

He shook his head. "I've got no idea. Honestly, I tried to know as little as possible about what she was up to. If you want to know more about her personal life, you should talk to May or Mitzi."

"When did Mitzi start seeing Paul Conrad?" I asked.

His brow shot up. "So you've heard about Paul, huh?"

"Yeah," I admitted.

"About a year after Heather left. Mitzi stopped hanging out with us then. Paul had just gone through a divorce—in fact, I think they started seein' each other while he was in the middle of it—and he didn't waste any time controlling her. He works for the sheriff's department, and he fits right in."

"What does that mean?" I asked.

"There's a core group of guys who are power-hungry assholes. If they don't like you, they'll torment you and make your life a living hell." He made a face. "And before you think I'm bitter because they busted me for something, you can back right on down that tree. They've left me alone, but I've seen them make other people's lives hell. Many of them moved away. Some of them are in prison on trumped-up charges."

I shot a look at Marco before shifting my attention back to Dick. "You're kidding."

"I wish I was. But Paul Conrad's part of the good ole boys club."

While I knew that there were corrupt deputies, it was eye-opening to hear Dick talk about it. Did Marco know any of this was going on?

"Do you happen to know who Paul Conrad was married to before Mitzi?" Marco asked.

"Yeah," Dick said. "He was married to Tammy Hershey. She works at the thrift store."

"Helping Hands Thrift Store?" I asked. The cashier there had been named Tammy.

"Yep. That's the one. I saw her in there last week. She was working at the register."

"Short dark hair?" I asked.

"Yeah, that's her."

I couldn't think of any more questions to ask him, so I cast a glance at Marco, who gave a small shake of his head.

"Dick if you think of anything that will help, would you give me a call at Max's Tavern and leave a message?"

"You work at Max's?" he asked, looking like he was having second thoughts about talking to us so openly.

"Carly does," Marco said, "but we're here for Hilde. My mom has been friends with her for years."

That seemed to appease Dick, but he still looked nervous. Like maybe he'd said too much. "Yeah. If I think of anything, I'll call."

We thanked him for talking to us and got back in the car.

"We're headed to the thrift store next, aren't we?" I asked.

"Yeah," Marco said in a gruff tone as he buckled his seat belt. "Paul Conrad's involved in this, and we're going to find evidence to prove it."

Chapter Twenty-Three

Tammy was working at the register when we walked into Helping Hands Thrift Store, and she recognized me right away. "Hey," she called out. "Did that recorder work out for you?"

She didn't have any customers, so I headed straight toward her, which was a one-eighty from the plan Marco and I had come up with—to buy something and talk to her as we checked out, but this seemed like a more natural segue to asking her questions.

"Actually," I said, stopping in front of her, while Marco stayed a couple of feet behind me to my right. "It did, but I was hoping to get some more tapes."

"I'm pretty sure we don't have any here, but you can check in the back." She thumbed toward the electronics section.

"Actually, that's not why I'm here," I said hesitantly, hoping I wasn't screwing this up. "I'm Carly and this is Marco," I said, gesturing to him behind me. "And we're friends of Hilde Browning."

She shook her head. "I don't know any Hildes."

"Hilde is Heather Stone's aunt," I said.

She shook her head again. "Should I know her?"

"Heather's body was uncovered at the Drummond resort construction site," Marco said.

"Oh, I heard about that. Awful business, but I'm not sure what it has to do with me."

"We heard your ex-husband is now married to Heather's best friend," I said. When she didn't respond, I asked, "Were you previously married to Paul Conrad?"

She made a face as though she'd just eaten something sour. "What do you want to know about that bastard?"

"I'm going to take that as a yes," I said.

"Oh, that's him all right. Fucking asshole." Her eyes narrowed. "This Heather's best friend was Mitzi Ziegler?"

"Yeah," I admitted. "We heard that he was sleeping with Mitzi while you two were getting divorced."

She snorted. "Much sooner than that. And I'm sure she wasn't the first."

"You think he had other affairs?" Marco asked.

"I know he did," she said in disgust, "although he would never admit it. But I found more than a few receipts for the Mountain View Lodge, so I followed him there one night. He went into a motel room for a few hours, and when he came out, he was with some woman." She shook her head. "Would you believe he still tried to deny it?"

"Was it Mitzi?" I asked.

"No," she said in a stern tone. "That was months before he was sleepin' with Mitzi."

"But you don't know who that woman was?" I asked.

"No. Never figured it out. I think he stopped seeing her after that...or he was more careful. He got sloppy with Mitzi."

"If I showed you a photo, would you recognize her?" Marco asked.

"I don't know," Tammy said, pursing lips.

"Could you take a look and see?" Marco asked as he pulled out his phone and let her have a look at it.

She handed the phone back to Marco. "I don't know if that was her or not."

"Do you know if Paul took a trip to Tulsa about eight years ago?" Marco asked.

She squinted up at him. "What? No. Paul hated to travel. Although he took Mitzi to Atlanta after we got divorced. He never took *me*, even after all my beggin'." Her jaw clenched. "Bastard. I left him after I caught them in my bed. My attorney petitioned for me to get the house, and the judge granted it to me while we were in mediation, but a few weeks later Paul broke in and claimed it was his. He had several deputies with him to have me physically removed, so I moved in with my mother." She shuddered.

I could have told her any judge would've had him thrown out, and maybe it was even true, but something about the way she glanced at the door told me she was still afraid of him. Marco must have picked up on it too.

"Did he ever raise his hand to you?" he asked.

She cringed and embarrassment washed over her face.

"I'm going to take that as a yes," I said. "No need for you to relive any traumatic experiences."

Nodding her thanks, she kept her gaze on the counter.

"Does he still bother you?" I asked.

She hesitated, then said, "From time to time. When he's drunk."

"Do you think Paul's capable of murder?" Marco asked.

Her eyes lifted and locked on Marco's face. "Why would you ask that?" Then her eyes lit up with understanding. "You think he killed that Heather girl?"

"We didn't say that," Marco said in an even tone. "I'm just wonderin' how much of a danger he is to the public."

"He's got a temper, and I suppose if he was mad enough... yeah. He could kill someone."

Marco pulled a card out of his pocket and handed it to her. "Tammy, I'm Deputy Sheriff Marco Roland." When fear filled her eyes, he lifted his hands and gently said, "Although we don't work together, I know your ex-husband, and I've never much cared for him. I detest men who abuse their strength and power. If you ever run into any trouble with him, please contact me using my personal number. I'll help you as best I can."

Taking the card, she looked it over before lifting her glare to him. "Everyone knows the sheriff's department in this county is a boys' club. I find it hard to believe you're still there if you're not playin' the game."

"You'd be surprised how many more there are like me," he said. "We're slowly building in numbers and strength." He pointed to the card. "Call me. If I can't get to you, I have a few friends who can."

She glanced at the card again, then back up to Marco. Something in her gave way, and the distrust leached from her gaze.

"Thank you," she said with tears in her eyes.

"And please call me if you think of anything else that can help us," Marco said.

She nodded.

"One more thing," Marco said. "Can you keep this on the down-low? We try not to publicize that there's a group of us who aren't following the boys' club rules."

Tammy clutched the card to her chest. "Your secret is safe with me, and so is your name."

"Thank you," Marco said with a nod, then turned and glanced at me before we headed out the door.

We didn't speak until we got in the car.

"Are you sure you can trust her, Marco?" I asked, struck by the full realization of what he'd told her.

"There's no way of knowing for sure, but she was scared, and I had to take a chance."

I was silent for a moment. "You're working to bring the good ol' boys club down—you and your friends."

"We've been workin' on it for a while," he said, rubbing between his eyebrows as if he had a headache. Then he rushed to add, "I didn't keep it a secret from you. I've mentioned things before."

He'd made no secret of the fact that he didn't see eye to eye with a good portion of the department. I knew he'd been held back from promotions because of it. But I'd had no idea that he was actively trying to change things.

"Don't be mad, Carly," he pleaded. "And please don't take this as a sign that you can't trust me."

I turned to him, shaking my head. "You're like me."

A soft smile filled his eyes. "Tryin' to right injustices, big and small?"

"My injustices are really big, Marco," I whispered, getting teary-eyed.

"I know, and we're workin' our way up to it, remember?"

Wyatt had said the very same thing to me, not so long ago, and I couldn't help but think about how that had turned out. "I want to believe you, Marco, and I do, but…"

"You've been burned," he said softly. "I know, and you have no idea how much I want to beat the shit out of every man who has hurt you, Wyatt included. But that won't prove anything other than I have a temper and know how to use my fists. The only way I know how to prove that you can trust me is to be a man of my word." He took a breath. "I know that's gonna take time, but I'm a patient man. I'm willing to earn it."

I turned away from him and studied the front doors of the building, knowing he was talking about so much more than earning my trust.

"So what do you want to do next?" I asked.

"I think we should see May," he said.

"Agreed."

He pulled out his cell phone and placed a call. "Hey, Darren, it's Marco. Can you look up an address for me?...Thanks, it's for May Agnew, maiden name May McMurphy. Last known address is in Piedmont, before that Ewing...yeah, give me a call. I'm in Ewing, so I'll be able to pick up."

After he disconnected the call, I asked, "Now what?"

"Let's do a drive-by of Mitzi's house."

"Won't it be a problem if Paul sees you?" I asked.

"We'll be fine," he said, "but maybe drive down the opposite side of the street so it's less likely I'll be noticed."

"Or we could not drive by it at all," I said. "What do we hope to accomplish?"

"I don't know," Marco said. "Just call it following my gut."

I flexed my hands on the steering wheel, my insides still twisting with anxiety from my newfound knowledge.

What if Paul found out what Marco and his friends were doing? Would he try to kill them to keep them quiet? The thought terrified me, but hiding from this wouldn't make it go away. If Paul was connected to Heather's death—

and we could prove it—it might help Marco dismantle the corruption in the department.

I had to trust that he knew what he was doing. "Okay."

I started the car and headed to the Conrads' house, on the other side of town. Just like we'd discussed, I drove down the opposite side of the street past their place.

"Two cars in the driveway," Marco said. "But his sheriff cruiser's not here."

"There were two cars yesterday, but no sheriff SUV," I said. "And Paul was waiting for me when I got there. I didn't even make it to the door."

"He must have left his patrol vehicle at the station, and Mitzi must have told him you were comin' after Abby's call."

"Agreed," I said as I kept driving past the house, going just under the speed limit.

"Drive around the block again," Marco said. "Only this time, pull to the side of the road about thirty feet down the block. We'll watch the house for a bit."

I made a loop and parked at the end of the street, the Conrads' house in view.

"What are we looking for?" I asked.

"Any signs of activity. To see who comes and goes."

"What if no one comes or goes?" I asked.

"Then we'll have a long, boring afternoon," he said with a teasing grin. When I seemed unimpressed, he added, "We're just watching until I get that address from Darren."

"Shouldn't he have it by now?"

"He might be busy. It's an unofficial request."

We sat in silence for a couple of minutes before Marco's cell phone rang.

"Darren," he said, picking it up and taking the call. He grinned at me as he wrote an address on the paper bag that had held our lunch. He hung up, and I was about to start the car to head to Piedmont, but Marco leaned forward. "We have activity."

I turned my attention back to Mitzi's house, surprised to see Mitzi walking out of the house with an infant car seat in her hands. A toddler followed behind her.

"Where's Paul?" I asked as she strapped her children into the backseat of an old green sedan.

"Good question," Marco said.

Mitzi got behind the wheel of her car and backed out, then drove past us to the end of the street.

"What do you want to do?" I asked, starting the engine.

"Start driving slowly to the end of the street so I can see which direction she's going."

"Okay." I did as he instructed, pulling away from the curb and heading the opposite direction as Marco angled the rearview mirror so he could watch her without turning around.

"She turned west," he said. "Turn right at the end of the street and we'll follow her."

"Okay." I turned right at the corner, and Marco told me to keep going a couple of blocks until the road dead-ended onto a busier street.

"Turn right here," he said. "Hopefully we'll catch up to her soon."

"How do you know she isn't going the other way?" I asked as I followed his instruction.

"Because she would've taken a different turn out of her neighborhood if she wanted to go that way."

I sped up a little, and I was relieved when I saw a green sedan farther ahead. "I see her."

"Let's hang back a bit," Marco said. "She's probably spooked, and we don't want to freak her out with those babies in the car."

"Good idea."

We followed her for nearly a mile until she turned into a grocery store parking lot.

"She's going grocery shopping?" I asked.

"Paul probably figures anyone who wants to talk to her will come to the house."

"Are we going to try to talk to her at the grocery store?" I asked.

"You bet your ass we are," Marco said with a grin.

I pulled into a parking spot, and we watched Mitzi struggle to get both kids out of the car and into the shopping cart she'd retrieved from a cart corral.

Watching her struggle irked me. "If Paul's home, then why on earth isn't he watching the kids so she can do her shopping?"

"You're seriously askin' that?" Marco asked. "You think a man like Paul is willin' to take care of his own kids?"

"I guess you have a point."

Marco reached for his door handle as Mitzi started to roll her cart toward the store. "Let's go."

I grabbed his arm. "Marco, wait. You can't talk to her. What if she connects you to this somehow? It could put you in danger with Paul and the corrupt deputies. Besides, if he's half as bad as he seems to be, I suspect she won't want to talk to anyone who works in the department."

He hesitated, thinking on it, then made a face. "Dammit."

"I can handle it," I said softly.

"I know you can. I just don't like you doin' it alone. Not with someone like Paul Conrad involved."

"But he's not here," I insisted. "At least let me try."

He drew a deep breath, then blew it out with a worried look. "Okay, but if you feel unsafe, then come straight here."

"Okay," I said as I reached for the recorder in my purse and checked the tape. "Dammit. I forgot the tape's almost full, and I don't want to record over my conversations with Emily or Thelma."

His eyes lit up. "Hey, your phone works here, right?"

I grabbed my cell phone out of my purse. "Three bars."

"Okay," he said, taking the recorder, "call me and tuck your phone into your purse. If you leave it on top, with nothing over it, I should be able to listen to your conversation. I can tape the conversation on mine."

"Oh! Good idea." I called his number, and as soon as he answered, I put the phone in my bag.

"Let's do this," I said, reaching for the door handle.

"Carly," Marco said, worry in his voice. "Be careful."

I nodded, then headed inside, feeling like a bundle of nerves as I tried to figure out how to approach her. Once I got into the store, I saw her turn down an aisle, so I grabbed a shopping cart and headed to the aisle next to hers, which turned out to be the chips and snacks aisle. I grabbed a box of crackers and some microwave popcorn, and then feigned serious interest in the ingredients listed on a jar of almonds. I snuck glances out of the corner of my eye, watching for her to turn down my aisle. After several seconds, I set down the jar and picked up a random can, still watching.

Had she skipped this aisle? Maybe she was picking up a short list of things instead of doing her weekly shopping.

Time to go search for her.

I set the can back on the shelf and started pushing my cart to the end of the aisle when a cart with an infant car seat locked onto the front turned down the aisle.

Mitzi.

She stopped to grab two different flavors of Doritos, so I pushed my cart toward hers, my heart beating frantically against my ribs. I really hoped I didn't blow this.

"Excuse me," I said as I stopped next to her. "Mitzi?"

Her eyes flew wide, giving me a panicked look that suggested she was on the verge of grabbing the kids and running.

I held up my hands. "I'm sorry. I didn't mean to scare you. I'm Carly. Abby told you I needed to talk to you."

Her head swiveled from side to side as though looking to see if we had any witnesses. "Why are you talkin' to me here?"

"I came by your house yesterday and your husband didn't want me to talk to you."

"I shouldn't be talkin' to you now." She glanced down at the little boy in her cart, who looked up at me with a curious scrutiny. Her gaze jerked up to mine. "Are you followin' me?"

"Mitzi, I only want to ask you a few questions about Heather."

Tears filled her eyes. "I don't want to talk about her in front of my kids."

"Okay," I said in a sympathetic tone. "I understand. Can we meet somewhere else?"

"I don't know." She looked doubtful. "Maybe when Paul leaves for work."

"Do you want me to come to your house?"

She shook her head with panic in her eyes. "No! The neighbors will tell him."

I slid between the carts until I was standing on the other side of her, away from her cart and her son's listening ears, and whispered, "Mitzi, do you need help?"

Tears slid down her cheeks. "You need to go."

"Okay," I said, "I will, but I'm worried about you. I can help you if you need it."

Her back stiffened, and she swiped her cheeks with the back of her hand. "I'm fine. Maybe we can talk about it next week when things die down."

"It can't wait until next week," I said. "I can walk with you while you shop, and we can talk in code if you like. So we don't scare your son."

The look on her face suggested she was about to shoot me down, but to my surprise, she nodded. "Okay."

She started down the aisle, and I said, "I'm going to just leave my cart here and walk with you."

"Okay."

"Were you and *her* close before she left?" I asked.

Her mouth twisted wistfully. "I thought so, but lookin' back, I don't know that she could be friends with people. Paul says she was a user, and even though he's guilty of a lot of things, he knows how to read people."

"Did Paul know her?" I asked.

"I don't think so. I didn't know him through our friends."

"But *you* knew him back then."

Her cheeks pinkened. "Not before she left, but we met soon afterward."

"How *did* you meet?"

She grimaced and leaned closer, lowering her voice. "Paul pulled me over for speedin', even though I wasn't, and made me get out of the car. He said he was goin' to let me off with a warnin', but only if I gave him my phone number."

I gasped. "Are you kiddin' me?"

A smile lifted the corner of her lips. "He told me that he'd seen me around town before and didn't know how else to approach me."

"And you said this was after Heather left?"

"About six months after." She leaned in further, her voice hardly more than a whisper. "He was married, but I didn't know it at the time."

"Did he take you to the Mountain View Lodge?" I asked.

She looked taken aback by my question, so I was surprised when she said, "No. He'd always come to my house. I always thought it was strange that we didn't go to his place, but he always had an excuse. Then the one time we went there, his wife found us." She sniffed. "Lookin' back, I think he planned it that way."

What a first-class asshole. But she clearly wasn't ready to talk about that yet, at least not to me, so I veered back to the subject at hand.

"Was Heather upset when Wyatt didn't propose at Christmas?"

She rolled her eyes. "Boy, was she. She'd been countin' on it. She'd already asked me and Abby to be her maids of honor."

"Really?" I said. "I didn't think she and Abby were close at that point."

"That's the sad thing. They weren't. But Abby came home over her Christmas break, and Heather asked us both then. When she told us that Wyatt hadn't proposed like she'd planned, I told her not to worry. He'd come around. And then he did, only Bart wouldn't give Wyatt the tavern or any piece of his inheritance, and Heather was fit to be tied. I tried to tell her that any woman in town would kill to have

Wyatt Drummond for a husband, with or without the money, but she said she wanted more."

"So she set him up to get arrested?"

Guilt filled her eyes. "I don't know for sure, but I've suspected."

"Do you know if Heather had another boyfriend after the arrest?"

"She met someone at the salon. She was always pretty vague about him. One night she got super drunk and admitted he was married. But it fizzled out, because the next thing I knew, she was askin' me to arrange a going-away party for her. She seemed excited about her plan to leave, even if she kept it close to her chest. I have to confess that part of me was happy she was goin'."

"But you threw her a going-away party anyway?"

"Yeah," she said with a sniff. "I'd just lost my job at the Mountain View Lodge after snatchin' a key and lettin' Heather use a room to meet her guy from the salon. They'd taken to meeting there, I guess, but she was running short on money and she seemed desperate when she asked me for a room that night."

What if she wasn't meeting the salon guy? What if she'd been meeting Paul? Or what if they were one and the same? It would fit with the timeline Tammy had given us. Although Tammy hadn't recognized the picture of Heather, she'd likely seen her in the dark. For all I knew, she'd been wearing a hat or her hair had been up. "And you have no idea who he was?"

"No. I tried to pry it out of her, and she would only tell me that he was a forty-three-year-old banker having a midlife crisis. She'd hoped he'd be her next ticket to livin' high on the hog."

313

Had Heather told her the truth? If so, that would definitely strike Paul out as her boyfriend. I'd guess him to be in his late thirties, early forties now.

"Do you know if she left Wyatt a note saying she was pregnant the day of her going-away party?"

"Yeah," she said with a frown. "Said she did it as a joke—one last way to get Wyatt. But I didn't know about it until after he left the party. I'd overheard them arguing in the room."

"Did you think she was *really* leaving town?" I asked.

"She acted so excited about it, but it was hard to imagine she'd just go. I knew five thousand was much less than she'd hoped for. I figured she still had something going. A plan to get more money. She admitted as much to me before the party. Said she might not have to leave after all if it worked out." She sighed. "But something changed. After the party, she collapsed on the sofa and said she was tired of it all. She just wanted to leave and get a fresh start. And for the longest time, I thought that was exactly what she'd done."

"Who else was in the room when she said it?"

"May. She really didn't want to see Heather go." She cast me a strange sidelong look.

"You want to tell me something else."

"It seems wrong to say it. Especially since Heather's dead."

"I won't say who told me," I assured her.

"It's not a fact, more like a suspicion."

"I understand," I said, "and I'll treat it as such."

She stopped pushing her cart and lowered her voice. "It's just that I got the feelin' May had an unhealthy attachment to Heather. She was furious with Heather when she said she was leavin'. Seemed invested in gettin' Heather to stick around and beat the Drummonds."

"When you say unhealthy obsession...?"

"I think she was in love with her."

I stared at Mitzi for several seconds. "Do you think Heather knew?"

She started to say something and stopped, cringing a little, and then said in a whisper, "I suspect May was Heather's *boyfriend*."

"Really?"

"The more I've thought about it, the more it fits. They started gettin' close, closer than Heather and me. And Abby was gone most of the time, so May took her place."

"So you think she made up the salon boyfriend?"

"Oh, I think she had him for a week or so, but then she started talking about her 'boyfriend' differently. Sweeter. Calling him 'Peep.' I wouldn't be surprised if she went from the salon guy to May and just kept up the ruse as a cover."

"How did May react at the party when Heather said she was really going to leave?"

"She started cryin', and the two of them talked outside by Heather's car for about ten minutes before they both left."

"In separate cars?" I asked.

She nodded. "Yeah."

"Abby said you'd told her Wyatt showed up drunk to the party, and that he and Heather had sex in the bedroom."

She was silent for a moment. "Really? I don't remember tellin' her that, but to be honest, when we finally talked and compared notes about everything, I was pretty drunk myself."

"How did May behave after Heather left?"

315

"She was really depressed for quite some time. Until she started datin' Tater."

Was it just sadness because Heather had left, or had May struggled with a guilty conscience?

A shadow crossed in front of us, and I glanced up to see Paul Conrad standing in front of Mitzi's cart. His face was an ugly mask of fury.

"Paul," Mitzi said, shaking with fear.

"I thought I told you to stay away from my wife," he growled, his hands fisted at his sides.

"I just had a few questions," I said.

"About that bitch Heather?" He took a step closer, his jaw clenched. "Wyatt Drummond did the world a favor when he killed her. And there's absolutely *nothin'* you need to be talkin' to my wife about."

I saw Marco out of the corner of my eye, about to rush toward us, but Paul couldn't see him—he'd turned to face his wife. Keeping my hand low, I motioned for Marco to stop. The last thing I wanted was for Paul to know Marco was working with me.

"Did you plan this, Mitzi?"

"No," she said, shaking her head violently.

"She didn't know," I insisted, my voice shaking. I couldn't let Paul hurt her because I'd ambushed her. "I came here to do some grocery shopping, and when I saw her, I decided to see if she'd talk to me."

His brow rose. "You were stalkin' her?" Some of his anger seemed to fade. "You realize that's a crime? I should place you under arrest."

Fear made my legs weak. I had no doubt he would follow through. And as soon as an arrest photo was taken, my father's people would begin to circle in. "Like I said, I saw her while I was here shopping. I wasn't stalking her. You must know that Drum doesn't have a grocery store. It was just a coincidence."

"If you were shoppin'," he said in a smartass tone, "then where's your cart?"

"Carly," Marco said, rounding the corner, pushing a cart with several items tossed inside. "There you are. Why did you take off like that?" He turned and feigned astonishment, as if only realizing Paul was standing there, then extended his hand, surprise lighting up his eyes. His reaction was so genuine, I almost believed it myself. "Hey, Paul. I didn't know you knew my girlfriend."

Paul motioned toward me. "You need to keep a better handle on your girlfriend, Roland. She's harassin' my wife."

Marco hesitated, and I knew he was struggling with whether to defend my honor. But the last thing he wanted to do, rightfully so, was draw negative attention from one of the cops he was trying to topple. My pride could handle Marco berating me in front of Paul Conrad. I refused to put Marco in any more danger.

"I'm sorry, Marco," I said in a meek tone, lowering my gaze. "I know you said to stay away from Mitzi, but I really wanted to talk to her, so I slipped away to ask her some questions."

Marco was silent for a moment, and I glanced up to see his stunned expression.

Paul laughed. "Gotta keep these women in line, ain't that right, Roland?"

I shot Marco a look that said *play along*.

He clenched his hands at his sides. "Yeah. Gotta show them their place."

Paul clamped Marco's shoulder. "Well, I'll let you get to it, while I deal with my own wife."

"She didn't do anything," I pleaded. "She told me to leave her alone."

His gaze hardened. "Believe it or not, the world doesn't revolve around you, Carly Moore." Paul shot a dark look to Marco. "If you don't get her under control, then you should find yourself another girlfriend."

"Carly," Marco barked, reaching out to me.

His tone scared me, but not because I was scared of him. It only proved how frightened he was for me.

I went to him and he wrapped a hand around my wrist, dragging me toward the exit, leaving the cart abandoned at the end of the aisle.

He didn't let go until he opened the passenger door of my car. I climbed inside, and he slammed the door shut behind me before stomping around to the driver's side. He didn't say a word as he pulled out of the parking lot, but he held the steering wheel in a death grip, his entire body so tightly wound I could bounce a quarter off it. He cast me a glance, fury in his eyes, and then made a pronouncement that caught me by surprise.

"You're done."

Chapter Twenty-Four

I blinked at him in confusion. "What do you mean I'm done?"

"Do you really believe you can keep lookin' into this?" he said, pulling into a strip mall parking lot. He took several deep breaths before he turned to me. "He just threatened your life, Carly!"

I'd figured as much, but I hadn't known for sure. "So we just *stop*?"

"*We* don't stop," he said, his voice shaking. "*You* stop. Clearin' Wyatt's name isn't worth you gettin' a target on your back with the sheriff's department."

"You're going to do this without me?" I asked in disbelief.

"I'm a damn deputy sheriff, Carly!" he shouted. "It's my job to do this!"

"No," I said, trying to control my anger, "it's not, because the good ol' boys club is keeping you under their thumb. They won't let you become a detective no matter how good you are."

"Well, they might now," he said in a dry tone, shaking his head as he stared out the windshield. "Why did you do that?"

I had no idea what he was talking about. "You're gonna have to be more specific."

His eyes burned with anger when he turned back to me. "Why would you make me look like such an utter asshole?"

I gaped at him. "I was trying to protect you, Marco!"

"At what price, Carly? Now he thinks I'm just like him."

"I'm sorry," I said, "but I'd do it again if I thought it would help you. If we'd stood up to him in there, you'd be in his sights too. You would have caught his attention, and then you'd never be able to bring them down from the inside." When I could see I hadn't swayed him, I added, "Marco, it's no different than being undercover. You played a role."

"I'm not like them, Carly, and it makes me physically ill to let anyone think otherwise. To let that man believe I'd treat you that way." His voice broke. "My character has to *mean* something. I have to *stand* for something."

Tears stung my eyes. "I'm sorry." I reached my hand up to his cheek and looked deep into his eyes. "You are a good man, Marco Roland. You *are* a man of character, and I'm lucky to know you."

His hand covered mine and some of his anger faded. "I nearly shit my pants when I saw Conrad walk into the store."

I pulled my hand away and sat back in my seat. "Do you think he knew we were there? Do you think he followed us?"

His shoulders tensed. "No. I think he was legit stalking his wife."

"I hope he doesn't hurt her because of me." My stomach churned at the thought of what might have happened after we walked out of the store.

"I tried to get to you as fast as I could. I had no idea what he would do to you."

I didn't want to open that can of worms again, so I focused on what I'd found out before Paul showed up. "Could you hear our conversation?"

"Yeah," he said, sitting back. Then, as if he'd only just realized the seat was adjusted for someone significantly shorter than him, he grunted and reached for the handle in front of the seat to push it farther away from the steering wheel. "She offered up some interesting facts. Like Conrad using his badge to threaten her with a ticket if she didn't go out with him."

I leaned my head against the headrest and sighed. "Yeah, I caught that too. He's a real peach."

"It's interesting that she thought Heather might have been in a relationship with May."

"Agreed," I said. "Do you think Mitzi was just tryin' to throw us off her husband?"

"You tell me," Marco said, leaning his head back too. "You were the one watching her."

"I think she was sharing what she saw as a possible truth."

Marco cracked a grin and turned his head to the side to look at me. "Good critical thinkin' skills."

I gave him a lopsided grin, but it collapsed. "We need to talk to May."

He sighed, the light leaving his eyes. "Carly."

"He already knows I wanted to ask Mitzi about Heather. It's not like I can hide the fact that I'm interested.

Besides, I think he was pissed because I ignored his orders, not necessarily because I'm poking around."

"So you think he's clear of this mess?" he asked in surprise.

"He's not our only person of interest. If May loved Heather to the point of obsession, and Heather refused to stay, she had motivation to kill her. Even if it was accidental."

"So who was Heather meetin' at the Mountain View Lodge?" Marco asked. "If it was the older boyfriend, it seems like he would have been able to pay. I doubt they'd need help from Mitzi."

"What if it wasn't a romantic rendezvous? What if Heather was meeting with her co-conspirator?"

His mouth twisted to the side. "I don't know. They could have met literally anywhere to discuss their plans. But you can get arrested for indecent exposure if you fornicate in a public place."

I laughed. "Fornicate?"

"There are lots of things besides sex that could be construed as a sexual encounter," he scoffed.

"True..." Sitting this close to Marco, thinking about "fornication" and all the things that would fit that definition, made my cheeks flush.

"We need to be careful about how we're fitting the puzzle pieces together," he said, oblivious to my thoughts. "It's good to make speculations, but not at the expense of ignorin' other possibilities."

He had a point. "So what theories do we currently have?"

"We can't overlook the possibility that Wyatt might have done it," he said. "He had plenty of motive and no alibi after he left the party."

"True." Even though I didn't believe he'd killed her, I'd acknowledge that he was a suspect until he was proven otherwise.

"We have the theory that Heather was working with someone to extort money from the Drummonds. And below that theory, we have a couple of possible co-conspirators. May. Paul Conrad, although we know of no connection between him and Heather other than our speculation that she might have been working with someone in law enforcement. From what I heard of your conversation with Mitzi, she doesn't think Paul and Heather knew each other."

"Yeah," I admitted grudgingly. "If we take her at her word."

"Another theory is that the Drummonds had her killed."

"But that one seems less likely," I said. "Based on the fact they didn't move her body when construction began. Sure, Bart could frame Bingham for it, but I'm not sure he'd risk bringing attention down on himself."

"True," Marco said, "but we also need to consider *where* her body was buried. Who had access to that land?"

"Plus, the person who did it would have to be strong enough to carry Heather's body to her grave site. May would've needed help."

"Unless her grave site was also the site of her execution, and the murderer simply had her walk there," Marco countered.

"And what happened to Heather's car?"

Marco grimaced. "Is it a coincidence that her body was found on the disputed land of a man who allegedly runs a chop shop?"

"So Bingham's a suspect again?" I asked.

"Don't rule anything out until you can prove it," Marco said.

"I need to ask Bingham if someone sold him her car."

"You really want to ask him that?" he asked in disbelief.

"Admitting to chopping up her car isn't the same as saying he killed her. It just means he has a good head for business."

"Now you're justifyin' his career choices?" he asked in disbelief.

"No," I said, insulted. "But the man is the alleged owner of a chop shop, an illegal venture. Do you really think he has a moral compass when it comes to where he gets his cars? Don't you think he just takes whatever he's brought?"

"I don't like the idea of you goin' back out there," he said, staring out the windshield again.

"Does that mean you're not gonna give me trouble about continuing our investigation?" I asked.

He was quiet for several seconds. "I still think you should sit this out. Paul Conrad has obviously done his homework on you. He used your full name."

"Because I introduced myself to him when I went to their house."

"Still… he's looked into you." He paused. "If you keep pressing, he could have you arrested for interferin' with an active investigation. Plus, you know he's going to pump Mitzi for what you two talked about. Who's to say that she won't tell him everything? If she does, it won't be hard for him to guess we'll go see May next." He turned his head to face me again. "He could have a deputy watchin' to see if we show up."

"I'm not stopping, Marco. I'm still lookin' into this."

"Then maybe we should call May instead of going to her house in Piedmont. See if she can give us some answers over the phone. We won't be able to see her body language, so it's far from ideal, but—"

"You want to do it anyway," I finished.

"Yeah. I kind of do."

"Okay, but I should be the one to call her." I pulled my phone out of my purse, realizing my call with Marco had been disconnected. "Did your friend Darren give you a phone number too? Because if not, I can try to get it out of Molly." Although I doubted Molly would be very cooperative.

"I can save you from that conversation. He had her number too."

I punched the numbers into my phone as he read them off. "So just keep the questions on the fact-gathering side, then turn more personal if it feels appropriate?"

The corner of his mouth tipped up. "Look at you becomin' a pro at this."

"I'm gonna take that as a yes."

His mood turned serious. "Yeah."

I took a deep, centering breath, then pressed send and put the call on speaker.

A woman answered with "Hello?" on the third ring, and my heart leapt into my throat.

"May?"

"Yes…" she said hesitantly.

"Hi, this is Carly Moore. I'm sure you don't know me, but—"

"Oh, I know who you are. You work with Molly at Max's Tavern. She says you've been nice to her."

I had to wonder what she'd have to say about me after our shift today.

"Molly's been great," I said.

"But I know why you're callin'," she said, her tone becoming more cautious. "Mitzi called me yesterday."

Marco's eyes widened.

"Honestly," she continued, "I've been expectin' to hear from you. I'll tell you what I know."

"Thank you," I said. "We can meet somewhere, if you'd prefer. It's just not a good idea to meet at your house."

"Paul found out, didn't he?" she asked wearily.

"I tried to be careful, so I found Mitzi at the grocery store and asked her some questions there."

"That was a good idea," she said, "because Paul is likely watchin' her every move. He's a controllin' bastard."

"He showed up at the grocery store."

"Not surprisin'. He likes to check up on her to make sure she's behavin', like she's a toddler who's incapable of taking care of herself." She paused before adding, "I'd rather talk on the phone."

"That's fine," I said. "I understand. She told me that you became close to Heather after the Christmas before she left town."

"You mean was murdered," May said, her voice tight. "She was murdered."

"Yes," I conceded. "She was, but most people only just discovered that."

"Most people?" she asked in surprise.

"Obviously the murderer knew."

"Yeah. I guess that's true."

I looked up at Marco to get his take on her reaction, but his face was expressionless.

I shifted sideways in my seat, holding the phone over the console. "May, when I heard about people who hung out with Heather, your name kept coming up."

"I'm not surprised."

"I know she was hoping Wyatt would propose to her that Christmas. Did she ever talk about it?"

"Wyatt didn't deserve her," she said, "or at least she had me convinced of that. Heather was really good at convincin' people she was right. I bought the whole 'no one understands me like you do' story hook, line, and sinker. She convinced me that we were best friends and she couldn't handle her life without me. She called or showed up at my doorstep at all hours of the day and night, expecting me to give her my undivided attention. And I did, because she had this gravitational pull that had a way of grabbing hold of you and not letting go. But it seemed like a kryptonite kind of thing. The more time you spent with her, the more the need to be with her increased, but if she drew back, you started to realize you didn't need her after all. That being around her was emotionally draining."

"May," I said, "are you speaking of your own personal experience or in general?"

A moment of silence, then she said, "Both. We've all discussed it over the past nine years. Compared our experiences with her. We think she'd have had hundreds of followers if she'd started a cult."

I cast a glance to Marco again and he mouthed, *You're doing great.*

Marco had been right about body language. I wish I could see her facial expressions. If she was nervous or reluctant, I couldn't tell. "When you say *we*, who do you mean?"

"Mitzi, Dick...Anna Faith."

"What about Abby Atwood?"

"I met her that Christmas when she came home from vet school. She wasn't back for very long because she had a job back in Knoxville. She was goin' to vet school and needed the money for her rent. I remember Heather was furious about her leavin'."

"Why?"

"Because Heather hadn't dismissed her. She dared to leave Heather's orbit without permission."

"Do you know who Heather's boyfriend was?"

"Everyone knows Wyatt was her boyfriend," she said slowly, like someone speaking to a child.

Was she insinuating there hadn't been another boyfriend? But if Mitzi was right and May and Heather had been sleeping together, I could understand why she'd dodge the question.

Ask about Wyatt and the tavern, Marco mouthed.

I nodded, then asked, "Did Heather tell you much about Wyatt's plan to ask Bart Drummond for the tavern?"

"She was the one who cooked it up. She manipulated Wyatt for weeks until he gave his father an ultimatum— either give him the tavern or he would walk away from the family. Neither one of them expected Bart to call them on it, which was shortsighted on their part. Bart doesn't let other people control him. Anyone from Drum knows that, but I think Heather had convinced Wyatt that his father had invested too much time and energy in him to just let him go."

"It backfired," I said, "but Heather had a plan B. Or she made one."

May didn't say anything for several seconds.

I decided to lie. "We already know that Heather set Wyatt up with the DUI and breaking and entering arrest."

She was silent for longer this time, and when she spoke, her voice was shaky. "Who told you that?"

Not an admission, but it was pretty far from a denial. "Someone who chooses to stay anonymous." It didn't take a genius to see I was scaring her off, so I switched gears. "The Drummonds paid Heather to leave town, but Mitzi told me that Heather said she had an idea for getting a bigger payout. Do you know what it was?"

"No, she wouldn't tell me, but she insinuated she was workin' with someone. While I wasn't crazy about the idea of manipulatin' people, I was happy she might be stayin', even if she was defyin' Bart Drummond. She said she wasn't afraid of him."

I took a moment, knowing that I needed to be careful with my next question. "How would you describe your relationship with Heather?"

"I know what Mitzi likely told you, but it ain't true," she said angrily. "I like men. Did I love her? Yeah, in a messed-up way, because she made me alienate everyone else in my life until there was only her, but we weren't like that."

"May, I don't care about your sexual preferences," I assured her. "Who you chose to love or sleep with is your own business. I'm just making sure I have all the puzzle pieces so I can figure out what really happened."

"Okay," she said in a softer tone. "Heather hooked up with some guy from her salon, but it only lasted a few weeks. He broke it off after his wife found out, but she didn't tell a lot of people because she didn't want anyone to know he'd rejected her. She was talkin' about someone called Peep by then. Most people thought it was some cute name for the salon guy, but I think it was the person helpin' her. Maybe even someone she'd found to get drugs for her."

"Drugs?" I asked in surprise. Marco looked just as shocked.

May was silent for a moment. "I heard her talkin' to someone on the phone, telling them she needed enough to make a grown man unconscious so she could put him in a compromisin' position without wakin' him up."

"She was planning to set up Wyatt?" I asked.

"No," she said slowly. "I think she was talkin' about Bart. She pulled me aside before she left the party. Said she'd been plannin' to blackmail Bart, but she was startin' to chicken out. She'd decided it would be best if she really did leave. I begged her to stay, but she said I'd been a good friend and then told me goodbye."

"Did she tell you where she was going?" I asked.

"No, but her aunt Hilde told me that she got a postcard from Tulsa. I was so hurt she hadn't sent me one, but then I realized it was just Heather being Heather. Honestly, Hilde was lucky to hear from her at all." She paused. "Although I guess maybe she didn't."

"Do you have any idea who she was talkin' to about the drugs?" I asked.

"No, but I know she was meetin' someone at the Mountain View Lodge. She got Mitzi fired over it."

"Do you know how many times?"

"Two. Maybe three...that I know about. But I think some of those times were with the guy from the salon."

"Do you know if she knew Paul Conrad?"

"She never mentioned him," May said. "But I wouldn't be surprised if she did. She mentioned getting stopped by a sheriff's deputy who didn't give her a ticket. In retrospect, I wouldn't be surprised if it was Paul pulling her over to get her number."

Marco's jaw tightened.

"Do you know when that happened?" I asked. "Before Christmas? Before Wyatt's arrest?"

"Definitely after Christmas... I think before his arrest."

"Did she ever say anything to make you think she might have been working with someone in the sheriff's department to get money from Wyatt or his family?"

She gasped. "I never considered that, but if that's what she was doin', she never mentioned him."

"Do you think she might have kept it a secret? She was meeting *someone* at the motel."

She paused, considering it, then said, "I don't know. But if it was him and she changed her mind, I can definitely see Paul gettin' pissed enough to beat and kill her."

I glanced at Marco, who sat stock-still.

"If you think of anything else," I said, "could you please leave me a message at Max's Tavern?"

"Yeah, I will."

"Thank you, May."

"Yeah."

She hung up, and I set my phone down and looked at Marco, my stomach tight. "She was lookin' for drugs."

"You think Hank was involved?"

"Maybe not directly," I said, "but he was still dealin' back then. I suspect she would have gone to him, or he would have heard something." Had she told him the drugs were for Bart? Had he thought they were for Wyatt?

"To be fair," Marco said in an even voice, "I don't think he was the only source around. Especially when meth came into play."

"But she wouldn't have asked for meth for that, and we know that he had pills, which could have included sedatives."

Marco didn't respond.

I swallowed, fighting my rising dread. "We need to talk to him," I said in a flat voice. "Now."

I only hoped I could handle what he had to tell me.

Chapter
Twenty-Five

There's no sense jumpin' to conclusions," Marco said as he headed toward Drum. "You don't know it was him."

"And I hope to God it wasn't." I turned to Marco. "But what if it *was*?"

He gave it a moment's thought. "Then I guess you need to determine your line in the sand, your deal breaker. We know it's unlikely he killed her, but he may have supplied her with the drugs. Especially if he believed she was going to use them on Bart. You know Hank's committed crimes, Carly. I think you need to figure out which crimes cross the line for you. Have you given it any thought?"

"Not as much as I probably should have," I admitted. "This shouldn't even be a question. A year ago, I would have been horrified by all of it."

"But a year ago, you were a different person. You've lived in Drum long enough to know the people here are desperate and unhappy enough to look for escape. Whether it's goin' to Max's Tavern three or four nights a week to shoot the shit, hanging out at a friend's house to get drunk, or finding an even deeper escape with drugs. I'm not condoning people gettin' high, but to combat that kind of behavior, you need to understand why they do it. And in this case, I think you need to look at Hank's motivation for dealin'."

"I thought you were a sheriff's deputy," I said in a dry tone as I sat on my hands to quell my anxiety. "Aren't you supposed to arrest criminals?"

"Unless you fix the disease and not just the symptoms, the cancer's just gonna keep spreadin'," he said with his eyes on the road.

"You sound like more of a social worker than a deputy."

"Some days I feel like a social worker. There's a lot of poverty and lack of education, both of which are contributors to crime. I'm no fan of Bart Drummond, but I sure hope his resort helps people around here get good jobs." He shot me a glance. "Now let's go over the rest of your conversation with May. Did you think she was on the up and up?"

"You didn't?" I asked.

"It was hard to tell over the phone. I would have preferred to talk in person, but it seemed too risky."

"Do you really think Paul would have May watched? Surely that would mean he was guilty of something. Do you think we have enough evidence to confirm that he was helpin' Heather?"

"We don't have *any* evidence. All we have are interviews, and there's nothing directly tying him to Heather," Marco said, "yet in my gut, I feel like he's part of this."

"Plus, his ex-wife confirmed that he met his girlfriends at the Mountain View Lodge, and we know Heather was meeting someone there."

"That doesn't necessarily mean anything," Marco said. "I'm sure a lot of cheatin' spouses go there."

"Classy," I said in disgust.

He turned to look at me for a second before turning back to the road. "There's nothin' classy about cheatin'. It's dark and dirty, and it tears lives apart."

"Why do I feel like you have personal experience with this?" I asked softly.

"My mother cheated on my father."

"I'm so sorry, Marco."

He shrugged. "She had a few boyfriends off and on over the years. I didn't realize what was going on until I was in high school. My father is a dreamer, and I can see how my pragmatic mother became disillusioned with him and found what she was lookin' for with someone else...and then another someone else. Mom said they stayed together for me, but it only made me feel like we'd all lived a lie. All along, she'd been cheating on him, and he knew about it. She'd end one and tell him never again. Then a year or two later, she'd start makin' excuses about goin' to help her cousin with her baby, or some such errand, when she was really meetin' her latest fling."

He paused before continuing. "I didn't put it together at the time. I only saw my father shrink deeper and deeper into his shell. And then my senior year of high school, she thought she found *the one*, the guy who was worth breakin' the cycle for, so she left. Left Dad. Left Drum. Left me the day after I graduated from high school. That guy didn't work out, but then she found her current husband. And Dad...he was left with nothing. He lost his house in the divorce. He'd lost his wife years ago. When I went away to college, he moved to Knoxville to be close to me, but I didn't visit him much because I blamed him for what happened. Since then, he's retreated from the world even more. Now he lives in a one-bedroom apartment with a couple of cats."

"You lost something too, Marco. That counts for something. That matters."

His mouth quirked to the side as he kept his eyes on the road. "I was a grown man. They both figured I was fine on my own. Neither one of them thought to make sure I was okay. Mom was too excited to be free, and Dad just wanted to ignore everything."

Which explained why he hadn't called either one of them to help him after he was shot. Why he hadn't allowed anyone to help him. He believed he couldn't count on anyone. Funny how I'd come to believe that too.

And yet here we were, counting on each other.

"When I first found out," he continued, "I thought, *Well, that's no surprise. Dad ignored her for years. Of course she went looking for love and comfort somewhere else.* But over the last few months, I've spent a lot of time thinkin' about their relationship and what I remember. And now I wonder if I got it all wrong. What if my father retreated deeper and deeper into his work because she broke his heart over and over again? What if I broke his heart when I chose her over him?"

"Oh, Marco…"

"I think it affected me more than I realized," he said, his voice thick with emotion. "It's made it hard for me to trust people. To accept them at face value. My parents seemed to have a decent relationship, and my mom always acted like a good, caring person. I realize that's why I've had trouble committing."

Was that why he hadn't been seeing women over the last few months? Because he'd been trying to sort out his feelings? Had I gotten everything wrong?

"My mother had an affair," I said. I'd told Marco that Randall Blakely wasn't my biological father, but I'd given him no details, and he hadn't pressed. "I have no idea why she cheated. When I was young, my parents always seemed so happy and in love. They were trying to have another baby and couldn't get pregnant, so they went to an infertility specialist. I don't know for certain, but I suspect they found out my father was sterile...and that's how he knew I wasn't his biological child."

I ran a hand over my head. "I was young, only eight or nine, so I only understood bits and pieces of their arguments. It wasn't until I was much older that I put the pieces together. I realized that the accusations my father had hurled at her were about his own brother."

I took a breath. "My uncle left Dallas around the time Mom died. I know he wasn't at the funeral, because I looked for him. He'd always been so nice to me. I don't know if he knew I was his child, but I'd like to think he didn't. That he wouldn't have knowingly left me with a murdering sociopath. But then again, maybe he never left at all. Maybe my father had him killed."

"Carly." Marco's voice sounded strangled.

"But your insight has made me re-examine my past relationships. I've never been in love, not really. The only person I felt comfortable committing to was Jake, because he'd been my best friend for years and I was sure I could trust him."

A new thought struck me.

I was repeating the exact same pattern with Marco.

"What?" he asked, noticing the change in me.

These feelings I'd noticed the past few days, were they my broken psyche's way of finding a relationship? Was I doomed to repeat every mistake of my past?

"What are you thinkin', Carly?" he asked, his question laced with anxiety.

No, I might be repeating my previous pattern, but Marco wasn't Jake. And there was no reason we couldn't remain friends. Just friends. These feelings I was experiencing couldn't be trusted—they'd tarnish and tear something beautiful. Not that Marco was looking for that anyway. His relationship patterns were just as messed up as mine.

I gave him a smile. "I'm thinkin' that you're a very insightful man. More so than most. I'm thinkin' that I have terrible judgment in men, so I'm very lucky to have stumbled into a friendship with such a good one," I said with a laugh.

"I'm not Jake," Marco said. "And I'm not Wyatt."

"No," I said. "You're Marco, and I need you in my life. I don't want to screw that up."

He glanced at me, his eyes filled with sadness. "I need you too, and I would never do anything to risk losing you." He shifted his gaze back to the road. "When I said I'll never lie to you, I meant it. No secrets. I won't give you a reason to distrust me."

"Thank you." I reached over and took his hand, squeezing tight. Some days Marco felt like my lifeline. But there was an implicit danger in relying on anyone that much—if I lost him, *this*, where would I be?

I didn't want to go to that dark place again, not when we still had so much to accomplish. "I think we should talk to Bingham after we see Hank. I want to ask him about Heather's car." I frowned. "Do we know what make and model car she drove?"

"I'm pretty sure that Wyatt was driving her car when he was arrested. I have a copy of the police report at home, but I think it was a late model Chevy Cavalier."

"Do we need to go by and get the report?" I asked.

"You could always ask Wyatt."

"I don't know where he's holed up. Only Lula does, although if he's hidin' on Bingham's land, we could look for him there."

"It's up to you," he said. "We can go see Hank, then drop by my house for the report. But I'm not convinced it's a good idea to visit Bingham unannounced. He tolerated an appointment. He might not be so keen on a drop-by visit." Before I could respond, he added, "I'm not sure how much mileage you'll have with the Lula card, so don't be countin' on that."

I had been.

"Let's just see what Hank says before we decide what to do next," I said. He agreed, and we spent the rest of the ride rehashing everything Mitzi and May had told me, not coming up with any new leads. For the first time since I'd started poking into this mess, I didn't have any new threads to pull. I wasn't sure what to do next other than talk to Hank and possibly Bingham and try to find out the identity of the banker. It felt like a dead end, although I refused to think of it that way. Whatever his flaws, Wyatt didn't deserve to suffer for a crime someone else had committed.

Hank was sitting in front of his TV, watching one of the afternoon talk shows he seemed to love so much. He glanced up at me in surprise. "What are you doin' home? I thought you were workin' all day." He braced his hands on the arms of his recliner and sat up straighter when he saw Marco was with me. "Max didn't fire you again, did he?"

"No," I said, walking around the sofa and sitting on the end next to him. "Nothing like that. I took the afternoon off to look into Heather's murder."

He glanced up at Marco, who still stood by the door. "You here as a deputy sheriff or Carly's friend?"

"Carly's friend, sir," he said respectfully.

Hank motioned him over. "Then come sit down. No need for you to guard the door."

Marco cracked a grin as he moved around the sofa to sit next to me.

"I take it you have questions," Hank said, clicking off the TV.

"Yeah."

He held his hands wide. "Ask away. I'll tell you what I can."

"When you were running your drug kingdom," I said, "you said you limited it to pot and pills. I remember you saying you didn't have the stomach to cook meth and that oxy was too hard to get. But surely people wanted those things."

He made a face. "True, but they had to leave the area to get it. I didn't tolerate anyone sellin' that nonsense while I was in charge."

"What about roofies?" Marco asked. "Or ecstasy?"

Hank's eyes narrowed.

"I don't give a shit about what you did in the past, Hank," Marco said. "There's plenty of bad shit floatin' around now to keep us busy."

Hank didn't look entirely convinced.

"Did the people buying drugs ever come straight to you?" I asked.

"No. Wouldn't bring the business into my home, and they had no reason to come to my place of business. There were too many other men around for anyone to get through."

Did Hank used to have bodyguards? Or maybe they were just his workers who acted tough. Either way, I had to wonder where they were now. Working for Bingham?

"So if someone was lookin' for something specific, would they go to their dealer and ask?" I said.

"This might go a little faster if you just spit out what you're tryin' to ask," Hank said gruffly.

The man I knew was all bark and no bite when it came to me, although I'd seen him shoot a man dead while protecting me, so I knew he was capable of violence.

"The Drummonds paid Heather five thousand dollars to leave, but she was cooking up a plan to stay. A witness claims to have overheard her talking on the phone, telling the other person she needed drugs to put someone in a compromising position without them waking up."

"And you think she called me?" he asked, his brow raised.

"Maybe. Or made the request of someone who could ask you. Do you remember anyone making any unusual requests around the time Heather left?"

"That question presumes I knew Heather, let alone gave a shit about her leavin' town. So the short answer is I have no idea what kind of requests were made back then. I didn't usually handle the little things. I was the big picture guy."

"Did you sell roofies, Hank?" I asked quietly.

He turned to me, his expression blank. "I sold a wide variety of pills, but I never sold anything that could be used to take someone's control from them."

I nodded in relief.

"If someone wanted something like that around here back then," I said, "where would they go?"

"I'm fairly certain Bingham was sellin' the things I wouldn't. I know he sells them now."

Further proof that Bingham was slime, but it also confirmed that I did need to talk to him again.

"Who was she hopin' to incapacitate?" he asked.

"We're not sure," I said. "Maybe Bart."

He released a short laugh. "If she'd come to me with *that* purpose in mind, I would have tracked the drugs down myself. Bingham had a horse in the race if she asked him. He very much wanted to eliminate Drummond. Still does."

Crap. That put Bingham back on the suspect list, but if he wasn't responsible, we still needed to figure out where Heather's car had gone.

"If someone was wanting to dump a car," I said, "what would be the best place to do it?"

"You can't be serious," he scoffed.

"Other than Bingham's chop shop."

He slowly shook his head. "Not many places. You'd want a deep lake or mine shaft, but you're not going to find either of those around here. You'd have to head up into Kentucky."

I cast a glance over my shoulder to Marco.

"You're gonna go talk to Bingham, ain't ya?" Hank asked. When I didn't respond, he said, "He ain't gonna like you askin' questions that insinuate he's a murderer."

Didn't I know it. "I'll be careful."

"Do you want me to go with you?" Hank asked.

I reached over and placed my hand over his. "No, Hank. That's not necessary."

He shot Marco a glare. "Are you gonna go with her?"

Marco hesitated, and I said, "No. He can't. Bingham will never talk if he's with me."

"I don't like the idea of you talkin' to him alone."

"I think she should wait to talk to him," Marco agreed. "Maybe you should actually go to work tonight. We can get Bingham to come to the tavern. Where I can keep an eye on him."

Hank nodded. "And remind him that I've claimed her as kin."

They were starting to irritate me. "I'm perfectly capable of making my own decisions."

"We're only tryin' to protect you," Hank said.

Giving him a soft smile, I leaned over and kissed his cheek. "I love you too, Hank." Then I stood. "What did you eat for lunch?"

Ginger had worked at the tavern today, which meant he'd probably been alone since yesterday afternoon.

"Some of that leftover casserole."

Guilt washed through me. If left to his own devices for too long, he was bound to eat something unhealthy.

"I'm going to make you dinner before I go."

"You don't need to do that," he said, sounding irritated. "I'll just have some of that leftover chicken in the fridge."

"Okay." I hated the thought of him being alone for so long, and then I remembered the kittens. "Hank, what do you think about cats?"

He made a face. "I don't have many thoughts one way or the other."

"Do you like them?"

He frowned. "I don't dislike them."

"What would you say if I asked if we could adopt a kitten?"

He studied me for a moment. "I'd tell you to go ahead and get it, so long as it's an outside cat."

I wasn't sure I liked the thought of that, but he hadn't said no.

His face softened. "You want a cat, girl? Get yourself a cat. I'll learn to live with it."

It didn't seem like the right time to mention I'd committed to two. I'd hoped he would be more excited about the idea, but I reminded myself that I couldn't expect Hank to get all giddy over a kitten. With any luck at all, the kittens would grow on him.

"Thanks, Hank."

"Are you comin' home tonight?" he asked.

"No," Marco said. "She's stayin' with me again."

I started to protest that I could make my own decisions, but I suspected he was worried after Paul Conrad's threat. And rightly so. While I knew Hank could protect me, it would be better if Marco defended me instead of an ex-drug lord. I could only imagine what kind of trouble Hank would be in if he shot a deputy sheriff.

"Yeah," I said, "I'm stayin' with Marco."

Hank gave me a long look, then nodded. "Just keep me posted so I know you're okay."

I headed into my room and packed a bag with a couple of days' worth of clothes, then added some toiletries from the bathroom.

"You headed to see Bingham after you leave?" Hank asked as I walked out of the bathroom.

"I don't know," I said.

"Call and leave me updates," he said. "Even if it's late. I'll just let the machine get it."

"Hank," I protested, "there's no sense in—"

"I'll call you, sir," Marco said. "I'll make sure that you know she's okay."

Hank nodded to him as I headed out the door to my car, leaving Marco to follow me.

"Are you really not goin' to see Bingham?" Marco asked as he got into the passenger side while I got in on the driver's side.

"Not yet," I said as I adjusted the seat.

Relief swept over Marco's face.

"Hank's right. He won't appreciate it if it sounds like I'm accusing him of anything," I said, "so I need to think this through." But time was not on our side, and the decision made me anxious.

Marco was quiet for a moment, then said, "We can try to find out who worked at the Mountain View Lodge. Maybe one of them remembers seeing Heather and whoever she was meeting." He shrugged. "It's also a long shot, and it'll be harder since it won't be an official sheriff's department inquiry."

"Have we hit a dead end?" I asked, my stomach sinking. What would happen to Wyatt if we failed to clear his name?

"No. We still have Heather's salon boyfriend. We still have Bingham. We just need to figure out the safest way for you to talk to him." He shot me a grin. "Bingham, not the salon guy." He turned his attention back to the road. "Before we do anything else, I need to swing by my house so I can get Wyatt's police report and pick up my police cruiser and a uniform. I'm covering a shift for a friend tonight, so I can go straight from the tavern to work. Since my Explorer's still in the tavern parking lot, maybe you can help me get it home later."

"Marco," I said, worry filling my head. "Of course I'll help you, but you should have taken a nap instead of running around the county with me."

"No," he said with a finality that told me it wasn't up for debate. "I wouldn't have been able to sleep knowin' you were lookin' into this alone." He cracked a grin. "Besides, you know how much I love investigatin'. But I really do think you should go to work tonight. Max and Tiny will keep you safe when I leave for my shift, and I'll hang out in Max's office and make some calls to further our own investigation while I wait for my shift to start. We can have Max call Lula and ask her to send Bingham to talk to you."

Bingham would likely be furious at that, but maybe Lula could convince him that it was to save her brother. "Okay. But I want to keep my car too. You can follow me into town. I feel anxious not having it."

We had a plan for the next few hours, but I couldn't shake the feeling that the last few grains of sand were drifting down in the hourglass.

Chapter
Twenty-Six

We didn't take long at his house, and Marco followed me into town. We walked in through the back door of the tavern at around four thirty. Marco headed to Max's office to get started on his research, and I made my way into the dining room.

Max's eyes widened when he saw me sliding behind the bar in my work shirt.

"I thought you were investigatin'," he said in a lowered voice.

"We decided to take a moment to figure out our next move," I said. "Plus, I need to talk to Bingham, and I was hoping you could call Lula and ask her to send him in."

His eyes darkened. "Are you sure you really want to do that?"

"I need to talk to him, and this seems like the safest way."

He scowled but didn't respond.

"Have you heard from Wyatt?"

A worried look filled his eyes. "No."

"Lula knows where he is—I'm certain of it. You can always ask her." I took a beat, considering his call with Lula. "In fact, when you talk to her, can you tell her to have him call me again? I have more questions that might help move things along."

"I'll see what I can do." His brow furrowed. "My mother called and left you a message."

"Really? What did she say?"

"She said to tell you the check was cashed two weeks later in Tulsa." His eyes narrowed. "Is she talkin' about the check they gave to Heather?"

"Yeah," I said. "That's very helpful."

"When did you talk to my mother?" he asked. He looked a little put out, but I saw some fear behind it. What was he afraid of?

I was about to answer him, but a customer was flagging him, and he reluctantly moved down to the other end of the bar to get the man a refill.

Ruth hadn't shown up yet, but Ginger had left for the day. Molly was working the dining room. She didn't seem as angry as earlier, but she ignored me as I scanned the dining room to gauge how busy we were.

Ruth came in a little before five, and I filled her in on how well Ginger had done, leaving out the part about Molly's sass. A rush of construction workers came in soon afterward, and the three of us were busy for the next two hours. Marco even came out and helped Max behind the bar, giving me a small shake of his head as if to say he didn't have anything yet. The men seemed to be in good moods and ordered plenty of beers to go with their dinners, then stayed after they finished to watch a Braves game on TV.

Business slowed down a bit, most of the families heading home, and Max sent Molly home at around seven thirty. Not long afterward, I noticed Marco talking on the phone behind the bar. A few minutes later, he headed me off as I was walking to the bar to get refills.

"I think I have a lead on someone who worked at the lodge," he said. "David Binion. I'm going to head over and talk to him."

"Do you think it's a good idea to go alone?" I asked with a frown.

He smiled. "I'll be fine. I'll need to start my shift when I get done, so I'll be in my sheriff's uniform. It's just a janitor for the lodge. Nothin' to worry about."

I nodded, still nervous. Marco had already been shot for me—I didn't want him endangering himself. "Okay. Just be careful, okay?"

His mouth lifted into a small smile. "I will. Do you feel okay with me leavin'? Bingham hasn't shown up yet."

"I'm fine. Max and Tiny are both here. If he drops by, they'll keep him in line. Don't worry about me."

I took the drinks back to the table, keeping an eye on Marco as he said something to Max and then left. I was going to be a nervous wreck until he came back.

About twenty minutes later, Bingham walked through the door with three of his friends. He searched me out, our gazes locking, and I knew he'd gotten the message.

His friends sat at a table, but he slid into an empty booth, still intent on me.

My stomach churned as I walked over to him with my chin lifted, then slid into the seat opposite him.

"So now you're usin' go-betweens to get me to do your biddin' instead of comin' to me outright." He cocked his head and gave me a pensive look. "That doesn't sound like you."

"I didn't think it would be wise to show up at your front door again. My questions are a lot blunter than usual."

A mock smile cracked his lips, and he held out his hand. "Try me."

I glanced around to see who might be close enough to overhear. His friends sat at the table next to us, and the booth behind me was empty. "Were you selling roofies nine years ago?"

His brow shot up. Then he looked amused. "You lookin' to buy some?"

"I said nine years ago."

"Maybe."

I resisted the urge to roll my eyes. "Let's say nine years ago I was lookin' for some—would I go directly to you to ask for it?"

He was silent for a moment. "If someone thought I could procure something, they would come to me."

"Shortly before Heather left town, did someone ask for some?"

Surprise filled his eyes. "You think someone roofied her?"

"No," I said, "I think she was trying to get some to use on someone else."

He leaned his forearm on the table, clearly intrigued. "Who do you think she was wantin' to drug?"

"First, you can tell me if someone came to you askin' for it."

He grinned. "No one came askin' for anything like that."

"How can you be certain?"

"Because it's never happened. Period."

"What about oxy?"

He sat back. "Well, that's another story, but if she was lookin' for something to make a person compliant, oxy wouldn't be the way to go. Now who was she wantin' to drug?"

"I'm not sure, but it looks like she was hoping to put Bart in a compromising position."

"You don't say."

"Obviously it didn't happen," I said.

"Or maybe Bart caught her in the act and left her murder to Carson Purdy, who buried her on my property to implicate me if she ever turned up." He held out a hand again. "See? That wasn't so hard, and it would have kicked up a lot less dirt if you'd come to me directly."

I wasn't so sure about that, but I wasn't going to call him on it. "There's something else."

He made a small shift in his posture. "Shoot."

"I know this was a long time ago, but did anyone bring you a Chevy Cavalier around that time? It would have been someone looking to dispose of a car."

He didn't say anything.

"I realize it was a long time ago."

"Who do you plan on sharin' this information with?"

"I can keep it between the two of us."

He pursed his lips and cast a glance toward the bar, a small grin lighting up his eyes. "Your boss ain't too happy with me talkin' to you."

Sure enough, Max was glaring at him, looking like he was prepared to vault over the counter to intervene. He'd known Bingham was coming, so this had to be for show.

"As long as you behave yourself, you'll be fine. Now tell me what you know."

Sucking in a deep breath, he leaned forward, resting both forearms on the table. "Between you and me, I got a phone call from a woman. She had a car that needed to disappear and wanted to know if I could help. I said sure, bring it by, but she wanted me to come get it instead. I told her that I didn't work that way. So she said she wanted to drop it off, no contact. I said fine, leave it at the end of my driveway, and I'll send a guy to drive it in the rest of the way. I asked her how she wanted me to pay her, and after some hemming and hawing, she finally said she'd pass on the money, even though I could tell she really wanted to take it."

A woman?

"I'll admit, I was damn curious, but I didn't ask questions. I figured it was a disgruntled wife tryin' to get back at her soon-to-be ex by gettin' rid of his prized Corvette or something. Only it turned out to be a Chevy Cavalier. A real piece of shit at that."

"And the time frame aligns with when she left?" I asked.

"It's been a few years, but I'd say yes. Plus, that's not how I do things, so it stuck out." He leaned even closer, his eyes alight with the knowledge he was about to share. "There's one more thing that I found odd."

"Okay…"

"When I said I was curious, I was curious enough that I hid in the woods, waiting to see who dropped off the car. It was definitely a woman, but it was the person who picked her up that caught my attention."

"Who?"

"Someone in a deputy sheriff car."

I sat back in my seat. Had it been Paul? Had he recruited a woman to help him dispose of the car? Was it Mitzi?

He released a short laugh. "Awww…the wheels are turnin'…"

"This has been more helpful than you know."

"Then my work here is done." He started to slide out of his seat.

"Why were you so agreeable?" I asked.

He paused at the end of the seat. "Lula. She likes you, and you gave her the benefit of the doubt. And she's fond of that fool brother of hers." He stood. "But don't push your luck in the future...unless it involves Bart Drummond. When it comes to him, I'm all ears."

He and his men left, and I hurried over to Max to assure him I was fine.

"Well?" Max grunted when I reached him behind the bar.

"He had some really valuable information. Something that could ultimately save Wyatt's ass."

Max looked skeptical, but I didn't have time to pacify him. I had a lot of thinking to do.

While I served my tables, I spent the next five minutes mulling over what Bingham had told me, trying to make it fit with what I knew.

A woman.

The top two women who came to mind were May and Mitzi, and May seemed the most likely suspect. By her own admission, she'd been upset about Heather leaving. Maybe she'd killed her in the heat of the moment. But who had Heather been talking to about getting drugs? Or had May made that up?

Would Mitzi answer more questions if I called her? Paul would likely be at work.

I headed over to the bar again. "Max, I need to make a phone call."

He gave me a wary look. "Okay."

"I'll be right back."

I grabbed my purse out of the back room and found Mitzi's phone number, then went into the office, my heart beating like a jackrabbit while I placed the call.

"Hello?" a tentative female voice answered.

"Mitzi?" I asked. "This is Carly."

"What do you want?" she demanded.

Obviously she blamed me for what had happened with Paul. "I had a few more questions."

"I'm not talkin' to you," she said. "You got me into all kinds of trouble."

"I'm sorry. I didn't want that to happen, but an innocent man is about to be arrested."

"Maybe he's not so innocent," she snapped.

"You and I both know that's not true," I said. Then, deciding to take a chance, I said, "We both know who killed her."

She was silent for a moment. "What do you know?"

Oh. Crap. "I know Paul helped dispose of her car."

"You can't prove that," she said.

Wait. Was Mitzi the killer? What if I'd gotten it wrong, and Paul had helped her dispose of the body rather than the other way around?

"How'd you come up with Tulsa?" I asked. "She never told anyone she was going there. Did you drive all the way there to mail that postcard to Hilde?"

"What are you talkin' about?" she asked. Then she gasped. "You think *I* killed her?"

"If you didn't, how'd you know about Tulsa?"

"Abby told me."

"How did she know? She wasn't even here at the time."

"I don't know. Probably on a phone call. I know Abby was really stressed about money at the time and didn't come back home much."

"Did Paul take a trip to Tulsa around the time Heather disappeared?" We'd already asked his ex-wife, but it seemed worthwhile asking Mitzi too.

"I don't know. I didn't even know him then, but I don't think he's ever been to Oklahoma."

If Paul hadn't mailed it, then it must have been done by his female accomplice.

Oh. God. Only one other person had known about Tulsa.

"I didn't kill her. I swear," she said, starting to cry. "The only thing I'm guilty of is calling the sheriff about Wyatt. I felt terrible about doin' it, but Heather convinced me that I might be savin' someone's life. Only the more I think about it…he was so drunk I suspect she drove him to the state park and then told the officer he'd been drivin'."

So she really *had* set him up.

"Why didn't you tell anyone?" I asked.

"I don't know," she said, starting to sob. "But Paul's on the warpath and out for blood right now, so if I were you, I'd lay low."

"Thanks for the warning," I said, but she'd already hung up.

I sat in the chair for several seconds, trying to figure out what to do with the two bombshells that had been dropped in my lap. I couldn't do much with the confession, but I *could* talk to Abby. Did I call and confront her? It didn't seem like a good idea. If she really had killed Heather, then she might run. I needed to wait for Marco.

But it turned out I couldn't. Much to my surprise, Abby was sitting at the bar when I emerged from the back.

What was she doing here?

I walked behind the bar and ignored Max as I sidled up in front of her. "Hey, Abby," I said, trying to sound breezy but not entirely sure I was pulling it off. "This is a surprise."

"I was just wondering whether you'd had a chance to talk to Mitzi."

"I did," I said, resting a hand on the edge of the counter.

"Did she tell you anything that proved helpful?"

"She did," I said. "She said that you were the one who told her about Tulsa."

Her face paled, her usual confidence draining away.

"I know Paul helped you," I said. "I have proof."

She looked like she was about to be sick.

"I guess the question is why," I said. "And how."

She glanced around the room. "I'll tell you, but not here."

"Then I guess you can tell the sheriff," I said.

Her eyes flew wide. "Carly. Please! Just let me explain what happened."

"I'm not going anywhere with you alone. I'm not stupid."

Her eyes flooded with tears. "Carly. I need your help. I'll tell you everything, but not here."

"Then how about Max's office in the back?"

She hesitated. "Okay."

I walked over to Max and whispered, "Abby's part of this, and she's going to tell me how in your office. I need you to get Tiny to watch the back door in case she decides to do something stupid."

His eyes flew wide and he whisper-shouted, "What the hell, Carly? Why are you goin' back there at all?"

"Because she knows what happened and we have no guarantee she'll tell the sheriff. Especially since a deputy was involved. This might be the only way to clear Wyatt's name."

I started to walk past him, but he stopped me. "Do you have your recorder?"

"No," I said, cursing my luck. "The tape was full and Marco took it."

Turning to his side, he dug his cell phone out of his pocket. He tapped on the screen and then dropped it into my apron pocket. "To record the conversation."

"Thanks," I said, looking for Abby and finding her at the end of the bar. Had she seen Max give me his phone?

"Back this way," I said when I reached her. I led her back to Max's office and motioned for her to sit in Max's chair while I took a seat on the guest chair.

"I'd like to shut the door," she said.

"That's not happening," I said. "But I assure you that we won't be disturbed."

She didn't answer, just twisted her hands in her lap.

"You were in town the night of Heather's going-away party?" I asked. "Why didn't you go?"

"We both agreed it would be better that way."

"You couldn't be tied to it if everyone thought you were in Knoxville. You came back to help Heather drug Bart so she could blackmail him."

She nodded, refusing to meet my gaze.

Now the drugs made sense. "She asked you to get a drug to put him out."

"I didn't want any part of it at first," she said, tears falling into her lap. "But Heather convinced me the payout would be worth it. She knew how desperate I was. I was behind on my rent, my next tuition payment was loomin', and I had a trip to Tulsa with my class."

"Which is why the postcard came from Tulsa."

She nodded.

"But she changed her mind," I said. "And you freaked out because you still needed the money."

"I was pissed, and truth be told, I was a little drunk. We were supposed to meet at the overlook and then go see Bart at his house. He thought Heather was coming to renegotiate, but we planned to drug him with a horse tranquilizer in his office and get photos of him with Heather, in the nude of course."

"Of course," I murmured.

"When she showed up, I was sitting on the hood of my car, staring out at the overlook, holding that stupid syringe full of ketamine as I tried to talk myself out of doing it. She sat down beside me and told me that after all the planning we had done, she'd changed her mind, and she was leaving after all, which was all kinds of ironic, since she'd kept needlin' me about not chickenin' out. She started callin' me Peep."

She shook her head and sniffed. "I was pissed. She'd treated me like a yo-yo for years. Hot and cold, but I always came runnin' back. So I shouted at her, telling her what a selfish bitch she'd been. I said I was done. She was furious and slapped me. We had a little shoving match, and the next thing I knew, she'd been stabbed in the belly and the plunger had been pushed down."

"So you're saying you accidently injected her?"

She nodded. "I panicked. It was a dose intended for a man a lot bigger than her. Plus, I'd stolen the drug—I'd be kicked out of vet school if they found out. So I'll admit that I stayed out there with her for a bit while I tried to figure out what to do. I decided I'd take her to the sheriff's office in Ewing and dump her off at the front steps."

"So what happened?"

"I took her car, figuring I'd hide it somewhere and find a way to get back to mine. I shoved her in the backseat and was halfway between Drum and Ewing when I saw flashing red lights behind me. I was being pulled over by a sheriff's deputy. I was terrified, but then he told me to get out of the car and move to the back. I was praying he wouldn't see Heather. So much so that I let him feel me up and do other things I'm not proud of. He seemed pretty satisfied with himself. He insisted on walkin' me back to my door, like he was a fuckin' gentleman. I tried to stop him, but he saw Heather."

Marco had to figure out a way to get that predator off the streets.

Abby continued, "He recognized her right away, not that I was surprised. It's a small town, and Heather was the kind of person people noticed. I told him that she'd overdosed and I was on my way to Ewing to get help. He checked her pulse and told me she'd never make it to the hospital in time. He knew she'd been paid off by the Drummonds, and he said he wouldn't turn me in if I gave him half the money. I didn't know what to say, but I *did* know she still had the check. I was scared enough that I agreed.

I followed him out to a section of Bingham land. He told me that Todd Bingham's daddy had buried tons of bodies out here. What was one more? Then he took the keys and left, tellin' me he was gonna get a shovel. I nearly left on foot while he was gone. Heather was dead by the time we parked there, and I was scared and upset. He was a sheriff's deputy. Could I really disobey and leave? When he came back, he had two shovels. He made me help him, but the ground was hard, and we only got the hole about three feet deep. He tossed her into the grave like a bag of potatoes, then made me cover her body with dirt. Told me it was a good reminder not to use drugs. Then he made me drive her car to his house and park it in his garage, and he took me back to my car. He told me to cash the check, and when I came back with his share of the money, we'd deal with the car together."

"And you deposited the money in Tulsa?"

"I had her debit card and I knew her PIN. So I used her debit card to buy several money orders while I was there. If anyone was looking into her disappearance, they'd see a footprint in Tulsa."

"Why didn't you turn him in?" But as soon as the words left my mouth, I knew it was a ridiculous question.

"He was a sheriff's deputy. Who would believe me over him?" She huffed. "It's one of life's awful coincidences that he ended up marrying Mitzi."

I wasn't so sure about that. Although Mitzi still claimed to have met Paul after Heather "left," she'd been involved with Heather's attempt to set up Wyatt, and I suspected Paul might have played a role too. Maybe he'd pulled the car over that night because he'd recognized it as Heather's, because he'd wanted or expected something from her. Still, I didn't feel any need to share that with Abby. I didn't want to destroy their friendship. I knew manipulative men, and they'd both been in the clutches of one.

I just nodded. "Would you be willing to testify against him now?"

Her face paled. "I could lose my vet license."

"An innocent man might go to jail, Abby. And Paul Conrad will just keep screwing people over. Literally." How many women had he accosted over the years?

"I can't!" she exclaimed in a panic.

"I know you're scared, but Marco will help you. And Detective White. She handled my case after Carson Purdy tried to kill me. She's not corrupt. I'm sure she'll be fair."

Her body was shaking and her face and neck were splotchy. "I don't want to go to jail. I don't want to blow up my life."

"I know," I said, "and maybe you won't have to. You didn't intentionally hurt her, and you tried to get her help."

"But I stole the drugs, and I didn't tell Paul she was in the car when he pulled me over."

"I don't know how the authorities will handle any of that," I said. "And I know you're scared, but aren't you tired of keeping this secret?"

She nodded. "Yes." Tears fell down her cheeks. "I am."

"Then let me help you figure out a way to do the right thing. Maybe you should talk to an attorney first and they can negotiate terms for your statement."

She nodded again.

"Okay. That's good," I said. "You stay in here, and I'll go see if I can get Marco to drop by."

I left her in the office and went back out to the dining room, heading straight for Max and handing him his phone. "I got a confession of sorts. Be sure to save the recording."

He took the phone and tapped the screen. "While you were back there, a sheriff's deputy dropped by and said to give this to you."

He pointed to a sealed envelope on the counter. I opened it and read the message, not surprised to see a typed note.

If you want to see Wyatt Drummond again, bring Abby out to Wyatt's hiding place. We'll both be waiting. And don't bring anyone else.

You have until ten, and then I start making Wyatt into a pincushion.

"What did the deputy look like?" I asked as I lowered the paper.

"I don't know. Medium height. Sandy-brown hair with a bit of a receding hairline."

Paul.

"How long ago did he drop it by?"

"Right after you went into the back."

Which meant he'd followed Abby.

"And you haven't heard from Marco?" I asked.

"No. What's goin' on?" He snatched the letter from my hand and quickly scanned it. "What the fuck?" His face lifted, his eyes wild. "He has Wyatt? Why does he want Abby?"

"She knows things, and he wants to clean up his mess. He wants to get rid of me and Abby along with Wyatt." But why hadn't he asked for Marco? Had our show at the supermarket been that convincing? Or did Paul know something I didn't? Had someone hurt Marco?

My heart hammering, I checked the time on the wall clock. Nine thirty. We didn't have much time, especially since I didn't have the first idea where Wyatt was.

Chapter
Twenty-Seven

I need to find Wyatt. Call Lula. *Now.*"

Guilt washed over his face.

"You already know," I said in a dry voice. The Drummond siblings and their damn secrets. And the answer suddenly occurred to me too. "He's out at Lula's shack, isn't he?"

He looked surprised.

"I figured he wasn't out at Bingham's place, so Lula's shack seemed like a logical next choice. Especially since hardly anyone knows about your newfound familial status. Do you know where David Binion lives?"

"Out toward Lula's place."

"I need to find him. Can you give me directions?"

"I want to go with you when you get Wyatt."

"Then meet us there," I said. "But make sure to ask Tiny to guard Abby."

"I'm not lettin' you go off by yourself!" he protested.

"I'm not going alone. I'm finding Marco."

"Why does the sheriff's deputy want Abby?"

"She knows how Heather died."

His mouth dropped open. "Is she willin' to testify to that?"

"I think so, but she wants an attorney to work out a plea bargain in case they want to charge her with something. We can't let anything happen to her."

"Tiny will protect her and make sure she stays put."

I nodded. "After I find Marco, we'll meet you at the entrance to Lula's property."

"Don't go in there alone, Carly."

"I won't. All I have is pepper spray. I'm not stupid enough to think I can take him on. We *need* Marco."

And I also needed to know he was okay. Mitzi had said Paul was out for blood. Oh, God. What if he'd hurt Marco? I tried to quell my rising anxiety. Letting my imagination take over wouldn't help anything. I needed to be calm and logical.

Max nodded as though reassuring himself. "Okay."

I convinced Abby to stay with Tiny, telling her that Max, Marco, and I were going to take care of Paul. Then I headed out to my car, once again cursing the lack of cell phone reception out here. When this was all said and done, I was getting us both long-range walkie-talkies.

Following Max's directions, I headed to David Binion's house, but Marco's cruiser wasn't out front and I hadn't passed a deputy sheriff on the road. Where was he?

I parked and walked up to the house. The front door opened before I could get to the porch.

"What do you want?" bellowed a man holding a shotgun.

I held my hands up. "I'm looking for Marco Roland."

"He ain't here. He left about fifteen minutes ago."

"Do you have any idea where he went?"

"Do I look like his daddy?" the man shouted, then slammed the door shut.

I could only imagine how well their interview had gone.

But now I had no idea what to do. I had no way of locating Marco, and it was now 9:50. I'd told Max to meet us outside of Lula's property so I headed in that direction.

I was on the county road that led to Lula's shack when I saw flashing red lights in my rearview mirror.

Adrenaline rushed through my blood, making me light-headed, and I struggled with what to do. Stop? Keep going? This was a pretty deserted stretch of road. Other than Max, no one would be coming along to help me anytime soon, not that anyone was liable to stop to help a woman who'd been stopped by a sheriff's deputy.

I pulled over, hoping and praying it wasn't Paul, but I wasn't surprised when I saw him approaching the rear of my car.

"Come out with your hands up," he called out.

I grabbed the pepper spray out of my purse and shoved it into my front jeans pocket before I got out and held up my hands.

"Where's Abby?" he asked, shining a flashlight in my eyes to blind me.

"I don't know."

"That's bullshit," he said, shoving me against the side of the car and patting me down. He found my pepper spray and slowly reached into my pocket to pull it out, lingering just a little too long for comfort. "Such a bad girl, Carly Moore. Now you have to be punished."

"Somehow I think you'd take any excuse to punish me. That's what men like you do, right? Punish women for ridiculous things so you can feel like a man?"

I wasn't prepared for the punch to the side of my head and it hurt like hell, but I realized that he'd held back when he hit me. This was about teaching me that he was in charge, not knocking me out. Nevertheless, my knees buckled, and he shoved me face-first on the asphalt as he zip-tied my arms behind my back, then roughly hauled me to my feet.

"Not so tough now, are you?" he asked with a laugh.

I didn't answer, mostly because I was trying to figure out what to do. Max would be here any minute. Would he be able to help me or would I get him killed?

Paul shoved me into the backseat of his deputy vehicle, and the next thing I knew, he was pulling away from the shoulder and in the direction of Lula's property.

When her lane appeared, he turned onto her property, and I started praying that Wyatt really was there because I didn't want to face this man alone.

He parked his car in front of the house, next to Wyatt's truck, then turned off the engine, but I noticed he left his keys in the ignition. He got out and opened the back door, giving me a dark leer. "Time to see your ex."

He wrenched me out of the car and led me to the dilapidated shack that looked even more run-down than it had back in December.

Paul's foot fell through a floorboard on the porch, and he released his hold on me while he bent down to pry his foot loose.

I took off running.

"You won't get far," he called out after me, sounding amused, "and the longer it takes me to catch you, the harsher your punishment will be."

I heard banging and shouting in the cabin, and for a moment I almost reconsidered my decision to escape—should I try to save Wyatt?—but every instinct I possessed told me to run, which was slowed down by the dark night and my arms bound behind my back.

Sure enough, Paul caught up with me as I reached the edge of the trees.

"Where do you think you're goin'?" He gave me a push and I fell, my shoulder colliding with a tree trunk before I hit the ground.

Laughing, he bent over and grabbed my ankles, then began to drag me out of the trees, the twigs and fallen branches scraping my stomach and face.

When I was out on clear ground, he rolled me over and loomed over me. "Don't be difficult."

But in placing himself over me, he gave me the perfect opening to deliver a vicious kick to his groin, and I didn't waste any time. He bent over and I sat up, struggling to get to my feet. I'd just made it to my knees when he straightened and kicked my arm, pushing me over.

"You bitch!" he shouted. "You want to play rough? I can play rough." And he gave me a couple more kicks to prove his point.

He grabbed my arm and jerked me up. "Think you're clever, huh? We'll see how clever you are inside."

Dragging me back to the shack, he cursed me every which way to Sunday, then shoved me through the front door.

I stumbled and fell to my knees, feeling slightly panicked that the room was so dark. I couldn't see Wyatt, or anything else for that matter.

"Drummond, you let the lantern go out," Paul said as he shut the door. Using the flashlight on his phone, he walked over to a table and lit a kerosene lantern, casting an amused glance toward the back corner of the room.

I looked that way and saw Wyatt was sitting on the floor next to the bed, his ankles bound with a nylon rope, his arms tied behind him.

Paul turned his attention back to me. "You were supposed to bring that bitch Abby with you. Now where is she?"

"She's on her way to the sheriff's department in Ewing," I said. "She's looking for Detective White so she can tell her everything you've done."

"You lie," he spat. "If she was going to turn me in, she would have done it already."

"She's tired of living in fear. You're the reason she came back to Drum, aren't you?"

"It was too easy. All I have to do is threaten to tell on her, and she does my bidding."

"You really are a psychopath, aren't you?" I asked in disgust.

He laughed. "If you think you're insulting me, guess again."

His radio squawked, and I heard Marco's voice. "Where is she?"

Paul grinned, then pushed his radio button. "Out at the overlook."

But as he spoke, I shouted, "Lula's shack!"

"Carly?" Marco's panicked voice cracked over the radio.

Paul gave me another kick, and Wyatt released a guttural sound.

"Where are we supposed to meet?" Marco called out.

Paul pushed me down on the floor and covered my mouth with one hand, reaching for his radio button with the other.

I chomped down on his fingers, hard enough for him to yelp and pull his hand away, and shouted, "Lula's shack!"

Paul turned off his radio and gave me a murderous gaze.

"Leave her alone, Conrad," Wyatt said in a bored tone. "She didn't do anything."

"Bullshit. She's done plenty." He grabbed a length of rope from the table and dragged me over to a support beam. Placing my back against the beam, he wrapped the rope around my chest several times and tied it off, which proved to be difficult since I fought him every step of the way.

"Damn," he grunted. "You're a hellcat." He cast a glance at Wyatt. "You like 'em wild, huh? Or maybe not, since you're not together anymore." He walked toward the door and glanced back at us. "You two have fun."

He shut the door behind him, and we sat in silence for several seconds until we heard his vehicle start. The sound of the engine got fainter as he drove away from the house.

"Are you okay?" Wyatt asked in a concerned tone.

I ached all over, and I was tied to a pole. I was far from all right.

"How did he find you?" I asked.

"I don't know. Maybe he followed me after I drove to Ewing to call you earlier. He drove out here around six in his sheriff's car. I didn't put up a fight, but instead of arrestin' me, he knocked me over the head and tied me up."

"I only found out where you were after he left a note telling me to bring Abby to where you were hiding. Obviously he thought *I* knew."

"Who told you?" he asked.

"Max, but I'd pretty much guessed." I paused. "Do you think Marco heard me?"

"I don't know," he said, sagging against the bed.

"Max knows we're here. He was supposed to wait for me on the county road, but he must have seen my abandoned car. Let's hope Paul doesn't catch him." I told him about Paul pulling me over. "Why not just wait until I pulled down the drive?"

"To make sure you were really alone? To intimidate you? All of the above?"

I would have nodded, but my face throbbed too much.

"Why does he want Abby?"

"She knows the truth about Heather." I paused, glancing at him, and added, "She accidently killed her." I explained what I knew about Heather's plan A (getting him arrested and blackmailing his parents) and B (setting Bart up in the hopes of a payout).

"Conrad was one of the deputies who arrested me," he said. "I wouldn't be surprised if he was part of the initial setup."

"He's a cancer."

"No argument from me," he said. "I'm sorry I dragged you into this. You know he plans to kill us. I suspect he intends to make it look like a murder suicide."

I wasn't surprised, but I felt a new adrenaline rush. "Then we have to get out of here before he comes back."

I'd fought him enough that my ropes weren't terribly tight. I just needed to figure out a way to free my hands. I lifted my butt and threaded my legs through my arms, which was difficult with my chest tied to the pole. When I finally got them free, I started tugging on the rope around my middle, trying to twist my bound hands so the knot was in front of me.

"I'm worried about, Max," I said as I kept fidgeting.

"Max is pretty scrappy. He can take care of himself."

"We haven't heard any gunshots, so I'm going to take that as a good sign." Paul had really tightened the knot, so I was struggling to loosen it. "If Marco heard me, he'll do everything in his power to get here."

Wyatt was silent for a moment. "You can break that zip tie, but first you have to tighten it."

I glanced up at him. "Tighten it? Are you crazy?"

"No. It'll make it easier to break. Tighten it, then lift your arms as high as you can and then swing them down and to the sides, as hard as you can. It should break the lock."

I'd heard it was possible, but I wasn't sure I could do it. I wasn't exceptionally strong.

"You can do this, Carly," he cajoled. "You just tried to fight off a violent man. You can definitely defeat a zip tie."

He was right. What was more, I didn't have much of a choice. I had to do this. I tightened the zip tie with my teeth, then lifted my arms and swung them down with all my strength. To my surprise, the lock flew off, freeing my hands.

"It would have been a hell of a lot easier to do that than untie knots in a cold shed last December," I said as I rubbed my wrists.

"Why were your hands tied?" he asked, his voice sounding strangled.

Crap. I hadn't meant to say that. I started picking at the knots securing me to the pole. "It was while I was looking for Lula."

"Why were your hands tied?" he repeated.

"Do you really want to know, Wyatt?" I asked, starting to get pissed.

His tone equally irritated, he responded, "I asked, didn't I?"

I'd kept this from him for so long. I was tired of carrying this burden. "I started out looking for Lula, but I stirred up enough shit that the people who were out to get her kidnapped Greta, thinking she knew where to find Lula. Since her disappearance had more leads, I started looking for her. Then they kidnapped me."

"What? Who was lookin' for Lula? Bingham?"

"No, Wyatt," I said in disgust, finally getting the knot a little loose. "Bingham saved me, although I had no delusions that he did it to save me. He wanted Lula, especially after I told him she was pregnant."

"So who the hell was it?"

"Are you telling me that you didn't find it odd that the funeral home director who had ties to Carson Purdy died around the time Lula went into hiding?"

He looked shell-shocked. "I…"

"Lula was running drugs for them. That's where she went on most of her trips when she took off. Only she didn't return with their money on her last trip. As you can imagine, they wanted it back."

"You're telling me that Pete Mobley was runnin' a drug ring? That he wasn't used by his employees like the sheriff said?"

"I'm not sure how much authority Mobley had in the running it. He didn't handle the pressure well, which makes me suspect Carson was in charge, but yeah, he and another guy kept it up after Carson died." He continued to stare at me in disbelief. "They wanted their money, Wyatt, and they were willing to do whatever they needed to do to get it."

"Which included kidnapping you out of the back of the tavern," he said in a flat voice.

"He drugged me to get me out. The same drug that killed Hank's daughter."

His face lost color. "Jesus, Carly…"

"He drugged Greta too, but thankfully she didn't react as badly as I did. I'd been talking to Bingham about my search for Lula, giving him updates, and when I was kidnapped, Marco humbled himself to ask Bingham for help. Bingham went to Mobley and found out where his partner,

Shane Jones, was keeping me and Greta. Sure, he did it because he thought Lula was there too, but he saved us nonetheless." I finally got the knot worked loose and pulled the rope free. "I would have died if not for Bingham. Twice over. Because if those drugs hadn't killed me, Shane would have."

I got to my feet and headed to the kitchen to look for a knife or scissors to cut his ropes, but it was the barest kitchen I'd ever seen, and I had to open multiple drawers to find a dull butcher knife. "But Bingham refused to let Marco take me to a hospital, probably because he killed Shane Jones too, and there would be too many questions. He sent a medic to stay with me at Marco's, and they hooked me up to an IV. I was unconscious until Tuesday, and then it took me over a week to recover. So, yes, Bingham saved my life, but it had nothing to do with me being on his payroll."

Wyatt watched me walk toward him, regret in his eyes. "Carly...I'm sorry."

"I really don't want to hear it, Wyatt," I said, my voice tight. "There's no apology that can make up for the way you treated me." Purging that out of my system had been cathartic, but also emotional and exhausting. Plus, I was really starting to feel the places where Paul Conrad's heavy shoe had connected with my ribs.

"Nevertheless, I'm sorry."

Ignoring him, I sawed through the ropes on his legs. He scooted forward a bit, and I worked on his arm restraints, setting the knife on the bed. When he was free, he swung his arms a couple of times, then rubbed them. "Where's your car?"

"Down the county road, but your truck's out front."

"The asshole took the keys."

"Then let's hope he didn't take my keys too. He didn't get them when he stopped me, but he likely stopped and grabbed them when he left."

We headed outside, and I was struck anew by the depth of the darkness. Lula's cabin didn't have electricity, and I had no idea how close her neighbors were. While it took a second for my eyes to adjust, there was no denying the sound we both heard: a car was approaching on the county road.

Chapter
Twenty-Eight

Wyatt snuck a glance at me, studied the lane leading to the county road, and then grabbed my arm. "Come on."

We raced down the steps, moving toward the tree line to the west, away from the creek.

The sound of the vehicle came closer and headlights appeared on the lane. My fear turned to relief when I saw it was a sheriff's SUV. A familiar face was behind the wheel.

"It's Marco," I said, pulling free from Wyatt's hold. "He heard me."

I started to leave the tree line to run to Marco, but a gunshot rang out nearby, shattering the driver's window of the SUV.

Wyatt dove on top of me as he pushed me to the ground.

"Marco!" I screamed.

Another shot rang out, and Wyatt's full weight held me flat on the ground. Marco's car continued on toward the shack, coming to a stop on the other side of Wyatt's truck.

Its headlights illuminated the sagging front porch. The back window of his SUV had been shot out.

"Son of a bitch," Wyatt growled. "It's coming from the trees close to the driveway." He rolled off me and got into a squat.

Another shot hit Wyatt's truck.

"He's aiming at Marco," he said, pulling me to a squatting position too. "Let's make a run for the trees ahead."

I got to my feet, hunching low to the ground, and Wyatt kept himself between me and the gunman as we ran for cover.

The next gunshot was aimed in our direction, and another shot quickly followed from behind Wyatt's truck. Marco.

"Give it up, Conrad," Marco called out. "Backup's on the way."

"And who are they going to believe?" Paul shouted. "A veteran deputy or a deputy who's thick as thieves with the Drummonds?"

"Maybe they'll believe this," Marco said. Paul's voice filled the air, radiating from his car's stereo system, turned up full blast, as the Explorer's headlights switched off.

"You stay away from Mitzi or I'll make your life a livin' hell. Trust me, girl, I've got the power to do it."

The words he'd said to me when I'd showed up at Mitzi's house to ask her questions.

The volume lowered and Abby's confession played. How had Marco gotten that?

Marco shouted, "You've been under investigation, Conrad. And Abby Donahey's statement will be the nail in the coffin. Come with me peacefully."

"And spend the rest of my life in prison on trumped-up charges?" Paul's voice carried across the small clearing.

Wyatt leaned into my ear and whispered, "Keep going around toward the back of the cabin."

"What are you going to do?" I asked, my heart in my throat.

"Get answers, but he'll know my location, so we need to separate. I can't risk him shooting at me and hitting you."

"I don't want him shooting *at all*," I protested.

"Me neither, but something tells me we're not going to get our wish."

"Be careful, Wyatt."

"I will. Go." He gave me a little shove, and I started walking through the trees while my voice and Paul's filled the air from the Explorer's speakers.

"Turn it off!" Paul said, his voice sounding closer, which meant he was moving through the trees toward Wyatt. "I've heard enough."

The recording stopped, and the silence was eerie.

"Who called in the anonymous tip the night of my arrest?" Wyatt asked.

"Mitzi," Paul said. "Heather convinced her to do it, but it's eaten her up ever since. Even though you could have easily bought your way out of it. You chose to be a stubborn ass. Just like that stupid Heather."

Sirens sounded in the distance.

"Give yourself up, Conrad!" Marco shouted again. "You might be able to get a plea bargain if you give up some of the other crooked deputies."

"No way in hell!" A barrage of gunfire followed.

I ducked down even though the house stood between me and the bullets. I considered running toward it. Would it be safer close to the house or here in the trees?

I held my breath as I waited to hear from Marco and Wyatt.

Nothing.

The sirens grew louder, and I inched my way closer to the creek, but the silence was overwhelming, and every step seemed to give me away.

"Wyatt?" Max shouted from in front of the house.

Max was here? Had he come with Marco?

Wyatt didn't answer.

Another round of gunfire came from the trees, closer this time.

Had Paul shot Wyatt? I tried not to panic.

One thing was certain, I didn't want to just sit in the trees and get shot. After the next exchange of gunfire, I made a run for the back of the house, then worked my way toward the front, stumbling on a few rocks scattered next to the house. I could see Max outside the Explorer on the passenger side, but Marco was out of view.

Max caught sight of me, his startled face illuminated by the dashboard lights. He held up his hand to motion for me to hold still.

The sirens sounded like they were on the other side of the tree line, and I wondered if Paul was going to give himself up or if they'd have to kill him.

I made my way to the edge and peered around to see Marco standing between his Explorer and Wyatt's truck, his service gun at his side.

Suddenly, Paul broke out from the trees, charging straight for Wyatt's truck and letting out a yell that sounded like a battle cry. He held his handgun aloft, with his arm straight out, but he hadn't fired a single shot. Was he out of bullets?

"Shoot me!" Paul shouted as he slowed down, firing a shot and hitting Wyatt's truck.

"No," Marco called out. "I'm not lettin' you off that easy."

Paul stalked toward the front of the truck, his gun still raised. "I'll kill you, Roland!"

My breath caught.

"Marco," Max said in a low warning.

"I'm not killing him."

I didn't want to kill him either, but I wasn't about to let him hurt Marco. While I didn't have a weapon, there were river rocks scattered on the ground around me. I picked up a hefty stone and hurled it at him, but I only managed to brush his arm.

He came to a halt, shifting his attention to me, and I scooted back around the corner and picked up two more rocks, ready to hurl them.

"Stop where you are, Conrad!" Marco shouted, but Paul ignored him, walking past the front of Wyatt's truck.

"Shoot him, Marco!" Max shouted.

Paul turned his gun toward Max and pulled the trigger. Another gunshot followed from Marco, but Paul remained standing.

Several deputy cars rounded the corner at the lane and streamed into the clearing, their headlights partially blinding. Paul turned and pointed the gun at Marco. Suddenly, Wyatt was behind me, and he threw his own rock, hitting Paul dead center in the back.

Two gunshots went off, and Paul fell to his knees, but Marco remained standing as the deputies flooded out of their cars and surrounded us with drawn weapons.

Paul was still on his knees, his gun pointed under his chin. "Stay back! I'll do it!"

"You coward," Marco sneered. "You need to be held accountable for what you've done."

"No, Roland, that's something you would do, which is why you'll never win at anything. It's a dog-eat-dog world, and you're nothing but a sheep."

The shot rang out and Wyatt jerked me to his chest, burying my face into his shirt as the deputies crowded around Paul, issuing orders to try to keep him alive until an ambulance arrived, but I'd seen his wound before Wyatt could pull my gaze away. I knew he wasn't recovering from that.

Then I remembered he'd fired at Max and Marco. I pulled loose and ran to Max first, grabbing his upper arms and searching him from head to toe, looking for any signs of injury.

"I'm fine, Carly. He missed."

I pulled him into a hug, holding him tight, even though it aggravated the pain in my ribs. I pulled away and searched the crowd of deputies for Marco.

"He's okay, Carly," Max said softly.

"Paul fired at him too."

"And he missed him, although I'm not sure why. Based on what I've recently learned, Paul Conrad was a first-class bastard who shouldn't have batted an eye at killin' either one of us."

He was right, but I had no answer for it.

Marco broke loose from a group of deputies and walked over to me, pulling me into a hug.

"You scared me to death, Marco! I thought he shot you! Multiple times!"

"I've already been shot twice, which is enough for me." He tilted my chin, and his eyes darkened when he saw my bruised face. "I'm gonna have an ambulance take you to the ER."

"I'm fine. I just want to go home."

Softness filled his eyes. "I'll get someone to get a quick statement from you, then have Max take you home."

"I can take myself. My car's just down the road."

"I realize you can do it yourself, but I'd feel better if someone took you. I'd do it myself, but I'm going to be here for a few hours, and I don't want to keep you waitin' that long."

"That's okay," I said. "I think I'll have Wyatt take me. We've got some things to discuss."

A shadow crossed his face. "Then I'll call you in the morning."

I grabbed his hand. "No. I need you to call me when you're done."

"It's going to be in the wee hours of the morning, Carly."

"I don't care. I'll wait up."

He conceded, but he didn't look happy about it. He found a deputy to take a short statement from me, telling me they'd want a more in-depth report the next day. The deputy didn't seem upset that I'd been asking questions, but it occurred to me that I might need to get an attorney myself to keep out of trouble.

Wyatt had given a statement, and after hearing about my conversation with Abby, they cancelled the arrest warrant and told Wyatt he was free to go, but he had to leave his truck since all the bullet holes made it part of the crime scene.

Max could leave too, but he'd ridden with Marco, which was how I ended up hiking the half mile to my car with the two Drummond boys. Wyatt had told us he could hot-wire it if the keys were missing.

"How'd you end up with Marco?" I asked Max as we walked.

"I barely made it out of town before my truck broke down, which I suspect was sabotage. Marco happened to see me on the side of the road. I told him what was goin' on, but he'd already gotten a call on his radio from Conrad. I had the recording you made with Abby on my phone, and he still had your recorder."

"Okay, but Abby's not sure she wants to give an official statement. She's worried about losing her veterinary license. She's going to need an excellent defense attorney first thing in the morning."

"I'll take care of it," Wyatt said.

The keys were still in my car, but to my irritation, Wyatt insisted on driving. We dropped Max off at the tavern, then drove in silence for a few moments before Wyatt said, "I owe you my thanks."

"No," I said, "you owe me answers."

"Carly…"

"You said if I helped prove your innocence, you'd give me answers. I got you off the hook and helped save your life tonight. The very least you can do is follow through on your promise."

"I can tell you some things, but not what you want to hear."

Same old bullshit. But I reined in my temper and asked, "And what do you think I want to hear?"

"Something that's goin' to give you some magical power to bring down my father," he said, his voice weary, "but you're not going to find it. It doesn't exist."

"That's what you think?"

"Carly," he said, sounding like he was getting pissed. "If you're stickin' around Drum because you're set on bringing my father down, then do yourself a favor and leave already, because we both know you're not stayin' for me."

"Pull over," I snapped.

"What?"

"I said pull *my* damn car over."

His hands tightened around the wheel. "Seriously? You're gonna leave me stranded on the side of the road in the middle of the night?"

"No, I'm gonna drive my own damn car like a grown-ass woman. For some reason, you suddenly think I'm some fragile flower, but I'm not sure why. You didn't seem to think that when you showed up at my bedroom door asking me to help you find out who killed Heather. You seemed to think I was capable of handling myself then."

"My father is different. You have no idea what he's capable of."

"I'm more aware than you think. Now *pull over*."

He jerked the car to the side of the road and came to a full stop, putting the car in park. "What the hell are you talkin' about, Carly? Has my father threatened you?"

"My personal life is none of your business!"

"It is if it involves my father!"

I opened my car door and got out, then walked around to the driver's door and jerked on the handle. "Get out."

He climbed out and stood beside me. "Has my father threatened you?"

"Why don't you ask *him*?" I slid past him and got behind the wheel, leaving him to walk around and get in from the passenger side.

He hesitated for a moment longer before he circled the car, and when he got in, he rested his hands on his knees. "I know you're not weak. And I know you mean well, but you *have* to leave my father alone."

"What happened?" I asked, pulling back onto the road. "At Seth's funeral you were all for helping me, but it only took you a few days to change your tune." I shot him a glance. "What did your father threaten you with?" I cast another look at him and saw the surprise on his face. "So I'm right?" How had I not realized this before?

He started to say something but stopped himself.

"What did your mother say to convince Max to come home from college and run the tavern? When I asked her, she told me she reminded him of his family obligations. What would those be?"

His body stiffened and he whipped his head around to face me. "When did you talk to my mother?"

I was tired of keeping secrets, especially from him. Maybe sharing a few of mine would jog some of his loose. "Yesterday."

"Where?"

"I went to their house for tea. Your father invited me when I saw him at the construction site."

"*What?*"

"Your mother and I had a lovely chat. For some reason, she thinks we're still dating. And apparently Max is perpetuating this illusion. You both have supposedly created a few excuses for why I haven't agreed to meet with her. If you're doing it to appease your father, he knows we're not together. He thinks I'm sleeping with Marco."

"Sometimes illusions serve their purpose. Sometimes everyone has a part to play, and when they stop playin' those parts, innocent people pay the price."

I shook my head. "What are you talkin' about?"

"When I broke free from my father, I didn't just hurt him. I hurt myself and other people in this town. I thought it was all about me, but it went deeper than that. Only I had no idea until recently."

"Let me guess…your father enlightened you," I said in disgust.

"I realize that for some reason you don't fear him like everyone else in this town, but he's still very much the boogeyman, Carly. Pretendin' like he's not doesn't make him any less dangerous."

"Oh, I know how he works, trust me. And he knows enough secrets to be powerful, but he's like a cockroach hiding in the shadows. Once you shine a light on him, you don't need a gun or even an army to destroy him. You only need a shoe."

"You can't be serious," he said in horror.

"I am. So you can either join me or hide in the shadows too."

"And what if you find information that could hurt my father, but also someone else? Someone who doesn't deserve it. What will you do then, Carly?"

"I'll cross that bridge when I come to it. Right now all I see is a pathetic excuse of a man who likes to use threats to control a whole town. But here's the truth: your father has lost most of his power and Bingham's waiting to swoop in and take the rest."

He released a bitter laugh. "You think Bingham gives a shit about this town? You of all people know that everything he does is to benefit himself."

"And you can't say the same about your father?" I asked in disbelief. "I don't for one minute believe he's building that resort for the town. He's doing it for himself, and the town just happens to benefit from it. Men like him aren't altruistic, nor are they compassionate. So he'll pay the lowest wages possible, all but indenturing the employees to him, and while they'll think he's helping them, he'll really be entrapping them, pinning their wings, but doing it so slowly they won't realize it's happening."

"What do you know?" he asked, and I could hear the hesitation in his voice, along with a hint of fear.

"Enough to know your father is vile, but not enough to pin him down yet."

"Carly, you're playin' with fire."

"Then I'll be sure to bring a fire extinguisher."

I turned onto the road that led to his house.

"What are you doin'?" he asked. "I'm supposed to be taking you home."

"I'm perfectly capable of taking my own self home." I took a deep breath before I continued. "While I appreciate your offer of help, I'm a strong, capable woman. Do I need help sometimes? Yeah, but so do you. I helped find out what really happened to Heather. I went to that cabin to save you from Paul Conrad. Surely I've earned your respect."

"Of course I respect you. How can I not? But you can't expect me to share everything I know just to make things more equal between us. Sure, your secret is huge, but mine? They affect more than just me. More than just my family. To expose them, I hurt far too many people."

"And you don't trust me not to hurt them?"

"No. You're on a one-woman mission to bring my father down, no matter the cost. Look at what you've already paid."

"What exactly have I paid?" I demanded. "A relationship with you?"

He turned to me and took my hand. "What we had was great, Carly. We could be great, if you'd only just let things be."

I snatched my hand away from him. "Like you've done since you came home from prison?"

"Carly."

I turned into his driveway and started down the lane to his house. "So here's what I'm hearing from you. I need to shut up and sit down and stop making waves." He started to speak, but I snapped, "No. I'm not done."

He crossed his arms and leaned back in his seat.

"You say you like me because I'm different than every other woman in this town, but you want to stifle the very thing that you like about me. Do you see how screwed up that is?" His house appeared in front of us, and I pulled into the drive and put my car in park.

"Oh," he said. "Am I allowed to speak now?"

I fought hard to keep from rolling my eyes.

"I like you for more than that, Carly, which is why I need you to stop this insane mission to take my father down. Don't you see how good we are together?"

"I'm attracted to you," I said. "And a year ago, I could have turned a blind eye and assured myself that I was but one woman and there was nothing I could do. I would have enjoyed my peaceful, idyllic life with a man who claimed to love me, all under the shadow of a tyrant, and pretended everything was okay. But I am *not* that woman anymore, Wyatt. That was Caroline Blakely, who chose to live her life with blinders on. I'm Charlene Moore now, and the blinders are off. And they're *never* going back on."

His jaw clenched. "Have you ever been happy, Carly? *Really* happy? I know I haven't, but I got a glimpse of it when I was with you. I liked it. What's wrong with bein' happy?"

"You know I've never been truly happy, because I've told you my deepest, darkest secrets. And maybe I would have known that about you if you'd shared yourself too. Your secrets are warning signs flashing in neon lights telling my psyche that I can't trust you. I need security in my relationships."

"You know I can't do that," he said, getting defensive. "There's just too much."

"I know," I said, my voice cracking with emotion. "Which is why you and I will never, *ever* work."

"Carly."

"I would love you, of that I'm fairly sure, if I could pretend that Rome wasn't burning around us, but I could never feel secure. I'd never feel safe with you."

"You think I'd hurt you?" he asked in horror.

"Physical pain isn't the worst kind, and you know it. I couldn't live my life always wondering what else you were hiding from me."

"Everyone has secrets. Everyone."

"True," I said. "But yours are way bigger than most people's."

"So you refuse to give us a chance because of my father?"

"No," I said softly. "*You* chose that." I took a breath. "It's not fair for me to make demands of you. You need to do what you need to do. But at the same time, you can't ask *me* to give up the things *I* need in a relationship. At the core of it, we need different things to make us feel secure, things neither one of us is willing or capable of giving."

"So that's it. We're really done?"

"We were really done last December, Wyatt. You just chose not to believe it."

He sat back in his seat. "I love you, Carly."

Pain filled my heart and I fought back tears. "We're not right for each other, Wyatt. Don't you see that?"

"Let me guess," he said in a dark tone. "Marco is."

"I think maybe he would be," I said, holding back a sob, "but what I said yesterday in the Greener Pastures' parking lot is true. I'm incapable of fully trusting anyone anymore, and without trust, there's nothing."

"And I was the final straw," he said with a bit of defiance.

"Now that I'm further away from it, I can see that you really thought you were protecting me, but it's like a child who catches a butterfly and holds it too tight. You were holding on too tight, and I saw it as deception. I still do, truth be told."

"Well, then I guess that's that." He opened the car door and placed a foot on his driveway.

"We're not done, Wyatt," I said in an even tone. "You *did* promise me answers, and I intend to get them. I realize part of the problem might be that you know so many things and you're so used to hiding them, you don't know where to start. So in the future, I'm going to come to you with specific questions and you'll answer them."

"I'll tell you what I can."

"No. You'll fully answer the question asked." I sat back in my seat, suddenly exhausted. "Now we're done. I'm going home."

He started to get out, then stopped, turning back to face me with soft eyes. "You think you're tough, and you are, but I see a woman who needs to be held. Needs to be loved. You deserve the kind of love I can give you."

"And if you loved me at all, you'd see I'd never feel truly loved until my deepest core needs were met. Something you're still incapable of giving me." I looked him directly in the eyes. "Good night, Wyatt."

He got out and headed to his front door, turning back to watch me as I left.

I headed home, trying to push all thoughts of what could have been from my mind.

Chapter
Twenty-Nine

Marco didn't call, but I was still up when his Explorer pulled into Hank's driveway a little after four a.m.

I ran out the door to greet him, and he got out of his truck, shaking his head.

"You should be in bed, Carly," he said softly when he reached me at the bottom of the steps. "You had a hell of a night."

I shivered. "So did you."

He ran his hands down my bare arms to warm me up, frowning when he saw the bruise on the side of my face. "How are you feelin'? I think we should run you down to Greeneville in the morning to see a doctor."

"I'm fine, just a little banged up. Are you headed home?"

"For a few hours of sleep. I need to head to the station in Ewing to give an official statement in the morning. You told me to call, but I didn't have access to a phone, so I decided to stop by. I'd hoped you'd be asleep, to be honest." he asked.

"I waited up to hear from you, and I'm nervous. I have to make a full statement too. Should I get an attorney?" My stomach clenched at the thought.

"No," he said, enveloping me in a hug. "You're not in any trouble. And I suspect Abby will be able to make a plea deal. Detective White thinks she can be beneficial, and she's pullin' lots of strings to get her off with just probation. Paul had Abby do a few things over the years that Detective White is hoping will help her root out more corruption. And it doesn't hurt that Max hooked her up with the Drummond family attorney."

I pulled away. "Oh, God. She won't owe Bart a favor, will she?"

"No. I've already asked. Wyatt's covering the expense."

"And where did he get all of this money he keeps doling out?" I asked. "Seth's funeral couldn't have been cheap."

He sighed. "Another mystery to solve."

A new fear hit me. "Does the thought of goin' after Bart worry you? Do you want to let it go? Cleaning up the sheriff's department is dangerous enough. You don't need to deal with my personal vendetta too."

He slowly shook his head. "No. I wouldn't be surprised if they're intertwined. Besides, his threat is still hangin' over your head. We'll find a way to bring him down."

"Thank you."

He nodded. "I won't be able to sit with you when you give your statement, but I'll be outside the room. Just answer the questions as truthfully as possible, and you'll be okay."

"What does 'as truthfully as possible' mean?"

He hesitated. "I would never tell you what to say in a statement—that would be illegal—but if you were to include anything about your vendetta against Bart... let's just say the corruption hasn't been rooted out of the department yet."

I nodded. "I understand."

He studied me in the moonlight for a moment, saying nothing. There was something beautiful about that moment, something pure and unbroken, and I didn't want it to end. But finally he said, "I better head home."

Still, he didn't make any moves to go.

I didn't want him to leave. I needed him. Yet I had nothing to offer him but my friendship, and I'd already abused that privilege.

"Thank you," I whispered, staring into his eyes. "Thank you for your help. Thank you for your understanding."

A soft smile lit up his eyes and he leaned forward and kissed my forehead. "Thank you for being my friend."

Then he got in his SUV and left.

***

The next morning, I woke to the sound of a car pulling onto Hank's land. I quickly jumped out of bed and grabbed my chunky cardigan before running out to see who it was.

Hank was sitting in his chair on the porch, nursing a cup of coffee.

Abby had pulled her pickup truck into the driveway, stopping about ten feet from the house. She got out of the truck, holding a wicker laundry basket. "I hope it's okay that I stopped by."

"Of course," I said hesitantly. I wouldn't be surprised if she was angry with me. Her chances of getting out of this free and clear might have been damaged by Paul's suicide, and maybe even by the fact that Max and Marco had shared all the details with the sheriff's department before she could.

"I come in peace," she said, lifting the basket slightly.

I walked to the bottom of the steps, realizing Hank hadn't said a word.

"Hank, this is Dr. Abby Donahey, the Drum veterinarian. Abby, this is Hank Chalmers, my…" To call him my landlord and roommate would almost be an insult. Friend didn't cut it either. Friend barely held up as a description for what I had with Marco, but what I had with Hank went beyond that. "My family," I said, with a lump in my throat.

She nodded. "Pleased to meet you, Mr. Chalmers."

"Call me Hank," he said. "Everybody does."

"Okay, then. Hank it is." She took several steps closer, turning her attention to me. "I wanted to thank you for helpin' me."

"I'm not sure I did," I admitted. "I said I'd keep your admission secret until you talked to a lawyer, but it got out anyway. I'm worried it will hurt your chances of getting a good plea bargain."

"I'll be fine," she said. "And I'm glad the truth is finally out. Paul hung it over my head every time he wanted something." She gave me a soft smile. "After this is over, I'll really be free. Paul can't keep me in Drum anymore."

"So you're leavin'?" I asked.

She laughed. "That's the thing. I don't think I will. It's just nice knowin' that I'm only here because I choose to be, you know?"

I nodded. Sadly, I did.

"In any case," she said, holding out the basket. "I'm going to be dealin' with all of this legal mess, though my attorney thinks that what I know about Paul will help me get off with just probation. But he thinks I need to stay somewhere else for my safety, and Detective White has given her permission. I'll be back once all the buzz dies down. In the meantime, I was wondering if you could foster some of those kittens you were playin' with the other day." She set the basket on the ground and I saw two kittens, the gray one I'd held at her office and a black and white one.

Happiness rushed through me as I scooped them both up and held them to my chest.

"I take it that's a yes?" she asked.

I turned to Hank, who was grinning.

"Anything that makes you that happy is an automatic yes," he said. He glanced up at Abby. "We'll take them."

"Thanks," she said. "I got someone to watch the others. You can bring them in when I get back to schedule them to be spayed. I left some food and kitty litter underneath the towel. You can get the basket to me when I get back." She took a few steps backward. "Thanks again, Carly."

I nodded. "If you ever need someone to talk to," I said, "I'm a great listener and Watson's makes some pretty decent coffee."

Abby smiled. "I'd like that."

As she backed out of the driveway, I cuddled and baby-talked to the kittens, both of which purred.

"You gonna let me see one of them furballs?" Hank asked.

Grinning, I climbed up the steps. "Which one do you want?"

"Do they have names?"

"No," I said, "but they're both girls."

"Which one is your favorite?" he asked.

"Seems wrong to choose," I said, but I held the gray one a little closer.

He grinned and reached out his hands. "Give me that black and white one."

I handed him the kitten, and he held her up so they were face-to-face. "Seems like you just found your new home, little one." He settled her on his lap and began to stroke her head and back. "They need names," he said gruffly.

I took a seat on the top step of the porch and put the kitten on my lap. "We could give them matchy names. Like Sugar and Spice." I made a face. "That's terrible."

He snorted but didn't otherwise comment. Instead, he seemed to forget about naming the kittens for the moment, sighing loud enough to have me looking back at him, arching a brow in question.

"Tell me about what happened last night."

So I told him, and by the time I stopped, his kitten had fallen asleep.

"You sure you ain't in any trouble?" he asked.

"Marco assures me I'm fine."

"That boy cares about you."

"I know," I said, keeping my gaze on the kitten in my lap.

"No, girl. He *cares* about you."

I lifted my gaze to his. "I know that too, but I can't be anything but a friend right now. He understands that."

He nodded, then said, "I'm gonna tell Wyatt I don't need him payin' for Ginger to come out here anymore."

"Hank," I said, jerking upright. "Don't do that." I liked knowing that Ginger was keeping an eye on him when I couldn't.

"She's working at the tavern now, and I can afford to pay her for a day or two a week. We don't need Wyatt." I heard the gravity in his voice, and I realized this was Hank's way of taking sides and making a stand.

"Hank, please don't do that on my account. You and Wyatt have been friends for years."

He nodded, his eyes glassy. "We've been friends, but we ain't family."

My throat burned and my chin quivered.

"I've declared you as kin," he said, his voice tight, "but now I'm declarin' you as mine. You may not bear my name, but you're like my daughter all the same."

"Hank." I reached over and put my hand on his knee.

He smiled down at me. "You've filled my life with love and happiness, girl. I never thought that would happen again." He nodded. "Thank you."

A tear fell down my cheek. "You have to know you're like a father to me. I love you, Hank."

He nodded, glancing down at the kitten. "I love you too." He sniffed and his tone turned gruff. "What's a man gotta do to get breakfast around here?"

Releasing a laugh, I got to my feet and placed my kitten on his lap next to her sister. "Coming right up."

I headed into the house, stopping in the doorway to stare down at the gruff man who had more love for me in his pinky finger than my father ever had, and I vowed I'd do everything in my power to protect him.

No matter the price.

Buried in Secrets
Carly Moore #4
October 27, 2020

Printed in Great Britain
by Amazon

65393005R00236